THE GIFTS OF PELICAN ISLE

THE GIFTS OF PELICAN ISLE

*Kathie,
my gift to you!
Fondly,
Padgett*

PADGETT GERLER

DISCLAIMER

This book is a work of fiction. Names, characters, places, and incidents are either products of the author's imagination or are used fictitiously. Any resemblance to actual events or persons, living or dead, is entirely coincidental.

For

MOM

Who felt the world should be fair and was saddened that it was not.

ACKNOWLEDGMENTS

Thanks to my friends in Wonderland. You make me think harder and dig deeper, and for that I will be forever grateful.

Alice Osborn, my sincerest thanks for your kind support and continued encouragement. Thank you, too, for sharing your time and talents with the Raleigh writing community. We cherish you.

Suzanne Boswell, my talented first reader, thank you for taking on this challenge and for holding my feet to the fire. You are such a gifted editor and writer, and I am so grateful for your help in making THE GIFTS OF PELICAN ISLE the best it can be.

Many thanks to my Tribe. You make me laugh and make me cry—in the very best way—and love me in the most sincere way. I am so blessed to have all of you in my life.

Thank you, Ed, for everything.

Juan, Victor, Javier, Hector, Roberto, Marcelo, Arturo, Maura, Gabby, Marta, Gloria, and Michely, you inspired me to write THE GIFTS OF PELICAN ISLE. So, thank you. Thank you so very much.

THE GIFTS OF PELICAN ISLE

For I was hungry and you gave me food, I was thirsty and you gave me something to drink, I was a stranger and you invited me in.

Matthew 25:35

Inasmuch as ye have done it unto one of the least of these my brethren, ye have done it unto me.

Matthew 25:40

ALLY

One

Nineteen, twenty, twenty-one.

I had just finished counting the odd vertical rows of pink roses that adorned the wallpaper of my childhood bedroom. Counting the roses kept me from thinking about anything else. So I spent my waking hours counting, counting, counting. There were twenty-one roses running from floor to ceiling on the odd rows, twenty-two on the even rows. I had tried counting the horizontal rows of roses, as well, but I got thrown off every time I reached the closet. I'd start at the door leading to the hallway and would be doing just fine until I got to that closet. So I tried starting at the closet, working my way toward the hall, but that didn't seem to work either.

"Honey, you just can't lie here forever."

Eight, nine, ten... I had started over, working on the even rows.

"Why, Mom? You getting tired of me?"

Eleven, twelve, thirteen...

"Of course not, Ally, but it's just not healthy to shut yourself away like this."

Fourteen, fifteen, sixteen...

"It's been six months."

No, it had not been six months. It had been six months, one week, three days, two hours, and some minutes, but who's counting, since a drunk driver had hit our car, killing my husband, Cam, and our unborn daughter a week before her due date.

We were heading home from Babies-R-Us where we had picked up a bumper for our baby's crib. Friends and family had given us every other conceivable gift, but no one had purchased the pink and brown polka dot crib bumper from our wish list. At the time that pink and brown polka dot crib bumper seemed so important to me, as if our child couldn't come into this world until she had a pink and brown polka dot bumper in her crib. And only the pink and brown polka dot one would do.

"Don't worry, we'll get it," Cam had assured me.

"Cam," I'd whined, "she's due in a week. She could come early, you know."

Certain I wasn't going to let it rest until that pink and brown polka dot bumper was safely in place in our daughter's crib, Cam said, "Okay, then, we'll go this afternoon when I get home from work. Is that soon enough?"

"Perfect," I said, putting my arms around my wonderfully accommodating and understanding husband and giving him a good-bye kiss.

I clock-watched all day long—which is what I did most days since I'd taken a leave of absence from my teaching job as I awaited our baby's arrival—and wandered into the nursery at least a dozen times, just to make sure we'd gotten absolutely everything we needed for our child—everything except the crib bumper.

So for over eight hours I waited impatiently and rotundly, watching from the living room window, until I saw Cam round the corner and pull into the parking lot. I was out of our apartment and into the car before he could turn off the engine and come inside to get me.

"Anxious?" he'd said as he smiled at my impatience and leaned in to kiss me.

"Very," I'd said, returning his kiss.

The stock boy had to rummage around in the warehouse until he unearthed the very last brown and pink polka dot crib bumper. We had gleefully—one of us more gleeful than the other—made our purchase and were on our way to get a bite to eat before heading home with the final piece to the baby-nursery puzzle.

We had already named our daughter Rory. I'd read the name in a children's book. It sounded like a girl with a purpose, perhaps even a super power. She sounded like a girl who knew where she was going and knew how to get there. That's the kind of daughter we wanted to raise.

Most men want boys. Not Cam. He'd always wanted a girl.

"A little girl to spoil," he had said and taken me in his arms. "A girl just like her mommy."

We were only a mile from home, and I was cradling my enormous, undulating belly in my arms, my legs splayed wide for comfort and balance.

"Quick, Cam, give me your hand." I'd cried. "She's doing flip-flops."

He'd reached over and gently patted our baby, saying, "See you soon, little girl."

Then he had taken my hand, kissed it, and placed it back on our baby, saying, "I love you, Mommy."

I love you, Mommy. Mommy. I was going to be a mommy.

That's the last thing I remembered. Then I was in the hospital, empty— in every way.

I tried to piece together the accident, as best I could, from snippets I'd overheard and reports I'd seen on WRAL-News and in the morning News and Observer. And in my piecing together, I learned about the person who had taken my husband and child from me.

He was a Fortune, a descendant of one of the First Families of North Carolina. He followed a long line of attorneys and politicians; he, however, was neither. He was a playboy, a junior college dropout, living a self-indulgent life on his mother's inheritance. To get him out of her house, she had bought him a tony flat in a high-rise in the center of the bustle of the city and gave him a generous allowance to assure that he'd stay away. Also with the help of Mom's financial assistance and his dad's connections, he had survived two DUI's before he missed seeing that stop sign.

Cam was one of the good ones. A standout on the football team, he was also President of the Student Government our senior year at Broughton High. But it made no difference that he'd graduated Summa Cum Laude from State and was a rising star at Enright Engineering, or that he spent his Saturdays building Habitat homes or holidays feeding the homeless. His family was transplanted from Virginia; he was not descended from a First Family. Name and money trumped goodness, and the Fortune heir was out of jail and back on the road before I was out of my bed in my childhood princess bedroom.

He never called, never visited, never expressed sorrow.

He left me closureless. He left me hopeless. He left me lifeless.

In the six months that felt like six years or maybe even six lifetimes since the accident, my physical wounds had healed, leaving only a small scar on my upper lip. But I was certain my emotional wounds were damaged beyond repair. So I had spent those six lifetimes lying motionless in my childhood bedroom, in my childhood bed, thinking that, perhaps, if I didn't use my organs, they would just stop working. And then it would all be over. Just like that. No more pain. No more loneliness. No more remembering. But, as hard as I tried to prevent it, my heart just kept on beating. I kept on breathing. I kept on aching.

And while I spent my endless days lying lifeless in my pink princess bedroom, my parents were kind and patient and loving. And scared, so very scared.

"I know healing takes a long time," Mom said, twisting her rings and biting her lip, "but Daddy and I just think you'll never begin to get back to your old self this way."

Seventeen, eighteen, nineteen...

She sat on the edge of the bed, caressing my arm, fresh worry lines creasing her still-youthful and beautiful face. But I had given her just cause for worry. I couldn't remember the last time I'd gotten up to eat, to shower, to wash my lank, greasy hair. My musky odor was beginning to offend even me. I can only imagine how repelled my mother must have been.

My folks had tried everything. "Please go to church with us, Darlin'. It'll do you so much good. Everyone misses you. They all ask about you. My Sunday school class has put you on the prayer list."

I'd refused, so church had come to me: a steady stream of well wishers whom I rebuffed so severely that they pasted on plastic smiles, said, "We are holding you in our prayers," and fled from my dark, musty room.

I was back to my flower counting before they could hit the stairs.

High school friends came, as well as college sorority sisters, but their visits were teeth-aching uncomfortable. I didn't feel I had the strength, much less the desire, to welcome them or make them feel at ease or listen to their sympathetic clucking; so when the tension became unbearable, they all hugged me stiffly, wished me well, and raced for the door.

"Ally, Madeline Forsythe says her grief support group did wonders for her when Bill passed away."

God, how I hated that term *passed away*. Or even worse, *passed. Cam *died*. Rory *died*.

"Maybe her group could help you."

I had been repulsed by the notion of my sitting in a circle in the First Baptist Church basement with its beige cinder-block walls, surrounded by a bunch of wrinkled, age-spotted, blue-haired women who would surely fawn over me, wanting to mother, or worse yet, grandmother me.

Still trying to coax me from my damp, fetid sheets, my mother said, "Just shower, Ally, and come on down for supper."

"I'm not hungry," I finally said, still lying motionless, trying not to stir my organs.

Twenty, twenty-one, twenty-two...

"I know that, but you can't go without eating much longer. You can't live without eating."

I gave her my that's-the-whole-idea look, the one she'd come to know so well.

I could see the pain and fear in her eyes when she said, "I know you feel life isn't worth living, but please give it a chance. Give *us* a chance. Please let Daddy and me help you. Please, Honey, please."

There were so many pleases in her request. She was frantic. I knew that I was being terribly selfish, so unfair. Yet I felt I had earned the right. But my parents had done nothing but love me, abide my grief, and care for me.

After Cam and Rory's deaths, the two of them had worked with Cam's and my apartment management company to dissolve our lease. They had also arranged to store or dispose of all our belongings, so that I wouldn't have to deal with that pain. But they had suffered tragic losses, as well. Their son-in-law, whom they loved like the son they'd never had, had been killed senselessly, along with their first grandchild. And now they were watching their only child waste away.

"Okay," was all I could manage as I dragged my near-atrophied limbs from my bed and headed for the bathroom to attempt my first shower in god knows how long.

I caught sight of myself as I passed the bathroom mirror. My once-blonde hair was now an indistinguishable color, somewhere between straw and gray. And my brown eyes that had once looked just like my dad's were dead, lifeless, and flat. My sallow skin hung loosely from my shrunken frame. No wonder my mother was frightened.

As I turned on the water and waited for it to warm, I could hear my mother cry out in relief as she began ripping my rank sheets from the bed. I peeled off my limp pajamas, dropped them into the hamper, and stepped into the shower. Then I closed the glass door against the flurry of activity that was going on in my bedroom. By the time I had washed away the weeks—months?—of lethargy and grief and toweled dry, my bed was remade, my room was straightened, and the once-putrid air smelled of spring flowers. Pink flowers, no doubt.

I rummaged through my drawers until I found a faded, rumpled tee shirt and a pair of gym shorts. Bypassing the underwear, I pulled the tee shirt over my head and stepped into my shorts, drawing the string tight around my shrunken waistline. I located flip-flops in the back of my closet, dragged them out with my toes, and stepped in. Closing my eyes, I took a deep breath into the lungs that refused to give up and made my way downstairs to my waiting, anxious parents.

"Hey, Sport, looking good," Dad said when I showed up at the dinner table in my baggy gym shorts, my wet, blonde-again hair dripping down my back.

"You mean looking *alive*," I managed and tried to form a smile, only to find that smiling had become foreign to me.

"It's a start," he said, leaning toward me and patting my arm. "I'm proud of you. I know this isn't easy."

"Come, sit. Supper's almost ready," Mom chirped in her faux upbeat manner.

I sat, my hands clasped uncomfortably between my legs. I'd forgotten where they were supposed to be.

While Mom busied herself at the stove, my dad and I sat across from each other, careful not to make eye contact, lest we be forced to engage in

5

painful small talk. But when the silence became deafening, he said, "Thanks, Honey."

"Excuse me?"

"Thank you."

"For what?"

"For trying."

"Oh, okay, sure," I said, shrugging, still unable to connect with him.

It wasn't much, but it was the longest conversation he and I had had in over six months. Sad, but a start.

Finally Mom bustled to the table, laden with bowls, saying, "Here we go," self consciously wiping her hands on her apron as she joined us.

She had fixed my favorites: split-pea soup and cornbread. I attempted a few bites while my parents watched me as though viewing an anthropological special on the nature channel. I felt as if I were a specimen, an untamed species in the wild that would accidentally stumble upon some human-like behavior and make the viewers clap and trill with awe and delight.

"Thanks, Mom. Tastes good," I said after only two spoonfuls, stirring around in my bowl, pretending I was just taking a break.

Not nearly delighted enough to clap and trill at my attempted human-like behavior, my parents soon sensed I'd reached my limit—of food? of conversation? of togetherness? They both leaned forward and took my hands and massaged them lovingly. Their kindness broke my heart. Their pain was palpable, but my pain was their only concern.

"Please don't shut us out, Ally," my father said. "You'll never forget Cam and Rory, but you can go on. Just let us help you. Okay?"

"I'll try. I promise," I said, attempting to hold back the tears that were always standing right at the backs of my eyes. I was humoring my parents, trying as best I could to help them feel better, struggling to make them think that I would really try.

I didn't believe, though, for a minute that I could move on, or even try, for that matter. But a promise is a promise, especially if it's a promise you make to your exhausted, loving, frightened parents.

Two

It had been four months since my mother had coaxed me out of my putrid bed and away from my pink-rose counting with her pea soup and kindness. And I had promised my parents that I would try, though I wasn't sure what trying would entail. As painful as it was, I kept that promise to my mom and dad. I actually got out of bed each morning, and while I was in bed, I attempted to cut back on my rose counting. I showered daily, though sometimes showering meant just standing motionless in the stream of warm water. I ate. Some days I ate baby carrots out of the plastic bag. Other days I ate a handful of cookies. But at least it was something. My parents didn't push.

And they were always there.

Much to my surprise, while leaning on my parents I had been able to take baby steps back toward life and had gotten as far as early morning walks around the mall with my mom. She would don her neon orange walking shoes and gray sweatpants and tee shirt and would be waiting in the car before I could drag myself from beneath the covers. A toot on her horn would propel me from bed, and I would climb unenthusiastically into my sweats and scrape my hair back with my fingers into a sloppy ponytail. I'd make my way down the stairs with my shoes in my hand, eye sand and morning breath still intact. She and I would drive to the mall in silence, and all the while I'd wish myself back to bed, back to sleep where I wouldn't have to think, to dwell, to remember. But mall walking, I figured, was part of the promise.

As we drove in silence, I'd watch the familiar sights whiz by, those same sights I'd known all my life, those same sights that once brought me immeasurable joy and comfort. Those sights marked the route we'd made to the mall to get my first shoes, my first bra, my first lip gloss, my first pierced ears. It later marked the route my friends and I made to hang out on Saturday nights, waiting for boys to notice us so that we could pretend we didn't notice them. I no longer got that going-to-the-mall rush. In fact, I just saw it as another source of pain, a reminder that my life had changed in every way and that I couldn't go back. But I felt it a necessity to appease my mother, who promised it was another essential step toward my healing. I didn't believe her for a minute, but, after all she had done for me, she deserved my cooperation. She deserved a promise kept.

At first we'd stroll the mall in silence, and I considered myself lucky if I were able to make just one loop.

"Great job! I'm so proud of you," my mother would say and give me a hug, as if I'd just completed the Boston Marathon or climbed the Alps.

As time progressed, we picked up the pace, dodging other early-morning walkers, losing count of our laps. Whereas our walks began in silence, we moved on to chatting a bit, even laughing occasionally. They weren't belly laughs, but we managed slight chuckles.

In time I even began brushing my teeth, washing my face, and combing my hair before leaving for the mall.

I had balked obstinately at first, not ready to part with my grief. I, somehow, felt it would be disloyal to Cam and Rory if I were to let my pain and sorrow go. Or even ease. Perhaps I felt unfaithful doing something that would divert my attention from my bereavement. I think I believed that the love for my husband and baby was measured by the depth of my despair. But my mother had persisted, patiently, and I grudgingly admitted that her therapy was working. I knew that I would carry my sadness forever, but time and my mother's love were making my load somewhat bearable.

After about four months of early-morning walking, I found myself up, dressed, and waiting by the door before my mother could get to the car and blast me from bed with her horn tooting. My calves were beginning to become lean and knotted, and my butt was tighter and perched higher than ever before. I felt invigorated, and I had to admit that I looked forward to Mom's and my early-morning outings. I was beginning to regain the grief weight I'd lost and my desire to get out of bed, and I had progressed to showering all over each day, changing my sheets regularly, and helping my mother around the house. And I had completely conquered my flower-counting addiction.

Both my parents and I were quite pleased and surprised by my progress.

But no matter how far I'd come, no matter my progress, I was still living under my parents' roof like a dependent child, a child who wanted to hold onto her security blanket forever.

"Ally," my mother called up the stairs, "you have company."

I'd just stepped from the shower—a real soap and water shower—and was toweling dry.

"Be right down," I called out as I briskly rubbed my dripping hair with a towel.

I hadn't had company in ages, since I had offended friends and church members alike with my rank room, my lack of hygiene, and my rude, off-putting behavior. But the thought of a visitor no longer made me want to burrow beneath the covers and cringe. So I rushed to dry my hair, jumped into a pair of jeans, pulled on a tee shirt, and headed downstairs in my bare feet.

"Dr. Brown," I said with astonishment when I saw my Teaching Methods professor sitting in my parents' living room, sipping a cup of tea. I had never seen her away from the University setting, and her presence in my parents' home seemed incongruous. I smoothed my once-again-blonde hair with my hands and immediately felt self-conscious about being barefoot. I'd never talked to Dr. Brown in my bare feet.

"Ally, I'm so sorry. I just got back from sabbatical and learned of your loss," she said as she stood and approached me to put her arms around me. She had hugged me only once before, the day I'd graduated from NC State, Summa Cum Laude. On that occasion she had smiled broadly and said, "One of my best students ever. I expect great things from you, Ally."

Not only had she expected great things from me, she had set her hand to making sure that I was on the road that could aid in my achieving some greatness. But I had not lived up to her expectations, had not achieved greatness in any way. After losing my husband and child, I had unceremoniously abandoned a prized teaching position she had helped me secure. I was sure she saw me as a huge disappointment, an abject failure.

"Can we talk?" she asked.

"Sure," I said, wondering why Dr. Brown had come to see me but suspecting that my mother surely was at the center of it.

My mother said, "Well, okay, then, I'll just leave you two to chat," and disappeared into the kitchen.

Dr. Brown sat back down and picked up her tea and took a sip. I sat on the sofa opposite her. Placing her cup back in its saucer and smiling at me, she said, "Oh, Ally, it's so good to see you again. My shining star," she said, beaming and making me blush. "The minute you spoke up in my class, I knew you were going to be an excellent teacher. And you are. Everybody sings your praises—parents, teachers, your principal." Then dropping her cheery attitude, Dr. Brown said, "They've really missed you, Ally. But they all understand. They send their warmest wishes."

"That was nice of them," I said. "You know, I really loved teaching."

"Loved?" Dr. Brown asked.

"Excuse me?"

"Loved. You said *loved*, as if your teaching career were in the past."

I opened my mouth, but no sound came out. Maybe teaching was a thing of the past, along with my husband and my child. I simply hadn't given it a thought since That Day. Teaching was my Life Before. I wasn't sure that teaching fit into my Life After. Being nurtured and protected by my parents felt like my Life After.

"Don't you plan to return to teaching, Ally?"

"I don't know. Maybe not. It doesn't feel like I want to." Then I took a deep breath and told her, "I haven't felt much like thinking about teaching—or anything at all, for that matter."

"Ally, I know you have suffered a tragic loss, and I am so sorry. But you haven't lost your gift for teaching. You're a teacher. You'll always be a teacher."

I knew Dr. Brown was right, but I didn't want her to be right. I didn't want to teach, or do anything, for that matter, that would require my leaving the safety of my parents' home. I wanted to walk with my mom, sleep in my pink rose-covered, childhood princess bedroom, and hold tight to my parents' hands so that I couldn't lose anything else or anyone else.

"I can understand your not wanting to go back to your old school."

"You can?"

"Of course, I can. I'm sure the memories would open painful wounds. Who would want such a thing?"

"Thanks for understanding."

"But just because going back to your old teaching job would be painful, that doesn't mean you're no longer a teacher."

But I really did feel as if I were no longer a teacher. Cam and teaching were my other life. Without one I felt the other didn't exist. But Dr. Brown was insinuating that the two were not intertwined, that I could still teach without Cam's existence.

Without his validation.

Without his approval.

As I tried to digest this, Dr. Brown leaned forward, took my hand and said, "I received a call from a principal friend of mine this morning. He needs your help."

"My help?"

"Well, he didn't know he needed your help until I told him. One of his teachers just gave notice that she isn't returning in the fall. He needs someone to take her class, and he hasn't much time to find a replacement. As soon as he described the position, I thought of you."

"Me? Why me?"

Smiling, she said, "It's a first grade class of bright kids who need to be challenged. Their parents are hard workers, and most of them have a house full of children and more than one job. But they know their kids' education is so important. They expect their kids to succeed, and they'll be involved as best they can. They sound like your kind of students, don't they?"

My kind of students—the kind of students who love story time and can't wait to show their teacher the words they've learned to read; the kind of students who love to hug their teacher and want to be the ones to hold her hand in line; the kind of students who always come to class prepared; the kind of students who fight to clean the boards and revel in the slightest praise from their teacher because their hard-working parents, as eager as they are to help, may be too weary or too preoccupied to praise their children when they get home from their second jobs.

The kind of students whose stories I loved racing home from school to share with Cam.

Out of politeness and awareness that Dr. Brown was not going away, I said, "Where is the school?"

"Pelican Isle."

Pelican Isle? The only Pelican Isle I knew was a little resort island off the northeast coast of North Carolina.

I said, "You mean the little vacation beach right near the state line?"

"That's the one."

"I didn't even realize Pelican Isle had a school. In fact, I didn't realize anyone lived there but summer vacationers."

"Yes, the island does have residents, and it also has a school, grades K through three."

I grimaced and said, "I just don't know," but I did know. I knew for certain that I didn't want to leave the sanctuary of my parents' home for an obscure island, even if the island were teeming with kids who needed my help.

"Ally, what's your alternative? Just stay with your parents and never teach again? That would be such a waste," she said.

I just stared at her, unable to respond, because in my emotional state I'd become incapable of responding to common sense.

"Will you just go take a look? Go talk with the principal?" When I just bit my lip and stared at my twitching hands without responding, she added, "His name is Carter, Carter Jolly. And he is—Jolly, that is."

Knowing that I owed Dr. Brown more than my silence and a blank stare, I said, "Can I think about it for a little while? This is a huge decision."

"Of course, but just a little while. Carter needs help right away. I promised to let him know if you were interested."

"Just overnight. That's all I ask. I'll call you tomorrow," I promised, so anxious was I to end our little chat and go back to being just Ally who lives with her parents in her rose-covered childhood bedroom, walks the mall with her mom, and doesn't have to respond to common sense.

"Fine, that'll be fine. Here's my cell number," she said, pulling a pad of yellow sticky notes from her purse and scribbling on it. Shoving the note in my direction, she said, "Call me any time."

I took the note and looked at it with feigned interest. It was just a diversion. A phone number is a phone number. Not remarkable.

"I'll call tomorrow," I told her. "No promises, but I'll give it some thought."

"A lot of thought. Please."

"All right," I said, as I anxiously ushered her out.

As soon as I shut the door behind her, my mother came bustling from the kitchen and trilled, "I *promise* I wasn't eavesdropping, but I just couldn't help but hear. How exciting!"

"We'll see," I said, as I trudged up the stairs, threw myself on my bed, and fought the urge to fall off the wagon and begin counting roses again, all the while attempting to push Dr. Brown's plea for help from my mind.

Three

I took the route from Raleigh to the northern end of Pelican Isle, the only part of the island accessible by bridge. Dr. Brown had told me that the southern end of the island could be reached directly only by ferry, and a foot ferry, at that. She said that motorists taking the ferry have to park their cars at the marina on the mainland side of Parmeter Sound. So I drove an additional thirty miles and in four and a half hours reached the narrow, rusting-with-age, two-lane bridge that would take me across the sound from New Oak, North Carolina to Pelican Isle.

The fact that I made the trip at all still baffles and amuses me. I knew, without a doubt, that I would not be accepting a teaching position on remote Pelican Isle. But Dr. Brown and my parents had been so persuasive, insisting that I was committing to nothing and what did I have to lose, that there I was, whizzing down Route 64 toward a job I didn't want and had no intention of taking.

As I drove, I recalled my first job interview. Dr. Brown and my student-teacher advisors had sung my praises, and I had waltzed right into my dream teaching job. I hardly had to break a sweat for it. But this was different. This was not my dream teaching job; I no longer had a dream teaching job. That's because teaching was no longer my dream. But, as a favor, I had told Dr. Brown that I'd go to Pelican Isle to talk with Mr. Jolly. But, more than my promise to Dr. Brown, I owed it to my mother to check it out. She had been my rock, the pillar of patience. She had put her life on hold to hold me up and bring me back to life.

She isn't named Grace for nothing.

I had to show her that her efforts had not been in vain, that I had been worth her saving.

My GPS told me that Mr. Jolly's office was at the north end of the island, and it directed me from the New Oak-Pelican Isle bridge to his front door in less than five minutes. The principal's office was housed in a tiny cottage that sat among the sand dunes overlooking the beach at Pelican Isle. I pulled into the small, sandy lot and parked my car in one of the few spaces that fronted the building. There were no other cars—just a small, red two-seater golf cart with a cheery, red-and-yellow striped canvas top. It looked like a toy, something Fisher Price might have designed. I noticed that the building's pale blue paint was peeling, and the wooden steps leading to the covered porch were sagging and worn. Not at all what I was expecting, but I figured I might as well get on with it, the sooner to get back to Raleigh and the comfort of my parents' arms and home. As I emerged from my air-conditioned car, a wall of humidity punched me in my face, and I could feel my hair begin to frizz. I slapped at a mosquito, but not before it had given me a welt on my arm.

As I stretched my road-weary back and slung my purse over my shoulder, the faded red door to the building flung open, and out stepped a short, squat, balding man with khaki Bermuda's belted high on his round belly. He wore a yellow striped polo shirt and red, rubber flip flops. He looked as though he belonged to the toy Fisher Price golf cart.

I wore a blue-flowered, cotton sleeveless dress, black flats, and bare legs. I was glad I'd decided against standard interview attire—navy suit and pumps.

I heard the boards squeak as the man stepped onto the porch and threw up a hand in greeting.

"Ally, you made it. Thanks for coming. Now, get on in here before you melt."

As I stepped up onto the porch, he grabbed my hand and pumped it, saying cheerily, "Carter Jolly. Good to mee'cha."

He ushered me into the small, low-ceilinged building that had a rusting air conditioning unit clanking in the front window. Condensation dripped from it into a galvanized bucket set on the worn, warped wooden floor. A large, scarred-and-cluttered oak desk, several mismatched plastic chairs, and a small kitchenette took up most of the main room.

"Sit, sit. I'll get you a Co-Cola. You must be parched from that long ride," Mr. Jolly said in his slow, welcoming, good-ole-boy southern drawl.

He reached into an ancient-looking yellow Norge refrigerator that appeared to have been hand painted with a brush. Spots of rust bled through. He grabbed two small, green glass bottles of Coke, the kind my Gramma always stocked just for my visits. He popped the tops with a bottle opener that was attached to the side of the cupboard with a frayed length of twine.

Handing me a Coke, he said, "There you go," as he took a draw on his bottle and pulled a large, white handkerchief from his back pocket and swiped at his glistening, broad forehead.

"Thank you," I said, as I tipped the Coke and soothed my throat, which was, indeed, parched from the drive and the oppressive heat. Only then did I notice the spectacular ocean view through the filmy kitchenette windows.

"Wow, what a view! It's breathtaking. How do you ever get any work done? I'm afraid I'd spend my days just staring and daydreaming."

"Stunning, isn't it? There are times I find myself drifting," he said, seeming to drift a little as he spoke. Shaking his head and returning to me, he said, "For the most part, though, it just has a calming effect on what can be a sometimes stressful job. Fact is, I get my best inspiration sitting here, looking out at that ocean."

Then remembering why I had driven over four hours to this deserted island, I said, "Thanks for seeing me, Mr. Jolly."

"And thanks for coming over. And, please, just call me Carter."

"All right, then, Carter," I said, all of a sudden feeling right comfortable in this very unconventional principal's office with what I was beginning to believe was a very unconventional principal.

"I've taken a look at your file. Pretty impressive," he said, smiling and raising his eyebrows at me. "Is there any award you haven't won? I do believe you were born to teach."

"Thank you," I said and felt my face flush. Even though I had been a good teacher, I'd never gotten accustomed to the accolades.

"But, Ally, I need to warn you, this isn't your ordinary elementary school. If you're expecting a big, well-organized classroom, new desks, up-to-date computer equipment, and all the resources that the big city schools have, this is not the place for you."

I had come to Pelican Isle as a favor to Dr. Brown and my mother. I came with no preconceived notions about what the post entailed. It was Carter's job to explain the job and convince me that I should want to take the position as first-grade teacher at Pelican Isle Elementary. As comfortable as I felt sipping a Coke with him, he was doing a lousy job of swaying me to jump at the chance to be his new first-grade teacher.

"We sort of fly by the seat of our pants here at Pelican Isle Elementary. We can get pretty daggone frustrated by the lack of attention from the State. But I guess they do the best they can," he said, shaking his head resignedly.

The picture he was painting was looking bleaker by the moment.

I was trying to find a polite way to thank him for the Coke and return to Raleigh and the security of my parents' home when he added, "But what we lack in resources, our kids make up for in enthusiasm. They love school, so they're always on time. They're polite and respectful. 'Course we have a little stinker now and then," he chuckled, his eyes sparkling, his round belly hopping up and down. I could tell he had a soft spot for the occasional stinker. I figured he'd once been a little stinker himself. Growing serious, he leaned forward in his squeaky chair and said, "Ally, if you'll come help these kids, they'll show you just how much they appreciate you—even the stinkers. They'll try so hard against all odds that sometimes they'll just break your heart."

He could have said anything but that. I didn't think I could stand for my heart to break any more than it had already broken. I certainly wouldn't take a job, on purpose, that had come with the warning that it would break my heart.

As if sensing my reluctance, he changed the subject abruptly.

"During the summer our population grows to about ten thousand, what with all the vacationers. In the off-season, though, less than a thousand folks live on the island. Most of them are Latino."

"I didn't realize that."

"Most people don't. Fact is, every one of our students is Latino."

"What do they do? I mean, where do their parents work?"

"Well, their moms wait tables or cook in the island restaurants or work in maid services at the local inns. But in the off-season work slows down, so they have to take second jobs over on the mainland. Now, the kids' fathers work either on the local fishing trawlers or they do construction on the island or over in New Oak."

I couldn't imagine having to work so hard to take care of my family.

"Sounds like a hard life."

"Yeah, it is," he said, "but not nearly as hard as the lives they've left behind. They came here to give their kids a better life. And some of those families have six, seven, or even more kids to care for."

I was astounded. First of all, I couldn't imagine abandoning my home and then trying to take care of six or more children in a foreign country, all the while juggling two jobs. It just didn't seem possible and certainly not fair.

As if he were reading my thoughts, Carter said, "But they manage. They seem to work as a great big team. Everybody pitches in. Anyone who has a few free hours between jobs will care for the whole neighborhood of kids while their parents are working."

I smiled and said, "Sounds like a pretty good set-up to me."

"It seems to work for them. And, of course, our little school is their salvation. Not only is it a safe haven, the parents know that education is the ticket to a better life for their kids."

"That's an awfully big responsibility for the teachers," I said, feeling that I wasn't ready for that kind of pressure, that kind of responsibility.

"Yeah, it is, more than you can imagine. These kids aren't privy to home schooling. Their parents aren't concerned about securing a spot on the waiting list of the best pre-kindergarten while their children are still in the womb. They just want the best education they can get for their kids."

I smiled, knowing exactly what he meant. I had done my practice teaching with privileged children whose parents had taught them Mandarin at three years of age and had sent them to the most expensive and most prestigious pre-K's in the state. By the time their children reached first grade, they were leaps ahead of the other children and were bored to tears while their less-financially-fortunate classmates worked to catch up with them—something the others could never do, because the privileged parents continued to push, push, push their mini scholars to excel, always to outshine the others. I knew even then that theirs weren't the children I wanted to teach.

Then Carter said, "A good many of these children come to school not knowing how to read or recite their numbers, like most kids do these days. Fortunately, though, they all know how to speak English. Some of their folks don't speak English well, but they insist that their children learn."

"That's good to know," I laughed, "because my Spanish is lousy," thinking that English-speaking students would always be a necessity for me—should I ever decide to return to teaching.

"And, Ally," he said, leaning toward me and lowering his voice, "Some of the families are here illegally." When he was sure that had sunk in, he added, "They live in fear of deportation."

"How terrible," I said, having never had a student whose living arrangement was so tenuous. "Do they...? Are they...?"

"Ever deported?" he said, helping me out. "Yeah, sad to say, they are, occasionally." He pursed his lips and furrowed his brow. That look, alone, told me how much he cared for the future, safety, and care of the children of Pelican Isle.

"Carter, what brought you to Pelican Isle?" I asked.

"Well, I was over in Greensboro, teaching and working on my master's. Soon as I got my degree, I started applying for a principal's job, from one end of the state to the other. I really wanted to stay in North Carolina. It's home, you know. Anyway, all the jobs were going to the tall, good-looking types." He chuckled, making his belly shake again, and said, "You know the type."

"Yeah, I know the type," I agreed.

"Then a colleague told me about this job. I came over, interviewed, and here I am—twenty-five years later. Glad those tall, good-looking types got those other jobs because I got the best one. Wouldn't want to be anywhere else."

I checked out his hand for a wedding band and found his finger bare. Not surprising. His existence on this deserted island didn't seem conducive to marriage.

"Never been married. Married to this job, this island, these kids," he said, apparently having seen me checking his marital status. I reddened with embarrassment. "It's been a great career, a great life. Wouldn't change a thing. And where else could I wear shorts and flip flops to work and drive a car that looks like a toy?"

Then slapping his thighs with his hands, he said, "How'd you like to see the classrooms?"

Really not at all interested since I wasn't planning to stay, out of politeness I said, "Sure, I'd love to, Mr. Jolly."

"Carter, remember, it's just Carter," he said, smiling and shaking a stubby finger at me. "We're real informal around here. Your kids, if you'll take them as your kids, will call you Miss Ally. No offense meant."

"Oh, I understand. That wouldn't offend me at all."

He hoisted himself from his worn, squeaky swivel chair, breathing heavily, and grabbed a key from a nail on the wall by his desk. He motioned for me to follow him, as his red flip-flops made slapping noises across the worn plank floor of his office. He yanked hard on the front door, and it made an agonizing *squeeee*, as if his tugging had pained it. We made our way across the sagging porch and down the equally sagging steps through a hedge of bright watermelon-pink oleander to the small house next door.

"Well, here it is. Pelican Isle Elementary," he said as he climbed the steps and stuck his key in the lock.

"This is it?" I asked.

I was accustomed to large, brick, multi-storied school buildings, not low, whitewashed houses with sagging porches and paint-chipped doors with leaded-paned windows.

"Yep, grades K through three," he said. Looking back over his shoulder at me, he added, "Surprised?"

"Very surprised. Why do the kids go to school in an old house?"

"Well, it's all we have to offer. Now, there's New Oak Elementary, right across the sound. You can even see the roof of the school from the ferry landing. But there's no bus service over here. And the kids are just too young to take the ferry all by themselves. So years ago some of the island's homeowners donated these two houses, the office building and the school building, so these kids could go to school."

Carter unlocked the door, and it screeched and scraped the sill as he shoved it hard. He beckoned me into the foyer.

"This is the third grade," he said, motioning to the first classroom on the right. It was spotlessly clean but lacked supplies. "Across the hall is second." It was as barren as the first. "Right down here is the kindergarten class, and this," he said, leading me into the last classroom on the right, "is your class. First grade."

He was assuming a lot when he called it mine, but still I followed him into the first-grade classroom, a room with two walls of windows that looked directly onto the white sandy beach and the sparkling blue ocean beyond. Little desks, apparent cast-offs with names scratched and carved into their tops, were lined up neatly, facing the teacher's desk and a freestanding blackboard on wheels. I had seen blackboards on wheels only in picture books of classrooms from way back when. The well-worn bulletin board had been cleared, for the summer, I assumed, and its emptiness made the classroom look sad and sterile. I noticed books lined up in an old, scarred wooden bookcase at the side of the room, so I approached, crouched, and slid several out to examine them. Some of their front covers were missing, and across most of the books was stamped in red the word DISCARD.

Looking up at Carter, I asked, "These are all the books these children have?"

"Yeah, but they don't know the difference. They have nothing to compare them to." Then he added somewhat defensively, "But the state will supply new text books when school starts."

"Well, that's good to know," I said, annoyed that the state couldn't do better for these children.

"They do the best they can. They figure they have a public school on the mainland but that it's our choice to educate our youngest children here on the island. They have just so much money to go around," he said, shrugging his shoulders, his hands turned up in resignation. "They give us what they can. Fortunately, they do provide us with a principal and four teachers." At that he smiled.

It still seemed so unfair, but his explanation softened me.

I hoisted myself back to standing and continued the tour of the sparsely appointed room. I noted a round table at the front of the class by the window; on it was a lone, outdated Apple computer.

"Is that it?" I asked.

"Sorry to say, it is. The kids just take turns."

I understood, as Carter had said, that education budgets were tight, but the city school classrooms were so much better equipped. Sure, the kids from Pelican Isle could go to the city school, but getting there would have proven most difficult for them. Something just had to be done for these children. They simply deserved better. I so hoped that Carter could find some help.

"Thanks for showing me around," I said, reaching to shake Carter's hand, anxious to get back to Raleigh.

"It's so nice meeting you, Ally. I hope you'll consider helping us out here, at least till we can do a search for a permanent replacement. The kids really need you."

"I'll think about it," I told him, as he walked me from the school building back through the hedge of lush oleander to the parking lot.

Just as I opened my car door, a bright yellow golf cart with a blue canopy wheeled in beside us and glided noiselessly to a stop. Out stepped a tall, blonde man wearing aviator sunglasses.

"Ready for lunch?" the man asked Carter.

"Just wrapping up here." Then to me he said, "Ally, this is Chris Cruz. Chris, Ally Albright. I'm hoping she'll agree to be our new first-grade teacher."

"Nice to meet you, Ally," Chris said, stepping around the golf cart and extending his hand. "Hope you'll consider Pelican Isle. Our kids sure do need you."

"Yes, that's what Carter tells me," I said, bobbing my head self-consciously and reaching to shake his hand. "Nice meeting you too, Chris. I'll sure give it some thought."

I didn't add that the thought would be, *Not a chance.*

"How about joining Carter and me for lunch?" he said, smiling for the first time, displaying a deep dimple in his right cheek. I've always been a sucker for a guy with dimples; it was the first thing I noticed about Cam when his family moved in down the street from my folks and me when he and I were just ten years old. "We're going over to Peli Pier. Best seafood on the island."

"Thanks, but I need to be getting back to Raleigh," I said, trying to ignore Chris Cruz's dimple.

"Well, then, we'll just take a rain check," he said, still smiling.

"Sure thing," I said, knowing full well I'd never return to Pelican Isle and certainly would never have lunch with Chris Cruz, even if he did know where to get the best seafood on the island. And even if he did have a deep dimple that brought back memories of Cam.

I climbed into my car and backed out of the parking lot as the two men waved good-bye, and I headed for the bridge that would take me back to the mainland and my parents' home.

When I arrived back in Raleigh, my mom was waiting with excitement, encouragement, and lemon meringue pie.

As she cut me a large, congratulatory wedge, I said, "Oh, Mom, I just can't do it."

Pausing mid-slice, as if I no longer deserved pie, she asked, "But, why? You're such a good teacher."

Still wanting my mother's approval and her pie, I sighed, "Thanks, but those kids just need so much—much more than I can give them."

My mother looked dejected but knew not to argue. She hadn't seen the conditions at Pelican Isle Elementary; she accepted that only I knew if I could handle it. So she acknowledged my decision to forego a year on an isolated island and, instead, stay on in Raleigh and walk the mall with her each morning. She even allowed me pie.

For days I tried to push the first grade children of Pelican Isle from my mind. I was pretty successful ignoring children I'd never met, but I could not ignore Carter Jolly's dedication to his students and his enthusiasm in providing the children with the best education possible. But he couldn't do that without a teacher for his first graders.

I knew that I was ill prepared to teach sixteen students under such challenging circumstances, but what teacher could possibly be equipped to tackle such adversity? But someone had to do it. Those kids could not teach themselves, and they *had* to go to school.

After five days of anguishing tail chasing, I said to my parents as we sat at the kitchen table for dinner, "Mom, Dad, I believe I've had a change of heart."

My parents turned to me, their eyes flashing with excitement and anticipation. They suppressed anxious grins.

"Those kids have to go to school, but they can't go without a teacher. So I guess I have no choice but to take the job," I said, shrugging my shoulders and lifting my palms in resignation. "I'll sign Carter's one-year contract. That'll give him time to conduct a proper search for a permanent replacement."

"Oh, Ally," Mom trilled and clapped her hands, "I don't think you'll regret this. It sounds like a wonderful opportunity."

I knew that she didn't mean a wonderful teaching opportunity. She meant it would be a wonderful opportunity to recover and to get back to normal, if that were at all possible.

"I think that's a wise decision," my dad said. "I know it was a tough one, but you're tough. I think it'll be real good for you."

"Thanks. I'm counting on your help, you know."

"Yes, we know. Whatever you need," Mom said, leaning toward me and patting my hand.

Four

So there I was, less than two months later, climbing into my packed-to-the-roof Honda, ready to head for the coast to fulfill a one-year contract to teach the first graders of Pelican Isle.

"Call us when you get there."

"I will, Mom."

"Better yet, Honey, call us when you make a pit stop, just so, you know…"

"Okay, Dad, I'll call you when I make a pit stop, just so, you know…"

My dad smiled broadly, but I could see the tears glistening in his eyes. He was ready for me to move on with my life, yet he still felt that need to protect me. The parent's conundrum. He took me in his arms and squeezed hard.

"I'm proud of you, Baby," he said into my hair.

"I know, Dad."

"Big step. Really big step. But you'll do great," he said, gripping my upper arms and shaking me firmly. "Now, you go knock 'em dead."

"They're first graders, Dad," I laughed.

He laughed too.

Edging him aside, my mother took over.

"Now, don't forget the oatmeal cookies, Darlin'. I tucked them under the passenger seat. And then there's that bag of fresh Farmer's Market tomatoes and peaches and cantaloupe in the trunk. Be sure you take them out as soon as you get there. Wouldn't want them to spoil in the heat of the trunk."

Small talk. My parents had struggled to bring me back to life. They had coaxed me out of bed and away from my flower counting to the shower and to the dinner table and to the mall. But this was no bowl of split-pea soup or a stroll around the shopping center. This was a huge leap. They were so proud of my decision; yet, at the same time, they were frightened for me.

And, understandably, they were sad to see their only child leave home. I had never left them, not even for overnight summer camp. And when it had come time to pick a college, I had chosen State, just two miles from my parents' front door. I had lived in a dorm on campus, but they had given me a car, so that I could bring my laundry home on weekends and stay for a home-cooked meal. And when we married, Cam and I chose an apartment within walking distance of my childhood home.

So my venturing two hundred thirty miles to take a job on a sparsely inhabited island was a huge step, even if I had signed only a one-year contract that would help Carter out and give him time to do his search for a full-time first-grade teacher. But the year away would help sever my dependence on my parents. We all knew it was for the best. For all of us.

"I'll take care of the tomatoes, peaches, and cantaloupe, Mom."

"I'll miss you so much, Ally," she said, pushing my hair back from my face and kissing my cheek.

The smell of her Chanel made a lump rise in my throat.

"I'll miss y'all too. But you'll be coming out to the island soon."

"I know, Sweetie. It's just the first parting that's the hardest," she said, her voice breaking.

So before she could cry, she patted my back and said, "Well, we'd better get this show on the road. Don't want you driving after dark."

It was ten in the morning, in August. We were on daylight savings time, and it wouldn't be dark for at least eleven more hours. And my destination was just four and a half hours away. But she didn't know what else to say.

"Bye-bye," I said as I climbed into my aging Honda, the same car that had made weekend laundry runs from college, and reached out to squeeze their hands one last time.

They each leaned down, in turns, to kiss me once more. Then holding onto the car window, they followed me as I backed out of the driveway. Only when I put the car in forward gear and gave their hands a final pat did they let go and begin their farewell waves. I watched them in my rear view mirror, waving, waving, as they got smaller and smaller and then disappeared as I turned the corner and made my way for the Beltline.

I would miss them and their caring with a painful ache. Even though they had granted me my independence at eighteen, I always knew, as did they, that they were only a hot meal and a load of laundry away. I shook the thought from my head to ward off weeping and turned my full attention to the journey before me.

I couldn't have picked a more beautiful day to start my new, temporary life. It was in the mid-80's with low humidity, something practically unheard of in North Carolina Augusts, so I was able to travel with my window down, my arm resting on the ledge. Since I was headed for the beach, I turned on the radio and scanned the dial until I hit upon 107.9 FM, WNCT, the beach music station out of Greenville, North Carolina.

The Embers wailed about loving beach music and sand between their toes, as the wind blew my hair like tumbleweeds and I streaked toward the coast. The trip was uneventful, with no sobbing and just one stop at a 7-Eleven to buy a bottle of water and call my mom and dad, just so, you know...

"Yes, Daddy, just two more hours. Right, making good time, real good time. I'm sure I'll be there before dark."

My father chuckled and said, "Oh, you know Mom. She loves you and just feels she has to say that."

"Yeah, I know that. Can you put her on?"

"Sure, Baby. Now, you stay safe, you hear?"

"I will. I love you, Daddy."

"Love you too, Honey."

"Hi, Sweetie."

"Mom, thank you."

"My pleasure, Darlin'."

"I couldn't have done this without you." And then I was crying, crying really hard. "Oh, Mom, I love you so much. Please come see me. Soon."

"Oh, I will." And I could hear her tears too. "Your daddy and I love you more than anything in this world. We'll miss you so much, but we'll see you before you know it."

"I know, Mom. I'll talk to you soon. Bye, now."

I reluctantly hit End Call and raked my sleeve across my eyes, sniffed back the tears real hard, and guzzled the rest of my water. I tossed the empty in the recycle bin, climbed back into my car, and headed out onto the highway, minding my no-sobbing-while-driving policy.

Turning up the volume on the radio, I tapped the steering wheel in rhythm as Maurice Williams and the Zodiacs moaned that I should *Stay, awwwwwww, just a little bit longer.*[1]

I was certain I could already smell the salt air.

Once I'd agreed to take the teaching job on Pelican Isle, Dr. Brown sweetened the pot by offering me her beach cottage, rent free, for the full school year. Granted, it wasn't the height of tourist season, your prime beach months, but it was the beach. And, it bears repeating, she offered it *rent-free*. Her home was located just five miles south of Pelican Isle Elementary, nestled among the dunes, overlooking the ocean. There has never been a sweeter deal in the history of sweet deals. What's more, the cottage came with its own golf cart for my personal use to get around the island. I wouldn't even need my car.

I made it to New Oak in slightly less than four hours and was just minutes away from saying good-bye to the mainland and hello to Pelican Isle. I pulled onto the ancient, rusted, two-lane bridge that connected the small town to the barrier island and listened as my tires clacked and bumped across decades of patches spanning the final one-half mile over Parmeter Sound to my new, temporary home. I exited the bridge on the island side and turned right, rather than left to the school, the route I had taken when I'd come to interview for my teaching job with Carter. That trip had revealed a laundromat, a snow cone stand, a putt-putt golf course, and a car wash. It was not an attractive landscape or an easy sell. But, somehow, Carter had managed to sell it to me.

I was expecting more of the same as I turned in the direction of my new home, but I was pleasantly surprised with the landscape. The strip of garish, concrete businesses to the north gave way to a southern expanse of well-worn, shabby-chic whitewashed cottages. They perched high on stilts dotting the shore to my left and were protected from the elements by a row of sea-oat-covered dunes. To my right stretched a string of sherbet-colored bungalows sitting low to the ground, overlooking Parmeter Sound. Each kiwi, tangerine, blueberry, lemon, raspberry structure sported a deep, wrap-around porch with a ceiling fan turning slowly with the gentle sea breeze over metal gliders, rope hammocks, or rush-seated rockers. Each home displayed a small, lush, green patch of front yard bordered by a low, white picket fence. The line of brightly colored homes was interrupted at intervals by a seafood restaurant, an ice cream parlor, or a small souvenir shop with bright, red banners emblazoning the windows, advertising END OF SEASON SALE. FLIP FLOPS, HALF PRICE. STOCK UP FOR NEXT SUMMER.

Dr. Brown had given me detailed directions to my new home, but she had not prepared me for the charm that was Pelican Isle. I craned my neck to take it in, smiling broadly all the while, until I pulled into the sandy drive of my new, temporary home. I parked my car under an arbor of lavender and white crepe myrtles and took an assessment of the cottage. It had seen better days, I was certain, but at least it was standing upright and looked as though it would hold me and my meager belongings just fine. It could have used a fresh whitewash, and one faded, blue shingle hung precariously by a single hinge, but that was just cosmetic, easily fixed. Or not.

I pulled the house key from my purse and decided to check out the place before unloading my car. I approached the stairs with caution and placed one foot on the bottom rung. I put my full weight on it and bounced lightly. The step squeaked and sagged a bit but held me. Each stair, in turn, complained under my weight, but they all appeared safe enough. When I reached the porch, I put the key into the rusty, salt-encrusted lock and heard the chalk-on-the-blackboard screech as I turned the key and shoved on the humidity-swollen door.

Then I stepped into the most wonderful, welcoming, charming room I'd ever seen. The floor was fashioned of well-worn, honey-colored wooden planks, and the walls were made of whitewashed, rough-hewn boards, running side-to-side, rather than up and down. The furniture was large and soft and squishy, all of it covered with rumpled, muslin slipcovers. There were colorful, braided rugs scattered about, and a large, functioning fireplace dominated one wall. And there were shells everywhere: on shelves, on tables, on the mantle, in jars, on window sills, in wicker baskets, as door stops, as drawer pulls, affixed to lamp bases, strung together and hanging from the ceiling and tinkling together as I stirred the air. It was the most magical place I'd ever seen. And, taking it in, I smiled to myself and figured I could use a little magic in my life. The magic of Dr. Brown's home on Pelican Isle would serve me just fine for one school year.

An examination of the rest of the small cottage revealed a kitchen that was tiny and dated but simply stocked with everything I'd need to prepare the uncomplicated meals I planned to cook for myself. The one bedroom was small, as well, with an ornate white iron double bed, a single dresser, and a miniscule closet. A bathroom with just a shower but no tub and an alcove off the living room, suitable, perhaps, as a small office, rounded out my new home.

Then I caught sight, for the first time, of the view from my living room windows. There, over the dunes, was the ocean, crashing, crashing toward the cottage, the sun casting blindingly bright rays of light on the turquoise blue waves. I closed my eyes and listened to the rumbling sound that I was confident would lull me into peaceful sleep each night. I stepped out onto the porch and breathed in the salt sea breeze. I leaned against the railing, closed my eyes again, and just listened to the sounds of real beach music.

Then I thought, *Yep, this just might work out, after all.*

"Hey, Ally."

I opened my eyes to find a tall, thin woman with long, snow-white hair and a flowing white, gauzy dress skipping barefoot up my stairs. She was waving her hand and carrying what appeared to be a pie. And she knew my name. When she reached the porch, she grabbed my hand and smiled as her startling, pale blue eyes sparkled.

And with a soft, soothing voice that sounded as if it were being filtered through butter, she said, "Welcome, Ally. We've been waiting for you. We're so glad you've decided to join us here on Pelican Isle. I'm Joy Summers, your next-door neighbor."

Then she let go of my hand and hooked her waving hair behind one ear.

"Hi, Joy, nice to meet you. I haven't even unloaded my car yet, but please come on in."

"No, my dear, I'm not staying—this time. Just wanted to drop off this pecan pie and say hey. We'll have plenty of time to visit soon. Now, you get yourself settled, and when you're ready, just come on over. My door is always open."

I loved her already. Instead of saying peh-con pie, like most people do, she said pee-can pie, just the way my mom did. And, of course, there was that buttery voice of hers.

Then she turned and floated down the stairs, her long, white dress and her long, white hair flowing out behind her. I watched as she padded across my yard and then her own, ran lightly up her stairs, waved to me once more, and disappeared into her house.

I stood on my porch, holding my pecan pie, still warm from the oven, and continued to watch the waves crash and listen to the surf rumble and the gulls screech overhead. Then I remembered the fruits and vegetables in the trunk of the car and my promise to my mother not to let them spoil. So I took my pie to the kitchen and placed it on the cracked, sky-blue ceramic tile counter and headed for my car to gather my luggage and produce.

By the time I'd unpacked my clothes and stored them in the dresser drawers and mini-closet, lined up my toiletries on the single bathroom shelf, made my bed with the new 1600-count Egyptian cotton sheets Mom and Dad had given me as a going-away gift, and stowed my tomatoes and peaches and cantaloupe in the fridge, it was close to supper time. I hadn't even eaten lunch yet, except for that bottle of water at the 7-Eleven halfway between my old home and my new home.

I was ravenous. I could either venture out in my golf cart to find food or settle for fresh produce. Neither appealed to me. So I found the silverware drawer, grabbed a fork and my pecan pie, and headed for the porch. There I sat in a weatherworn Adirondack chair with faded, red peeling paint and ate my supper: one-quarter of a pecan pie, right out of the ceramic pie plate. Though I promised myself I wouldn't make a habit of eating a quarter of a pecan pie for supper, that pie, eaten from a worn, red Adirondack chair, straight from the pie plate, overlooking the turquoise Atlantic Ocean was, without a doubt, the most delicious meal I had ever had in my life. Or planned to have for the rest of my life.

I took the remaining three-quarters of my pie to the kitchen, leaving the fork in the plate—just in case I felt the need for a bedtime snack. Then I returned to the porch to watch the seagulls swoop, the waves crash, and the sun go down.

I awoke with a jolt. I remembered the horizon turning from gold to fuchsia to black, but I didn't recall falling asleep in the Adirondack chair. As I looked around, I discovered that the houses dotting the beachfront were fast asleep. Not a light shone for as far as I could see. I squinted at my watch. The green, illuminated hands told me it was two forty seven in the morning. I hoisted my contorted, aching muscles out of my chair, stretched, breathed in the warm, salty air once more, and headed for the bedroom. Too tired to shower, I climbed out of my clothes and dropped them on the floor, pulled my cotton nightgown from the top dresser drawer, slipped it over my head, and collapsed onto my cool, new sheets.

Five

The sun was high in the sky when I awoke the following morning. I squinted at the bedside clock. Ten o'clock. Though I had recently spent months in bed, I hadn't actually slept until ten o'clock in the morning since high school, that fount of irresponsibility. Apparently, moving day had rendered me exhausted. But now I needed coffee. Lots of coffee. I had none. In fact, I didn't even know if my new home was equipped with a coffee maker. Or even a coffee pot. I showered and quickly toweled dry. Reaching for my hair dryer, I changed my mind and gave my head a good shake. My hair was capable of drying on its own. After a quick once-over of sunscreen, I jumped into shorts and a tee shirt and stepped into my pink-and-red flowered flip flops, a last-minute purchase at the Rite-Aid Drug just before leaving Raleigh for the coast. I grabbed Dr. Brown's key ring and the overpriced tan canvas Coach purse that I had coveted and Cam had bought for me when we'd learned that we were expecting a child. Then I headed for my golf cart. And coffee.

At a blazing 18 miles per hour my cart streaked silently toward the village. Dr. Brown had told me that the village of Pelican Isle was less than three miles away from my house, at the south end of the island near the ferry landing. So I just drove south on Beach Road, the only fully paved road on the island, and soon the little village of shops and restaurants came into view, just as Dr. Brown had promised. And it wasn't difficult to find a breakfast restaurant that served coffee. The low, cinder block building on the right was bright, sunshine yellow with the word BREAKFAST emblazoned in red across the front. And beneath that, also in red, were the words HOT COFFEE.

The village was bustling with locals, as well as late-season vacationers, mostly older couples who no longer had the responsibility of getting children ready to head back to school. They looked like seasoned veterans, true beach worshippers, affluent and tanned to the shade and texture of burnished leather. They appeared to be milking the very last remnant of beach out of the season.

I joined them in the BREAKFAST restaurant and found a small two-seater booth by the back window, overlooking Parmeter Sound. My bare thighs squeaked across the red vinyl upholstery as I slid in, and I did that silly thing we all do—cleared my throat—in hopes of masking the suspicious sound. I pulled the laminated menu from between the catsup and the Texas Pete bottles and perused the pictures of the more-colorful-than-they-could-possibly-be breakfast selections. Pancakes, crepes, French toast. I decided I'd had enough sweets to hold me for a while.

"Good morning, may I get you something to drink?"

I turned to face the most beautiful young woman I'd ever seen. Her hair was dark and shiny and held away from her round, rosy cheeks in a long, wavy ponytail. Her eyes were huge and black, her lashes long and thick. And her welcoming, full smile revealed perfect, white teeth. Her name tag told me that her name was Bianca.

"Yes, please, Bianca, I need some coffee. Lots of coffee. Right now."

She laughed and said, "Yes, ma'am, I get that a lot. Hang on. I'll be right back."

She returned quickly, carrying a mug, a plastic, insulated carafe of coffee, and a tall glass of ice water with a wedge of lemon clinging to its rim.

"Here you go. This ought to hold you till I can get you some breakfast," she said, smiling, flashing her beautiful, white teeth, and pouring me a cup of coffee. "Now, have you decided what you'd like, or do you need some more time to look over the menu?"

"What do you recommend?"

"Well, the southwest omelet is delicious," she said, pointing with the eraser of her pencil toward the neon-yellow eggs pictured on the menu, "but I'm a little partial. It has jalapenos and onions and cheese. And, of course, you'd want to shake a little of that Texas Pete on it."

Sliding the menu back into its catsup-Texas Pete slot, I said, "Very persuasive. I believe I'll give the southwest omelet a try."

"I think you'll like it, but if you don't, I can always get you something else." Jotting my order on her pad and then stabbing her ponytail with her pencil, she said, "And you'd like some orange juice, maybe?"

"Sure."

"Okay. It won't take long."

All alone, I sipped my coffee and came to life, looking out at the crystal blue water of Parmeter Sound. I assumed that most of the commercial fishing boats had already headed out to sea for the day as I watched only a few pleasure boats moored to the pier or scooting past, their happy passengers smiling and waving gaily to one another. They seemed overjoyed to have no responsibility other than keeping their boats upright and in the middle of the sound.

And then I realized, for the first time, how the island had gotten its name. There, perched on every wooden piling lining the waterfront wharf, was a pelican, sitting perfectly still, as if each were a permanent fixture or performance art.

"Here you go," said Bianca, as she placed my fluffy, yellow omelet and a tall, thin glass of orange juice in front of me. "Brought you some corn sticks too. On the house, of course. They're sort of like fried cornbread, but a little spicy."

"Thanks. They look delicious."

"Hope you enjoy it. Let me know if you need anything else."

First I slathered butter on a corn stick and took a bite. And I knew, for certain, that I had found my new favorite food, next to Joy's pecan pie, of course. Then I tasted my southwest omelet and decided that, no, southwest omelet was my new favorite food, next to Joy's pecan pie. It appeared that Pelican Isle was helping me locate my lost appetite. I'd be lucky if I could waddle back to Raleigh at the end of the school year.

"How is it? More water? Juice? Anything else?"

"Nope, it's perfect. Don't need another thing. But thanks. And thanks, too, for recommending the omelet. It's delicious. The corn sticks too."

"I was hoping you'd like it." Then she asked, "You new to Pelican Isle? Don't recall seeing you in here before."

I was certain my pasty skin gave me away, told Bianca that I hadn't been vacationing.

"Yes, I'm new, but I'm not visiting. I've moved here to teach first grade at Pelican Isle Elementary."

Her eyes widened and she cried excitedly, "Miss Ally. You're Miss Ally! Oh, it's so nice to meet you," she said, grabbing my hand and pumping it, her shiny, black ponytail jumping with glee from shoulder to shoulder. "We have been waiting for you. My Cara will be in your class this year. She is so excited. She already knows her alphabet, and she can write her numbers and read some words."

I was delighted to be meeting the mother of one of my students, but I just couldn't believe Bianca was old enough to be the mother of a first grader. She looked like a schoolgirl herself.

Then she added, "And my Mateo will be in third grade. He's a smart boy."

"Well, Bianca, I'm so glad to meet you," I said, "And I can't wait to meet Cara. And Mateo."

Before I left the BREAKFAST restaurant, I'd met all the employees. Even the fry cook, a huge, bald man named Angel, came to greet me and give me a great bear hug. They were all so happy that someone had agreed to isolate herself on Pelican Isle so that their first graders could go to school and learn to read and write.

Angel said, "People love Pelican Isle in the summer, but they forget all about us in the winter. If we can't give them warm weather and calm, blue seas, they don't want to have anything to do with us. Thank you for accepting our cold weather and gray, choppy seas, Miss Ally."

Already taken by the warmth and charm of the islanders, I said, "My pleasure, Angel. I'm pretty sure we're going to have a good year."

I left BREAKFAST even more confident that I had made the right decision. I was certain that I was supposed to come to Pelican Isle so that I could teach little Cara, who already knew her alphabet and numbers and could read some words.

Bianca had told me that the only grocery store on Pelican Isle, Island Grocery, was a block south and around the corner to my left. I hopped into my golf cart, and, sure enough, I found it as easily as I'd found everything else on the island.

I pulled into the partially filled parking lot, grabbed my purse, stepped from my golf cart, and headed for the entry.

It's always hard to become acquainted with a new grocery store. It's somewhat like meeting a new boyfriend. You're not quite sure you're going to like him or feel comfortable with him at first. But, over time, he's finishing your sentences and you don't mind his seeing you without make-up. I felt disloyal giving up my Whole Foods, my old boyfriend, for Island Grocery, but I had no choice. So I'd grudgingly accept the inevitable change. We'd go slowly until we got to know each other well; I'd just take my time, cruise the aisles, buy, very cautiously, only those items that were familiar to stock my new kitchen.

"May I help you find something?" a handsome, young stock boy brandishing a price gun asked me as I tentatively entered aisle one.

"Thanks, I think I'm fine."

"Well, my name is Miguel. Let me know if I can help, Ma'am," he said, and went back to clacking his gun across a case of pinto beans.

Island Grocery cemented our relationship immediately. I warmed to the new market that smelled of fresh fruit and herbs and local seafood and had a handsome young boy with a price gun who wanted to help me and called me Ma'am. When I approached the check-out, my cart was overflowing with familiar items and a few unfamiliar ones that had looked too enticing to pass up. I was so hoping everything would fit into my four-seater golf cart.

"Miss Ally?"

"Yes?"

"I'm Ramona Diaz," said the cashier, as she reached to shake my hand.

"Hi, Ramona, nice to meet you," I said.

But before I could ask how she knew I was Miss Ally, she said, "Angel, you know the cook over at the diner, he's my cousin. He called to tell us you were coming over. He said we better take real good care of you."

I laughed and said, "Word sure does spread fast, doesn't it?"

"Yes, ma'am. But we've been waiting for you, Miss Ally. Our kids needed a teacher so bad."

"Will you have a child in my class?"

"Oh, no, my children are big now—three girls and two boys, two sets of twins and a single. They go to New Oak High." Then smiling proudly, she said, "They're all honor students. They all plan to go to college. But everyone of them went to Pelican Isle Elementary."

"They sound like terrific kids."

"Oh, they are," she said before adding, "that'll be eighty-four dollars and nineteen cents, please. Paper okay? We don't carry plastic. Bad for our environment, you know."

"That's great to hear. Paper's fine." I told her as I swiped my credit card through the machine.

As Ramona handed me the receipt and began bagging my groceries, she called, "Miguel, come help Miss Ally get her groceries to her cart."

Before I could protest and tell her that I was perfectly capable of toting my own groceries, Miguel was at my side, his price gun now protruding from the hip pocket of his jeans. He deftly loaded my bags into the basket and headed for the door.

"Thank you, Ramona. See you again soon," I called, as I ran to catch up with Miguel.

I followed him to the parking lot, where he transferred my groceries to my golf cart and secured them with bungee cords that he'd found in the compartment under the back seat.

When he finished, he gave the bags one firm shake to make sure they were secure and said, "That ought to do it."

I reached into my wallet and pulled out of couple of dollar bills and offered them to him.

"No, ma'am, I can't."

"Oh, please, Miguel, I really appreciate your help."

"Thank you, Miss Ally, but I can't take your money. You're doing something special for us. Please let us do something for you."

Six

After unloading my groceries and finding a spot for everything in my small kitchen, I drove my cart in the opposite direction—to the north end of the island, to Pelican Isle Elementary. I needed to ready my classroom for my students. Having met some of the island residents, even the mother of one of my students, I had become intrigued, if not altogether excited, about the upcoming school year.

The weather was picture-perfect, the sun high in the clear-blue sky, the crystal waves rumbling and crashing to shore. I couldn't have ordered a more beautiful day to get settled in my new home.

I found the small, sandy parking lot in front of the school building empty when I pulled my cart in and cruised to a silent stop in front of a huge, blue hydrangea bush. I hopped out and headed up the worn, sagging stairs, pulling out the key Carter had entrusted to me. I shimmied the key into the lock, only to find that it also screeched and screamed with salt and rust. I had begun to believe that Pelican Isle was made up of old, worn, sagging stairs and salt-encrusted locks.

I made my way to my first grade classroom and experienced fresh despair over its emptiness. Never had I seen such an under-equipped space. Of course, I had seen it when I was just a visitor, but now that it was my responsibility, it's barrenness made me shudder. How could there be just one outdated computer for sixteen children? And instead of shiny new tables and colorful chairs, my first graders would sit in old, defaced, cast-off wooden desks. I wished I'd had time and the proper tools to sand them smooth and refinish them so my students would have clean, new surfaces to start their clean, new year. Their bookshelves had books, all first-grade appropriate, but they were a disgrace—tattered and worn. There was ample bulletin board space, but I had no dry-erase boards and just the one chalkboard on a stand.

Something had to be done.

But what? The weight of my predicament sank me to the floor where I wrapped my arms around my legs and rested my head on my knees.

What just the day before had seemed like a good decision now had me saying out loud, "What have I gotten myself into?"

So I did the only thing I could think to do: I reached into my pocket, pulled out my phone, and dialed.

"Mom, what are you and Dad doing this weekend?"

"I don't think we have plans, unless your dad has something up his sleeve that I don't know about."

"And we both know that he doesn't, right?"

"Yeah, guess not," she chuckled. "But why do you ask? You need something?"

"Sure do. Do you think y'all could come to Pelican Isle?"

"Oh, Ally, we'd love to. We've been talking about a visit ever since you pulled out of the driveway. We just didn't want to intrude, though, until you were settled."

"Well, I'm as settled as I'm going to get, and I really need your help."

"Of course, Honey. What do you need?"

"Get a pencil because my list is long."

I heard her rummaging through the junk drawer for a pencil and a scrap of paper. She had been promising to clean out that disorderly drawer since I'd been in middle school. From the sound of things, she still hadn't gotten around to it.

"There. Ready. What'cha need?" she asked, sounding out of breath from her rummaging.

"My old laptop. It's in a green canvas case on the shelf of my bedroom closet."

"Got it."

"And my globe."

"Okay, I know where that is. I saw it in the attic the last time I was up there."

"And, Mom, can I have my old dorm fridge?"

Since the state didn't provide hot meals to our students and teachers, I was going to have to carry my own lunch to school. I figured I'd need a fridge to store my bag lunch and a drink.

"Certainly, Daddy and I have no use for it. I'm sure it's still in the attic."

"Great, thanks."

"Okay, what else?"

"Books. Books, books, and more books. I know you haven't thrown away a single book since PAT THE BUNNY. Just find anything you think would be appropriate for first graders."

"Oh, my goodness, that's a lot of books. It'll take a good, long while for me to sift through all those boxes."

Remembering that a retired librarian lived in my parents' neighborhood, I said, "Mom, maybe Mrs. Mayhew could help you."

"Oh, sure, I didn't think of Mildred. I'll give her a call."

"Thanks for your help."

"It'll be fun, Ally. But I'd better get to work," she said, sounding anxious to get to her tasks. "Dad and I will see you Saturday."

"Unless he has something up his sleeve."

We both laughed out loud at the absurd notion and said good-bye.

I returned my phone to my pocket and surveyed my blank slate. Cold and institutional, its only redeeming feature was the view of the ocean through the back windows.

Then something Carter Jolly said the day we met came to me: "I get my best inspiration sitting here, looking out at that ocean."

With that in mind, I hopped up from the floor and began spinning all the worn little desks, facing them toward the back of the room. My students may be short on supplies, but they would not be short on inspiration. Then I pushed and shoved and dragged my desk from the front of the room to the back, causing it to screech and moan as I inched it across the wooden floor. When the desk finally came to rest in its new home, I was bathed in perspiration and panting for breath. I was certainly glad that the chalkboard was on a wheeled stand so that I could easily roll it along.

When I had the furniture where I wanted it, I laid a blanket on the worn, wooden floor and upended three huge tote bags of supplies from my years of teaching. I had no idea what I'd find, but I knew I'd surely have the makings for a bulletin board. After covering the space with brightly colored squares of construction paper, I gathered gold-painted, wooden letters and spelled across the top of the board: MISS ALLY'S ALL STARS. Then I cut sixteen paper plates into the shape of stars, covered each with aluminum foil, and scattered them across the bulletin board. And then on each star, in colorful foam letters, I spelled the name of each of my new students, copied from the roster Carter had emailed me the week before I left Raleigh for Pelican Isle. Children love bright, colorful bulletin boards, especially when they can find their own names. It makes them feel as though they belong. I so wanted them to feel as though they belonged. And I figured if I could give them a sense of belonging, we'd be on our way to having a great year together.

As I was putting the finishing touches on my handiwork, I heard the front door of the building screech open. Hearing footsteps in the hall, I called out, "Hello, who's there?"

Carter popped his head in the door and said, "Hey, Ally, hope I didn't frighten you."

"Oh, hey, Carter. No, you didn't frighten me. Just wasn't expecting anyone today."

"Well, I saw your cart out front and just wanted to check and see how you were doing."

As he stepped into my classroom, I noticed that he was wearing the same uniform he wore during our interview: striped Polo shirt, khaki Bermudas belted high on his pudgy tummy, and rubber flip flops. He approached my bulletin board. Spreading his legs and crossing his arms, he surveyed my display, shook his head approvingly, smiled, and said, "I'd say you've done this before."

"Yeah, a few times," I told him.

"Good job. Very good job. The kids are going to love it."

"Hope so." Then I added, "Hey, you notice anything different?"

Glancing around, he said, "The desks are facing the back of the room."

"That's right, thanks to you."

"Me?" he said, cocking his head.

"Yes, you. You said that you got your best inspiration looking out at the ocean from your office window. I figured it would inspire my kids too."

He grinned and said, "It probably will. I'm betting their teacher will inspire them as well."

I smiled and felt myself blush from the compliment.

"Well, what can I do to help?" he asked.

I had brought cleaning supplies, so I said, "Want to help me clean, sort of spruce the place up a bit before the kids get here?"

"I'd love to. Where do we start?"

Handing him the bag of supplies, I said, "Anywhere you'd like."

So we dusted all the desks and baseboards, Swiffered the floor, and Windexed the classroom windows, inside and out. As we worked, Carter and I laughed and chatted amicably, as if we were old friends. The sun was setting when we finally surfaced for air. Exhausted but pleased with our day's labor, we stowed the cleaning supplies in the break room and headed for the parking lot.

"Thanks for your help. I don't think I could have finished today had you not shown up."

"My pleasure. And thank you for coming to the island. We're so grateful."

"Glad I could help, Carter."

I crawled into the golf cart and made it home with just enough energy for a shower, a peanut butter sandwich, and a topple into bed.

My parents showed up on Saturday, mid-morning, their car groaning from the weight of my wish list.

"Well, let's get that classroom ready for the kiddos," my dad said, once he'd had a chance to place his stamp of approval on my magical beachfront home.

I wedged myself into the back of their SUV, between the mini fridge and a tower of books, and the three of us set off for the schoolhouse.

"Great job on the bulletin board, Ally, but this place sure does need some filling up," Dad said, as he wandered among the desks. "But look at that view. Lucky kids."

"Yep, they are lucky. That beach is going to be our playground, as well as our inspiration for creativity. Isn't it wonderful?"

"Oh my, Ally, it's just spectacular," Mom said, clasping her hands and beaming with delight at the children's and my good fortune.

"Well, let's get the car unloaded."

Dad was anxious to do his part.

He and I hauled in the mini fridge and wedged it into the corner of the break room. Then we set up my laptop on the lone table, alongside the only other computer. My mother put the globe on my desk, for lack of any other available surface. Then the three of us set about arranging gently-worn and much-loved books on the bookshelves. Mom had brought all my childhood favorites, and I had to resist the urge to sit on the floor, cross-legged, and re-read them all.

When we felt the room was ready to receive sixteen fresh, new first graders, we stepped back to survey our handiwork.

"Looks good," pronounced my father.

"Yep, I think so too," I agreed.

"Nice, really nice," Mom said.

I put my arms around them and said, "Thanks for everything. I'd never have made it this far without you. Love y'all so much."

"We love you too," my mom said, "and we're so proud of you."

She'd never tire of telling me just how proud she was.

My father just hugged me tighter.

Releasing me and looking at his watch, he said, "My, it's later than I thought. I don't know about you girls, but I've worked up quite an appetite."

Mom and I told him that we were pretty hungry too, and, as a thank you, I offered to treat my parents to dinner at Peli Pier. I recalled Carter's friend saying that they served the best seafood on the island.

"Sounds perfect," they both said.

I locked the classroom, and we headed for my parents' car. We made it to Peli Pier in less than ten minutes, and the hostess seated us in a booth by the huge bank of windows overlooking Parmeter Sound. I was grateful for the view because I so wanted my parents to be rewarded for their efforts with one of the most beautiful sights on Pelican Isle.

"Well, Ally," my dad said, "I believe I could get used to a steady diet of this."

"Oh, I agree. Breathtaking, isn't it?"

I was so happy that my parents approved of my decision to leave Raleigh for a remote island. I still wanted, even needed, their validation, a lifeline still connecting me to them.

We ate clam chowder and broiled flounder, the day's specials. I was grateful for Carter and his friend's recommendation. It was truly delicious.

As we were eating and chatting, I heard someone say, "Hey, Ally."

I followed the voice to a very attractive man with shaggy, blonde hair and the most disarmingly beautiful green eyes I'd ever seen. He looked somewhat familiar, but, for the life of me, I just couldn't place him.

But when he smiled, flashing his dimple, I remembered.

"Chris, Chris Cruz, right?"

"Right," he said, still smiling, taunting me with that dimple. "Good memory."

"Chris, these are my parents, Grace and Gray Macklemore. They came from Raleigh to help me ready my classroom."

"Nice to meet you," he said, coming forward and shaking both of my parents' hands. "We are just so grateful that Ally agreed to help us out. Our kids really need her."

"Well, thanks, Chris. We're awfully happy she accepted the job," my mom said.

Then smiling at me, he said, "Good to see you again. Wish I could stay and chat, but I really have to run. I just came in to grab a take-out order." And to my parents he said, "So nice meeting you. Hope you'll come back to visit often. There's just no place like the island."

I watched him head for his take-out order at the checkout counter. Once he had paid, he turned, pointed at me and winked, and called across the restaurant, "Carter and I are going to cash that rain check you owe us."

I was embarrassed that he'd caught me staring as he retreated, so I just lowered my lids and gave a half-hearted wave.

When he disappeared, both my parents gave me a what-was-that-all-about look.

"Well?" they both said.

"Well, what?"

"What aren't you telling us?"

"Nothing!" I gasped. "When I was leaving the school after my interview, that guy pulled up in a golf cart to take Carter to lunch. They asked me to join them—just to be polite, I'm sure. That's all. Nothing more," I added, waving my hands in the air, trying to sweep the notion out of my parents' heads.

"He remembered you, so he apparently wasn't just being polite," my mother said, the notion apparently still in her head.

"Well, Mom, I didn't go to lunch with them then, and I have no intention of cashing his rain check."

"Wouldn't hurt," Mom said, and I knew I had to change the subject immediately.

"I don't know about y'all, but I'm stuffed," I said, leaning back in my chair and patting my stomach."

"Me too," my dad said, "but it sure was delicious."

"Thanks for the help," I told them again, though I'd never be able to thank them appropriately for all they'd done for me.

And I wasn't referring only to their help getting my classroom ready for my students. They understood that I was thanking them for nurturing me and holding me up until I was, once again, able to stand alone. But before we could dwell on that dark place, I caught our waiter's eye and motioned for our check. I wanted to get far away from the past, but I also wanted to get far away from Peli Pier before my mother could revisit the idea of my dining with Chris Cruz.

When we got home, we kicked off our shoes, and the three of us collapsed on the porch, lined up in my weatherworn Adirondack chairs. Preparing a classroom for sixteen six-year olds can be exhausting.

Sitting quietly, nodding to the rumble of the waves, we heard, "Hey, neighbor, how you doing?"

We stirred and found Joy skipping down her steps and heading toward us.

"On my way out and wanted to check first to see if you needed anything from the market."

"Thanks, but I don't need a thing. But come over and meet my mom and dad. They came to help get my classroom ready."

She floated up my stairs, hair and skirt flowing out behind her, hand already extended in greeting by the time she reached the porch.

My parents stood to meet her as she grasped their hands and said, "Welcome, I'm Joy Summers. And it is such a delight to know the parents of this wonderful lifesaver. We are so grateful for Ally," she said, releasing their hands, smiling, and patting my cheek lovingly.

"So nice to meet you, Joy. I'm Grace, and this is Gray."

"Well, Grace, Gray, I would love to visit with you, but I have a to-do list *this* long," she said, spreading her arms wide. "But we'll have plenty of time to catch up later. Bye, bye now," she said and sailed back down the stairs.

Once Joy pulled out of her driveway in her cart, Mom, Dad, and I settled back in our chairs to enjoy what was left of our afternoon and evening. We chatted about the beauty of Pelican Isle and my wise decision to accept the teaching position, as well as my good fortune in having such a warm, welcoming next-door neighbor. We steered clear of painful memories and focused on what lay ahead.

But as my mother got quieter and her eyes began to droop, she said, "If you don't mind, Ally, I believe I'll turn in. I'm a little weary from our trip and busy day."

"I believe I'll join your mom. I'm pretty pooped out myself," my dad said.

"'Course, I understand. I'm a little tired too," I told them. "I've made up my bed for you. I'll sleep on the couch."

They didn't protest and insist that I sleep in my own bed but made their way to my bedroom where they quickly passed out from exhaustion. I could hear my dad snoring softly within minutes. I guess I'd asked a lot of my parents, but they'd come through for me, once again.

The following day we had a leisurely breakfast and spent our remaining hours together walking on the beach, collecting shells to add to the magical-cottage collection, riding around Pelican Isle in the golf cart, and getting acquainted with the island.

We milked our day for as long as we could, until Dad said, "I'd love to stay, Ally, but Mom and I need to head on out. Don't want to be on the road after dark, you know."

He and I both chuckled at his and Mom's standard excuse.

Seven

As soon as they pulled out of my drive, I went to the kitchen to see what I had in the fridge for supper. I didn't want to cook, so I decided to make myself a sandwich to eat out on the porch and enjoy the beach as the sun went down. That's when I noticed Joy's pie plate sitting on the kitchen counter. I really needed to return it to her before I got bogged down in school and forgot it altogether. I had hoped to return it with some baked goods, but I didn't know when I'd get around to baking. So I decided to wait on that sandwich and picked up the empty plate and headed over to Joy's house.

When I knocked on her screen door, she called with her buttery voice, "Come in. Be right with you."

I opened the creaky door and called, "Hey, Joy, it's Ally. From next door. Just returning your pie plate."

"Oh, hey," she said, appearing in the kitchen door with tongs in her hand. "Come on in. I'm back here frying fish."

When I got to the kitchen, I found that Joy was not alone.

"Ally, this is my friend, Chris Cruz," she said, pointing with her tongs in his direction. He was leaning against the kitchen counter, his ankles crossed, his arms folded across his chest, watching Joy fry fish. When he saw me, he untangled himself, stepped forward, and extended his hand.

"You're everywhere, aren't you?" I said. "I'm beginning to think you're following me,"

"Well, I could say the same about you, now couldn't I, Miss Ally?" he said, flashing his green eyes and, once again, showing me his dimple. I was beginning to think he knew the power of the dimple and was merely taunting me.

"Did I miss something?" Joy asked. "I feel as though I've just walked in in the middle of Act Three."

"Carter introduced us when Ally came for her interview. And then we ran into each other yesterday at Peli Pier."

"Well, good, we have the awkward intros out of the way. We're all just friends now." Joy said, concentrating on her fish.

"Guess she's right," Chris said, still holding my hand and adding, "friend."

I smiled and blushed and withdrew my hand.

"You came just at the right time, Ally," Joy said. "We have more supper than the two of us can possibly eat. Join us?"

"Well, that's awfully nice of you, but I don't think I deserve it. I've returned your pie plate empty. I don't have the hang of my new kitchen yet and haven't done any baking."

Joy waved her tongs in the air, saying, "Oh, please don't bring me anything to eat. I can cook for myself. And the pie was just a welcome to the island. I don't need a welcome pie. I've been here forever."

Missing my parents already and not wanting to spend the evening alone, I said, "Thanks, Joy, I'd love to stay, if you're sure you have enough."

"More than enough." And to Chris she said, "Make yourself useful. Grab the tea pitcher from the fridge, and fill some glasses with ice."

While Chris was making himself useful, I said, "Joy, your pie was delicious. I ate every bite of it all by myself."

"Yeah, my pecan pies are good. No bragging, just fact."

"Well, how can I help?"

"Get us some plates and silverware," she said, pointing me in the direction of both, "and there's a bowl of slaw in the fridge. By the time you two set the table, the fish ought to be about ready."

Joy's kitchen was not built for three, and Chris and I banged elbows, backed into each other, and stepped on each other's toes, all the while muttering, "'Scuse me, oops, sorry, my fault."

When the two of us finally managed to set the table without injury, Joy bustled over to the cozy little booth in the corner of her kitchen carrying a sizzling platter of fish.

"Hurry, sit. Gotta eat it while it's hot."

Chris motioned for me to sit and then slid in beside me, while Joy sat across from us and passed heaping plates and bowls of food our way.

"Ummm, ummm, Joy, this fish is as delicious as your pecan pie."

"Well, I wouldn't go that far," she chuckled, "but I do love fried fish, even if broiled or grilled is better for us. But a little grease every once in a while won't hurt us. Kind of keeps the pipes lubed, right, Dr. Cruz?"

Chris rolled his beautiful, sparkling green eyes and said, "Well, I don't know if I'd go that far."

"Doctor? You're a doctor?" I asked between bites.

"Yeah, I work at the clinic here on the island."

"A medical clinic? I didn't realize there was a clinic on Pelican Isle."

"Sure is. North of here, the last thing on the island, not too far beyond the school."

"Well, that's convenient. I'm happy to know that."

"We treat the locals, even an occasional student, as well as our summer visitors. Business soars during tourist season with sun poisonings and jelly-fish stings."

"I'll bet it does."

"In the off-season we just have the regular old colds, flu, and occasional stitches."

"Good to know where to go if I ever need some stitches."

Between bites of Joy's almost-as-good-as-her-pecan-pie fish, Chris asked, "How are you liking your new home?"

"To be honest, I like it a lot better than I'd expected."

"Really? Why is that?"

"I actually came here to teach just to help out a friend, but this place is so beautiful. And who could say no to a free beach house? And the people are so nice and friendly."

"Yes, we are, aren't we?" Joy said, and we all laughed in agreement.

"I went to the breakfast restaurant down in the village, and the employees already seemed to know who I was. Everyone was so welcoming."

"You met Bianca?" asked Chris.

"Yes, I did."

"What a sweetheart, "Joy said. "You're going to love her little Cara. She's a darling. Too bad you didn't have Mateo in your class. He's a smart little boy."

"Yeah, she told me about her children."

"Terrific people. Sad story, though," said Chris.

"How's that?" I asked.

Joy laid her fork on her plate, dabbed her mouth daintily with her napkin, shook her head slowly, and said, "She and her husband both came to the island when they were small. They were both darling children, so charming and full of life. They were childhood friends and high school sweethearts. They got married after they graduated, and Juan joined the Army right away. He was so proud to be an American citizen, excited to serve his country. He did three tours of duty in Afghanistan. Three, can you believe that? He had a very impressive military record and was highly decorated. But he was killed by a road-side bomb just two days before he was scheduled to return from his final tour."

"Oh, no, how tragic," I cried, my hand flying to my mouth.

"Yeah, it sure is, but you'd better get used to it," Chris said. "Pelican Isle is a wonderful place to live, but there is a great deal of grief here. You'll see it, and you'll cry over it. But you have to be strong for these kids. It's just part of the job."

Another person telling me about the heartbreak, the sadness. I didn't want to hear that. I didn't come to Pelican Isle for more sadness. I didn't come here to cry. I had finally stopped crying and was trying to put my pain behind me. I refused to take on someone else's pain. I didn't even want to talk about someone else's pain. So I returned the conversation to fried fish, pecan pie, and a free beach cottage.

"I need to run around the block. Afraid I've over-eaten."

"Well, maybe drying the dishes will work it off. Grab that towel, will you? I'll wash. You dry. Chris can put away."

So as we bumped hips and rubbed shoulders while we tidied the kitchen, Joy said, "Do y'all have time to visit for a bit?"

"Sure," I said, "sounds great."

Chris said, "Count me in. I don't have to be back at the clinic until nine o'clock rounds."

"Great," Joy said, "let's sit on the porch and enjoy the end of the day."

On our way outside, Joy grabbed a canvas bag from a big basket beside her living room sofa. When she'd settled herself in a creaky, paint-chipped rocker, she reached into the bag and pulled out a handful of yarn.

"What have you got there?" I asked her.

"The beginnings of a sweater."

"You knit? Or is that crochet?"

"It's knitting, one of my indulgences. Been knitting most of my life. My grandmother taught me when I was just a little girl. I couldn't have been more than six years old. I've always loved watching a ball of yarn transform into something special."

"May I see it?" I asked, and she held up a tiny, partially completed pink sweater.

"Oh, isn't that adorable!" I said and reached over to caress the soft yarn. "Are you making it for a friend's baby?"

"Lots of friends. I make them for the babies who are born in the clinic," she said, smiling over at Chris.

Chris said, "In addition to treating jelly-fish stings and colds, we also deliver babies, lots of babies."

"Really? Do you deliver them yourself?"

"Yeah, I do a little of everything."

"And you knit stuff for all the babies?" I asked Joy.

"I make the caps the babies wear right after they are born. I also like to make a little something for each of them to take home."

"Oh, that's so sweet."

"Well, it's my delight. It keeps me busy, keeps me out of trouble."

As we talked, I watched her hands fly across the yarn, listened to the needles click together with a soothing cadence. It fascinated me to watch the little garment take shape, as we all sat quietly and relaxed to the rhythm of Joy's knitting, as well as the rhythm of the surf. In no time at all, Joy finished the sweater, smoothed it across her knee, and handed it to me. It was lovely, so precious and tiny—no bigger than my two hands placed side-by-side. I held it to my cheek. It was so soft, like all the little sweaters and shirts and onesies I'd collected and arranged neatly in the drawers of Rory's white dressing table. I felt a lump rise in my throat as tears gathered behind my eyes. I handed the sweater back to Joy quickly, before I could go back to that place of pain and despair.

"It's beautiful, Joy."

"Well, thank you. Have you ever knitted?"

"No, I'm all thumbs. I could never do anything so delicate, so intricate."

Chris chuckled and said, "Joy even tried to rope me into knitting. Our one and only lesson was a bust. What a mess. I told her I'd stick to delivering babies, and she could do all the knitting."

"Oh, hush, Chris. It's really quite simple. I'd be glad to show you, if you'd like. I could have you making baby caps in no time. And the clinic can always use more caps."

"Thanks, but I think I'll pass. Don't believe knitting is my thing. I'll stick to teaching. That I know how to do."

"Okay, but if you change your mind," she said, on to another project, this one a tiny yellow cap, her needles already clicking and flying so fast they were a blur.

"Well, if you don't feel that knitting is your thing, perhaps you'd like to rock the babies. The clinic is always short-handed, not enough nurses to go around. I go up in the late afternoon and on weekends to lend a hand. There's always a fretful little one who needs some one-on-one cuddling. Want to join me?"

"What a great idea, Joy," said Chris. "I'm sure the nurses would love to have Ally's help."

I froze. I should have been cuddling my own child. Cuddling someone else's baby would break my heart. I had no intention of sharing my painful past with people I'd only just met, but I had to let them know, in no uncertain terms, that I would not be rocking babies at Pelican Isle Clinic.

"Thanks, but I don't believe so. I've never spent much time around babies. Six is my minimum age limit. I never even baby sat when I was a teenager. Don't think I'd be too good at it."

"Doesn't take much, just a couple of arms and a willingness to rock," said Chris.

"Well, I'll think about it," I said, my stock answer to changing the subject and avoiding self-disclosure.

And, as I promised, I would think about it, but the answer would always be *no*.

We sat in silence, Joy's needles click, click, clicking in time to her squeaky rocker and the crashing of the waves on the shore. Shortly my eyes began to droop from my frenzied weekend, and I stifled a yawn.

"Well, this has been so nice, but I've had a very tiring couple of days. I'd better get on home. I need to be up and at 'em and ready for sixteen kiddos early tomorrow morning." And rising from my chair before either of them could talk me into staying, as polite southerners are wont to do, I said, "Thanks for supper, Joy. As soon as I can find my way around my kitchen, I'll return the invitation." And extending my hand to Chris, I said, "Nice seeing you again."

Standing, he took my hand, flashed his beautiful green eyes and dimple, and said, "Good seeing you too, Ally. Good luck with your first day of school."

Standing and dropping her knitting back into her bag, Joy stepped forward and, towering over me, gave me a gentle hug, saying, "Thanks for coming, Ally. We love making new friends, don't we, Chris?"

"That we do," Chris agreed, flashing his dimple at me once more—on purpose, I was certain.

I skipped down the steps and across Joy's yard in the warmth of new friendship, looking back once to wave good-bye.

Eight

I was awake the following morning long before the alarm was scheduled to annoy me. I hopped from bed with an excitement I hadn't felt in a long while. My life had purpose; I realized that I had missed a life of purpose.

After I showered, I had plenty of time for coffee and toast on the porch. Several seagulls perched on the railing and asked if I might share my breakfast with them. I was in such a great mood that I gladly obliged—though I told them I didn't plan to make a habit of it.

Once we'd finished our toast, I shooed the birds away and headed indoors to dress and pack myself a lunch. I made my bed, washed my coffee cup and toast plate and set them in the dish drainer to dry on their own, and checked to make sure the water was turned off, the lights were out, and the toaster was unplugged. When I was a child, our neighbor Mrs. Griffin left her toaster plugged in and went to her circle meeting at the church. When she returned two hours later, her house was ablaze, apparently the result of a faulty toaster cord. I always check my toaster before leaving the house. Confident that I was as ready as I'd ever be, I grabbed my lunch and purse, stepped out onto the porch, and locked my door with a screech. Then I skipped down my sagging steps and set off in my golf cart to meet my first graders.

They tumbled from the tram and thundered into the school building, eager to begin their new school year. They knew the drill better than I since they'd all been kindergarteners at Pelican Isle Elementary the year before; so they raced into the classroom, claimed a desk, and waited patiently for first-grade instructions.

They were adorable. I had never seen a cuter bunch of kids. They all had shiny, black hair and large, dark expressive eyes, and their taut, smooth, fresh-from-babyhood skin was the color of honey. They smiled broadly, some already sporting gaps where baby teeth used to be, all of them looking at me with anticipation, as if I were the one with all the answers. I hoped I had enough answers to make a difference in their innocent lives.

All sixteen were present. And as I scanned the room, I could already see their sixteen personalities emerging. Some sat quietly, hands folded on their desks. Others fidgeted with excitement, their sturdy legs pumping back and forth. Several scanned the room, checking out the new teacher's handiwork, pointing out their names on the bulletin board. A few giggled excitedly and whispered across the aisles. One little girl, a beautiful child with dark, cascading curls held away from her face with a large pink bow, sat quietly, her hands in her lap, her eyes focused on her desk. I would learn hers and all the others' stories soon.

"Good morning," I called to them, smiling broadly and clasping my hands in excitement, and most of them responded with an enthusiastic, "Good morning!"

The beautiful little girl with her eyes focused on her desk did not.

"My name is Miss Ally."

I had decided not to tell my students that I was Mrs. Albright since Carter had already told me that they would be calling me Miss Ally. I'd learned that it was best to keep it simple. Then I pointed to my name on the bulletin board.

"You have just one name to learn, but I have sixteen. So until I get to know all of you, I'd like for you to wear your names for me. Okay?"

Most nodded or said, "Yes, Miss Ally," as I called their names and passed out stickers for them to wear on their shirts until I came to know each of them.

When I got to Martina, there was no answer.

"Martina? Martina Gonzales? Where is Martina?" I chirped merrily.

Then a boy pointed at the quiet little girl, still staring at her desk, and said, "She's Martina. She don't talk much."

So I walked down the aisle, crouched beside her desk, and said, "Hi, Martina. Here's a sticker with your name on it."

She didn't move or look up from her desk.

So I removed the backing from the sticker and affixed it to her new-for-the-first-day-of-school pink tee shirt.

"There you go," I said and made my way to the other students.

Carter and Joy had told me that some of these children had sad stories. I so hoped this precious little girl with the dark, cascading curls held back with a crisp, pink bow wasn't one of them. I wanted to believe that Martina was just experiencing first-day jitters and was shy around strangers.

Knowing that I could not dwell on the emotions of one child because I had sixteen students to consider, I set about getting to know all the children and assessing their learning levels. I soon discovered that their favorite activities were giggling and fidgeting, just like every other first grader I'd ever taught. But I was trained to channel my students' attention toward more educational endeavors, and soon I would have them enjoying, if not loving, their lessons in language arts, reading, numbers. By morning's end all sixteen were relatively attentive, and we were well on our way to learning.

When it came time for lunch, I said, "Okay, kiddos, time to put away your writing tablets."

They obediently put them in the openings under their seats and folded their hands on their desktops, waiting for further instructions.

"Who's ready for lunch?" I said, as I grabbed my big bottle of hand sanitizer and walked the aisles, squirting a dab into each child's palm.

They rubbed their busy little hands together, smacking them to a rhythm they'd made up, giggling all the while. I giggled along with them, at their silliness, their adorableness.

There was no cafeteria with a hot lunch waiting for my first-graders. That was one of the things that the state couldn't provide for the school students of Pelican Isle Elementary. They had to bring bag lunches each day.

So when I said, "Okay, then, let's get out our lunches," my students scrambled to pull their crumpled, brown paper bags or canvas totes from their desks.

Thinking some of the children might not have been able to bring along a drink, I had brought in a stack of paper cups and put them in the break room beside the sink. I was glad I had. Some of the children had juice boxes or mini bottles of water, but there were some who had nothing at all to drink.

I said, "Does anyone need a drink of water," and a good many hands shot up.

"Okay, then, go ahead and start eating, and I'll get you some water."

I went to the break room and began filling cups and passing them around the room. That's when I noticed that one little boy was sitting at his desk, hands folded, with no lunch. Then I noticed another child, and another. There were three children who didn't have lunches. Had they forgotten them? Had their moms been too busy to pack them? Did they even have lunch to bring? The reason didn't matter. I couldn't let them watch the other children eat and spend the afternoon hungry, but neither could I leave them alone to drive down the island to buy lunch for them.

So I returned to the break room where I'd stowed my lunch in the mini fridge. I emptied the contents on the counter: a whole-wheat-bread sandwich with deli ham and mustard, an apple, a piece of string cheese, and a Little Debbie oatmeal cake. I tore three paper towels from the roll and placed them on the counter. Then I went to my desk for my scissors, since there was no knife in my classroom. I cleaned the scissors with hand sanitizer and began making three little lunches out of my one. I was sorry I didn't need to make two or four lunches because I had a hard time cutting a square sandwich into three pieces. Geometry had not been my strong suit. But I managed. Then I cut the apple into twelve slices and gave them each four pieces. A third of a piece of string cheese isn't much, but at least they'd each get a bite.

As I was preparing mini meals, I realized that for three hours—three full hours—I had not grieved, had not even thought of Cam and Rory. Since my sixteen tiny students had thundered through my classroom door, they had occupied my every thought. That realization made my emotions swing back and forth between joy and guilt, joy and guilt. As if I were filling out a survey, making deliberate choices, I consciously ticked the joy box.

Yes, I choose joy, I told myself.

I hadn't chosen joy in 10 months, 21 days, 19 hours, and some odd minutes. It felt exhilarating, liberating to choose joy.

I arranged a bite of oatmeal cookie on each paper towel, and balancing the tiny meals on my outstretched hands, I made my way to my waiting students.

As I placed the lunches on the children's desks, they each, in turn, said quietly, "Thank you, Miss Ally."

No, thank you, I said to myself, smiling and really meaning it.

I finished passing out cups of water while the class ate silently. Guess a no-talking-while-eating rule had already been established. And who was I to challenge such a marvelous rule?

After lunch and a romp on the beach, where the children twirled and leapt themselves into exhaustion, I let them rest while I read a story aloud. A few of them nodded off, their heads drooping to their desks. Some fidgeted a bit, but most listened attentively. Then I noticed that Martina, the quiet little girl with the sad eyes, was no longer looking at her desk but was paying close attention to me as I read. She was a stunning child with full, pink lips and huge, black eyes surrounded by thick, curly lashes. I could tell by the way she listened with obvious anticipation that she was going to love books. I hoped she would be an excellent reader. Reading had always erased my childhood sadnesses; perhaps it could do the same for her. I so hoped it would.

The rest of that first day flew by, and I was unaware until I herded my students out the door to their waiting tram that I was starving. A day of energetic teaching without lunch can work up a mighty appetite. I watched as the children clambered aboard their ride and waited for Mr. Ruiz, their driver, to pull out of the school yard and round the bend and disappear down Beach Road. Then I sprinted back to my classroom, grabbed my purse, yanked my warped door closed with a screech and locked it, and headed for my cart. I needed to find food, and I was certain I didn't have time to drive home and cook before full starvation set in. I motored to Peli Pier because I knew the food was excellent, by recommendation and from actual experience. I also knew that it was filling and fast. And fast was most important.

"Welcome, Miss Ally," the young man at the door greeted me. "I'm Emilio."

"Hi, Emilio, nice to meet you," I said, no longer surprised that everyone on the island knew that there was a new teacher named Miss Ally at their elementary school.

"Dining alone?" he asked as he led me to a booth by the window, overlooking Parmeter Sound.

"Yeah, just me, and I'm starved."

"Well, we're kinda slow, so it shouldn't take too long. Menu?"

Not at all interested in taking time to study the menu, I said, "No thanks. What do you recommend?"

"Got some fresh whiting. Cook can make you a great fish sandwich. Comes with fries and slaw."

"Sounds perfect," I said with a wave of my hand.

"Okay, then, I'll rush your order. Want some sweet tea?"

"Sure, with lemon, please."

"Okay, then, I'll be right back."

A few late-season stragglers were out on the sound in their boats, taking advantage of the balmy weather for as long as they could. I was watching a small craft jump and rock over the wake of a larger passing boat when Emilio returned with my tea and said, "Your sandwich shouldn't take too long."

"Thanks, Emilio," I said and took a gulp of tea.

It was delicious; it tasted just like my mother's sun tea, so sweet it curled my tongue and made my jaw ache.

As Emilio had promised, my dinner was ready before the larger boat had disappeared behind a cluster of sherbet-colored bungalows and its wake had settled to a smooth, glassy finish. He placed before me a platter—not a plate—with a fried fish the size of a small shark protruding from the sides of a regular-size bun. Next to it was a huge mound of fries and a good-size bowl of cole slaw. I was already thinking to-go box.

I hefted the sandwich with both hands, not sure where to start. I began nibbling at the ends, trying to wrestle my dinner down to a manageable size, but after several bites I still had not reached the bun.

"Good, isn't it?"

I looked up to find Chris Cruz standing by, smiling, watching me eat. I immediately dropped my sandwich, grabbed my napkin from my lap, and began dabbing at my greasy lips.

"Join you?" he asked, pointing to the empty seat across from me.

Still chewing and dabbing, I shook my head up and down, motioned to the seat across from me and mumbled, "Um hum."

He was wearing green scrubs, similar to the color of his shockingly green eyes, and he had big, white Crocs on his feet. His gold-blond hair was disheveled, and he sported a day's stubble the same blond as his hair. Even in his work-worn state, he was still quite handsome.

Finally able to speak, I said, "Delicious, but huge. I had no idea what I was getting myself into."

"Just think of it as a week's worth of groceries. The leftovers will go on and on."

I laughed self-consciously at the absurdity of my meal and the embarrassment of my gluttony.

"Hi, Dr. Chris."

"Hey, Emilio. I'll have what she's having," he said, pointing at my still-heaping platter.

"Sweet tea?" Emilio asked, his pencil poised over his order pad.

"Sure."

I paused to wait for Chris's meal to arrive, but he waved his hand and said, "Oh, please don't stop on account of me. You don't want your dinner to get cold. There's nothing better than hot fries, but there's nothing worse than cold fries."

I so agreed with him and picked up a hot fry saying, "If you insist."

"I do insist. I'll just sit here and stare at you. I might even entertain you with my witty banter."

I covered my mouth with my hand and laughed.

"This isn't too witty, but how was your first day of school?"

"Great. The kids are wonderful—all of them. I usually get a whiner or two, but all my students are so well behaved and seem eager to learn. And I didn't have a single child cry for mommy. And that's quite unusual for a class of first graders."

"They are a great bunch. I delivered a good many of them."

"Really?"

"Sure did, and I know all of their families. They've all made their way through the clinic for one reason or another. I agree, they're a good bunch of kids. They're going to steal your heart."

Just then Emilio brought Chris's meal.

"Thanks, Emilio, looks great."

As Chris lifted his sandwich to take a bite, I raised my hands to him and said, "No heart stealing here. Can't afford to get attached. I'm here for just a year. My contract will be up in June."

"So you're not staying?"

"Well, I'll be staying this school year," I said, taking a gulp of tea and lifting my still-mammoth sandwich. "I'm just doing a friend a favor until Carter can find a permanent replacement. I've signed just a one-year contract."

He put his sandwich back down on the platter without taking a bite and leveled me with his gaze. His look made me uneasy.

"A favor, huh?"

"Well, the school needed a teacher, and one of my college professors asked if I'd be willing to help out. And I agreed."

"A favor. Agreed to help out. That's what all you teachers think about this job." As he spoke, a vein appeared in his forehead and his jaw began to twitch. He continued to speak to me through clenched teeth. "You don't see it as the fulfilling opportunity that it is—as a chance to learn something that might enrich your life. No, you see it as a do-gooder's favor, an obligation to give back to society."

I was taken aback by his outburst, but he wouldn't give me a chance to jump in and defend myself.

"Well, these kids don't need a favor. They need a commitment. Their families are hard working, but they live day to day, financially and emotionally." I opened my mouth to speak, but before I could say a word, Chris kept on, railing at me. "They feel they can't trust the system. Some of them live in fear that they could be sent away at any minute. These kids need to trust that they can at least count on their teacher to stick with them. They need to know that their teacher isn't going to be deported!"

By now Chris had pushed his platter away, and his voice was ringing with his passion. His beautiful, green eyes appeared cold and flushed with rage. Embarrassed by his outburst, I looked around the restaurant to find that the few other diners had turned to stare curiously.

Then I became furious. How dare he point a finger at me and make such an accusation. He didn't even know me, didn't know what I'd been through. He had no right to make assumptions about me and expect me to give up my life for Pelican Isle Elementary just because *he* thought it was the thing to do.

In my anger I couldn't respond, didn't want to respond. So, without a word, I dropped my sandwich on the plate, reached into my purse, pulled out a twenty, and slammed it on the table, causing our tea to slosh. I slid out of the booth, stood, and strode across the restaurant and out the door without looking back or asking for a to-go box.

When I reached my cart, I hopped in, slung my purse onto the floor, its contents spilling out. I didn't care. I just let my belongings slide and roll around the cart floor as I crammed the key into the ignition, started the motor, and stomped my foot on the accelerator. Only I didn't accelerate much. Instead of careening out of the parking lot, spewing gravel as I so wanted, I silently cruised out of the lot onto Beach Road and puttered along mutely toward the village.

When I reached the south end of the island, I was still angry from my altercation with Chris Cruz, but time and space had somewhat cooled my anger. I pulled into the Island Grocery parking lot, grabbed my purse, scooped its contents back inside, and headed for the door. I tried to put the passionate doctor out of my mind and concentrate on making certain that none of my students would ever again go without lunch.

"Hey, Miss Ally," Ramona called from behind the cash register.

"Hi, Ramona."

"How was your first day of school?"

"Great. I have a wonderful group of kids. It should be a really good year," I said, as I grabbed a cart and headed for the aisles.

"Hi, Miss Ally," Miguel said, looking up from banging his price gun across a case of peaches. "How'd school go?"

"It was a good day, Miguel."

"You know, my nephew Leandro is in your class. I told him he better behave for you or he'll be hearing from me."

"I don't think you need to worry, Miguel. Leandro is a very nice, polite boy."

"He better be," Miguel said, smiling broadly at my compliment, and went back to pricing his peaches.

I breathed deeply and tried to clear my mind of Dr. Cruz's unpleasant, finger-pointing guilt trip as I filled my basket with lunch and snack foods to stock the mini fridge. I dropped in some fruit cups, as well as a large bag of low-fat string cheese. I stayed away from sugary cookies, but fruit roll-ups seemed like a good snack to have on hand. I tossed a box of whole-wheat crackers into my basket and figured I'd need a loaf of bread too. I grabbed a giant jar of peanut butter and made a mental note to ask my students' parents about nut allergies and gluten-free diets. Teaching was far more complicated than it used to be. I cruised through the produce department and picked up a bag of oranges and another of apples. Then I made my way to the drink aisle, where I got juice boxes—lots of juice boxes. Kids love juice boxes. I headed for the checkout with a brimming basket that would assure that my students would not go without lunch again. Neither would I.

After I settled up with Ramona, Miguel helped me to my cart, secured my bags with my bungees, and, once again, refused a tip.

"Just keep an eye on Leandro for me. He's a good boy."

"I'm sure he is, Miguel. I promise I'll keep an eye on him. We're going to have a really good year together."

As I waved and pulled out of Island Grocery parking lot, the breeze picked up and whipped my hair about my face. I smoothed it back with my hand and breathed in the wonderful, salty air of Pelican Isle. The sea breeze and the relaxing ride home released my tension, as I tried to concentrate on my students and forget about my altercation with Dr. Chris Cruz.

Nine

"What's he doing here?" I snapped at Joy, making a point of avoiding eye contact with Chris.

Joy batted her eyes rapidly but responded in her always-buttery voice, "He's here because he's my friend."

I blistered with embarrassment at my outburst and could feel the heat rising in my cheeks. Then I mumbled, "Sorry," and headed for the door.

"Please, Ally," was all Chris said as he rose from the sofa and stepped cautiously toward me.

It had been only three days since our Peli Pier confrontation, and I realized as I faced Chris that my wound was still raw. I believed it had been unfair of him to put me on the spot and make me defend myself. What's more, I felt as though I were being sabotaged, having been invited to Joy's and finding Chris there when I showed up.

I was a grown woman; I knew what was best for me. And not being around Chris Cruz at that moment was best for me. I turned to tell him that I really needed to go and saw the look of abject sorrow on his face.

"Please don't leave, Ally."

"Why?" I snapped.

"Because I stepped over a line, and I want to apologize."

"Well..." I said but, surprised by his contrite demeanor, didn't know where to go from there.

I looked down at my sandal and uncomfortably nudged the frayed edge of Joy's rug with my toe.

"Please, sit," he said, and I cautiously eased myself onto the comfy, over-stuffed sofa where he joined me. I usually enjoyed sinking into those downy cushions, but on this occasion there was nothing at all comfortable about it. I avoided eye contact, for fear Chris would flash his dimple and unhinge me. I couldn't allow that to happen. I wanted, needed to cling to my anger.

Perched ramrod straight on the edge of Joy's sofa, I felt myself bristling and ready to bolt at the slightest hint of Dr. Cruz's accusation. I grabbed a throw pillow, wrapped my arms around it, and pressed it hard to my chest, a wall of protection between the two of us. Chris reached to touch my arm. When I shot his hand a withering look, he withdrew as if he'd been scalded. I squinted angrily and finally looked him in the eye. I said nothing, just waited to hear what he had come to offer.

Joy turned and retreated to the kitchen. We could hear her banging pots and pans for no other reason than to afford us our privacy.

"I really don't know where to start, Ally."

"Well, now that you've apologized, maybe you could explain why you talked to me the way you did. But an explanation still won't excuse how rude you were. And you were really rude," I said, my chin up, my teeth clenched.

"You're right. I don't expect to be exonerated for my rudeness. But I do want a chance to explain why I said what I did."

"Okay, so explain."

"Ally, I'm just so passionate about Pelican Isle but, mostly, about the island's children. Like I told you, I delivered a good many of them. I feel as if I have a stake in their lives. Most of them have a hard life, an uncertain life. Their parents struggle to give them a better existence than they had before."

"I know that," I said, defensively.

"The kids see their parents live in fear of uncertain futures, and that fear rubs off on them. Their world, as they know it, could unravel tomorrow. They could be deported. They've seen it, watched their little friends spirited away, never to see them again. Granted, it doesn't happen often, but the possibility is always there. The fear is real."

"I understand. Carter told me all of that the day I met him. But I don't have any control over my students' legal status or their fear of deportation. All I can do is care for them and teach them as long as I'm here.

"As long as you are here…"

"So?"

"You can stay, Ally," he said, ducking his head and speaking softly. "These kids need constants in their lives. They need to believe that you're not going to be deported next year."

"But my contract…"

"Yes, I've heard that so many times. 'I signed up for only one year. I can't spend my life on this deserted island. But I want to get married and have kids of my own. They're not my responsibility.'"

That's the one that stung the most.

Then Chris said very quietly, "They may not have been born your responsibility, Ally, but you can make them your responsibility."

"But, Chris, I understand everything those other teachers have said. Why, I could have said them all myself. I just haven't been backed into a corner and forced to say them out loud."

"I know that, but surely you can understand my feelings, can't you?"

"Of course, I can. But you had no right to push your ideals on me with such hostility. And you were very hostile, Chris," I said, crossing my arms in defiance. "I have every right to live the life that's best for me."

"Best for you…" he said, and drifted off.

I was certain he had more that he wanted to say, but, instead, he just clenched his jaw. I watched the muscle jump.

"All first graders love their teacher. I'm sure your kids already love you. Then that teacher leaves them when her contract is up. When that happens, the children aren't quite so open and trusting with their next teacher. They're not so quick to give their hearts, for fear they will be dashed again. Of course, their fears are founded when that teacher leaves, as well. Eventually they lose all faith that their teacher will stick around for them and their younger siblings. They still perform in class, but by then they are closed off, no longer cheerful, loving little children who hang onto their teacher's hand and say, 'I love you, Miss Ally.'"

I understood what Chris was telling me and even agreed with him up to a point, though I'd never let on. And I would not allow him to manipulate me into feeling I had to commit permanently to Pelican Isle Elementary. I just would not let him lay a guilt trip on me.

"Now, you have a perfect right to work out your contract and leave. And I'm so sorry if I made you feel guilty about that. But, Ally, I'll never be sorry for telling you how I feel about these kids."

"Thanks for your apology. I accept it." I said. "But you didn't make me feel guilty because I don't have anything to feel guilty about. I did a friend a favor. How could that make me feel guilty?"

I watched his lips tighten and his nostrils flare at the mention of my favor, but he let it pass this time.

"Well, thanks for accepting my apology. It wasn't my intent to hurt you."

Smiling at him for the first time, I said, "And thank you for explaining your passion."

Then he smiled back, his beautiful green eyes flashing, his dimple springing to life for the first time that evening.

Then he stuck out his hand and asked, "Still friends?"

I reached for his hand and said, "Sure, still friends."

Covering my hand with both of his, he said, "Well, Friend, I really have to run. I'm going to be late for my shift."

"You came all the way down here just to apologize to me?"

"All the way down here just to apologize to you." Releasing my hand and heading for the door, he yelled over his shoulder, "Bye, Joy."

She stuck her head around the kitchen door and said, "Bye-bye. We still on for Saturday?"

"You bet," he said, smiling and winking at her.

When he reached the porch, he turned and smiled once more. He opened his mouth to speak but must have changed his mind. Instead, he bounded down the stairs, hopped into his cart, and sped off at a brisk eighteen miles per hour. I watched till he disappeared onto Beach Road; then I closed the door.

I was so glad Chris had come to apologize and was equally glad I'd stayed. I was also glad that I'd listened to his explanation. But there was one thing I was not glad about. I was not glad that I had been so rude to Joy. I needed to make amends.

"I'm so, so sorry," I cried as I entered the kitchen and found her at the stove, gently stirring a pot of clam chowder.

She tapped the wooden spoon on the side of the soup pot, laid it gently in the spoon rest, and turned to me. "It's okay, Honey. We all have our moments," she said, reaching for my hands and holding them gently.

"But I was so rude," I cried, "and I'm so embarrassed."

"Oh, goodness, don't be. I know you didn't mean it. It was just a knee-jerk reaction. I'm certain it won't ever happen again," she said, smiling with her beautiful blue eyes.

"Thank you, Joy. I promise that it will never happen again."

Tucking an errant strand of hair behind my ear, she said, "Now, come pour us a glass of wine while I dish us up some chowder," as if my petulant outburst had never occurred.

When we sat down in Joy's warm, cozy kitchen booth, I said, "That was awful nice of Chris to come all that way just to apologize."

"Yes, Chris is very polite, a nice young man. I feel blessed to call him my friend. But if you plan to be his friend, you'll need to understand his passion for this island."

"I believe I understand."

"Good."

"By the way," I said, "how did you and Chris meet?"

"Oh, Chris and I go way back," she said, breaking eye contact with me and waving her hand in the air.

"Way back?"

"Um hum," she said, now concentrating on her chowder.

That didn't answer my question, but I could tell by her tone and her dismissive attitude that that was all she was going to offer.

So, to change the subject, she said, "Why don't you join Chris and me for dinner Saturday night? Nothing fancy. Maybe lasagna. What do you think?"

I thought about it, not sure I was ready to spend the evening with Chris Cruz. Despite his apology, the still-raw wound needed time to heal.

Ten

But I'd accepted, reluctantly. I figured if Joy could forgive my disrespectful behavior, then I could suck it up for one evening and agree to disagree with Dr. Cruz. What's more, missing my parents and adult human contact and conversation, I didn't relish the idea of spending my Saturday night alone.

When Saturday evening came, Joy and I were in her kitchen chopping salad, buttering Italian bread, and waiting for the lasagna to come out of the oven, all the while nursing a glass of wine.

"Anybody home?" Chris called and let himself in.

"In the kitchen," Joy yelled. "Come on back."

I caught sight of him striding through the living room toward us. As he shed his jacket, I saw that he was wearing khaki slacks and a crisp blue cotton shirt with the sleeves rolled up, instead of the hospital scrubs or shorts and tee shirts I'd seen him wear on other occasions. His generally shaggy, golden-blond hair was styled neatly, fresh comb tracks visible in his wet-look do. With his hair away from his face, his startling green eyes were more vibrant than ever.

"Well, aren't you pretty?" Joy said and gave him a one-armed hug as she continued to toss salad with her free hand. "You smell good too. Who are you trying to impress?"

I watched Chris blush pink. I felt my own face flush when I realized I just might be the person he was trying to impress.

But he made a plausible save when he said, "Not trying to impress a soul. Just thought it would be impolite to dress like a slob in the company of two lovely ladies."

Joy rolled her eyes, took a bottle of wine from his hand, and returned her attention to our meal, while she said under her breath, "Yeah, right."

"Hi, Ally," Chris said, reaching for my hand. I reached back to shake, but, instead, Chris just held my hand in both of his and held my gaze with his penetrating eyes. I felt the heat rise in my face and knew, from experience, that I was blushing bright red. Surely he sensed my uneasiness, but still he held my hand, his smile widening, his dimple deepening.

"Hey, Chris," I finally sputtered, my wound from our last encounter miraculously scabbing over as we held hands.

Joy clucked her tongue, shook her head, and said, "Y'all grab those plates and silverware and toss them on the table, will you?"

Chris finally released my hand, and the two of us began setting the table, making small talk, bumping into each other.

"Good week?"

"Yeah, but the kids were a little rowdy yesterday, for some reason."

"You?"

"Delivered four babies. All girls. One set of twins."

"Four babies in one week? Isn't that a lot of babies for an island this size?"

"Well, we're the clinic to the island, but we serve some of the mainland population too."

"Isn't there a hospital in New Oak?" I asked.

"Yes, but a lot of patients don't have insurance, so they come to us."

"No insurance? Does that mean you treat them for free?"

"Well, sometimes, but most pay what they can. We're sort of on the honor system. And our patients are very honorable," he said, smiling with pride.

"But how can the clinic afford to treat people who can't pay?"

"We operate, for the most part, on donations—one very large donation, in particular."

"What do you mean?"

"One of our benefactors provided for the clinic in his will. The interest alone covers over half our budget."

"That's amazing."

"Yeah, he was amazing."

"Move so I can put this down. It's hot," Joy said and elbowed us aside, interrupting our conversation. "And sit so we can eat it while it's still hot. Not a fan of cold lasagna. Chris, pour us some more wine, please."

The lasagna was scrumptious and hot, and the conversation was light and relaxing, with no mention of my plan to defect. I was relieved.

"Ally, you should see the set of twins Chris delivered yesterday. So tiny, so precious. I rocked them both at the same time, and I swear they were cooing in harmony. You don't know what you're missing. Rocking the babies can heal your soul. Sure you won't join me?"

"Well, I think we can all use some soul healing, but I believe I'll pass on the babies. But thanks, again, for asking," I said, and immediately and awkwardly changed the subject to something light and frivolous.

While we ate, I noticed the ease between Joy and Chris. They finished each other's sentences, reached out and touched each other's hand or arm as they talked. They shared inside jokes that they attempted to explain to me and laughed great big, sincere belly laughs at each other's silliness. I grinned giddily and attempted to follow their banter and soon found myself drawn into their easy, warm, comfortable friendship.

"Tell Ally about that time we waded out to the sand bar with our bottle of champagne, got tipsy, lost track of time, and the tide came in and nearly drowned us."

"I think you just told her," Joy laughed, and they collapsed into a fit of giggles, both a little tipsy, once more, from Chris's wine.

"Oh, what about that time..."

"You gotta tell Ally about..."

"Do you think she'd believe for a minute..."

By the end of the evening, I was so relaxed with the two of them that my wound had healed so well it hardly left a scar.

"Hey, my friend."

I smiled at Chris's voice.

"Hey, my friend," I said.

"You busy Saturday night?"

"Don't believe so."

"How about dinner at my place? I make a mean pot of gumbo," Chris offered.

"Sounds good. What's the occasion?"

"Well, I figure I owe you dinner since I spoiled your meal at Peli Pier."

"I believe we've moved beyond that, Chris."

"Yeah, I do too, but it's a good excuse to invite you for dinner. Sorry this invitation has taken so long, but I've been on call every night for a month. I finally cried uncle and told the staff I needed a few hours away."

"And you want to share your few free hours with me?"

"Well, we're friends. Friends have dinner together, share free time together, don't they?"

"I believe they do."

"Okay then, Friend, see you at my place at seven, unless you want me to pick you up."

"Nah, a friend is capable of making her own way. But thanks for the offer. Can I bring anything?'

"Just yourself."

"Sounds easy enough. Then I'll see you at seven."

He'd insisted dinner was casual, so I pulled on jeans and a turtleneck sweater and hopped into my golf cart. The air coming off the ocean made the night feel chillier than the unseasonably cool fifty degrees that the weatherman swore it was, so I was grateful for the clear, plastic curtains that I could roll down around the cart. I closed myself in and cruised silently toward Chris's home. The moon was full, so I hardly needed the small headlights of the cart to guide me down deserted Beach Road.

Chris must have been watching for me because as I pulled into the crushed oyster shell driveway in front of his house, he stepped out onto the porch and threw up his hand in greeting.

"Right on time. Come on in where it's warm," he called, hugging his arms and stepping gingerly from bare foot to bare foot.

I pulled the plastic curtain back, hopped out of the cart, and ran up the steps to the front porch.

"Come in, come in," he said, one hand on the open door, the other gentle on my back. "Take off your shoes and drop them right there," he said, pointing to a mat by the front door.

"You don't allow shoes in your house?"

"The house has nothing to do with it. I don't allow shoes at the beach. You're at the beach. You're not supposed to wear shoes at the beach. Sand between your toes and all that stuff."

"But it's not summer anymore."

"But it's still the beach."

So I shed my shoes, wishing I had given myself a fresh pedicure, and made my way to the sofa in front of the fireplace.

"A fire at the beach when it's fifty degrees?"

"Sure, that way we can go barefoot."

I laughed at his circular reasoning.

"Make yourself at home," he called over his shoulder, as he headed for the kitchen. "The house is a little drafty, so if you're chilly, just grab one of those afghans."

There were two afghans draped across the back of his blue-plaid sofa, one blue and white checked, one red and blue striped.

Chris returned with a bottle of white wine and two glasses.

Pointing at the afghans, he said, "Joy made those. She wraps her feet in them because of my no-shoe policy."

"I may take you up on it later, but I'm good for now. I will take a little of that wine, though. Wine seems to warm my toes."

After he poured us both a glass, he said, "Would you object to eating our gumbo here in front of the fire?"

"No, not at all. That sounds great. May I help?"

"Thanks, I can manage, but you can come on in the kitchen and keep me company," he said, smiling over his shoulder.

I followed him into his tiny galley kitchen with a huge window overlooking picturesque Parmeter Sound.

"Beautiful," I said, as I leaned across the counter and peered out at the water. I watched as the choppy wake jumped up and down with shards of gold cast by the full moon, and small crafts, tied to docks, rocked bumpily back and forth. "This view just takes my breath away."

"I understand. I've been looking at it for years, and it still takes my breath away. Sometimes I stand here at this window, plate in hand, and eat my supper, just so I can watch the day disappear into the water. I'll never get tired of it."

"You really love Pelican Isle, don't you?"

"There's just no place like it. There's nowhere I'd rather be."

Chris ladled gumbo into two bowls and placed them on a tray with silverware, napkins, placemats, bread plates, and a basket of cornbread. I followed as he returned to the living room and the warmth of the fire. He set our places at a big, square coffee table, lighting small votive candles and arranging them between us. Then he placed cushions on the floor and took my arm to help me ease into place.

"Help yourself, before it gets cold," he said, passing the cornbread to me and motioning to the gumbo.

Taking a spoonful, I said, "Yum, this is scrumptious. I didn't know you could cook. I'm so impressed."

"Oh, you needn't be impressed. Joy taught me how to make this. If I can cook it, Joy taught me. This is one of the few things I've really mastered."

"Well, yes, you have truly mastered this. It's delicious. I've lived in the South all my life and have tasted my share of gumbo. I believe this is the best I've ever had."

"So glad you like it," he said and flashed his turn-my-knees-to-jelly dimple.

"Joy's afghans, Joy's gumbo. Y'all are really tight. Just how did y'all meet? When I asked her, all she'd say was, 'Oh, Chris and I go way back.'"

Chris laughed and said, "Yeah, Joy and I do go way back—way, way back."

"Way, way back? How far is way, way back? And how did y'all become friends? No offense, but the two of you seem an unlikely pair."

"No offense taken. We get that a lot." Then he smiled wistfully and stared off into the distance. Then, all of a sudden, he jumped up, saying,

"Hold on a minute. I'll be right back."

He padded out of the room in his bare feet, and I could hear him opening and shutting drawers in the next room. When he returned, he was carrying a small, yellow baby blanket. He handed it to me.

"Joy knitted this blanket."

"Oh, it's beautiful."

But, then, all of Joy's baby blankets were beautiful. She made them each a little different, a personal gift for each baby, all intricate and delicate and created from her heart. I watched her night after night weaving tiny blankets and sweaters and hats for the babies at the clinic, and I could see the love and caring she put into each piece. But why would Joy give Chris a baby blanket? He didn't have a baby. Or did he?

So I asked, "Why did Joy give you a baby blanket? Do you have a baby you haven't told me about?"

Smiling shyly, he said, "No, I don't *have* a baby, Ally, but I *was* a baby at one time."

"Okay...," I said, confused.

"My mother brought me home from the clinic in that blanket."

I was still baffled, and Chris could tell.

He reached across the low table, took my hand in his, and said, "Ally, I was one of Joy's babies."

"I don't understand, Chris."

"Joy's husband, Dr. C, delivered me right here on Pelican Isle, in the Pelican Isle Clinic."

"You mean Joy's husband was a doctor at the clinic?"

"Sure was."

"And you were born there?"

"Yep, right there. And Joy rocked me and sent me home wrapped in this blanket."

"But you're..." I started, but Chris read my thoughts.

"A doctor?"

My cheeks flamed as I withdrew my hand in embarrassment.

"I was born here, went to Pelican Isle Elementary, grew up here, went away to college and medical school, and became a doctor. You really can come from Pelican Isle, Ally, and become a doctor, as long as you have people around you who believe in you and encourage you."

"I'm sorry, I..."

"It's okay," he said, holding up his hand to silence me, "I hear that from a lot of people. No one can believe that a Pelican Isle kid can do anything but fish and clean rooms for strangers."

"I didn't mean that, Chris. I just had no idea. You never told me. It was an honest mistake."

"You're right. I should have told you."

"That would have helped me understand your passion for this place."

"Well, now you know. So you see, Ally, you may have some doctors in your class. I sat right there in your classroom when I was a first grader, sat in those same scarred desks, read the same cast-off books. Like I say, you may have doctors in that class of yours, but they can't make it on their own. They can't realize their potential if the people who can help them keep abandoning them."

I was so hoping Chris and I could get through an evening without his accusing me of abandoning my students or being deported and dashing their hopes of being successful. I guess it was just too much to ask, considering Chris's connection to the island and his passion for its kids.

Then he said, "Joy was my Miss Ally. She's been with me from the start, from the moment she wrapped me in that blanket and rocked me in the nursery at the clinic."

Joy had rocked Dr. Chris Cruz when he was a newborn at the Pelican Isle Clinic. I imagined a much-younger Joy Summers cradling a tiny Chris Cruz in her arms, and the vision made a lump rise in my throat. I swallowed hard and fast, before the tears could come. He was not her child, yet she had cared enough to love and comfort another young woman's fretful baby.

"Joy has rocked lots of babies. Out of all the babies, why did she pick you?"

Thinking for a moment, he said, "She and Dr. C didn't actually pick me. They picked my mother. My mom—her name was Elena—waited tables at Peli Pier from the time she was fourteen years old. She was the oldest daughter in a family of eleven children. My grandmother cleaned rooms at the Pelican Inn, and my grandfather was a shrimper."

"So your mother was a local?"

"Yes, my grandparents brought their family from Mexico when my mother was very small."

"But, Chris, you don't look at all Latino."

"Yeah, I've also heard that before, many times. Apparently, my father was very fair."

Apparently? Didn't Chris know for sure? As curious as I was, I wouldn't ask. I'd already stuck my foot in my mouth.

"Anyway, Dr. C and Joy just took a liking to my mom, saw something special in her."

"She was fourteen when she went to work? That's awfully young, isn't it?"

"She needed to help her family."

"Amazing. But that's a lot to ask of a fourteen year old."

"That's what family is all about, Ally. They help each other."

"Even so, that says a lot about your mom, taking on such a load at fourteen."

"She was very ambitious. She was also a straight-A student at New Oak High. I don't know how she did it. Guess she just wanted to make something of herself."

I couldn't imagine a fourteen-year-old girl having to work so hard just to exist, but Chris seemed to beam with pride as he told me about his hardworking, industrious mother.

"So Joy and Dr. C would come to the restaurant several times a week, and Mom would wait on them. They grew very fond of her. Joy said that she was bright and personable, and they were impressed that she could work so hard and still maintain a straight-A average."

"That's really remarkable."

"Dr. C offered to send her to college, anywhere she wanted to go, to study anything she wanted to study."

"How generous."

"Yeah, he was generous, all right. Mom told him that she wanted to be a doctor, just like he was. She wanted to come back to Pelican Isle and help her people."

"So where did she go to med school?"

"She didn't."

"Why not?"

"She had me."

"Oh."

"She met a guy," Chris said, a look of sadness on his face.

"Ah, a guy…"

"His family came from Connecticut on vacation, and they were regulars at Peli Pier. He stayed for two months, just long enough for him and my mom to fall in love. They'd meet at night in the dunes because they were certain their families wouldn't approve. Mom said she knew from the beginning their love couldn't live past the summer."

"But why, if they were in love?"

"She was just sixteen. He was eighteen. She was a poor Latina waitress with parents who could barely speak English. He'd just graduated from some private school and was on his way to Harvard."

I was so touched by Elena's story. It reminded me of Romeo and Juliet.

"Sounds like an opera, doesn't it?" he said, as if reading my thoughts.

"What happened when your mom told him that she was pregnant?"

"Oh, she didn't tell him."

"Why? He was your father."

"No, he wasn't, Ally. He was just a boy named Chip that my mother loved for a summer. She knew that telling him would destroy his life. He had a promising future in a world she couldn't even imagine."

"But what about your mother's promising future. She wanted to be a doctor. She deserved that chance," I snapped, perhaps a bit too passionately.

"She didn't see it that way. She didn't feel she had a choice. She would never have considered abortion or adoption. She was going to be a mother. And once she learned that, that's all that mattered to her."

"It just doesn't seem fair, though."

"She never considered the fairness of it. She did what she had to do, what she felt she was supposed to do. That's what my people do. She had a commitment to me. She gave birth to me and never looked back, never resented me or the boy she loved for a summer."

"Did she ever get to college?"

"No. Dr. C still offered to send her to school, even offered to take me in until she could graduate."

"He really was generous."

"Yeah, but she wouldn't hear of it. I was her responsibility. She chose to have me, chose to care for me. She made me her life. She was so smart and beautiful, Ally, but she never finished high school, never dated, never married. Of course, her family loved us and helped in any way they could, and Joy and Dr. C were like my family, as well. But all of Pelican Isle loved beautiful Elena Cruz and her little one. They supported my mom, and me too. I owed it to my mother and to this island to come back, to be a part of the place that gave me such a good life, to be the doctor she had planned to be."

His story was so touching.

"Is your mother...?"

"Gone. She died...four years ago. Cancer," he said, his eyes reddening with emotion.

"I'm so sorry, and I'm sorry I couldn't have met her. She sounds like a remarkable woman."

"She was remarkable, and I'm sorry too that you couldn't have met her. You'd have loved her. Everyone did."

"Did you ever meet your father?"

"Before she died, Mom offered to help me find him, if that's what I wanted to do."

"Did you? Find him, that is?"

"I didn't even look. He's not my father, Ally. He's just the boy who loved my mother and made her very happy for a summer."

"But, Chris, everybody deserves to know his father. Every father deserves to know his son."

"Maybe," was all Chris would say before changing the subject abruptly. "I wish you could have met Dr. C too. He was an amazing man, the kindest, most caring person I've ever known. Everyone on the island loved him."

"Why did you call him Dr. C?"

"Everybody called him Dr. C."

"Didn't he have a name?"

"Sure."

"What was it?"

Smiling, Chris said, "Christopher."

Eleven

"Anybody home?" I called, peeking my head in Joy's door before strolling on in.

"In here, making the bed. Come on in and help me, and I'll give you coffee. Just brewed a fresh pot."

Joy actually had an old-timey coffee pot that brewed the most delicious coffee I'd ever tasted.

"Good, I brought my mug along."

I crossed to Joy's bedroom and found her unfurling fresh-out-of-the-dryer sheets.

"Here, grab that corner."

While we were tucking and smoothing, she said, "Well, how was the date with your *friend*?"

"Dinner, not a date, with my *friend* was very nice, thank you," I said, tossing the pillows on the bed and turning away as I felt my face redden at her implication that Chris was more than just a friend.

I grabbed my mug and headed for the coffee pot.

Joy followed and said, "Didn't mean to embarrass you. I won't pry. Just tell me what you want me to know. I'll fill in the blanks."

Helping myself to coffee, I said, "There's nothing to tell and no blanks to fill in. We really are just friends. He hugged me goodnight and gave me a brotherly kiss on my cheek. That's all. Nothing more. He was a perfect gentleman."

"That's my Chris."

"Your Chris?"

"Hmmmm?"

"You said, 'Your Chris.'"

"Oh, well, you know what I mean. He's my friend too."

"Yes, I know. Chris told me what good friends you are. He told me about how you became friends."

"I see," she said dismissively, turning away and brushing imaginary crumbs from the kitchen counter into the sink.

"Why didn't you tell me, Joy?"

"Well, I didn't think it was my place to tell Chris's family history. It's his story, not mine. He deserved to be the one to tell you. I figured when he was ready, he'd fill you in."

"It's quite a story."

"Yes, it is. First I loved his mother, Elena. Then I fell in love with Chris the moment I held him in my arms. Something about him just tugged at my heart. He was so beautiful, and he had the best disposition. And the fact that he was fatherless saddened my Christopher and me and made us want to protect him. I knew from the start he'd always be special to me."

Once again, that vision of young Joy rocking baby Chris came to me, and the tenderness touched me so.

"And, Ally, he was a blond-haired, green-eyed baby in a sea of black-eyed brunettes. I was afraid he'd be an outcast, that he'd need protecting."

"Did he? Need protecting, that is?"

"Oh, my goodness, no," Joy chuckled, "I couldn't have missed that one any further. Chris was leader of the pack from the get-go. He was always the tallest and most outgoing and a born leader. The other kids looked up to him and wanted to do everything he did. And, of course, he was so handsome, as you well know. All the girls just swooned over him. I needn't have worried about him for a minute."

"Was Chris the first baby you rocked?"

"Oh, no, he was just my favorite."

"Then you've been baby rocking a long time."

"A very long time."

"You must love it."

"Oh, I do. I love my babies. I believe you'd love them too, if you'd give rocking a try."

"Sorry I can't help, Joy."

"But you can help, Ally," Joy said, reaching out and resting her hand tenderly on my arm. "It doesn't take any special talent. We're all born knowing how to cradle a baby."

I knew what she was saying was true. I couldn't remember a time I didn't want to be a mother, to cradle an infant in my arms. When I was a little girl, I'd swaddle my doll in a blanket, hold her close to my heart, and rock her in my child-size rocker, the one that played Rock-a-Bye-Baby, as we toddled back and forth.

When I learned that the baby I was carrying was a girl, I bought a baby doll to store safely in tissue paper until my little girl was old enough to rock her dolly. From time to time, I'd take her out of her wrapping and hold her close and rock her in my now-adult-size chair, practicing till my own baby could fill my arms.

"But I can't. I just can't," I said, my voice cracking.

"Why not, Ally?"

I couldn't answer.

"Did something happen?"

Joy took my hand and held it gently in both of hers and looked at me with such tenderness. I had hoped not to share my sadness, my loss with the people of Pelican Isle. My tenure would be brief. I could slip in, teach the children, and slip back out without making waves or memories and without leaving behind my history.

But Joy's kindness splintered my reserve, and in a rush that was out of my control, I said in a cracked, ragged whisper, "My baby, oh, my baby."

"Oh, Honey, what happened?" Joy said in that buttery, comforting voice of hers, cradling my shaking hand in both of hers.

"I had a baby." By now the tears were coursing my cheeks, and the sobs were beginning to erupt from my throat. "She died, killed in an automobile accident. A drunk driver." Now I was sobbing uncontrollably, squeezing Joy's hands tightly. "I can't rock someone else's baby. It would break my heart."

Joy didn't say a word, just patted my hand. She sensed I needed to talk, to finally get it out.

"Oh, I'm so sorry. I didn't mean to do this," I said, snuffling and trying to dry my eyes with the heels of my hands, to no avail. The tears just kept coming.

And then, through my sobs, I was telling her about Cam and Rory. She didn't even know that I had been married and certainly didn't know that I had carried a baby to term. I told her about my slow recovery and about how my wonderful parents had brought me back to life. And I shared the story of how I'd come to Pelican Isle—not to pursue a dream job but to help out a beloved professor and her friend, Carter Jolly.

She guided me to the living room sofa and sat down beside me, one hand caressing my back tenderly, the other holding my hand for comfort. She pulled tissues from her pocket, just as my mom had done when I was a hurt, sniffling little girl, and, offering them, let me sob. I knew that I would always love and miss Cam and Rory, but I thought that my sobbing days were behind me. But they weren't, and Joy did not begrudge me my unexpected tears.

"I'm so sorry, Ally. I know how devastated you must be, but I hope you won't let your loss keep you from living. You'll miss so much if you let that happen."

"You don't understand, Joy. There's just no pain like it."

"I know, Ally. I'm just so very sorry."

"No, you don't know, Joy. You'll never know," I snapped, angry that someone would presume to know my pain.

So she just held onto my hand and let me shed grief that I thought I'd already shed.

When I had slowed to a sigh, Joy patted my hand and said, "Come with me. I'd like to show you something."

Grabbing her jacket and handing me her extra, she said, "Here, put this on. It's right chilly outside."

"Where are we going?"

"You'll see. Just follow me."

She led me outside, down her steps, and across the back yard toward the dunes. At the base of the dunes, among a stand of waving sea oats, she knelt and, with her bare hands, began brushing at the sand. Soon she uncovered two small, smooth, flat, granite stones. On one was engraved

CHRISTOPHER JOHN SUMMERS, III
April 10, 1968 – April 11, 1968

The other read

FAITH JOY SUMMERS
April 10, 1968 – April 17, 1968

She stared at the small stones, tracing the names with her finger, and said nothing for the longest time.

Then she whispered, "I understand, Ally. I understand all too well. It never stops hurting, but I promise you that the pain does ease a bit over time, if you let it."

"Oh, Joy, I didn't know."

"Of course you didn't, my dear. I don't talk about them much. I lost them a long time ago. But, Ally, they'll always be in my heart. I'll always ache for them."

When she looked my way, I noticed that her cheeks were damp with tears.

"How did you get through it?"

"It wasn't easy, but I had the love of my wonderful husband and my friends to help me. And I had the babies at the clinic."

"But, Joy, how could you rock other mothers' babies when you'd lost your own?"

"Just because I'd lost my babies, Ally, didn't mean I wasn't a mother. I still had arms to cradle an infant, a heart to love a child. It's a gift all mothers share. You have the gift. Don't squander it. You don't know what you're missing."

"I can't. I'm sorry, I just can't."

"No need to apologize. It's all right," she said, standing and putting her arm around me and drawing me close. "Grief takes time. And, Ally," she said, smoothing the hair back from my face and looking me in the eye, "you have friends to help you through it. I just hope you'll let us. Now, let's get inside, out of this cold. I need another cup of coffee. How about you? Maybe we'll even light a fire in the fireplace. Does that sound good?"

"Yeah, that sounds really good. It has gotten awfully chilly out here."

We trudged up the stairs, arms around each other. I thought of asking her not to share my story with Chris, but I knew there was no need. She wouldn't say a word. This was my story, not hers. She would let me share it, if and when I felt I was ready. When we reached the porch, we stamped the sand from our shoes before returning to her cozy living room.

"Go pour us another cup of coffee while I get the fire started," Joy said.

I went to the kitchen to refill our mugs and returned to the living room to kick off my shoes and curl up under one of Joy's brightly colored afghans. I warmed my hands around my mug while I watched Joy kneel at the hearth, her skirts fanning out around her, and begin to build us a fire.

"There's nothing I like better than a nice fire on a bone-chilling day. Good for what ails you," she said over her shoulder as she stacked wood in a meticulous crosshatch pattern and added some dry sticks and several wads of balled-up newspaper.

She struck a long match with a whoosh and nestled it among the wood and paper and watched until it took hold. Once the flames were dancing and the embers were popping and hissing, Joy joined me on the sofa and gathered her legs beneath her billowing skirt. She grabbed her mug and began warming her hands as we both stared into the flames, transfixed and silent.

Finally I asked, "What happened?"

"My babies?"

"Yes."

"They came early, too early. They just weren't strong enough. We knew from the start that Christopher wouldn't make it, but after six days, we had such hope for Faith."

"I'm so sorry."

"Thank you, Ally." Then she added, "I lost seven altogether."

"Seven babies? Oh, Joy…"

"I didn't have trouble getting pregnant, just couldn't seem to stay pregnant. Miscarried all of them. My twins were the only ones who came close to term."

"And rocking babies helped?"

"Yes, it helped a lot. It still does."

As she mentioned rocking her babies, she smiled into the flames and seemed to get lost in her memories and the comfort that the rocking gave her. A log shifted in the fireplace, causing sparks to fly and a large ember to explode onto the hearth and fizzle as it hit the cool slate.

The explosion shook us from our daydreaming, and I said, "I better get on home."

"You sure? Stay and I'll fix us some lunch."

"Thanks, but I think I'll just grab a sandwich at home. I haven't even showered this morning, and I have to get to the grocery store. My fridge is bare. And I promised Mom and Dad that I'd give them a call this afternoon."

I was just making up excuses to get away, something I'd learned so skillfully. I needed to stop talking about having babies and losing babies and rocking babies. And as I babbled, I stood and began backing toward the door, toward my escape.

"Well, okay, Honey," she said, standing and reaching to hug me. "I hope I didn't upset you, Ally. I don't talk about my babies often, but I felt you needed to know." Then shrugging her shoulders and smiling sweetly, she said, "Perhaps I just needed to tell you."

"That's fine, Joy. Maybe I did need to know."

"And thanks for telling me about Cam and Rory. I'm so sad for you, Honey, but, I promise, your friends are here for you."

"Bye-bye, Joy," I said, kissing her on her soft cheek. Then I gave her a quick hug as I made my way out the door and to the solitude of my own home.

I didn't make myself a sandwich or take a shower or go grocery shopping or call my parents. Instead, I stood at my living room window, staring out at the ocean, my arms wrapped tightly around me to ward off the chill of the day and the chill of my memories.

I felt so lonely, the loneliest I'd felt since my arrival on Pelican Isle. Thinking about Cam and Rory always seemed to make me forlorn, so I tried to steer clear of thoughts of them. But they had crept up on me, and I had spilled my life to Joy, and it had ripped at my heart—again.

At my saddest, though, the beach and the ocean usually heal my soul, but even they seemed lonely to me. We were well into autumn, and even the most avid beach goers had shuttered their cottages and headed inland for their winter homes. The sandpipers that normally scurry at the edge of the surf, poking their needle-sharp beaks into the sand in search of micro meals, were nowhere to be seen. And the seagulls that swoop and dive were gone, probably having followed a fishing trawler out to sea in hopes of scavenging the decks for snacks. Even the ever-present pelicans were missing. How could Pelican Isle exist without its namesake? And the ocean, usually glistening aquamarine with diamonds dancing on the waves as they crash to shore, was a placid, waveless pewter gray, the loneliest color the ocean can possibly be.

As my sorrow tried to undo my healing, I heard Joy's screen door slam and watched her skip down the stairs. She was bundled in her heavy coat and a woolen scarf and mittens. Stopping along the way to crouch and pick up something to put in her pocket—a shell or a colorful pebble, perhaps— she pulled back the plastic curtain of her golf cart, climbed into the driver's seat, and chugged down her sandy drive. I watched her take a sharp right onto Beach Road and disappear out of sight. I knew that she was headed to her babies at the clinic.

I went to my bathroom, shed my jeans and sweatshirt in a pile, and stepped into the shower. The water was like icy needles, and I danced around them until the spray ran warm.

I thought about what Joy had said. I am a mother. A mother. Just because I lost my baby doesn't mean I am no longer a mother. I ran my hand down my flat abdomen. I carried my baby for nine months. I nurtured her. She was my child. I was her mother. I didn't stop being her mother because of a horrible accident. I will always be Rory's mother. I will always be a mother.

I showered quickly. After toweling I reached for my hair dryer; it was too chilly to let my hair dry naturally. I took clean jeans and a turtleneck from my dresser and pulled them on. Stepping into my boots, I grabbed my purse and warm, hooded jacket and headed for the door. I made my way down the stairs to my golf cart, peeled back the plastic curtain, and climbed in. Heading down the driveway and turning onto Beach Road, I followed Joy's route.

Carmen Jimenez was working the front desk when I arrived at the clinic. "Hey, Miss Ally. How you doin'?"

"Fine, Carmen. You okay?"

"Can't complain."

"Will you direct me to the nursery, please?"

Standing and leaning over the reception desk, she pointed to her left and said, "Sure, just go down this hallway and take the second right. Go through the double doors, and the nursery is on the left. Can't miss it."

"Thanks."

I hurried down the corridor, shedding my jacket as I went. I took the second right, pushed through the double doors, and there it was.

There they were.

All lined up, there were four of them, cocooned in pink or blue blankets, Joy's little caps on their heads. Two slept soundly while one batted large, dark eyes. The last, a boy, wailed and flailed chubby arms. In the distance, their backs to me, sat Joy and another volunteer, cradling infants. As I watched, Joy stood, kissed the sleeping infant she was holding, and placed her back in her crib. Then she leaned over the fretful little boy, removed his cap, kissed him, and caressed his downy head. He calmed instantly.

Then she looked up and noticed me standing at the window. She waved and then turned to say something to the other volunteer, who turned, looked my way, and smiled, flashing his beautiful green eyes and dimple.

Joy stepped to the door, cracked it, and said, "Change your mind?"

"Not sure. Maybe."

"You're welcomed to observe, if you'd like. Or if you want to come in, there are sterile caps and gowns next door and a sink where you can scrub your hands."

Thinking about it for a moment, I said, "I think I'll watch, for now."

"Sure, Sweetie, you do that," she said and slipped back into the nursery.

I watched as she made her rounds of the tiny plastic cribs, tucking blankets, smoothing caps, patting backs. She looked like a natural. She looked like a mother.

I looked like a mother too. That's because I am a mother.

Flexing my fingers and taking a deep breath, I turned from the window and went to find a sterile cap and gown and a sink where I could scrub my hands.

Twelve

I won't say that it was easy in the beginning. It wasn't. It was truly heart wrenching. Holding that first newborn in my arms brought on a deluge of tears and an ache in my heart, but Joy and Chris were there to help me through. Especially Chris. That first day I held an infant I began to shake. Chris crouched beside my chair and put one arm around my back as he helped me cradle the baby with the other.

As I shook with fear and sadness, he held me so gently, saying, "Doing just fine."

He had no idea why I was having such a difficult time cradling a baby, but he had the decency not to ask. He just comforted me and helped me work through whatever my issues might be.

And as he looked from me to the infant with so much care and kindness, I finally came to feel, to understand the passion he felt for the people of his island home. In time I relaxed into his care and was rocking babies with confidence. I comforted them, and, to my surprise, they also comforted me.

But once I'd rocked those sweet, tiny, mewling infants, my six year olds—though still precious and adorable to me—seemed so huge and loud and rowdy. I tried not to compare because who would want six-year olds to behave like helpless infants? But on some days I prayed they'd chill out.

On one day in particular my students had been wired—loud and argumentative and dissatisfied with school, me, and one another. Uncertain how to tame them, I release them to the beach so that they could romp and twirl and run away their aggressions. They raced and spun and threw things for about thirty minutes, yet when it was time to return to their work, they brought their abundance of energy and rowdiness right back into the classroom. I needed to calm them somehow.

Not at all certain if anything would work, I breathed a sigh and said sternly, "Okay, I want each of you to go to the book shelf and choose a book. We're going to have quiet time now." Several looked as though they weren't through being wild, so I said, "And anyone who doesn't want to settle down won't get a book."

Surprisingly, each of them became quiet at the thought of being forbidden from choosing a book to read. They had all become enamored with the books my parents had brought from their attic—books with covers, books without tattered pages, books that didn't have DISCARD emblazoned across them—and they cherished the times I allowed them to pick one to read quietly at their desks.

"Okay, first row, go pick your favorite book. Quietly, please. No pushing, Cara."

When row one had made their selections, I said, "Okay, row two, your turn."

"Row three? Ready?"

And row three, including beautiful Martina with the sad eyes, rose and approached the bookcase. While others scrambled and elbowed one another to find a book to their liking, Martina reached, without hesitation, and pulled out a small book. As she returned to her desk, I smiled when I realized she had picked my all-time favorite children's book, THE SURPRISE DOLL.

It was an old book, a simple little Golden Book that had been published back when my mother was a child. Her mother had read it to her, and then she had bought a copy for me because she thought that Mary, the little girl who owned many dolls, looked just like her little girl. She had blonde hair, brown eyes, and a turned-up nose, just like mine. I had so loved the book because it was a special gift from my mom. I cherished the book. It would always be my favorite.

I watched as Martina sat at her desk and opened the book gently on her desktop. Then she, painstakingly, pointed to word after word and mouthed each to herself. I knew that she enjoyed books by the way she watched so attentively when I read to the class. But I had no idea she could read so well. Sure, she could read our spelling words, but we had not yet progressed to reading books in class. But I knew she was reading, because I had memorized the book word for word and could read her lips, mouthing each word correctly. How long had she been reading? How had I not realized? Perhaps her shyness had caused her to keep her gift to herself.

When all the children were engrossed in their books, I approached Martina and crouched by her desk.

"You've chosen my favorite book," I whispered.

She didn't say a word or look my way.

"Will you read some to me, please?"

Without responding, she turned back to the beginning of the book and placed her tiny finger beneath the first word. Then she began reading, very slowly and deliberately, in a near inaudible voice.

"Mary lived in a little house on the side of a hill, right over the ocean."[2]

She turned the page gently, as if THE SURPRISE DOLL were as precious a book to her as it had been to me.

And she continued: "Mary had big brown eyes, a nose that went up like this, eyebrows that went up like that, hair as yellow as butter, and cheeks that were pink from the sun and wind. And when she smiled, she smiled all over her face."[2]

"Where did you learn to read so well, Martina?" I whispered, so as not to disrupt the other children.

"My mommy," she said quietly, without taking her eyes from the page.

"Do you have books at home?"

"No, ma'am."

"What do you read?"

"Magazines from Miss Virginia's house."

"Miss Virginia?"

"Mommy cleans Miss Virginia's house. She lets Mommy bring magazines home for me to read."

Magazines for a six-year old? What kind of magazines was she reading? People? Newsweek? Good Housekeeping?

Martina needed age-appropriate reading material, not cast-off adult magazines. I assumed her mother could not afford to purchase books for her, and taking her to the library over at New Oak was probably out of the question. I hadn't allowed the children to take books home from school because we had so precious few, and I didn't want to run the risk of having them lost or ruined. But Martina loved to read, and she needed children's books. Did I dare break my rule for just one child? I decided that it was my rule; I could break it if I wanted.

"Martina, would you like to take a book home to read to your mommy?"

"Yes, ma'am," she said, her eyes still downcast.

"Okay," I said to her quietly, "we're going to put our books away now, so that we can work on our numbers. But before you leave this afternoon, pick out a book to take home."

"Yes, ma'am," she said and rose to return THE SURPRISE DOLL to the bookshelf.

For the rest of the afternoon, Martina worked quietly at her desk, but I noticed that from time to time she'd steal glances at the bookshelf, as if she couldn't wait to pick a book to take home to share with her mother. When the day ended, without prompting, she headed straight for the bookshelf. With all her choices, she, once again, picked THE SURPRISE DOLL. I smiled to myself. Martina and her mother would read THE SURPRISE

DOLL, just as my mother and I had read it when I was a little girl.

The following morning I watched the children tumble from the tram and thunder into the classroom. Quiet Martina brought up the rear, as she always did. While the others slung lunches and backpacks into their desks, Martina went straight to the bookshelf and returned THE SURPRISE DOLL to its empty space. Then she took her seat.

At the end of that day and each day thereafter, she'd approach the bookshelf, remove THE SURPRISE DOLL, slip it into her pink backpack, and take it home with her, only to return it to its slot the following morning.

During the second week I approached her and said, "Martina, wouldn't you like to take another book home with you?"

"Yes, ma'am," was all she said, still not looking my way.

That afternoon she knelt before the bookshelf and removed a new book to take home with her to read to her mother. But she took THE SURPRISE DOLL with her, as well. Day after day she chose a different book, but THE SURPRISE DOLL always took the trip home with Martina.

One day as the children worked quietly at their desks, I took THE SURPRISE DOLL to Martina and crouched beside her desk.

"You like THE SURPRISE DOLL a whole lot, don't you, Martina?" I asked her.

"Yes, ma'am," she said, running her finger across the cover, tracing the letters.

"What do you like best about it?" I asked.

Without hesitation, she turned the pages and pointed to the doll named Teresa, the one with dark eyes and dark hair, and whispered, "She looks like me." She smiled for the first time as she showed me Teresa, the little Spanish doll.

"She sure does," I said. And then I turned to Mary, the little girl with many dolls, and said, "Who does Mary look like?"

Still smiling and looking up at me for the first time since she had joined my class, Martina batted her huge, dark eyes, pointed at me, and said, "She looks like you."

I can't describe the joy a teacher feels when she realizes she has reached a child she thought unreachable. I held back tears and the urge to grab her and hold her to me and just said, "That's right. My Mom bought this book for me when I was a little girl because she thought Mary looked just like me."

"I know," she said and turned to the front of the book and the inscription from my mother. Then she pointed to each word as she read aloud, "To Ally, my surprise doll. I love you, Mama."

"This is my favorite book," Martina told me.

"I know, Martina. It's my favorite book too."

And this time, I didn't resist my urge to hug her.

"Okay, kiddos," I said before I began to cry, "time to gather our belongings and get ready to go home."

Martina slipped THE SURPRISE DOLL into her backpack and headed for the bookshelf to find another book to take home to read to her mother.

"Bye, Miss Ally," they all screamed as they streaked from the classroom and headed for the tram. Even Martina smiled shyly and waved to me as she left the room.

I watched as my little scholars clambered for a seat, and Mr. Ruiz pulled out and rumbled down Beach Road to deposit his passengers along the way. When I knew that they were safely on their way, I grabbed my purse, locked up for the night, and hopped into my cart. I pulled onto Beach Road and cruised toward home, waving cheerily to passersby, anxious to share my news with Joy. I pulled into my sandy drive and parked my cart in my yard and, without even stopping by my house, headed next door.

"Hey, Joy, you home?" I yelled, as I opened the door.

While I knocked when I first moved to Pelican Isle, I soon learned that the island's inhabitants have an open-door policy. Doors are never locked, and visitors just poke their heads in and yoo-hoo in greeting. It reminds me of the neighborhoods of my parents' childhoods. I'd always envied their neighborly warmth and camaraderie, and I was overjoyed to find that familiarity in my new home.

"Back here," she called and stuck her head around the kitchen door. "Making a pitcher of tea. Come on back."

I stepped in, closed the door behind me, and ran with excitement to the kitchen.

"Oh, Joy," I said, grabbing her hands and jumping up and down, "you aren't going to believe what happened today."

"So tell me."

"Remember my telling you about Martina?"

"Yeah, I know Martina. Gonzales, right?"

"Yep, that's the one."

"Beautiful little girl. Real quiet, though."

"Well, today, for the first time, she smiled in my class."

"Oh, Ally, that's wonderful."

"And that's not all, Joy. She actually looked me in the eye."

"Fantastic."

"She seems so withdrawn. I thought I'd never get through to her."

"See, Ally, you're a great teacher, and these kids need you."

"I know, but it's always gratifying when a child shows me that she needs me."

"I'm just so proud of you. Job well done," she said, taking me in her arms and giving me a warm hug.

"Thanks, Joy. That means so much, coming from you."

"I believe this calls for a celebration. Let's celebrate with soup. The pot is steeping right now."

"Sounds great."

"Let's call Chris and see if he can join us."

"Good idea," I agreed.

Joy pulled her phone from her pocket, put it on speaker, and hit Chris's number.

"Hey, what's going on?" he said when he answered.

"Not much. Just thought you might like to take a break at suppertime for some soup."

"Gonna have to take a rain check. We're slammed here, and it doesn't show any sign of letting up."

"Oh, come on, everybody's got to eat."

"Thanks for the invitation. I'd love to, but we're short-handed."

Then I said, "It's she-crab, your favorite."

There was a silence on the line before Chris said, "Ally?"

"Yeah?"

"Didn't know you were there."

"Just came in from school with some good news for Joy."

"What's the good news?"

"Come for soup, and I'll tell you."

Another pause.

"Well...I guess I can find someone to cover for me. What time is supper?"

I looked to Joy and she whispered, "How about six?"

So I said, "Would six work?"

"Sounds good. Let me find a replacement, and I'll see you girls around six o'clock."

"Great, see you then," I said.

"Bye, Ally."

"Bye, Chris."

When I hit the OFF button, I looked up to see Joy shaking her head and rolling her eyes.

"Oh, brother, that boy's got it bad."

"Nuh uh."

"Oh, yes, he does. He'd still be saying *no* to my soup if he hadn't found out you were here."

"Well...," was all I said and blushed at the notion that Chris was coming

85

for supper because of me.

He must not have had trouble finding a replacement because he was in Joy's kitchen at six on the dot, sporting his green scrubs, white Crocs, and a hint of golden stubble on his chin.

"Okay, what's the great news?" he asked, grabbing my hands. "Oh, hi, Joy," he added.

"Oh, hi to you too," she said in her faux-hurt voice.

Chris ignored her and returned his attention to me.

His grasp on my hands grew tighter and tighter as I told him about my breakthrough. When I finally said that Martina had looked me in the eye, Chris grabbed me in a bear hug and began chanting, "Told you so! Told you so! Told you so!"

Pulling myself away, I said, "Okay, I get your point."

He took my hand again and said, "Oh, Ally, I knew it. I knew you'd be perfect for these kids. I knew you were just what they needed. Great job."

"Soup's on," Joy called. "Get it while it's hot."

But, for some reason, I didn't want to eat soup. I just wanted to stand there, holding hands with Chris Cruz, talking about making a difference in the lives of Pelican Isle kids. But holding Chris's hand soon became awkward, so I said, "Better do as Joy says or she won't feed us."

Pulling away from Chris, I scooted into the booth, and he slid in after me. Sitting side by side, eating Joy's scrumptious she-crab soup, we chatted animatedly and laughed easily. Then I realized that every time our knees brushed together, I would feel a tingle surge through my body. Was I feeling an attraction to Chris Cruz? I dismissed the notion, though, and accepted the feeling as residual excitement over Martina's and my connection.

As soon as we finished eating, Chris swiped his mouth with his napkin, carried his soup bowl to the sink, and said, "This is great fun and I hate to leave you ladies, but I really need to get back. Thanks a bunch for calling."

Then Joy said, "Ally, I'll clean up here. Will you please see Chris out?"

I didn't think Chris needed seeing out, but I followed him from the kitchen as he headed for the door.

He grabbed the doorknob, but instead of twisting it, he released it and turned to face me. Taking my hand, he said, "I'm so happy for you, Ally. And for Martina. What a day, what a day."

"Thanks. I can honestly say that this was the best day of my teaching career. This is why teachers teach."

Then he put his arms around me, hugging me to him, and said, "Job well done, Teacher. Congratulations."

We continued to hug, and I got lost in his arms, until he whispered, "Better run."

I sadly released him and watched him leave. Once he'd disappeared down the stairs, I wandered back into the kitchen where Joy was finishing up the dishes.

"Can you stay a while?"

"Sure, I'd like that."

"Then come on in the living room and chat with me while I knit."

Then I said, "Better yet, Joy, teach me to knit. If I can rock babies, and I can, maybe I can learn to knit."

"Of course you can. We can start with simple little baby hats?"

I picked up one of Joy's little hats, a tiny pink one with a white flower on the ribbed cuff, and began to get cold feet. "This looks a little complicated for a beginner, at least this beginner. Can we start with something basic, something real easy?"

"Well, okay, then. How about a scarf? You just knit and knit and knit until you get tired of knitting, and, voila, you have a scarf."

"Sounds more my speed."

"Hold on, and I'll be right back," Joy said, as she disappeared into her bedroom. Soon she returned with four huge canvas bags full to overflowing with colorful yarn.

"Take your pick," she said, as I fell to my knees and plunged my arms elbow deep into her cozy, soft stash of vibrantly colored yarn.

I was into the fourth bag when I came upon a beautiful brown tweed yarn with orange, green and turquoise flecks. It was soft and rich, and I knew it was the one, the one I wanted to knit and knit and knit until I got tired of knitting.

"Great choice," Joy said as she pulled out needles and began showing me how to cast on stitches and then begin knitting my scarf.

It was slow going, very slow going. It took me three attempts to cast on all my stitches, but on the third try I had a nice little row of yarn teeth all lined up on my needle.

"Well, look at that!" Joy cried, as if I'd made some monumental scientific discovery. "It's perfect. I knew you were a natural, Ally."

And then there was the knitting and knitting and knitting till I got tired. I'd drop stitches, and Joy would help me pick them back up. I'd twist stitches, and Joy would show me how to untwist them. I'd split stitches, and Joy would fix my screw-ups and explain that everybody, even the most veteran knitter, splits stitches. I didn't believe her for a minute. I was all thumbs and knew it.

But before the end of the evening, I was getting the hang of it and was starting to see some progress—about three inches of scarf. Granted, the progress was slow, but it was progress nonetheless.

I soon learned that it doesn't take long to get hooked on knitting, and night after night I'd appear at Joy's door, eager to add to my project, anxious to improve, excited to see the finished product. In time I could create that rhythmic, click-click cadence that I loved hearing Joy make with her needles, and my slow-going project was beginning to take shape. It no longer looked like a potholder. It was actually beginning to resemble a scarf.

I looked forward to the day when I could say, "Voila, it's finally a scarf!" and begin tackling one of those cute little baby hats.

Thirteen

"Hey, Joy," Chris said, "Ally can help us decorate the tree this year."

"Well, of course, she can," Joy agreed.

"Oh, I'd like that. I've always loved helping my mom decorate our tree. But she has a very specific way she likes it decorated—same red and silver balls and strings of white lights in the same place year after year. Dad drags the tree down out of the attic the week after Thanksgiving and gets it steady in the stand, and then he puts the scratchy, old Bing Crosby and Nat King Cole Christmas albums on his ancient stereo turntable."

I could feel myself getting nostalgic as I recalled my family's favorite annual traditions. Joy and Chris just smiled at me and let me reminisce.

"Then he and Mom and I spend the whole evening decorating and drinking eggnog. Even when I was a little girl, Dad would put a drop of rum in my eggnog. It made me feel so grown up. He'll build a fire in the fireplace, which we rarely need in Raleigh. Some Christmases he's even had to turn on the air conditioner to counteract the raging heat. But a fire in the fireplace is a must," I said, punctuating the air with my finger, the way my dad always does, "a huge part of decorating night. And though it rarely snows back home, I always imagine that it's snowing right outside our window while we get the house ready for Christmas."

I sighed, thinking how I'd missed our tradition this year.

"Sounds like fun," Joy said and put an arm around me and gave me a warm, motherly hug.

"Sorry you weren't able to be at home for your family's tree decorating, but Chris and I will try to make it up to you."

"Great, when do we start?" I asked, looking around for the artificial tree and box of ornaments and twinkly lights.

"Well, not quite yet. Christmas eve afternoon Chris and I go over to

New Oak to Leonard Robinson's tree lot. We've been buying our Christmas trees from him since he opened for business, back when Chris was just a tyke."

"That's right. I think I was four. I still remember my first time. Mr. Robinson gave me a candy cane."

"But why do you wait so late?"

"So we can get the puniest tree on the lot," Chris said, and he and Joy looked at each other and laughed at what appeared to be a private joke.

"The puniest?"

"Yeah," Joy said, "we wait till all the big, perfect trees are gone, and then we take the most pitiful, scrawniest tree that nobody else wants."

"Aw, that's sweet," I said, "sort of like Charlie Brown's tree."

"Yeah, sort of," Chris said, smiling. "Mr. Robinson knows to save the runt for us."

Then I remembered that I'd be leaving for Raleigh Christmas eve morning.

"Oh, no, you guys, I won't be here. I'm going to visit my folks that day."

Without skipping a beat, Joy said, "No problem, we'll just have our decorating party the night before, won't we, Chris?"

"Sure, why not?" he said, in agreement.

"But it's your tradition. I don't want you to change your tradition just for me."

"Oh, nonsense," Joy said, with the wave of her hand, "we made the tradition. We can change it if we want to, can't we, Chris? There's no one here to punish us for breaking the rules."

And Chris proclaimed that rules—especially theirs—were meant to be broken.

"Well, that's awfully kind of you."

"So, it's settled," Joy said. "We will be having our tree decorating celebration the night before Christmas Eve. Are we all in?"

"I'm in," Chris said.

"Me too," I said.

But before tree-decorating night, I hoped to have a Christmas party for my kids. Knowing that Christmas could be politically incorrect for some, I first checked with Carter.

"Oh, goodness, Ally, by all means have a Christmas party. Everyone here on the island celebrates Christmas with church services and trees and lots and lots of food and gifts. School without a Christmas party would be tragic," he said, laughing. "All the children have come to expect a party."

"Carter, will you come to our Christmas party?"

He grinned broadly and said, "Just try to keep me away. And let me know if there's anything at all I can do to help."

"Thanks, Carter, I'll be sure to let you know."

I had brought in a tree from a lot by the ferry landing, a little small but one I could tie to the top of my golf cart. The children loved it, though, and had made ornaments out of construction paper and magazine cutouts and shells and glitter and anything else we could find that looked like it belonged on our tree. Once we had it groaning under the weight of the children's decorations, they proclaimed it beautiful, the most *beautifulest* tree ever.

"Oh, Miss Ally, I love it!" Cara, my drama queen and one of the most charming, adorable students I've ever taught, crowed and threw her arms around my waist.

Joy and I set to making sixteen red felt stockings on her old Singer sewing machine, writing my students' names in glue and glitter on the cuffs. Then we drove over to the Dollar Store in New Oak for stocking stuffers: pencils, barrettes, candy canes, scratch pads, games, crayons, Silly Putty. While we were there, we picked up festive red Santa napkins and paper plates. The night before the party, Joy, Christopher, and I baked cupcakes, decorated sugar cookies, and cut up a gigantic bowl of fruit.

"My kids are going to love this. Thanks so much for all your help. Chris, won't you come? Joy will be there. And Carter plans to drop by."

"Sorry, but I just can't make it. I'll be the only one on duty tomorrow, and I just can't leave my patients."

"I understand, but you don't know what you'll be missing."

"Oh, I know it's going to be a blast. But I just don't have a choice."

The day of the party the children were like a bucket of worms. There was just no settling them down. So when Joy strolled into the classroom shortly after lunch, I was grateful that we could call it a day.

So I crowed, "Okay, kiddos, it's party time!" and threw up my hands.

They jumped up and began dancing and squealing, and I had to close the door and tell them to pipe down to keep them from disturbing the other classrooms. They obediently returned to their desks and fidgeted as Joy prepared plates of cupcakes, cookies, and fruit and passed them around while I doled out juice boxes. I powered up the computer and found some Christmas music to serenade us as we partied. And while the children ate, Joy and I gave out stockings to sixteen very surprised first graders. Eating with one hand and plundering through their loot with the other, they had a grand time and made a glorious mess.

And as they were squealing with excitement, Carter stuck his head in the door and called out, "What's all this racket going on in here?"

Knowing that Mr. Carter wasn't scolding them but was eager to join in their fun, they called out, "Hey, Mr. Carter! Come play with us, Mr. Carter! Look, Mr. Carter, what we got!"

Some of them jumped from their seats, raced to him, and grabbed onto him with their sticky little hands. He clucked over them all and let them usher him into the classroom.

"What's in your bag, Mr. Carter?" Cara called out.

"Well, I have a treat for all good boys and girls," Carter said, smiling and raising a big, red gift bag. "Now everyone sit down so I can share my goodies with you."

Once the children were seated, Carter went from desk to desk, calling each child my name, handing each a chocolate Santa, and tousling their hair or patting their backs.

When he had reached my last student, he said, "I have just enough time for a cupcake and a juice box. Then I have three more parties to go to."

So I grabbed Carter and me each a cupcake and a juice box, and we sat side-by-side on my desk, chatting and making our teeth red with Christmas icing.

"Thanks, Carter," I said, as I watched my precious students jittering with excitement over their party. "I'd have missed so much had I not accepted your offer."

"Yeah, I know. They're a special bunch, aren't they?"

I agreed they were.

Wiping his mouth with his Santa napkin, he called out to the children, "Thanks for inviting me, but I'd better be off."

They all yelled their good-byes to him as he left us with a wave and a huge grin.

When the kids were just about finished with their snacks, I said, "Martina, would you like to read a Christmas story to the class?"

She smiled broadly and said, "Yes, ma'am."

Since Martina's and my breakthrough, she had blossomed and gained a confidence I never dreamed she'd find. When I first asked if she'd like to read to the class, she was reluctant, but she agreed when I told her I'd be right there to help. Immediately the children were mesmerized by a child their age reading so well, and they became transfixed as she commanded the reading circle.

Day after day as reading time came, my students would cry, "Let Martina read. We want to hear Martina."

So she became our classroom reader, soon assuming her position at the head of the circle without my coaxing.

"Well, go pick a favorite," I told her.

She smiled at me and scurried to the bookshelves. As she crossed the classroom, the other students called out, "THE NIGHT BEFORE CHRISTMAS, THE LITTLEST ELF, HOW THE GRINCH STOLE CHRISTMAS."

But when Martina held up CHRISTMAS IN THE MANGER, her fellow students agreed, "Yeah, read that one. That's the one. I like that one."

So Martina took her place in my chair at the front of the classroom, crossed her ankles, and opened CHIRSTMAS IN THE MANGER on her lap. The rest of the children scooted their desks close to her so that they could hear her soft voice and waited quietly for her to begin. And then Joy and I watched Martina draw in her audience with her exceptional gift, reading flawlessly, sharing pictures with the others as she read. I looked on with pride and astonishment as my once painfully shy and withdrawn student glowed with assurance. Our Christmas party just couldn't get any better.

Or so I thought.

From beyond the closed door we heard, "Ho! Ho! Ho! Are there any good little girls and boys in there?"

Then the door burst open, and Santa stepped into our classroom, eliciting squeals from all my students. Dressed in his customary red suit, he had burnished black leather boots to his knees and a lush, curly, snow-white beard and wig. Who was he and where had he come from? I looked at Joy, thinking she had invited him, but she shrugged her shoulders and looked as clueless as I felt.

"Here, Santa," Cara called, as she ordered Martina from my desk chair and dragged it toward Santa so that he could sit and share whatever he had in that big canvas bag. Cara was not only my drama queen but my self-appointed class leader and social director, as well.

"Thank you, Cara. I'm awfully weary. That trip from the North Pole is a long one. Ho! Ho! Ho!"

"You know my name!" Cara screamed and grabbed him around the waist.

"Of course I know your name. I know the names of all good boys and girls. And I have lots of children to visit this afternoon, so y'all come here and let's see what Santa has in this big old bag."

Y'all, huh? Santa must be from the southern part of the North Pole.

And one by one Santa lifted my children, calling each by name, and set them on his knee, bellowing to each of them in his rich, southern-accented baritone. He held them close and asked what they'd like for Christmas, laughing at each of them, making his whole body shake with every chuckle. This guy was good.

And as each child finished reciting his Christmas wants, Santa would reach into his bag, pull out a wrapped surprise, and say, "Here's a little something to tide you over till Christmas morning. Now, you be a good girl and do what your mommy says. Okay? And Merrrrrry Christmas!"

What a ham. And what a perfect addition to our Christmas party.

When all the children had sat on Santa's knee and torn into their packages, littering the floor with their wrappings, Santa said, "I believe there are two more good girls I haven't talked to."

Then all the children began hopping up and down, chanting, "Miss Ally, Miss Joy, Miss Ally."

Joy lifted her long skirt, skipped over to Santa, hopped up on his knee, and started rattling off Christmas wishes—a Porsche, a mink coat, a trip to Spain. All the children laughed, and Santa promised that he'd see what he could do.

Swept up in the excitement of the moment, I shrugged and crossed the room to sit on Santa's knee. I felt myself blush as I perched on his lap and all the children began giggling and clapping.

Then Santa said, "And what does Miss Ally want Santa to bring her this year?"

When I opened my mouth to answer, Santa looked up at me and, without breaking character, winked a startlingly beautiful green eye.

I opened my mouth to speak but could only mutter, "I uh-uh…"

"Looks like the cat got this girlie's tongue. How 'bout I just surprise you on Christmas morning?" he said, pinching my cheek with his white-gloved hand.

Giggling like a schoolgirl, I felt myself blush.

To save me from further embarrassment, Santa bellowed, "Well, I'd better be getting along. I have three more classrooms to visit. But I'll be back. Ho! Ho! Ho!"

And he was off to spread joy to all the rest of the children of Pelican Isle Elementary.

Fourteen

At five o'clock on the day before Christmas Eve, Chris came rumbling into Joy's yard in his old beat-up, rusted, and faded red Chevy pick-up truck. It was the only vehicle he owned, other than his golf cart that he drove back and forth from home to the clinic. Before he swung down from the cab, he gave his horn one long honk that screamed *Ah-ooooo-guh!*

Joy and I had been waiting for him at her house, so we grabbed our jackets and headed for the back porch, just in time to see Chris stride toward us wearing jeans, cowboy boots and hat, and a suede jacket.

"Going to brave the wilderness to chop you down a big old Christmas tree, pahdnuh?" Joy called out to him.

"Some'pm like 'at, Miss Joy. Care to mosey along with me in my pick-em-up truck?"

"Sure do, but I think you forgot your jingling spurs."

"You two are so silly," I said.

Tipping his hat, Chris called out, "Well, Miss Ally, we'd be much obliged if you'd agree to join us in our search for the most perfect Christmas tree."

Deciding I'd best play along with their foolishness, I fanned my face with my hand and said, "Well, Dr. Chris, I'd be raht pleased to be a part of the hunt for that there Christmas tree of yourn."

Joy rolled her eyes and said, "Good lord, we've made her one of us."

"Well, let's get going before somebody snatches our tree," Chris cried, to which Joy replied, "You know there's no rush. Who would want our tree?"

But we rushed to Chris's truck just the same, hopped in, me wedged in between the two of them, and headed to the north end of the island, toward the narrow bridge that would take us over to New Oak and to Mr. Robinson's Christmas tree lot.

As we bounced along on worn-out shocks and Chris ground worn-out gears, I said, "That was quite a show you put on the other day."

Chris said, "Show? What show?"

"You know, Santa."

"Santa?"

I looked at Joy, and she just shrugged.

I knew I would never get him to admit to being Santa, so I just dropped it and began fiddling with the AM radio until I found a station that was playing Christmas music. And all the way to New Oak the three of us sang, to the top of our lungs and way off key, *Rockin' Around the Christmas Tree, I Saw Mommy Kissin' Santa Claus*, and *Grandma Got Run Over By a Reindeer*. It was perfect beat-up-truck Christmas music.

And we never mentioned Santa Chris again.

We rattled across the rickety bridge from Pelican Isle, Chris's truck shimmying on its wounded shocks. We thumped off the end of the bridge into quaint, Christmas-bedecked New Oak, its street lights adorned with greenery and seasonal banners, its storefronts decorated with trees and Santas. Christmas music blared from outdoor speakers as last-minute shoppers wrestled with packages and twirling, hyper children. Between Beemis Hardware and the Delightful Donut Shoppe, we careened into the Christmas tree lot, bouncing over the curb and hitting our heads with a bonk on the roof of the truck. Gene Autry wailed *Here Comes Santa Claus* from the truck radio in his recognizable nasal twang.

"You folks is early this year. Wudn't 'spectin' y'all till tomorrow," the lot proprietor said in a voice so deep that James Earl Jones would have sounded like him, had James Earl Jones been able to speak one octave lower.

"Well, we had a little change of plans," Joy told him. And turning to me and winking, she said, "Mr. Robinson, this is our new friend, Ally. She's going to help us decorate our treasure this year."

"So nice to mee'cha, Miss Ally," Mr. Robinson said in his one-octave-lower-than-James-Earl-Jones voice. "And as luck would have it, I have the perfeck tree for y'all. Come on back heah. I've been saving it for ya."

When we got to the back of the lot, past perfectly-shaped, full, lush six-, eight-, and ten-foot Christmas trees, Mr. Robinson picked up off the ground the scrawniest, most pitiful, most lopsided Christmas tree I'd ever seen.

"It's glorious!" cried Joy

"You think the needles will hold up through Christmas, Mr. Robinson?" Chris asked.

"Prolley not, Dr. Chris," Mr. Robinson said, looking it over and shaking his head.

"Perfect! We'll take it," Chris and Joy cried in unison.

"Sounds good to me," Mr. Robinson said, chuckling.

"How much do we owe you?" Chris asked as he pulled his wallet from the back pocket of his jeans.

"No charge for you, Dr. Chris," Mr. Robinson told him, handing over the scrawny tree.

"Then twenty bucks it is," Chris said, giving him a crisp bill.

Mr. Robinson grinned real big, showing a smart gold tooth. Then he reached into his overalls pocket, pulled out a candy cane, and handed it to me.

"Newcomers always get a candy cane."

"Well, thanks, Mr. Robinson. That's awfully nice of you."

"Bye now, folks, see you next year. Mighty nice meeting you, Miss Ally," he called as we headed for the truck.

Chris gently laid our tree in the bed of his truck and cried out, "Next stop, Wendy's!"

"That's tradition too," Joy said. "Always have to have a Wendy's hamburger and fries on Christmas-tree night.

So Chris pulled out of the lot to the right, then made a quick left directly into the Wendy's parking lot. We climbed back out of the cab of the truck, leaving our tree in full view in the bed, unattended. But there was scant chance that anyone would want to pilfer our pitiful tree.

It felt warm and inviting and greasy in Wendy's. The restaurant was full of holiday shoppers, happy and bustling and talking loudly. Christmas music belted from ceiling speakers, competing with the chatter of boisterous diners. As Joy and I shed our jackets and tossed them into a booth, Chris stepped to the counter and ordered for all of us—hamburgers all the way, fries, and large Cokes. I would have preferred a salad, but I didn't let on, for fear of screwing up their tradition even worse than I already had. By the time Joy and I grabbed napkins, straws, and catsup and returned to our booth, our order was waiting for us. The fries were hot, the burgers juicy, and the Cokes enormous and brimming with calories. But I had to admit that it was perfect, pre-Christmas-tree-decorating food. A salad would not have been festive or rib-and-thigh sticking enough.

When we finished our supper, we jumped back into Chris's truck and began our bouncy return trip to the Isle on a grease-and-sugar high. On the way I reached into my pocket and pulled out the candy cane that Mr. Robinson had given me. As I broke it into three pieces, I handed one to Joy and another to Chris.

"No, I don't want that one. I want the crookedy piece," Chris said, holding out his hand.

Handing him the crookedy piece, he popped it into his mouth and began slurping. Then he winked, smiled at me, and playfully poked me in the ribs with his elbow. I was enjoying the lighthearted feel of the outing, so

I smiled and poked him back. And as we bounced along, Chris's and my thighs began rubbing together, recreating that tingle that I recalled from our last meal at Joy's. Perhaps it really had nothing to do with my breakthrough with Martina. But I tried to ignore the tingle and joined Joy and Chris singing along to silly Christmas songs as we headed back to our island.

When we reached Joy's yard, Chris carefully lifted our sad little tree from the truck bed and headed for the house, shedding needles along the way. Joy ran ahead of us and placed her old, rusty tree stand in the corner of her living room.

I had brought a bottle of wine for the evening, but Joy said, "No wine on Christmas tree night. Only mulled cider. We have to have all our faculties about us when we decorate our tree."

So while I put the wine in Joy's cabinet for future consumption and Chris steadied our tree in the stand, Joy heated our cider.

When she returned carrying a tray with three steaming Santa mugs and a festive, red plate of iced gingerbread men, Chris took a cup of cider and a cookie for each of us, raised his mug, and said, "To best friends and the world's most perfect Christmas tree." Then to Joy he said, "Okay, now show us what you've got."

Then each of them grabbed a cardboard box and plopped down on the floor, Joy saying to me, "Come, sit right here," patting the space between the two of them.

They both opened their boxes and then, for some reason unknown to me, took turns presenting random stuff to each other.

First Chris handed Joy a huge mushroom about the size of his hand, the top bright orange, the underneath a rich, dark purple.

"Oh, a shroom!" Joy cried. "We're going to party tonight."

"Calm down, Joy. You know it's only cider and cookies tonight."

"Looky here," Joy said, pulling from her box a branch with four dried magnolia leaves with three flower pods attached.

Chris took them from her and said, "They're wonderful. Where'd you get 'em?"

"Remember when I went to Wilmington to visit Marilyn? She has a huge magnolia tree in her front yard. She graciously donated these."

"Perfect," Chris agreed and reached once more into his box, pulling out a handful of Spanish moss. "Got this when I went to that medical conference in Charleston. Apparently, it's not protected like our sea oats. They don't mind at all if you pull this stuff off the trees. Isn't it magnificent?"

"Love it," cried Joy, grabbing it from Chris and examining the gray, hair-like mass closely.

"Betcha can't top this," Joy said, reaching into her box and pulling out two stones, a round green one and a pale, blue oval.

"Oh, my gosh, sea glass. Where'd you get these?" Chris said, taking them from her and rubbing the smooth surfaces against his cheek. "They're beautiful."

"Found them in the cove down at the south end. You just gotta know where to look."

"Excuse me," I interrupted. "What are y'all doing? And what is all this stuff?"

"Stuff? This isn't *stuff!* These are Christmas tree decorations," Chris said, and they both looked at me as if I were from another planet, a planet where people didn't put strange, random objects on their Christmas trees.

Sensing my confusion, Joy said, "Chris and I decided long ago that we want only natural materials on our tree. Throughout the year we keep our eyes open for *stuff* to add to our stash. Soon our tree is going to topple from the weight of our collection."

"But until it does, we'll keep on adding more *stuff*," Chris said.

They weren't the red and silver glass balls and strings of white lights I was accustomed to seeing at Christmas, but, then, their tree wasn't a perfect, eight-foot, faux Douglas fir either. So I decided to keep my opinions to myself and reserve judgment until I saw Chris and Joy's finished product.

"Oh, okay, then. What else you got?" I asked.

"Driftwood," Chris said, presenting a rich piece of smooth driftwood about a foot long. It was marbled with swirls of browns and greens, with four small, amber knotholes.

"It's exquisite," Joy said, taking it from him and examining it closely, turning it over and over in her hand. "I believe you've topped my sea glass, Chris."

Then Joy handed Chris a perfect, white starfish, the largest I'd ever seen. In return, Chris gave her a bright yellow scallop shell, still perfectly hinged, opened to display a rich, purple and blue interior.

When they had come to the bottoms of their boxes, Joy reached into hers and cried, "Ta dah!" and lifted two perfect hydrangea blooms, dried to a beautiful pale green.

Taking them from her, Chris said, "These win the prize," and gazing at their little Charlie Brown tree, he told her, "and I know exactly where they belong."

Then Chris and Joy disappeared into Joy's bedroom and hauled out two more cardboard boxes and set them beside the tree. They opened the lids, and Joy said, "Dig in."

I peered into the boxes and found pinecones and moss-covered bark and seaweed and sea grass and colorful stones and feathers. There were beautiful yellow and blue and red butterflies, as well as more dried flowers of all sorts. And there were shells—lots and lots of shells, dangling from hangers made of pine needles or seaweed, since the rule stated that we could use only natural materials. There was even a bleached-white bird skull, its beak half open.

I was close to saying, "Yuck!" but I'd promised myself that I would not make disparaging remarks about Joy and Chris's decorating efforts, as kooky and unorthodox as I believed them to be.

So I joined in, and for well over an hour we gently placed the delicate objects among irregular, shedding branches of our tree and hung shells from spindly twigs. I steered clear of the bird skeleton and let Chris decide where that belonged. To my surprise and delight, as it began to take shape, as our *ornaments* filled in gaping holes, our Christmas tree no longer looked shabby. Or pitiful. It looked surprisingly lovely. It looked like it belonged. It looked, well, it looked perfect.

Just as I placed the last handful of seaweed on a bare branch and stood back to survey our creation, Chris said, "Almost done. Just one more thing."

And as Joy and I watched, Chris placed the green hydrangea blooms at the very top of the tree. They were more beautiful and looked more appropriate than any aluminum star I'd ever seen at the top of a Christmas tree.

When Chris joined us to admire our finished product, Joy said, "You know, Chris, I think that's the most wonderful Christmas tree we've ever had."

Chris put his arm around Joy and hugged her tight. Then he looked at me, smiled, and said, "She says that every year."

"Well, it's true," countered Joy. "Each year is better than the last, don't you think?"

"You're right," said Chris, and kissed her on the cheek.

"Okay, presents, I want presents!" Chris screamed, as if he were a little boy.

He ran for his gifts, which he'd hidden under his jacket on the sofa. Mine, too, were on the sofa, but in plain sight. While I'd been home for Thanksgiving, I'd pilfered some of my mother's most beautiful gold and purple designer paper and gold, wired ribbon to wrap my friends' gifts, so I wanted them shining and visible for them to see. Joy retreated to her bedroom to get her gifts for the two of us. I went to the kitchen to freshen our cider, and when I returned, the two of them were seated on the floor in front of the Christmas tree, drumming their fingers in anticipation.

As soon as I put down our cups, Chris cried, "Me first," as he handed us identically-shaped gifts, Joy's wrapped sloppily in colorful funny papers, mine wrapped in brown butcher paper. Each was tied with twine.

"Oh, Chris, where did you find it?" cried Joy, when she pulled back the paper. Then she leaned over and hugged his neck.

"In the storeroom of a musty old bookstore in Charleston. It took some rummaging, but I finally found it."

"Oh, look, Ally, it's a leather-bound edition of Shakespearean plays. Isn't it wonderful!"

I ran my hand over it and smelled its must and agreed that it was, indeed, wonderful. Guys usually grab a gift card at Victoria's Secret or a certificate to a day spa. But not Chris. He had put thought into Joy's gift, had gotten her something that she really wanted.

Then I pulled back my butcher paper to reveal a leather-bound book, as well, this one a volume of sonnets. I thought the gift was lovely, but I'd never shown any interest in poetry and wouldn't have known a sonnet had it jumped out of a bush and bitten me. I'd never understood poetry, never quite gotten the point. I was certain Chris had found it in Charleston, along with the book of Shakespearean plays. Its burgundy leather binding was rich and rubbed to a burnished hue. It was a kind gift. An easy gift. A safe gift.

"Thank you, Chris. It's lovely," I said, rubbing its soft leather cover with the palm of my hand.

"I hope you like it," Chris said.

"Oh, yes, I do, I do. Thanks. Thanks so much." And changing the subject so that I wouldn't have to commit too madly to a book of sonnets, I said, "Okay, me next."

I handed my beautifully wrapped gifts to Chris and Joy, all of a sudden feeling that they were so out of place. With all the natural wonder of our Christmas tree, my wrapping appeared garish, even ostentatious.

So I joked, saying, "Sorry, but I ran out of kelp and rags."

They both laughed, and reassuring me with a gentle pat on my knee, Joy said, "Ally, they are absolutely lovely. I can't wait to see what's inside."

I had gone to the yarn shop, Ewe Knit, in New Oak and had told the proprietor, "I want the loveliest blue yarn you have for one of the loveliest women I know. Enough for a sweater." I must have added, "And cost is no object," because the price of the yarn she chose was commensurate with that of a new compact car. But I didn't care. It was gasp-inducing beautiful, royal blue raw silk. I'd never seen anything quite so gorgeous, and I knew right away that it was made for Joy. I was certain that it would make her startlingly blue eyes look like sapphires and her hair shine as white as snow.

"Oh, my gracious, Ally, you just shouldn't have," she said, cradling the skeins gently in her hands and presenting them for Chris's awe, as if she were bearing priceless jewels. "Isn't it exquisite?" she asked him, her beautiful eyes reflecting the striking blue of the yarn.

Chris reached out and caressed the yarn, saying, "It sure is. Bet that'll make an awfully pretty sweater."

"Oh, it will, it will," she said, leaning forward and hugging me. "Thank you so, so much, Ally."

Then Chris said, "Okay, my turn," as he smiled and showed me his dimple before carefully pulling away the purple and gold wrapping from my gift.

"Love it!" Chris yelled, wrapping my brown tweed scarf round and round his neck. "It'll be perfect for those chilly, middle-of-the-night rides to the clinic when I'm too lazy to put the curtains down on the golf cart. Thanks a bunch, Ally."

Glancing Joy's way, I detected the look of surprise on her face. I hadn't told her that I was making the scarf for Chris. Guess she surmised it was for my father or, perhaps, a friend in Raleigh.

"Joy helped me make it," I said.

"You made this?" Chris said, apparently shocked that I was capable of such an undertaking.

"Yes, but, like I said, I had a lot of help."

"Don't listen to her, Chris," Joy clucked, waving her hand and clearing the air of my compliment. "She was a really fast learner. Once I got her started, she took off like a pro."

Fingering the ends of the scarf, he looked over at me and said, "I really love it, Ally. Really love it. I can't believe you made this just for me." And leaning toward me, he wrapped his arms around me and kissed me on my cheek. When he released me, I smiled and touched my hand to my cheek as I watched him return his attention to his scarf.

I looked at Joy and mouthed, "Thanks."

She just smiled and winked.

"Well," Joy said, "guess mine are all that's left."

She handed me a soft package bundled in burlap and Chris a very irregularly shaped object wrapped in iridescent purple silk. It appeared to me that she'd mixed up our wrapping, but I had long ago stopped second-guessing my unconventional neighbor.

I pulled back my burlap to find a gorgeous, intricately hand-knit green sweater. Joy picked it up, held it to my face, and said, "I was right. This green makes the gold flecks in your beautiful brown eyes just pop."

I flushed from the attention but agreed that green had always been my color.

"Oh, Joy, it's so beautiful. I'll wear it Christmas day. Thank you, thank you."

"Me, me," Chris cried and began peeling back his purple silk. "Where did you find it?" he screamed at Joy and held up a silver faucet handle with a white porcelain button on top with an H engraved in it.

"I was so tired of turning on the hot water in your kitchen with a dish rag. I was determined to find a matching knob for that spigot. I scoured antique stores from northern Virginia to the South Carolina line. Found it in Asheville."

I stifled a laugh at the absurdity of Joy's gift but then realized that it was very useful and most thoughtful, and she had gone to a lot of effort to locate it. It was truly a heart-felt Christmas gift.

As we finished our cider and gathered our gift-wrap, I said, "Hey, isn't burlap natural?"

"Why, I believe it is," Chris said.

So I bunched up my burlap wrapping and began fashioning it into a nest. Then I found a gaping, empty limb on our tree and gently placed my nest up against the trunk. Finally I had contributed something to the all-natural Christmas tree.

"Ta dah!" I cried.

Then Joy hopped up and said, "Hold on a minute," and began searching among the branches. "There they are," she said, and plucked the two polished pieces of sea glass from a tuft of pine needles. Then she gently placed the sea glass eggs in my burlap nest. "*Now* the tree is perfect."

And it was no longer just Joy and Chris's Christmas tree. It was mine too.

"This has been so much fun, y'all, but I really have to get to bed. My mom and dad will be expecting me for lunch tomorrow, so I'll need to get on the road to Raleigh pretty early in the morning. Thanks so much for letting me help you with your tree."

"Our tree, Ally, our tree," Chris said, including me.

"Well, thank you, and thanks for the wonderful gifts too," I said, standing and hugging them both.

Chris held me extra long and gave me a sweet kiss on my temple. Hmmm, what had gotten into him? Two kisses in one night. Was he high on cider? In the Christmas spirit? Perhaps decorating the world's most perfect Christmas tree made him especially loving.

I gathered my Christmas gifts and headed for the door, saying, "Merry Christmas, y'all. See you next week."

Fifteen

I crossed Joy's yard to my house. The night was so chilly I could see my breath. I rushed up the stairs, but before letting myself in, I glanced back toward Joy's house. Chris was standing on the porch, leaning on the railing, looking my way.

"Just wanted to make sure you got in all right," he called.

"Thanks, Chris. I'm fine."

"And thanks for helping us, Ally. It was fun."

"I had a good time too."

And lifting the end of his scarf and waving it at me, he said, "Love it."

"Merry Christmas, Chris."

"Merry Christmas to you too. Have a safe trip."

Finding it hard to pull myself away and bring an end to a most magical evening but knowing I needed to get some sleep, I let myself in and went straight to my bedroom, disrobed, and pulled my nightgown over my head. My suitcase was open on the floor, waiting for my last-minute packing: make-up, toothbrush, hair dryer. I gently placed my beautiful new green sweater that brought out the gold flecks in my brown eyes and my book of sonnets on top of my neatly folded clothes. I stepped to the bathroom to wash my face and brush my teeth before returning to crawl into bed. I pulled up the covers and leaned over to flip the bedside light switch but paused.

I slid out of bed and reached for the book that Chris had given me. If he were thoughtful enough to buy me poetry, I owed it to him to try to enjoy it. I climbed back into bed, pulled up the covers, and let the book fall open at the middle. I began reading. The cadence of the lines felt lovely as I spoke the words, so soft and tender. The poems were of love, and they touched my heart. Maybe I'd just never given sonnets a chance. Perhaps I just needed someone special to give me a gift of sonnets to make me appreciate them.

Just as I was placing the book on my nightstand, the pages ruffled and something caught my eye. I retrieved the book and opened it at the beginning. There on the inside cover was a message written in a beautiful flowing script, in ink that had faded with age to a soft, pale blue. It read:

Wishing the merriest of Christmases to my dearest
Allison
I shall miss you most profoundly in your absence.
Affectionately yours,
Christopher
Dec. 25, 1910

I read it again.

And again.

And again.

And again.

And with each reading my pulse quickened and my heart raced.

Instead of returning the book of sonnets that I was hoping had absolutely nothing to do with sonnets to my open suitcase, I placed it on the nightstand, just in case I were to awaken in the night and wish to read the inscription again.

And again.

But before turning out the light, I reached for my cell phone and texted: *Thanks, Christopher. Affectionately yours, Allison.*

Within moments my phone dinged. The return message read: *Likewise, Allison. Affectionately yours too, Christopher.*

Fighting the urge to continue playing this game, whatever this game we were playing might be, I reluctantly returned my phone to the nightstand and turned out the light. I slid deeper beneath the covers and touched the place on my cheek and then my temple where Chris had kissed me.

I didn't sleep much, and I did read the inscription in my sonnet book again and again and again throughout the night. What did it mean? Had Chris just happened upon the book in the used bookstore and found the century-old inscription to be a coincidence that he just couldn't resist? Or was there more to it? Well, he had responded to my text immediately that he thought of me affectionately too. But was he just being polite because I had signed my text *Affectionately yours, Allison*? Perhaps he wanted more than friendship, but, then again, it could have been just happenstance.

I played this circular game until I felt as if I were a dog chasing its tail. At about five in the morning, I headed for the bathroom, having given up on sleep and my attempts to figure out Chris's motives. Within an hour I had showered, washed and dried my hair, put on a little make-up so that my mother would think I was trying, dressed, finished packing, and made my bed. I zipped my luggage and rolled it to the door, checking along the way to make sure all the small appliances were unplugged and all the faucets were turned off. I locked the door behind me, out of habit and not out of any need, breathed in the salt air one last time, and headed to the garage for my rarely-driven Honda. I was hoping it would crank and get me to Raleigh.

The motor turned over with just one flick of the wrist, and I was off to New Oak and the nearest McDonald's for a giant black coffee. I was hoping I could make it the few miles without nodding off.

Though I was certain the south end of Pelican Isle had been bustling with vendors and fishermen for hours, the north end of the island was just awakening as I made my way to the bridge. The sky was beginning to glow purple at the horizon as I crossed from Pelican Isle into New Oak. I turned right shortly after leaving the narrow bridge, making my way to the McDonald's, about a half block off the main road. There was only one other car in the lot, a vintage seventies dark green Oldsmobile the size of a tank. When I entered the restaurant, I found the owners of the tank standing at the counter, ordering sausage biscuits, hash browns, and orange juice. A look-alike husband and wife team with fluffy tufts of white hair, each at least eighty years old, both bent and shrunken to no taller than five feet, greeted me with identical thin smiles and crinkly eyes.

"Morning, Miss," the old man said, as the woman added, "Hi, Sweetie, you're out awful early this mornin'."

"Yes, ma'am," I said, out of southern politeness and habit. I would never be too old to say ma'am and sir to my elders. "I'm going to Raleigh to visit my mom and dad for Christmas."

"That's nice. I bet they're real anxious to see you," the wizened little lady said.

"Yes, ma'am, they are."

I was grateful when their order arrived and they turned their attention to settling up with the cashier. I'm not an early-morning chatterer.

"That'll be $6.50 with your senior discount, Mr. Herb."

"Oh, Gloria, I think you just make up that senior discount," Mr. Herb chuckled and crinkled up his eyes at the young woman behind the counter.

"Well, Mr. Herb, anybody comes in here as much as you and Miss Effie deserves the senior discount."

Mr. Herb pulled his wallet from his back pocket with a palsied hand and slowly took out six ones. Returning his wallet to his back pocket, he then reached into his side pocket and pulled out an orange, rubber coin purse. He held it close to his face and squinted, squeezed the ends, and painstakingly fished out fifty cents in dimes, nickels, and pennies with gnarled, arthritic fingers. He handed the bills and change over, and the cashier put the money in the register.

Then Mr. Herb returned the orange coin purse to his side pocket and reached once again into his back pocket for his wallet, unfolded it, pulled out a crisp one-dollar bill, and grasped Gloria's hand.

"And a little something for you, my dear," he said, depositing it in her palm without fanfare and reaching for his tray. "After you, Mother," Mr. Herb said, as his wife steadied herself on her cane and shuffled off ahead of him to find a table.

I ordered an English muffin and a large coffee. I had planned to eat my breakfast in the car on my way to Raleigh, but since it was so early and my parents weren't expecting me until lunchtime, I decided to hang around for a while. After paying for my meal—Gloria didn't offer me the senior discount—I took my tray to a nearby booth and slid in. Then I unwrapped my English muffin and pulled out my cell phone.

I found Chris's text: *Likewise, Allison. Affectionately yours too, Christopher.*

I still chased my tail. Was this a game? And, if so, what kind of game? What were the stakes? Was there a winner? Or was Chris's finding the book just a fluke? A happy accident? Well, there was just one way to find out.

I texted: *Christopher, hope you have the merriest of Christmases. Affectionately yours, Allison.* I read it three times, very carefully, before hitting *send*.

I slipped my cell back into my purse and reached for my coffee. After only several sips, I heard a *ding*.

I pulled out my phone and read: *Allison, have a safe journey and a joyous Christmas. Please come back to us. Affectionately yours, Christopher.*

I felt my face flush as my heart raced. His response was so quick that he must have been anticipating my text. I still didn't know just what this was and where it was heading, but I knew, for sure, that it was heading somewhere. He hadn't asked me to come back just to the children of Pelican Isle. He had asked me to come back to him—well, to *us*, and us would most certainly include him.

And one thing I knew for sure: we would never again be Ally and Chris. We were officially Allison and Christopher.

I was smiling, touching my temple, my cheek, and re-reading Christopher's text when Mr. Herb and Miss Effie approached me.

"My dear," Miss Effie said, "we will pray for a safe journey as you head for Raleigh." Patting me gently on my shoulder, she smiled and said, "You have a very blessed Christmas."

I thanked them and wished them a blessed Christmas, as well, and watched them join hands and shuffle out to their big, green Oldsmobile.

Cam and I had talked about growing old and shuffling off together into the sunset. I quickly shook the thought away before I could become melancholy on Christmas Eve and tried to concentrate on my English muffin. But suddenly I found that I really wasn't hungry at all, so I rewrapped my breakfast and stuck it into my purse. I picked up my coffee, slung my bag over my shoulder, and headed to the condiment island for a couple of napkins.

"Merry Christmas," Gloria, the cashier, called and waved as I turned to leave. "Would you like a refill to go?"

"No thanks, I'm good," I said and smiled at her kindness. "And Merry Christmas to you too, Gloria," I called back as I heaved the heavy, glass door with my hip and headed for my car.

The sun was rising at my back. I was most grateful since I hate driving with the sun in my eyes. And I was equally glad it was daylight. I also dislike driving in the dark. So sun at my back, daylight all around, I set my cruise control to an acceptable speed and settled back for an uneventful trip to my childhood home. I drank my coffee, finally got hungry enough to eat my muffin, and made one stop to fill up my gas tank and empty my internal tank.

And then there was Raleigh and my parents' driveway.

Mom and Dad were out of the house and clinging to the side of the car before I could come to a complete stop.

As I climbed out, Mom clutched at me, crying, "Oh, Darlin', I can't believe you're home," as if I'd been away for years, instead of just the month since Thanksgiving. "Here, let me look at you," she said, releasing me from her hug and holding me at arm's length. "Oh, my, that salt air really agrees with you. You look perfectly glowing," she told me, smiling and smoothing my hair from my face.

Then I was in my father's arms, where he repeated what my mother had just said—that it had been a long time, the salt air agreed with me, and that I was looking good.

Grabbing my hand, Mom said, "Now give Dad your keys so he can bring in your bag. And you come with me. I have to get back to the kitchen before the cornbread burns."

And she hustled me into the house before I'd uttered a single word in greeting.

"Now, Darlin', you go freshen up and rest, and I'll call you when lunch is ready."

"Thanks, Mom, I'll do that," I told her and climbed the stairs behind Dad, who was already hauling my bag up to my pink-flowered bedroom.

Nothing had changed. Pictures of me aging from birth to college marched up the wall, in time with the steps. At the top of the stairs, I turned right and tripped on the rolled corner of the burgundy-flowered runner that led to my room. We'd been tripping on that same rolled corner since it had begun to roll when I was a small child. It never occurred to anyone to tape it down or to put a piece of furniture on top of it. We'd just say, "Watch your step," to anyone who lost footing.

"Watch your step," Dad said, as I stumbled slightly.

I smiled. I was home.

My mother had put a fresh Whole Foods mixed bouquet in a cut-glass vase on my dresser. Other than that, my room hadn't changed. I assumed the same number of flowers still marched up and down the walls, but I no longer had a desire to confirm my assumption by counting them.

"Good to have you home, Ally," my father said as he put my bag at the foot of my bed and turned to give me a hug. "I've missed you, you know."

"I know, Dad. I've missed you too."

"This is the first time you've been this far away," he said, and I could hear his statement catch in his throat. "But, Ally, I'm just so proud of you."

"Thank you, Dad. It was a hard decision, but going to Pelican Isle was the right thing to do."

It was the first time I'd said it out loud, but I knew, for certain, that it was true.

Before he could choke up, he said, "Well, you get settled now. Mom and I will be waiting downstairs. I'll go rev up the old stereo."

"That'll be good, Dad. Be right down."

Just as he tripped on the hall runner and warned himself to watch his step, I heard my cell ding.

Did you make it okay? Affectionately yours, Christopher.

Without hesitating, as if we were life-long texting buddies, I responded, *Just touched down. Mom and Dad waiting lunch for me. Later. Affectionately yours, Allison.*

I was beginning to feel that Christopher and I had started a new Christmas tradition. I was hoping it would extend past the holidays.

Christmas eve lunch is always the same: Mom's homemade three-alarm chili, sour-cream cornbread, and mincemeat pie. And, of course, no matter the time of year, tongue-curling, jaw-aching sweet tea. We'll take our lunch to the living room and sit on cushions around the coffee table as we praise Mom's beautiful tree and her chili, all the while fanning our mouths, and listen to Dad's old Christmas record collection.

After splashing water in my face and brushing my teeth, I went back downstairs to find that my mother had already laid the coffee table with our lunch, and Dad had lit a fire and revved up the old turntable. Bing Crosby crooned *I'm Dreaming of a White Christmas.* Mom had plugged in the Christmas tree lights and lit candles on the mantle.

"Everything looks beautiful, Mom."

"It does, doesn't it? There's just nothing like Christmas decorations and music to put us in a festive mood. Come. Sit. We don't want our chili to get cold."

I kicked off my shoes and sat cross-legged by my place at the coffee table. It was the same seat I'd always had—the one with the best view of my mother's perfect Christmas tree with the red and silver balls. We joined hands as Dad said his standard blessing and Bing competed with him for our attention. Then we dined on Mom's delicious chili and cornbread. It felt so comforting to be back with my parents, to indulge in all those simple Christmas traditions that made me feel safe and loved and nurtured.

Mom and Dad wanted to hear all about my students and Pelican Isle, and before I could answer each question, they would be on to another. But I understood their excitement: I had exceeded their expectations. So I happily answered all of their queries and delighted and astounded them when I ate two bowls of chili and a huge piece of pie. But as much as I loved my parents and wouldn't have traded my Christmas with them for anything, I found myself having a hard time concentrating on lunch and our conversation.

I kept listening for my phone to ding.

Sixteen

"Sweetie, our guests will be arriving soon. Don't you think you'd better go get dressed?"

My parents and I had had our traditional Christmas morning breakfast of cranberry scones and hot chocolate while we opened gifts and Eartha Kitt growled *Santa Baby* at us.

I found that Mom and Dad had had a tough time shopping for me. I was no longer a little girl or a wife or an expectant mother. When I was any of those, they found an abundance of appropriate gifts. But now I was a grown, widowed, childless woman, roughing it out on the very fringes of our state. So they gave me mittens and a toboggan, a bottle of the cologne that my girlfriends and I had loved in junior high, a journal, and a pair of purple Crocs. The generic or nostalgic nature of each gift tugged at my heart and made it hurt in a sad sort of way. They also gave me a Yankee Candle in a jar; the scent was Sea Breeze. I felt it sad that the irony of giving someone who lives by the sea a sea-breeze-scented candle went right over their heads.

Then Dad reached forward and handed me an envelope.

"Here, Sweetie, a little something extra for you. We had a tough time figuring what you'd like. Hope you'll buy something nice for yourself."

Inside the envelope, tucked within the pages of an ornate and elaborate card that praised, in iambic pentameter, my cherished daughterhood were five crisp one hundred dollar bills.

"Oh, Mom, Dad, this is way too generous."

Pushing my hands toward my chest, Dad said, "No, no, Ally, Mom and I want you to have it. Do something good for yourself. You deserve it."

"Well, thank you, thank you so much," I said as my heart hurt deeper because I had become that relative you feel obligated to buy gifts for even though you don't know her well enough to know her needs or likes. How had I become that person to my parents? I'd been gone only three months. Had my circumstances changed that much? But I thanked them again and wondered what I'd buy myself that cost five hundred dollars. I didn't need a major appliance or a piece of semi-fine jewelry or a new Coach bag or two.

I tucked the card with the bills between the Crocs and the Yankee Candle as we began tossing wrapping paper, saving our ribbons and bows for my mother's wrapping closet, and dust busting our scone crumbs.

Before I had gotten out of bed that morning, Mom had set up the finery, the silver and crystal and china, on the dining table for the all-afternoon heavy hors d'oeuvres bash, and Dad had emptied the liquor cabinet onto the buffet. Its contents had not been set free since last Christmas's get together. All we had to do was transfer the food from the kitchen to the dining room, and we'd have the makings of a Christmas party.

Mom looked on proudly at the beautiful display, ready to receive her guests. That's when she turned to me and said, "Well, Honey, you'll probably want to go get dressed for the party. The guests will be arriving soon."

It wasn't until then that I realized that the distant relative who roughed it on the outer fringes of the state wasn't dressed properly. I was wearing jeans and my new green sweater that brought out the gold flecks in my brown eyes. Since my departure from Raleigh, I'd forgotten that jeans, my wear-for-every-occasion beach attire, was not appropriate Christmas-party-at-the-Macklemores attire. But I'd absentmindedly brought along nothing but jeans.

I smiled at my mother and said, "Oh, sure, lost track of time," and headed upstairs to see if I could find something appropriate in my bedroom closet.

I located at the very back of the rod of outdated and unwanted clothing a black pencil skirt, flung over a wire hanger where I had discarded it years before. There was a perfect line of dust where it was bent in half, so I shook it and swiped at it with a damp washcloth until the dust line disappeared. I also found a pair of scuffed black kitten heels that had been retired at about the same time as the pencil skirt. But I hoped that, paired with my new sweater, they'd look Christmas-partyish enough. Then I rummaged through my drawers for a pair of panty hose or black tights. No luck. So I pulled on my skirt and stepped into my heels and headed back downstairs, hoping that my mother and her guests wouldn't notice that I was bare legged on this very special and festive occasion.

Before my dad could create his play list and Mom and I could arrange the food, Ray and Glenda Rupert from next door, always the first to arrive, were at the door. They both bellowed, "Merry Christmas," kissed and hugged me, told me how lovely I looked, and said my mother's decorations were the prettiest in the neighborhood. It was exactly what they'd said to me every Christmas since they'd moved into their house twenty-five plus years before. Except back then they'd called me cute as a bug instead of lovely. The Ruperts and I hadn't finished our pleasantries before the masses began pouring in, placing bottles of wine and decorative tins of rum balls beneath Mom's perfect tree. By day's end there would be enough wine for Mom to re-gift to a year's worth of dinner-party hostesses.

It was wonderful seeing my parents' friends who had watched me grow up. They were all so kind and loving and had tried their best to support me through my grief. I did not doubt their care for me, since they had all watched me grow from cute as a bug to lovely; and I knew that they were all sincere in their interest about my new life on Pelican Isle. And the more I talked with my former neighbors, the more I realized that's just what they were: former neighbors. Their children, my contemporaries, had moved on. And I had moved on, as well. As loved and cherished as my parents and their friends made me feel, I knew that Grace and Gray Macklemore's house was not my home anymore, knew that Raleigh was not my home anymore.

Pelican Isle was my home.

There, I'd said it, if only inside my head. But I knew that Pelican Isle was my home and that it was where I belonged.

And not just for one year.

At the end of a very long day of standing in toe-pinching, arch-sagging shoes, I helped my parents usher the last revelers out the door. I turned to my mother and said, "Mom, I hope you don't mind if I go change my clothes. I'm just not comfortable in skirts and heels anymore. I've found that I'm really a jeans kind of girl."

She looked sad that I was no longer her preppy, big-city girl but said, "Sure, Honey, run along and change, and then you can help me put all these leftovers away."

I pulled off my shoes, inspected the fresh blisters on my heels, hiked up my skirt, and took the stairs two at a time. I really did want to get out of that skirt, but that wasn't the only reason I wanted to escape to the solitude of my bedroom. After tripping over the rug and warning myself after the fact to watch my step, I closed the bedroom door behind me. I reached into my purse and pulled out my phone.

Merry Christmas, Allison. Miss you. Hurry home. Affectionately yours, Christopher.

I held the phone to my heart and felt my pulse quicken. I touched my temple, touched my cheek. Tears came to my eyes. Out of joy? Fear? Anticipation? I still didn't know what was happening. And I wasn't sure I was ready for It, whatever It was.

I looked at the one and only picture on my dresser, a photo of Cam and me on our wedding day. Cam had shed his tux jacket, rolled up his sleeves, and untied his tie, leaving it hanging loose around his neck. I had kicked off my shoes and gathered the full skirt of my wedding gown around my knees. We were laughing and dancing and hopeful for our future together. We were so in love and confident that we had our lives figured out. We'd have successful careers, a house full of kids, a dog or two—but not a cat because Cam was allergic to cats—and a long, happy marriage.

I placed my phone on the dresser, picked up the picture, and touched my lips to Cam.

"I love you, Cam. I miss you," I whispered, as I felt tears fill my eyes and spill over my lashes. I wiped my lip smudge from his face and told him, "I didn't want to live without you. I didn't think I could." I paused. Waiting for him to answer me? Hoping he'd give me a sign? When he just continued to stare, I sighed and told him: "But I think I can now. I think I can be happy again. I so want to be happy again, Cam. Please want that for me too. Please give me your blessing."

Then I crawled onto my childhood bed and curled into a ball, clutching the picture of my only love and me to my heart. Then I allowed myself a good, purging cry. And as I cried, I remembered all the wonderful times I'd had with my childhood buddy, my only boyfriend, the only guy I'd ever dated.

I knew when I was ten that he was the one for me. By high school everyone knew that he was the one for me. I was certain that there were still spiral notebooks in my parents' attic on which I'd written in colorful balloon letters ALLY + CAM, ALLY ALBRIGHT, MRS. CAMERON ALBRIGHT. I was confident, even as a tenth grader, I'd someday be Mrs. Cameron Albright. And I was.

Was.

When I'd exhausted myself with my sobbing, I grabbed a wad of tissues from the box on the bedside table, raked my eyes, blew my nose, and gave Cam one more kiss before replacing the picture on the dresser.

Then I picked up my phone and texted *Merry Christmas, Christopher. Miss you too. I'll be home soon. Affectionately yours, Allison.*

I put my phone away, changed into my jeans, and skipped downstairs to help my mom put the house back in order. Since we had hosted all afternoon and hadn't had a thing to eat since our breakfast scones, the three of us were ravenous. So we fixed ourselves a plate of leftovers with a glass of sweet tea and headed for the living room. The tree was still twinkling and Andy Williams was crooning when we sat around the coffee table and joined hands for Dad's blessing.

As soon as he'd said, "Amen," he pronounced our party one of our best ever, just as he did each year.

And Mom and I both agreed, as we did each year.

We ate our supper and made superficial chitchat. Mom told me that Mavis Childress had died, so that had made room for Doris Epworth to join the bridge club.

"You know how it is. We just have so many hands, but poor Doris has been so patient."

Poor Doris? But what about poor Mrs. Childress? I just bit my tongue and didn't say a word. I didn't want to encourage that particular line of chatter. I was ready for this topic of conversation to die right there, along with poor Mrs. Childress.

Then Dad said, "My lawnmower died right after you left home," as if my leaving had had something to do with it. Apparently, though, talk of Mrs. Childress's death had reminded my father of his dead lawnmower. "Looks like I'm going to have to spring for a new one come spring. I'm thinking, at my age, I ought to be looking into one of those fancy riding machines."

"That sounds like a good idea, Dad."

"Well, your mother thinks I should stick with a walking mower. Says that's the only exercise I get. Right, Mother?" Dad said, as he looked at my mom with a resigned look on his face.

And my mother just smiled and patted my father's hand.

I could have rescinded my agreement with Dad and transferred my allegiance to Mom because I did think Dad needed the exercise, but lawnmower purchases and the benefits of owning a push versus ride were also topics of conversation that didn't interest me.

So I said, "Whatcha say we get these dishes cleaned up? I'll wash. Dad, you dry, and Mom can stash the leftovers. Sound good?"

"Sounds great to me," they said in tandem, the way they did most everything after forty years of marriage.

After cleaning the dishes and putting them away, we watched a few reruns on TV. But by nine thirty and three episodes of Big Bang Theory, I'd had enough. I loved Sheldon and Leonard, but since I'd moved to Pelican Isle, I had not turned on the television. Not once. In fact, I'd lived in Dr. Brown's house for three weeks before I'd even noticed there was a TV in my magical home. So not feeling the need for a fourth episode of Big Bang Theory, I kissed my parents good night and headed for bed.

I washed my face, brushed my teeth, and slipped into my pajamas. Before crawling into bed, I picked up the picture of Cam and me. I looked like the girl next door, with my flyaway blonde hair, freckled nose, teeth straight from three years of braces, and my wedding gown strap slipping off my shoulder. Cam, on the other hand, looked as if he'd just stepped off the pages of GQ. His clothes fit as though they were made on him, his teeth were naturally straight and blindingly white, and his dark hair was freshly groomed and styled, every hair in place. He looked at the camera with black eyes rimmed with double rows of curly, black lashes while I looked directly at him, my love for him captured forever in black and white. I smiled at the memory of his giving me butterfly kisses on my cheek with his long, thick lashes. I touched my cheek. I loved his butterfly kisses. I loved him.

"I'll always miss you, Cam. I'll always love you."

Then I kissed him again and placed the picture back on the dresser, this time leaving my lip smudge across his face.

I climbed into bed and slept soundly in the pink princess bedroom.

Seventeen

I awoke early to the smell of bacon and coffee. I climbed out of bed and headed downstairs in my pajamas and bare feet. I didn't bother to comb my hair, brush my teeth, or wash my face. It's what my little-girl self would have done. And I felt the need to be my little-girl self once more before heading back to my big-girl life.

I found my mom at the stove, stabbing at the bacon in her iron skillet and Dad at the kitchen table, drinking coffee and reading the newspaper. Nothing had changed.

I shuffled in, the kitchen tile cold on my feet, put my arms around my father's neck, kissed him on the cheek, and said, "I love you, Daddy."

He reached up and patted my frowsy hair, saying, "I know, Honey. Love you too."

My mom turned and smiled, and I approached her and gave her a smooch. "And I love you so much, Mom."

She put down her bacon fork and took me in her arms.

I could hear the tears in her voice as she said, "I love you so much, and I'm so glad you're here."

Before I could answer her and before she could cry, she returned to her bacon stabbing.

I poured myself a cup of coffee, sat at the table, tucked my bare feet under me to warm them, and waited for my mother to serve me little-girl style.

Breakfast was delicious, just as I remembered all the breakfasts I'd eaten right there at our family's aqua Formica kitchen table with the chrome legs. Mom had bought it at a local antique shop back in the 80's, calling it her Mid-century Modern find. She still loved it, and I still thought breakfast tasted better at Mom's table than anywhere else. It helped that she fed us real bacon, not that stiff turkey stuff that didn't taste to me anything at all like bacon. And she fried our eggs in real butter, the same real butter she slathered on our white-bread toast. We also had peach preserves for our toast, preserves Mom had made from the peaches she'd bought back in June at the Farmers Market. And, of course, there were stone-ground grits with more real butter. I could feel my arteries narrowing as I ate, but I promised myself that I'd ream them out with oat bran and grapefruit just as soon as I crossed the narrow, rickety bridge from New Oak to Pelican Isle.

I took a bite of toast, licked the preserves from my thumb, and said, "Mom, Dad, I've decided what I want to buy with your generous Christmas gift."

"Oh, good, Darlin'. We hope you'll get yourself something real nice."

"Well, it's not for me, exactly. I want to do something for my kids."

"Your kids?"

"My students."

"Oh, well, Honey," my dad said, "if your students need supplies, your mother and I will be glad to help out. But we want you to get something special for yourself."

"Thank you, Dad, but I don't need a thing, honest. This is what I'd like to do. It would mean so much to me. And to my kids."

"Well, okay, then."

"All the schools are short of supplies, and the teachers have to supplement their classrooms out of their own pockets. And Pelican Isle Elementary has a greater shortage than most. Your gift would go a long way in making a difference in my kids' education."

"We understand, Darlin'," Mom said, smiling, her joy and pride for me shining through.

"Will y'all go to Staples with me this morning to help me shop for some supplies?"

"Well, Honey, I promised I'd help take down the tree at the church," Dad said, "but you and your mom go right ahead."

"Mom?"

"Sure thing, Ally. I'd love to go."

"Thanks, I'd really appreciate your help."

"Then you run along, Darlin', and get your shower," she said. "I'll clean up here, and I'll be ready to go whenever you are."

So, without argument, I headed for the shower, leaving her to clean up the breakfast dishes. When I finished showering and dressing and headed back downstairs, I found my mom perched on a chair in the living room, her pocketbook resting on her knees.

"Is Staples still at the corner of Six Forks and Wake Forest Road?"

"Far as I know, they haven't moved it," she said.

So we headed for my car and took off in the direction of where I remembered Staples to be.

Along the way Mom said, "Ally, I just can't tell you how proud Dad and I are of you. What you have done is remarkable."

Looking over at her and smiling, I said, "Thank you, Mom. I didn't feel I was ready, but I'm glad I took the leap. I have an incredible classroom of kids."

"Well, the change certainly agrees with you. You look simply wonderful," she said, reaching over and patting my leg maternally.

"I feel good."

"That's great, but you know, Honey, Dad and I will be so happy to have you back home. I'm sure you won't have any trouble at all getting your old teaching job back."

I knew this conversation was coming, but I wasn't ready to discuss it. I couldn't bear the thought of disappointing her by saying, "Mom, I think I'm already home," so I just stared straight ahead and said, "Umm hmm."

Very noncommittal. Nothing she could hold me to later.

For the rest of the drive, my mother chattered about church, recipes, her friends who were retiring, her friends who were dying and making room for new members at bridge club. I just *umm hmmed* from time to time, watched familiar and comforting sights whiz by, and somewhat guiltily listened for my phone to ding.

The Staples parking lot was full of shoppers, there to take advantage of the after-Christmas specials, I assumed. We drove around and around until we saw red taillights flicker. We sped down the lane and grabbed the coveted spot, infuriating four other motorists, just as the driver backed out and I glided in.

Hopping out and ignoring the scowls and icy stares, we made our way to the entrance, grabbed one of the few remaining carts, and headed in the direction of the school supplies. They reached from floor to ceiling and stretched for as far as the eye could see, and I was delighted to find that all the provisions my kids could need or want were on sale. I was in teacher's heaven as I began tossing in note pads and pencils and colored markers and construction paper. I bought scissors and flash cards, as well as science sticker books. Kids love sticker books, no matter what age they are. I bought glue sticks and glitter. My little girls would squeal with glee. Then I pulled out my phone, tapped my calculator app, and started tallying up my purchases. I found that I had just passed one hundred dollars. I had a long way to go.

Maneuvering the aisles around throngs of shoppers, many of them most likely teachers on tight budgets, we approached a young clerk who was setting up a new display. He installed a sign that read:

One-hour special.
e-tablets.
$39!

I picked up one of the tablets and said to the clerk, "You mean to tell me I can get an electronic tablet for just thirty-nine dollars?"

"Yes, ma'am, but just for an hour. They're normally eighty-nine, but we got in a special order just for today because, you know, it's the day after Christmas and all."

"Now, be honest, is it worth it?"

"Yes, ma'am. 'Course, it doesn't have all the bells and whistles you'd get on, say, an iPad, but you can do lots of stuff on it." Then he handed me the display tablet, the one tethered to the shelf by a cable and already loaded to the hilt with apps, and said as he tapped the screen and swooshed his finger back and forth, "See, you can surf and download books and manage your email. And look at all the apps you can put on it."

"Could I download math and spelling and reading apps to it?"

"Sure. Any app you can get in the App Store, you can download to this tablet. Then looking at his watch, he said, "But the sale will end in fifty-four minutes. And once word gets out, these things are going to disappear like crazy."

For four months my students had been taking turns on two antiquated computers, the one Apple and my old laptop. They would love having new tablets to learn their spelling words and do their math lessons. I could get ten pads with the money I had left. My kids would still have to share, but it certainly was better than what they had to work with now. I thought about it a minute, but I couldn't procrastinate because the special was winding down and the stock was already moving fast. Word must have gotten out.

"You're very persuasive," I said to the clerk. "So are they," I said, pointing to the shoppers, as I hovered around the tablets so all of them wouldn't disappear.

But I really did not want my kids to have to share anymore—they deserved what other kids had—so I decided to toss in a little money of my own and spring for six extra tablets so there'd be one for each of my sixteen children.

"Help me, Mom," I said. "Grab eight before they're all gone. I'll get eight more."

Elbowing our way in, just as the other shoppers were doing, we began snatching tablets and filling our basket. Finally, with sixteen new tablets and a basket full of supplies, we headed for the checkout.

"Darling, let me get those extra tablets."

"Thanks, Mom, but you've already done so much. I'm fine. Honest."

"Well, okay, Dear," she said, shrugging, "but it would be my pleasure."

I put my arm around her and pulled her to me.

"Love you, Mom."

She patted my hand, sniffed, and looked away before she could tear up again. I'd come to realize that tears are the fallout of children leaving home and becoming independent, no matter how old and self-sufficient the children are.

We wrestled the huge plastic bags to my car and arranged them in the trunk. My kids were going to be beside themselves with delight when they returned from vacation to find all of their new supplies. And I was certain they were going to be especially excited with their tablets. While I was admiring our stash, three cars honked for me to move it and added hand gestures to make certain I got the message. So I smiled sweetly, waved, hopped in, threw my car in reverse, backed out, and sped off, leaving the three drivers to fight over my vacated space.

As we pulled out of the parking lot, I had a sudden ache to be home—Pelican Isle home. After my shopping trip for my kids, I knew, without a doubt, that it was where I belonged. I needed to see my kids. I needed to see my magical home. I needed to see my beautiful beach that calmed and soothed me. I needed to see Joy. I needed to see Christopher—really needed to see Christopher, to see where this thing was going.

Taking a deep breath to steel my reserve, I said, "Mom, I know I'd planned to stay till tomorrow, but I think I need to get on back today."

"But, why, Darlin'? Did Dad and I do something?"

I reached over and squeezed her hand and said, "Oh, no, Mom, not at all. This has been just wonderful, but I really need to get back. The kids will be coming back to class next Monday, and I have so much to do to get ready for them. I have to undecorate the tree and figure out how I'm going to dispose of the tree itself. And I need to take down all the Christmas stuff on the walls and redecorate the bulletin boards. And, of course, I need to make room on the shelves for all the new supplies. And thank you, again, Mom, for making my kids' supplies possible. And our snack shelves are getting depleted, so I need to make a trip to the grocery."

By now I was babbling, just making up excuses for why I needed to leave, to get back to the Isle. Back to where I belonged. Back Home. I was getting better and better at making up long lists of excuses when I was anxious to make a getaway.

"It's okay, Honey, I understand," she said.

I could see sadness in my mother's eyes, but I also saw something new: I saw a resignation. I knew at that moment that my mother realized I wasn't going to work out my one-year contract and come back home. Because Raleigh was no longer my home. My parents were no longer my home.

We rode in silence the rest of the way, the silence broken from time to time by my mother's self-conscious throat clearing. When we pulled into the driveway of my childhood home, she reached over and took my hand. When I turned to her, I saw that her eyes were red, an indication that she was fighting back tears.

"Ally, Darlin', Daddy and I were so scared. We thought we were going to lose you. I don't believe we could have endured that. You are our precious angel."

"I know that, Mom."

"Even when you left, we still worried. You were so sad. You had lost so much. We knew your grief was unbearable."

By now I was crying, not even attempting to hold back my tears.

"But, Ally, we're not worried anymore. You are an amazing young woman. Your father and I know that you are going to be all right."

She stopped short of saying, "And I know you're not coming back home," though the words hung heavy between us.

Instead, she reached for me and enfolded me in her arms and let me cry into her neck just one more time, the way she comforted me when I was my little-girl self.

When I was cried out, Mom took a handful of tissues out of her jacket pocket and mopped my face, saying, "Are you going to be okay?"

"Yes, ma'am, I'm fine. Just a little nostalgic."

"I understand."

"What'll Dad say?"

"Don't you worry about your dad. You do what you have to do. I'll handle him," she said, smiling through now-watery eyes.

We found Dad pulling ham biscuits, fruit, and sweet tea from the fridge.

"It didn't take long to put away the Christmas decorations at the church. And I figured you girls would be good and hungry after your morning of shopping. Come. Sit. Fix yourselves a plate."

"Thanks, Dad, I am a little hungry."

My mom and I dropped our purses and sat down at the table that my father had loaded with food. I reached for a ham biscuit and the bowl of pasta salad.

"Ally is going to have to head on back to the coast after lunch."

Dad began to protest, but I could see Mom out of the corner of my eye giving him her let-it-drop-I'll-explain-later look.

He just smiled at me and said, "Well, then, I guess we'd better get you good and fed before we put you on the road."

Mom's ham biscuits are the best, made from scratch and loaded with good old, salty country ham. Knowing I wouldn't be eating more any time soon, I downed two.

"That was delicious, Mom. I love your ham biscuits."

"I know, Sweetie. You always have."

We sat at the table long after we were through with our lunch, making small talk, getting a good dose of one another to last till our next visit.

Finally, I reached for their hands and said, "This has been wonderful. Thanks for making Christmas so special. You always do. But I'd better be getting on the road. Don't want to be out there driving in the dark."

Dad chuckled, and Mom blushed and waved her hand at the two of us.

With my parents' help, I gathered my belongings and my Christmas gifts and headed for my car. I tossed my bag in the back seat, since my trunk was full of school supplies, and placed my gifts from my parents on the passenger-side seat, along with my purse.

"Let us know when you get there."

"I will, Mom."

"Now, you be careful. There's going to be a lot of holiday traffic on the road."

"Yes, Daddy."

"Here, I've packed a tin of M&M cookies to take to your students."

"Thanks, Mom. They'll love 'em."

"Love you."

"Love you too."

I backed out of the driveway and watched my parents watch me pull away from Home for the last time.

ALLISON

AND

CHRISTOPHER

Eighteen

And then I was off, eager to get home, eager to move on, eager to find out where my moving on would take me. The trip was uneventful. The holiday traffic that Dad warned me about stayed on its own side of the road and left me alone, and I made it to Pelican Isle safe and unscathed in just under four and one half hours. As I tick-tick-ticked across the uneven pavement of the New Oak bridge, I felt the stress, stress I didn't even know I had, melt away. I let my breath out in a whoosh, as if I'd been holding it in for the last several hundred miles.

I pulled onto the island and smiled as I said out loud, "I'm home. Hello, Pelican Isle. Hello, Home. It's so good to be back."

Turning onto Beach Road, I cracked my window and breathed in the brisk salt air. I didn't need the scent of potpourri or Glade cinnamon vanilla plug-ins. Or a Yankee Candle in a jar that smelled like sea breeze. All I needed was the scent of the murky salt marsh and that sea air.

I passed by the weatherworn beach cottages nestled in the dunes and the low, colorful cottages lined up along the bank of Parmeter Sound. Most were shuttered and dark. They'd wait in hibernation for five more months until vacationers would return to wake them, to bring them back to life. But for now they rested.

As I drove past Christopher's cozy cottage, I was surprised to find smoke curling from his chimney and his sunshine-yellow golf cart with the sky-blue canopy parked on his crushed-oyster-shell drive. I'd assumed he'd be at the clinic with his patients.

Peli Pier was open and doing a brisk business. Cars, probably owned by mainlanders tired of ham and turkey and suffering from Christmas cabin fever, lined the parking lot. Christmas lights encircled the windows as the red OPEN sign blinked off and on. I found the open Peli Pier dependable and comforting. The food remained delicious, abundant, and always the same; and with each visit I could count on a warm, inviting welcome from the waitstaff.

When I reached my house, I hopped out of the car and breathed deeply. Then I just listened. I much preferred my beach music, the sound of the crashing surf and screeching gulls, to Dad's much beloved Christmas crooners. So happy was I to be home, I grabbed my purse and my luggage, leaving my kids' loot in the car, and ran up the stairs.

"Hey, neighbor," I heard Joy call from her back porch. "Saw you pull up. You're back a little early."

"Yeah, I had a nice Christmas with my folks, but I just wanted to get back home."

"Home, huh?"

I just smiled and said, "Yeah, I believe so."

"Well, I'm off to rock some babies," she said, heading down the stairs to her golf cart. "Want to join me?"

"Thanks, but I need to unpack. Catch you next time."

"Okay, then, I'll talk to you later. And welcome back. I missed you."

"Missed you too."

I let myself in and was delighted to find that nothing had changed. My magical home was still magical. The rumpled muslin slipcovers were still rumpled. The well-worn plank floors still shone honey-gold. The seashells still covered every surface, and the garlands that were suspended from the ceiling tinkled as I stirred the air. Smiling at my good fortune and so happy to be back, I headed to the bedroom to unpack. I had just unloaded my belongings and tucked my suitcase in the back of my closet when I heard my phone *ding*.

When are you coming home? Miss you still. Affectionately yours, Christopher.

I'm home. Affectionately yours, Allison.

Here home?

Yes, here home.

You mean Pelican Isle home?

Yes, Pelican Isle home.

When?

Just now.

May I come over?

Yes.

When?

Now.

Really?

Really!

Soon! Bye!

He must have sprinted from his house and driven faster than the posted eighteen miles per hour speed limit because he was at my house before I could brush my teeth, run a comb through my fly-away hair, and call my folks to let them know that I'd arrived home before dark and unharmed by the holiday traffic.

I had just said good-bye to my mom and dad when I heard Christopher take the stairs two at a time. I opened the door before he could knock and stick his head in to yoo-hoo. His face was red. From rushing? From blushing? His green eyes sparkled. His dimple taunted me.

"Hi, Allison."

"Hi, Christopher."

And then I was in his arms.

"I've missed you so much, Allison."

"I've missed you too, Christopher."

"I had no idea how much I'd miss you."

"I know. Me, either."

Then cupping my cheek in his hand, he said, "This is where you belong, Allison. This is your home. Don't ever leave us. Please stay with us. Your kids need you. Joy and I need you. And I think, I hope, you need us."

I knew he was right. I loved my parents and I loved Cam and Rory, but the time had come for me to move on. I could no longer live in the past where there was no hope. I couldn't live in the past where no one needed me. I had students who needed me, a neighbor who cared deeply for me, and a man who missed me when I was gone. And, yes, I needed them all. I needed Pelican Isle.

"Yes, yes, this is my home," I said, the tears spilling down my cheeks.

Then his lips were on mine.

"What will Joy say?"

Christopher propped himself on his elbow, showed me his dimple, and kissed me lightly on the lips. Then, running his fingers through my hair, he smiled impishly at me and said, "She'll say, 'What took you so long?'"

"No, she won't!"

"Wanna bet? She's been asking me for months when I planned to make a move."

I swatted at him and said, "You're just making that up. Now, stop teasing me."

"Not teasing at all, Miss Allison. Joy has said since the moment we met, 'Good grief, I'm surprised the sparks don't set y'all on fire. It's just a matter of time, you know. You might as well go ahead and get it over with.'"

"Then why did you wait so long?"

"Didn't want to spook you, scare you off. Didn't want to pressure you. And, Allison, I was afraid you wouldn't stay." And kissing me once more, he said, "And I honestly didn't want to start something we might not be able to finish. I just felt I couldn't take loving you and losing you."

"Loving me?"

In answer to my question, he took my hand and kissed my palm. Then he gathered me in his arms and covered my mouth with his. We moaned as he threw back the covers and traced the curve of my hip with his fingers.

I didn't know that a man could be so tender, his hands so gentle. Perhaps he had learned tenderness from delivering and cradling babies, from comforting sick, fragile patients. I was neither sick nor fragile, but I melted under his touch.

For the next two days we got out of bed only to shower and eat. We did very little of either, and the showering we did together. We shut out the outside world and let our phone messages go straight to voicemail.

"But what about the clinic?"

"Dr. Cummings is taking over for me. I told him I couldn't be reached so he need not even try. I haven't taken a full day off in six years, and I don't want to think or talk about the clinic. I've earned this, don't you agree?"

"You wanted to spend your first days off in six years with me?"

"Isn't that obvious?" he asked, as he took me in his arms again and pulled me on top of him, smoothing my hair away from my face and kissing my eyes.

Knowing that our time together would soon end and that he'd have to leave me for the clinic, I said, "I need to tell you something, Christopher."

"Uh oh, sounds serious."

"Yes, it is serious. But it needs to be said. You've told me about your past. It's only fair I tell you about mine."

Looking nervous, all he said was, "Okay, then."

"I was married."

"Oh?"

"Yes. And pregnant."

He said nothing but held me close and let me weep as I told him about Cam and Rory and my painful journey after their deaths.

I told him that Cam had been my only love, that I'd loved him since I had been a child and that he was the only boy I'd ever dated. I told him that when Cam and Rory had been killed, that I was certain my life was over— had hoped it was over. I even told him of my flower-counting obsession and my attempt to stop my organs from working. I figured if Christopher could hang around after that admission, he would stay around after anything.

Then I told him about my wonderful parents who had patiently loved me back to life. "I owe them everything, Christopher. They are my rocks."

He caressed my back and said, "I just had no idea, Allison. It's no wonder you were reluctant to commit to more than one year when you came to Pelican Isle. And that certainly explains why you had such a hard time rocking the babies. That must have been so difficult. I'm just so sorry. Thanks for telling me, for trusting me."

"I needed for you to know, Christopher."

"You're so lucky to have such wonderful parents. I believe I'm a good judge of character. I knew when I met them at Peli Pier, that they were special, just like their daughter."

He could tell that I was exhausted from recounting my grief, so he smiled and kissed me and held me in his arms until I fell asleep. I was still in his arms when I awoke the following morning.

"My two days are up. I have to get back to the clinic," he whispered and kissed the end of my nose.

"I knew the time was coming, but I don't want you to leave," I said, stretching myself awake.

"I know. Me either. But I'll be back."

"You'd better."

Laying me gently back on the pillow, he caressed my cheek and kissed me tenderly one last time.

"Thank you for trusting me, Allison."

"Thank you for being so understanding."

And then nuzzling my neck, he said, "I dreamed of this, but I never dreamed it could be this good."

"It's been wonderful, Christopher."

"And it'll only get better," he said, kissing me once more.

He reluctantly left the bed, and I lay naked and watched as he pulled on his jeans. He was beautiful—his startling green eyes, his dimple, his shock of honey blonde hair so disheveled after our days of tumbling in the covers, his chiseled chest covered with golden down. He smiled when he saw me studying him.

When his dimple sprang to life, I pointed and said, "You know that drives me crazy, don't you?"

"Yeah, I know," he said, grinning broadly.

Then he stepped into his shoes and pulled on his jacket, knelt on the bed, leaned over, and gave me a good-bye kiss.

"Walk me to the door," he said, pulling the sheet from the bed and wrapping it around me. I slid out of bed and walked with him, our arms encircling each other.

"I'll miss you," he said, as he kissed me once more at the door and walked backward across the porch.

"I promise I won't go far," I called and waved after him.

When he'd disappeared from sight, I went to the bedroom and pulled on jeans and a sweatshirt. I had brushed my teeth and was brushing two days of tangles from my hair when I heard a yoo-hoo at the door.

"Okay, I want to know everything," Joy said, charging right in. "But first, coffee. And I know you don't have coffee made because you've just been too busy, so I'll go put on a pot myself."

As I watched her charge toward the kitchen, brandishing her thermal coffee mug, I collapsed on the sofa and laughed till I was out of breath, from her excitement and from my giddiness.

When she reached the kitchen door, she turned and said, "He must be *real* good."

While she rummaged around in the kitchen for coffee and filters, I composed myself and went to the bedroom to find my book of sonnets. When we met back in the living room, we sat side-by-side on the sofa, and she handed me a cup of coffee and said, "Start talking."

"Okay, I will. Remember this?" I asked, showing her Christopher's Christmas gift.

"Of course," she said, taking the book from me and turning it over in her hands. "Chris gave it to you for Christmas."

"You asked what happened, Joy. This is what happened," I said, opening the cover and showing her the inscription.

She read it, and a grin spread across her face. "Oh, my, it's beautiful," she said, squeezing my hand and smiling at me.

"I didn't know when he gave it to me what it meant. I thought, perhaps, it was just a coincidence. I spent the entire Christmas holidays playing that nerve-wracking, what-does-it-mean game. Well, I know now that it wasn't just a coincidence. He meant it, every word of it."

"Oh, Ally, I knew it was only a matter of time—a matter of time before you realized you belonged here with us, belonged here with Chris. I'm so happy for both of you," Joy said, confident that I had told her all she needed to know.

But I added, blushing, "And, yes, he's *real* good."

Nineteen

It was for the best that Christopher returned to the clinic. He wasn't the only one who had work to do. I had to do all those things I'd told my parents I needed to return to Pelican Isle to do: take down my classroom Christmas tree, redecorate the bulletin board, replenish the snacks, and tidy my classroom. Our budget didn't allow for a janitor, so I was the maid, as well as its teacher. I also needed to read the instructions for the new tablets and download some apps for my students. I wanted them all up and running when my kids returned from the holidays on Monday.

I threw myself into a frenzy of activity, and by Sunday night my classroom smelled of 409 and Lemon Pledge and I was panting from my efforts. I had even washed the windows, inside and out. Everything was so clean I could almost see my face in the sixteen little scarred desks. I had stored the Christmas ornaments on a high shelf in the break room where they would wait until next year, and I had dragged the tree to the curb for pick-up. The holiday bulletin board had made way for a winter theme, and the mini fridge was full of juice boxes and fruit. I had also made room in the bookcase for all the children's new supplies. Best of all, I had understood the tablet instructions, and they were all full of apps that I was certain my kids would love.

I was sitting crossed-legged on a pallet on my classroom floor, playing with one of the tablets, when I heard footsteps in the hall. Had I been all alone at night in a classroom anywhere else, I'd have been frightened by footsteps in the hall. But Pelican Isle footsteps didn't scare me, no matter how dark it was, no matter how alone I was. No one on the Isle wanted to hurt me. I was confident I was hearing the footsteps of a friend.

"Hey."

"Hey, yourself," I said when Christopher shuffled into the room, still wearing his scrubs and Crocs, a day's stubble on his face. He looked tired, but even tired he was gorgeous. I smiled in my newfound happiness.

"I was on my way home and saw your light. I wanted to make sure you were okay," he said, joining me cross-legged on my pallet.

"Thanks for checking," I said, leaning forward. He met me halfway and kissed me. "I'm fine," I told him. "Just wanted to make sure I'll be ready for my kiddos when they return tomorrow."

"Everything looks great. Smells nice too. I remember classrooms smelling like tennis shoes and BO, not lemons. I like this," he said, perusing my room, bobbing his head approvingly.

"My kids deserve the best. And look at this," I said, passing the tablet to him.

"Oh, wow, this is fantastic. And you got one of these for each of your students?"

"Yeah, aren't they great? And look at all the apps," I said, swiping the screen with my finger. "I just know they are going to love them. And they'll be such a great teaching tool. I worry that my children aren't going to be able to keep up with the tech-savvy students in the city schools, but these little gizmos will help bridge that gap."

"Fantastic." And, taking my hand, he said, "They'll be so happy."

"They're an incredible bunch of kids—the best class I've ever taught. They deserve this. You know, I really love them."

"And they love you."

"Yeah, I know, and they're going to love me even more when they see all their new goodies."

Christopher laughed and said, "You're probably right. Kids are mercenary little stinkers. And they are lucky little stinkers to have you."

"These kids are so lucky that someone cared enough to provide this school for them. Wish I knew who that generous person was so that I could thank him, but I guess that was way before my time."

Christopher furrowed his brow, looked at me questioningly, and said, "You mean you haven't figured out who donated the school building and Carter's office?"

"Uh, no. Carter just told me it was an anonymous donor. I figured anonymous meant no one knew because the donor didn't want anyone to know."

"Well, lots of people know who gave this property to the island, but the donors gave them out of love, not for any kind of recognition."

"But who…?"

"One guess, Allison," Chris said, showing a sly smile, his dimple creasing his cheek.

I gave him a how-would-I-know look, but that expression told me.

"Christopher, was it…?"

"Yeah."

"You mean?"

"Yep. Dr. C and Joy."

"They *gave* these houses for the school?"

"Exactly."

"But what? How? Where did they get them?"

"They belonged to their parents. This building was Joy's parents' home. The one next door was Dr. C's family cottage."

"I don't understand. I thought they moved to Pelican Isle when Dr. C got out of med school."

"They did. But that wasn't the first time they'd been here. This island has Dr. C and Joy's name metaphorically stamped all over it. But you'll never hear that from Joy."

"Well, how did they come to Pelican Isle? How did they decide to donate two houses for a school?"

"I'll tell you all about it over dinner. I haven't eaten and it's seven o'clock, and I'm starving."

"Good idea. I haven't even had lunch. I'm a little hungry too."

"Peli Pier okay?"

"Peli Pier is always okay."

I made one last sweep of my classroom to be sure it was ready for my children. Then I turned off the lights, locked the door, took Christopher's hand, and headed for the parking lot.

"I'll follow you in my cart."

"Okay," he said, giving me a quick kiss, "see you at the restaurant."

As I drove, I touched my lips. His kiss was so casual, so natural, like he'd been kissing me forever. I smiled at the memory of our brief time together and hoped that it would never end. I cruised silently down Beach Road, smiling all the way, and pulled into the lot right behind Christopher. We hopped out and walked with our arms around each other into Peli Pier.

"Hey, Emilio."

"Hey, Dr. Chris. Hey, Miss Ally. A table by the window?"

"That'd be great."

"Business is kind of slow tonight. That means great service."

"Slow? That's an understatement. We're the only customers," Christopher laughed.

"That means you can sit anywhere you'd like, and you'll have my undivided attention. Here are your menus. I'll be right back with your water."

Christopher said, "Will you split a seafood platter with me? I've been dying for fried seafood."

"I'd love that."

So when Emilio returned with our water, Christopher told him, "One seafood platter, two plates, please."

"Sounds easy enough. Be right back with that," he said, collecting our menus.

When I was sure Emilio was out of earshot, I said, "Okay, so tell me."

"Well, let's see," Christopher said, hunching toward me, his elbows on the table. "Dr. C's parents came from upstate New York to vacation here on the island. Joy's came from Connecticut. The two couples met when they bought side-by-side cottages."

"The school house and Carter's office, right?"

"That's right. Dr. C and Joy didn't remember a time when they didn't have cottages on Pelican Isle because they were babies when their families moved here that first summer. They also didn't remember a time when they didn't know each other."

"Really? That's amazing."

"Each June the families would come south and get set up in their summer homes. After several weeks the fathers would return to the north and their jobs, leaving their wives and children here for the season. At the end of August, Joy and Chris's fathers would return to the island to retrieve their wives and children."

"Sounds like great fun for the moms and kids, not so much for the husbands."

"I agree, but it seemed to work for them. Each summer the moms would play bridge and sit on the beach or go to the mainland to shop, leaving the children in the care of a nanny."

"A nanny?"

"Yeah, her name was Rosario? She lived on the island and watched out for the two children from the time they were babies until they were teenagers and able to take care of themselves. Even then, though, she came to the cottages each day to cook and clean for the families and boss Dr. C and Joy around."

"Boss them around?"

"Joy said she was wonderful, even her bossiness. They loved her and loved that she never tired of taking care of them. It was Rosario who introduced the two children to the island. She'd take them to the village where they'd meet the fishermen and dock workers, as well as the women who cooked and cleaned for the island."

"I'm guessing that's when Joy fell in love with the island people."

"Exactly," Chris said. "She also taught them how to crab and dig for clams in Parmeter Sound, and at night she'd take them gigging for flounder. It was also Rosario who introduced Joy to sea glass and shell collecting."

"What fun. I wish I'd had a Rosario when I was a kid."

"Yeah, Joy said they were so lucky. They loved this place so much that they always knew they'd one day come back, for good."

"Together, right?"

"But, of course. They'd always been a couple. Joy said she couldn't remember not loving Dr. C. The feeling must have been mutual because Dr. C proposed to her when they were just nine."

"You mean nine years old?"

"That's right. He took her hand and walked her out to the dunes behind their cottages. He gave her a shark's tooth on a thin leather cord and asked her to marry him."

"A shark's tooth?"

"Yes, the same shark's tooth she wears around her neck to this day. She has never taken it off."

"Oh, Christopher, that's wonderful."

"Every year, on the same date, Dr. C would walk Joy to the dunes, where he renewed his proposal. Then the year they graduated from college, he walked her to the dunes, got down on one knee, and slipped a diamond on her finger."

"I think I'm going to cry," I said, fanning my eyes with my hand.

"That's not the best part."

"How can it get any better?"

"Dr. C could have finished med school, opened a private practice in New York or Connecticut, and lived the rich, high life."

"But he and Joy didn't do that."

"Nope, they wanted to come back to Pelican Isle, to the place they loved, to the people they loved."

"That sounds like Joy."

"And Dr. C. He was just as loving and generous as she is. And he adored this place every bit as much as she does."

"Oh, Christopher, I wish I could have met Dr. C. He sounds wonderful."

"He was wonderful, Allison. You'd have loved him, and he would have loved you too," Christopher said, his voice cracking with emotion.

As if on cue, Emilio rushed to the table with our seafood platter and extra plate, just as Christopher pressed his napkin to his eyes.

"Awesome, Emilio," Christopher said, "y'all have outdone yourselves this time."

"Only the best for Dr. Chris and pretty Miss Ally."

I blushed at Emilio's compliment and gave him an awe-shucks thanks.

Christopher divided our platter, and I picked up my fork. I speared a scallop and waved my hand in a go-on motion.

"Okay, now, where was I?"

"Instead of getting rich up north, Dr. C and Joy chose to come back to Pelican Isle."

"Oh, yeah," Christopher said, popping a shrimp into his mouth. "The closest doctor to Pelican Isle was over on the mainland, and it was so inconvenient and expensive for the islanders. So Dr. C returned so that the locals would have a doctor, one nearby and one they could afford. But there was no facility on Pelican Isle where he could practice. So he and Joy decided to start a clinic."

"Just the two of them?"

"Well, not exactly. They were young and didn't have money of their own, except for their trust funds, so the two of them solicited donations from their parents' rich friends. And with an enormous amount of financial help from their parents, they started construction on the Pelican Isle Clinic."

"I had no idea they had *built* the clinic? I thought that Dr. C just worked there and Joy knitted for the babies and rocked them."

"Nope, it was all theirs."

"Their clinic? Wow!"

"Yeah, but they never took credit for it. They hired only local workers to construct the building and gave them all the recognition. If you'll look at the plaque in the lobby, you'll see that it says, 'In honor of all the citizens of Pelican Isle who dreamed Pelican Isle Clinic and made it a reality.'"

"Well, if Dr. C and Joy's parents helped fund the clinic, they must have supported their children's coming to the island permanently."

"Oh, yes. They were so proud of their kids. They were generous people themselves, and they taught their children to share their good fortunes. They couldn't have been happier with Joy and Dr. C's decision."

"And their cottages?"

"Both couples left their estates to their only children, including the beach cottages. But there was one stipulation—that the cottages would never be sold but used only to benefit the residents of Pelican Isle. It was Joy and Dr. C's idea to turn the cottages into a school for the island kids."

I was speechless. I had heard of generosity of spirit, but I had never personally known anyone as giving as Joy and her family. And in all the time I'd known Joy, she'd never hinted at all she had done for the island and its residents. She'd just told me that she knitted hats and rocked babies.

"I just had no idea," I said, reaching for his hand. "Joy has looked after me since my arrival to Pelican Isle, a sad, lonely, lost soul. But don't you see, Christopher, even her parents were looking out for me by leaving their cottage to the residents of the island. I'm a resident of Pelican Isle, and no one has benefitted more than I have from those little cottages."

Christopher squeezed my hand, flashed that dimple, and said, "Why, Miss Allison, I've known that all along. I was just waiting for you to figure it out yourself."

"Thanks. And thanks for sharing."

Emilio appeared at the kitchen door. He saw that we didn't need anything from him and retreated.

"Why do you suppose Joy has never told me?"

"Joy has never told anybody, not even me. I heard it through the grapevine, just like everyone else. She doesn't think there's anything to tell."

"Nothing to tell? But look what they've done for so many people."

"I agree, but you'd never convince her that she's done anything extraordinary. That's just Joy."

"Yes, loving, giving Joy."

Christopher gave my hand a squeeze before he returned his attention to his seafood. We ate the rest of our meal in silence while I thought of my friend Joy's generosity and how it had transformed my life.

"Well, this has been great," Chris said, wiping his mouth with his napkin, "but I need to run. I have to shower and shave and get back to the clinic. I have two mothers in labor."

"Well, thanks for supper. I didn't realize I was so hungry. I cleaned my plate. And thanks again for sharing Dr. C and Joy's story."

Emilio approached and handed Christopher the check saying, "No rush. Just pay me when you're ready."

"Here, Emilio," Christopher said, reaching into his pocket. He handed him some bills and said, "Keep the change."

"Thanks, Dr. Chris. I hope you and Miss Ally will come back to see me soon."

"Thanks, Emilio, it was delicious," I told him.

Christopher walked me to my golf cart and took me in his arms.

"It's chilly tonight," he said, holding me tighter. And, then kissing me, he said, "Hope my stubble isn't scratching you."

"I love your stubble," I said, running my hand across his cheek. "But don't let your beard get so thick that I can't see that dimple."

Christopher smiled and turned his cheek to me. I kissed his dimple, his stubble tickling my lips. Then he pulled me close and kissed me tenderly once more before helping me into my cart. He watched until I drove out onto Beach Road before he climbed into his own cart and headed for home.

When I pulled into my driveway, I noticed that Joy's lights were on. That meant that she was home, not rocking babies. I slipped out of my cart and headed her way.

I crossed her yard, climbed the stairs, tapped on the door, and let myself in, calling, "Yoo hoo, it's just me, Ally."

"Come on back. I'm in the kitchen," Joy answered.

"Hey, hope it's not too late."

"Oh, goodness, it's never too late for you. My door is always open. So glad you came over. I'm just having some chowder. Want some?"

"No thanks. Chris and I just shared a seafood platter at Peli Pier."

"Then sit and keep me company while I eat."

I slid into the booth opposite her and shed my jacket and scarf.

"Did you get your classroom all set up for tomorrow?"

"Sure did. I think I'm finally ready for my sweet kiddos to come back."

"You sound anxious to see them," she said, smiling slyly.

"Oh, you know I am. I miss them even on weekends. Christmas break has been interminable. Can't wait to have them back."

It was true. I had grown to adore all sixteen of them, and I hated seeing the tram take them away each Friday afternoon. I envied their families the time they shared with them and wondered all weekend what fun they were having, what mischief they were up to. I'd bound out of bed extra early on Monday mornings and would be standing in anticipation at the door to Pelican Isle Elementary when the tram brought them back to me. I'd hug each one to me before they took their seats. And I'd spend the first thirty minutes of each Monday morning insisting they tell me what they'd done over the weekend, what I'd missed of them while they were gone from me. Yes, I loved them so much. I was meant to be their teacher, to stay on the island so they would know that they could depend on me—and that I could depend on them to love me back and heal my soul.

"They're lucky to have you, Ally," Joy said, smiling and reaching out to lovingly pat my hand.

"And I'm so lucky to have them."

"Yes, yes you are."

"And they're lucky to have you, Joy."

"What? To substitute every once in a while? Piece of cake."

She averted her eyes and waved her hand. I was getting too close. I knew that she would not volunteer anything about the part she played in taking care of the island children.

"Joy, Christopher told me, told me all that you and Dr. C have done for the island."

"Oh, fiddle," she said, "we did what we wanted to do. If what we did helped others, so be it. But, Ally, this is where we wanted to be. Practicing medicine was what Chris wanted to do. And I wanted to be with him. It was no sacrifice at all for us."

"What about the school? Carter's office?"

"Oh, that. Chris and I had nothing to do with that. We'd already bought this house when our parents left the cottages to us. And we didn't need three houses, now did we? And, anyway, our parents wanted them to be used for the people of Pelican Isle. So I guess you could say that it was our parents who were the generous ones."

I knew that no matter what I said, she was just not going to take credit for doing anything extraordinary for the residents of Pelican Isle. So I figured I might as well just accept that.

"Well, I just stopped by to see how you were doing. I guess I'd better get on home. I've had a tiring day, and I want to be rested for my kids tomorrow."

"Sure you don't want some chowder?"

"I really can't, Joy," I said, patting my full stomach. "But thanks."

"Well, here, then, let me send a little home with you," she said, hopping up and scurrying around her kitchen.

I smiled as she floated around, slamming cabinet doors, ladling chowder, testing plastic lids, wiping the container with a sponge, so that the drippings wouldn't get on me. Then I realized that helping others, doing kindnesses for people for no personal gain and no praise, was just what Joy did. Second nature. No big deal.

Twenty

"But where do they live?"

"Here," was all Christopher said.

"What do you mean, here?"

My students just showed up each morning—from somewhere. For months I'd watched them arrive in their tram and then leave me each afternoon to return to their homes. But where was that tram taking them? Where were their homes? As I cruised the island in my cart, I saw nothing but the shabby-chic beachfront homes that rented for an obscene amount during peak tourist season. Most were deserted during the school year, waiting for well-to-do vacationers to take up residence when summer returned. So I was certain my little scholars and their families did not live on pricey Pelican Isle.

But Christopher assured me, "Here on the island."

"But where?" I said, spreading my arms and waving them across the deserted strand.

"In the village."

"The village? Where in the village? Island Grocery? The Breakfast restaurant? The hardware store?"

Smiling and shaking his head in mock exasperation, Christopher took my hand and, heading toward the door, said, "Come with me."

The afternoon was unseasonably warm and balmy, a luscious breeze coming off the ocean. As we motored toward the village in Christopher's cheerful blue and yellow golf cart, my hair blew around my face, sticking to my lips and flapping at my eyes. To tame it I made a make-shift hair band out of my arm, wrapping it over the top of my head.

In ten minutes we turned left at Island Grocery, where we saw Miguel out front collecting carts. He threw up his arm in greeting as we passed.

Once beyond the parking lot Christopher took a sharp left between the grocery and Mr. Cortez's bait shop-taco stand. I had never noticed the oyster shell path sandwiched between the two buildings, a drive wide enough for only one car. As we cruise along, listening to the oyster shells crunch beneath our tires, the narrow path opened upon an enclave of pristine, miniscule bungalows and duplex homes. Each was painted confetti orange, raspberry, lime, lemon, with equally-bright contrasting shutters. Mariachi music wafted from open, screenless windows, as blindingly-white curtains waved like flags in the sea breeze. Scents of cooking spices and herbs foreign to my southern palate filled the air, making my mouth water. The homes hugged one another tightly, leaving little room for yards or gardens. What scant space there was grew single rows of vegetables, dormant for the winter. Porches and window boxes were lined with pots of herbs I couldn't identify.

In the center of the grouping of homes stood an enormous live oak, under which a group of children, all resembling my students, jumped rope in the sandy soil and took turns swinging high on a single tire suspended by a rope from one of the tree's high branches.

I looked at Christopher and shook my head in bewilderment. "Why didn't I know about this?"

"It's a safely guarded secret," Christopher shrugged. "We don't want the tourists to know about this place. If they found out it was here, they'd probably want it, just like they want everything else."

"But I'm not a tourist," I said, defensively.

"Not anymore. But, Allison, until recently you told us that you were temporary, just passing through. This place is not for temporary people. This place, this enchanted place, is for Pelican Islanders only." Then he leaned over, put his arm around me, and said, "But you're no longer temporary. Pelican Isle is your home. You are most welcomed to *el lugar de la familia.*"

"What does that mean?"

"Well, roughly translated, it means *the family place.* You're family now, Allison."

As he leaned in to kiss me and seal me as family, we heard, "Hey, it's Dr. Chris. Welcome!"

I turned to see a handsome young man with jet-black hair, a deep tan, and rippling biceps straining his tee-shirt sleeves. He stepped from his porch onto his sandy walkway and strode toward us. Four small children, all miniatures of the beautiful man, each appearing to be under six years of age, clung to his legs. He herded them along as he approached us, his smile wide, his hand outstretched in greeting.

"Allison, this is my cousin Jorge. Jorge, Allison Albright."

Reaching for my hand, Jorge said, "Oh, I already know Miss Ally. I just haven't had the pleasure of meeting our wonderful teacher in person. So good to make your acquaintance, Miss Ally."

"And it's so good to meet you too, Jorge," I said, as he grasped my hand in both of his and gave me a warm, inviting welcome.

Then he turned to Christopher, and the two men opened their arms in familial greeting. As they embraced, I watched as Christopher palmed a bill—I don't know the denomination—and slipped it into Jorge's back pocket. The men continued to hug and cry out greetings.

Neither acknowledged the exchange.

"Oh, look who is here!" I heard and turned toward the voice. Stepping from Jorge's home was a very beautiful, very pregnant woman. She smiled broadly as she shuffled forward, bracing her back with her hands. Her well-worn, pink flowered maternity top stretched across her protruding belly, displaying her distended belly button, a sure sign that she was not far from giving birth to baby number five, if I had counted correctly.

"Lorena, come, meet Miss Ally," Jorge called as Lorena's face lit in recognition and she stepped gingerly from the porch. I slid out of the cart and approached in order to cut her journey by half, and we embraced as if we were good friends.

"Oh, Miss Ally, I am so happy to see you, to finally meet you." And, turning to Christopher, she said, "Hi, Dr. Chris. Thank you for bringing our teacher to see us."

Smiling, Christopher approached Lorena and wrapped her in his arms. "Hey, Lorena. You look as beautiful as ever. If Jorge hadn't gotten to you first..." he said and winked, watching her blush at his flirtation. Then he kissed her on the cheek and released her.

"You gotta stay for dinner. Nothing special, just chicken and tortillas."

"Sounds great," Christopher said. "We'd love to stay."

"Are you sure it's no trouble?" I said, as true southerners always do when one shows up at dinnertime unannounced and uninvited.

"No, no trouble at all. And we have plenty. Please, come on in."

The four little children, still clinging to Jorge's legs, hadn't uttered a sound but had just stood politely and listened to the adults chat. Now, though, they each released their father and stepped forward to take my hands. Still silent, they ushered me into their home.

To call it small would be a gross understatement. We stepped directly into the living room-dining room combination. In the living area stood an overstuffed sofa and a small, dated television on a rolling stand. The dining area, though, held a long, well-worn plank table and ten mismatched chairs lined closely together, as well as a small, red plastic child's table with four matching miniature chairs. The dining area was, by all appearances, the hub of the family's activity. From the dining area door, I could see a small galley kitchen. Two cramped bedrooms—one with two sets of bunk beds—and one bathroom were attached to the living room area. It was hard to imagine six—soon to be seven—people living in such a miniscule space.

"Run wash your hands," Jorge said to the children, smiling sweetly at them and tousling their hair as they scurried toward the lone bathroom.

"Lorena, it smells wonderful," I said, following her as she waddled into the tiny kitchen. Backing up against the counter to make room for my very-pregnant host to peer into the oven and poke at our supper with a long fork, I said, "What can I do to help?"

Yanking out a drawer, she said, "Here, you can put the forks and napkins around. The little forks are for the children."

"Sure," I said, gathering the forks and napkins and heading for the dining area, leaving the tiny kitchen space for Lorena.

When the men saw me coming, Christopher took the forks from my hand and began setting the table as I folded the napkins. Jorge retreated to the kitchen where we heard him say, "Here, Lorena, let me get that for you. You don't need to be lifting that." Then there was silence. I imagined a tender embrace and kiss from a man who clearly loved his family.

The couple soon returned, Lorena carrying plates and tortillas, Jorge following with an earthenware roaster full of the most delicious-smelling chicken imaginable.

"Please sit," Lorena said and motioned to two chairs for Christopher and me, as the four well-behaved and newly-scrubbed children found their places at the small, red table. While Lorena prepared plates for her children, cutting up their chicken and placing a tortilla on each plate, Jorge returned to the kitchen for four small glasses of milk for his children, and then for four larger glasses of tap water for the adults.

So accustomed was Lorena to waiting on others, she prepared plates for Christopher and me and passed them to us. She did not, however, cut up our chicken.

"Oh, my goodness, this is melt-in-your-mouth delicious. I've never tasted anything like this."

"Thank you, Miss Ally."

"Oh, please, just call me Ally."

Lorena blushed and ducked her head. I knew she would never feel comfortable calling me Ally. I would forever be Miss Ally to the Islanders.

"The chicken," Lorena said, clearing her throat of our uncomfortable conversation, "is made with herbs that my mother-in-law grows in her window boxes. But you must come back for Sunday dinner—that is on a Sunday when I don't have to work."

Lorena told me that she waited tables at a fancy restaurant on the mainland and that she had two Sundays off per month. On those Sundays she and Jorge's mother would cook all their favorite dishes for at least sixteen people.

"It all depends on who doesn't have to work and who doesn't have family to eat the Sunday meal with."

I couldn't imagine sixteen people wedging themselves into this tiny house to share a meal.

Lorena smiled and said, "It can get kind of crowded in here, but it's more fun when we have many people enjoying our cooking. I hope you and Chris will join us sometime soon."

As we ate, Christopher and Jorge shared a camaraderie that appeared to be between brothers, rather than cousins. They laughed at private jokes and recalled fond memories of their childhood.

"This is where I grew up," Christopher said to me.

"Really? Which house was yours?" I asked, peering out the window.

"This one. This is the house I grew up in. That was my bedroom," he said, pointing to the small room with the bunk beds.

"This was your home?" I said, a lump of tenderness rising in my throat. Dr. Chris had been a little boy growing up in the colorful, enchanted village on Pelican Isle, in this very home.

"When Aunt Elena passed, she left this house to me," Jorge said proudly.

Christopher said, "Jorge's dad is Roberto, Mom's oldest brother. Mom adored Uncle Roberto, and she loved Jorge as if he were her own child. Jorge spent more time here than he did at his own home next door. We even shared a single bed in that room till we were in high school." Both men laughed at the memory. "I finally had to kick him out and make him sleep on the sofa." Christopher added

"Chris was the best man in our wedding," Lorena said, reaching out to touch his arm and smile the smile of a sister for her beloved brother, if only by marriage.

Christopher took her hand in both of his and smiled sweetly at her. They didn't need words. Their tenderness touched my heart.

"I learn more about you every day," I said, when Christopher and I said good-bye and cruised back to our part of the island.

He reached over and took my hand, saying, "This is who I am, Allison—just a Pelican Isle boy who can never leave home."

I squeezed his hand and smiled, knowing he was so much more than that.

"Thanks, Christopher."

"For what, Allison."

"For calling me family."

He released my hand and put his arm around me, pulling me to him. I rested my head on his shoulder as we cruised toward home.

Twenty-one

To my delight, my students were hysterical over all their new supplies, especially their tablets. I passed them out and thought that we'd need a practice session before they were able to navigate their devices. But before I could return to the front of the classroom, they were all hunched over their tablets, playing games, viewing flashcards, reading stories, adding and subtracting on their math app. I was overjoyed and delighted that Mom's and my purchase was such a success.

Martina had located her reading app, a special, more challenging app that I had downloaded to her device only. There was a series of stories about girls from all over the world who had succeeded against all odds. I wanted her to read about smart, strong girls and believe that she, too, could be one of those girls.

I crouched beside her desk and whispered, "I put a special reading app on your tablet."

Smiling conspiratorially, she whispered, "I know. I'm reading already."

"What are you reading?"

"A story about a girl who wanted to go to school, but girls in her country weren't allowed to go to school. Her name is Malala."

"I've read about Malala," I told her.

Her eyes wide, Martina smiled and said, "You have?"

"Yes, I have. But, Martina, there are many places in the world that don't allow girls to go to school."

Her smile disappearing, she said, "That isn't fair, Miss Ally."

"I agree. Would you like to read the story about Malala to the class?"

"Yes, ma'am, when I'm through reading."

"You can let me know when you're ready to share with everyone."

"Okay, Miss Ally," she said and went back to her story.

I allowed the children thirty more minutes of unstructured play before I said, "All right, kiddos, time to put your tablets away. We have work to do."

They all began to whine, and I said, "I promise we'll work on them later. How about we do our math lesson on our tablets this afternoon?"

With my promise they obediently placed their new gadgets in their desks.

One morning about a month later the children tumbled into the classroom, as usual, and went straight for their tablets. They'd been a bigger hit than I had dreamed they'd be—the first things my students reached for in the morning, the last things they put away each afternoon before leaving for home. Martina brought up the rear, shuffling her feet, head down, as she made her way to her desk. When she sat down, she didn't grab her tablet and begin reading as she usually did but, instead, just folded her hands on her desktop and stared at them. I looked closely. I could tell that her eyes were red and swollen. She had been crying. But kids cry. I couldn't get involved in every child's hurt feelings, but, for some reason, Martina was different. I'll admit, she was my favorite, always would be. Finding her despondent troubled me. I had watched her come out of her shell as she read to the class; I didn't want anything to happen to make her lose her new-found confidence.

I approached her desk and crouched by her side and asked her casually, "Hey, Martina, how are you coming on your story about Malala?"

"Okay, I guess."

"Are you ready to read for us?"

"No, ma'am."

That was a surprise. Once she had read to the class and had seen how the other children reacted, she would jump at any chance to read out loud. Something was wrong. But I couldn't pry.

One of my first lessons of teaching was that I couldn't fight my many children's battles, couldn't get involved in their hurt feelings, couldn't be responsible for their emotional well-being. If Martina needed my help, she'd let me know. Until then I'd just have to let her deal with her feelings in her own way.

However, as the days wore on, Martina became more and more subdued and withdrawn. I'd ask her if she were ready to read, and, without making eye contact, she'd just shake her head to let me know that she was not. She didn't even say politely, "No, ma'am," as she usually did. But, still, I told myself that I could not get involved.

"Miss Ally?"

I jumped. I was alone in my thoughts and wasn't expecting visitors. I had seen all my students onto the tram and had waved to them as they trundled out of sight down Beach Road. The day had been exhausting. For some reason, the children had been more energetic than usual, all but Martina. She was more withdrawn than ever and did nothing but stare at her desk or read silently. I was tired from the super-active children and from worry over Martina, and I was ready to head for home and a hot shower. I had planned to rock the babies with Joy after school, but I was just too weary even for babies.

"Mrs. Gonzales, you startled me."

"I'm sorry, Miss Ally. Can I speak to you, please?"

"Why, of course, come on in."

I watched Martina's very pregnant mother waddle across my classroom, her feet shuffling, legs splayed wide, her arms cradling her bulging abdomen. I remembered the feeling well, those last days of pregnancy when I was certain that I just couldn't endure expectant motherhood one more minute. I felt sorry for Mrs. Gonzales in her swollen state, yet I envied her, as well.

"Here, Mrs. Gonzales," I said, taking her arm and helping her to the chair by my desk, the only adult-size seat in the room. When she was settled, I pulled one of the children's desks near and wedged myself into the pint-size seat.

"How are you doing?"

"Not so good, Miss Ally."

"Oh, I'm so sorry. Difficult pregnancy?"

"No, the pregnancy is fine."

"Then what is it?"

She held a wad of tattered tissues, and she twisted it and stared at her red, rough, work-worn hands without speaking.

After an uncomfortable silence she whispered, "We have to leave."

"Leave?" I asked. "Why do we have to leave?"

"My family, Miss Ally. We have to leave Pelican Isle. Leave the country. We are being deported."

Christopher, Joy, and Carter had tried to prepare me, but there was just no way that I could have been prepared for the imminent deportation of a student, especially my favorite student.

"Oh, no, that can't be," I cried.

But I knew that it was true. That explained Martina's crying, her despondence, her withdrawal. It also explained why she was no longer interested in reading to the class. Why be involved, only to leave? My heart broke for my precious, favorite student. She should not have to bear the pain of her family's deportation. She was just a little girl, only six years old. Her life should be happy, cheerful, free from adults' worries. But she knew; clearly she knew.

"Is there anything I can do to help?"

"Yes, Miss Ally."

"What? Anything. I'll do anything," I said, frantic for a solution.

"My Martina loves you," she said, but that didn't explain what I could do to help.

"I know. I love her too. She's a wonderful little girl. So special. So smart. I wish all of my students were just like her."

It was true. Martina was so special, like no other child I'd ever taught. She showed up prepared for class each day and worked harder than any of my other students. She paid attention and didn't fidget or giggle or whisper. She had an inner drive to succeed that most children her age don't possess. Would her new teacher, whoever that might be, recognize her specialness, give her the attention she would need to thrive? And would she encourage her to read about brave girls? I was confident Martina would believe that she could be a brave, successful girl. But a little girl needs reassurance as she pursues her dreams.

I fantasized about keeping her with me on Pelican Isle, nurturing her drive, giving her stacks and stacks of books to indulge her love of reading. But I knew it was just a fantasy. She had to be with her mother. She belonged with her family.

Shaking me from my thoughts of Martina, Mrs. Gonzales, caressing her unborn child, said, "My baby will come soon."

"Yes, I know. Martina told me."

"We have to leave as soon as the baby is born."

"But isn't there something someone can do to help you stay?"

"No, nothing can be done. We have tried. No one can help. We must leave."

They had turned for assistance to anyone they thought could help them. They had exhausted all avenues at their disposal to avoid deportation but had failed in their efforts. It was so unfair. After eight months of struggling to stay in the home they had come to love and call their own, a home where the parents worked hard to provide a good life for their children, their battle had come to a tragic end. They would be leaving.

"But you can help, Miss Ally."

"Anything. Just name it," I said, hoping that it was true, that, even though I couldn't help them stay in America, I could do something to help precious Martina and her family in their transition.

"Just love my baby like you love my Martina," she said, wrapping her arms protectively around her growing child.

"Excuse me?"

"My baby, she is an American citizen. She has a right to be here. This government can never deport her," Mrs. Gonzales said triumphantly and defiantly, sitting straight, her chin in the air. "My baby must stay here in America. Even if I cannot, she must."

"But, Mrs. Gonzales, your baby belongs with you. You are her mother. She needs you."

"No, Miss Ally. I can't give her the life she deserves. I can't take her where I am going. It is not her home. This is her home. Pelican Isle is her home. America is her home."

"But how can a tiny baby stay here?"

"With you."

It took me a moment to realize that Mrs. Gonzales was asking me to care for her child.

"Me? Mrs. Gonzales, you're asking if your daughter can stay with me?"

"Not stay with you, Miss Ally. I'm asking you to be her mother."

"Her mother? You mean adopt her?"

"Yes, please," she said, her eyes welling with tears, her arms still cradling her unborn daughter.

And then she was crying, crying hard at the only choice she felt she had. And as she wept, her straight, defiant back shrank as she folded herself around her unborn child. Mrs. Gonzales no longer looked triumphant. She looked small and defeated. She looked desperate, desperate to protect her baby from the fate that her family faced. I slipped from the desk and went to her. I crouched beside her and placed my hand on her back.

"Oh, Mrs. Gonzales, there must be some other way."

"No, it's the only way. She deserves to be here. And I know that you will love her the way you love my Martina. You will teach my baby to read. You will tell her the importance of an education. You will help her go to college. You will show her how to be a brave girl. And she will always be an American citizen," she said, the defiance returning to her voice.

I could not believe what she was asking of me. I had never witnessed, had never even imagined such selflessness. Mrs. Gonzales was willing to make the ultimate sacrifice for her child. She was prepared to hand her over to America so that she could have the life that she and her husband had worked so hard to provide for their family, a life that only her unborn daughter could realize legally.

"Mrs. Gonzales, I'm not even married. I live alone."

"But you are the perfect mother for my little girl. I know that you are."

"Why me? Don't you have friends? Family?"

"Yes, I do, but you will teach her. You will give her books to read. You will make sure that she goes to college. And you will never be deported."

She quickly wiped her eyes with her shredded, twisted tissues, composed herself, and said, "Please. Please, Miss Ally."

"I'll think about it, Mrs. Gonzalez," was all I could say.

When she realized that was the best I could offer at the moment, she hoisted herself from the chair and steadied herself by clutching my desk. She shuffled toward the hall, and when she reached the door, she turned. Taking a deep, ragged breath, she said, "Her name is Eloisa."

Then she trundled out the door and down the hall. Once she was out of sight, I stood motionless, trying to wrap my head around what had happened, what I'd just been asked to do. I'd been charged with what seemed an impossible task. Mrs. Gonzales wanted me to rescue her unborn child so that she might claim her legal birthright: America. It was my legal birthright, as well, a gift I'd done nothing to earn, a gift I accepted casually and took for granted blatantly.

Slapped in the face by my embarrassment of riches, I sank to the floor, buried my face in my hands, and began shaking. Then the emotion of the moment poured from me as I began to weep. The whole conversation had seemed abstract, a situation that was tragic but completely out of my control. I had been thrust into the tragedy without my permission and asked to do something that, by all measures, appeared implausible. But the desperate mother had said the one thing, the only thing that could have made it all seem so very personal and real to me.

She had said, "Her name is Eloisa."

Eloisa. Her name is Eloisa. Why, Mrs. Gonzales, did you have to tell me her name?

Twenty-two

I sat on the floor of my classroom till my butt became numb and my crossed legs began to tingle. I'd lost track of time and was shocked to discover that it had been well over an hour since Mrs. Gonzales had said, "Her name is Eloisa," and had disappeared from my classroom.

But even after an hour I still couldn't make sense of her request. She wanted me to adopt her unborn child. And, to her, my primary qualification for being her child's mother was my American citizenship. I couldn't be deported. How tragic that something we take for granted could be her number one condition for motherhood. But Mrs. Gonzales also knew that, in addition to my being a citizen, I was a teacher who could encourage her daughter to read, to excel, to go to college, to be brave. I knew that Mrs. Gonzales could do all those things for Eloisa—she had done them for Martina—but she just could no longer do them in the United States. Having her daughter claim her rightful American citizenship was of utmost importance to Mrs. Gonzales, and she would make the ultimate sacrifice to ensure her child could claim her birthright.

My head still buzzing, I picked up my purse and headed for my cart. I pulled into my driveway, not remembering the trip but grateful that I'd reached my home unscathed. I prayed that if I'd passed anyone along the way, they were safe, as well.

I climbed the stairs to my porch and began shedding my clothes at the doorway, leaving a trail of garments to the shower. I stepped in and turned on the water, not waiting for it to warm. I didn't mind the iciness; it served to heighten my senses, to shock me into an alertness I felt I needed to tackle the situation. When, after the water had warmed and then cooled again and I was no closer to a solution than before, I stepped out and toweled dry. I slipped into a clean pair of jeans and a tee shirt and padded barefoot to the kitchen to make myself a cup of tea.

As I drummed my fingers nervously on the kitchen counter, waiting for the water to boil, I heard, "Anybody home?" at the door. I looked up to see Christopher striding toward me.

"You ready?" he asked when he reached the kitchen and gave me a peck on the cheek.

"Oh, my gosh!" I cried, having forgotten our dinner date. "I'm so sorry, Christopher. Something came up, and I just forgot to call you. Can I take a rain check?"

I still wasn't ready to share with him the conversation I'd had with Mrs. Gonzales and was hoping I could convince him to leave me to my thoughts.

But when he asked, "What's up?" and I burst into tears, I knew there'd be no hiding Mrs. Gonzales or keeping the news from him.

"Allison, what happened?" he asked and wrapped his arms around me, letting me weep against his shoulder.

"Oh, Christopher, I just don't know where to start."

"You're shaking. Sit down while I fix the tea. "

Without hesitation or argument, I sat on the kitchen stool and let Christopher fix us both a cup of tea and carry it to the living room. I followed and eased myself onto the sofa.

Joining me and handing me a cup, Christopher said, "Now, what's going on?"

So I told him, told him everything.

"Oh, Christopher, it's so sad. Her heart is breaking, but she is willing to sacrifice her own happiness for her unborn child."

"Yes, that is sad. But it has happened before, many times. We tried to prepare you, but there just isn't any way you can be prepared for such tragedy."

"But, Christopher, she wants me to adopt her baby," I cried out, still not able to grasp such a request.

"That's quite a sacrifice for her, but it's also an awful lot to ask of you," Christopher said, "a major commitment."

Commitment. I'd heard Christopher use that word so often. Commitment was awfully important to him.

"Do you think you could be this little girl's mother?" he asked.

Before I could answer, Joy stuck her head in the door and said, "Glad I found y'all at home. I just baked sugar cookies for the nurses and went overboard. I have enough to feed the whole island. Thought y'all might like some."

Sensing the tense atmosphere and our lack of enthusiasm for sugar cookies, Joy crossed the room to us and said, "What's the matter, you two? Did something happen?"

Willing myself not to begin crying again, I told Joy about Mrs. Gonzales's visit, Christopher filling in when I skipped over a detail.

"Oh my, Ally, I can understand why you are so upset." Placing the plate of cookies on the coffee table, she sat beside me on the sofa and said, "What can we do to help?"

"I don't know, Joy. I just don't know."

Taking my hand, she asked, "Are you really considering adopting Mrs. Gonzales's baby?"

"I don't know that either. I don't know anything at all. I'm just so confused," I cried.

"It's okay, Ally," Joy said, understandingly. "It isn't every day that someone asks you to adopt her baby."

It was true. Mrs. Gonzales's request was shocking, something I couldn't have anticipated. I'd been warned, but Christopher was right when he'd said that no one could have prepared me for this.

"Have you called your mom and dad?" Christopher asked.

"No, I haven't had a chance, and, to be honest, I need time to think about what to say to them."

"That makes sense. Maybe you'd like some time alone to sort this out," Joy said, signaling Christopher with her eyes.

"Maybe so. Do y'all mind?"

Joy said, "Oh, absolutely not. We understand, don't we Chris?"

I noted a look of sorrow and rejection on Christopher's face, yet he said, "Oh, sure. You need time to think."

"Thanks, Christopher," I said.

Then he rose, leaned to kiss me, and said, "Please call me. I'll need to hear from you. I'll be up, waiting. Any time…"

Then he took Joy's arm, helped her from the sofa, and ushered her to the door. Then he turned, smiled wanly at me, and the two of them left me to think.

I sat alone, holding my tea, untouched, until it turned cold. Placing the cup on the coffee table, I crossed to my bedroom where I pulled my coat, scarf, and boots from my closet. Bundling up for the brisk breeze coming off the ocean, I headed for the beach, my best thinking spot.

As I followed the rumble of the powerful surf, I could feel my muscles relax, the tension melt from my throbbing temples. Cresting the dune, the brisk salt air caused my eyes to water and made me shiver. Wrapping my coat tighter and pulling my scarf around my face, I began walking north, in the direction of Pelican Isle Elementary.

The night was clear, and the stars looked like a canopy of fireflies overhead. Back in Raleigh the stars are dimmed or completely washed out by the glow of street lights and the lights from houses and businesses. But on that night, on Pelican Isle, with no street lights and houses darkened for the winter, the sky was an explosion of sparkles, the likes of which I'd never seen. About a mile from home, I sat on the packed-sand beach and stared out at the crashing waves. As the pounding calmed and lulled me, I pulled my hood over my head, lay flat on my back, and stared up at the sparkling sky.

"What am I going to do?" I asked out loud, so hoping I would hear a booming voice giving me a clear solution.

But when I heard no voice, I knew, for sure, that I had to decide what I should do. This was my decision—not my parents' decision, not Joy's decision, not Christopher's decision. I had to be the one to say *Yes, I can be Eloisa's mother* or *No, as much as I want to help Martina and her family, I just can't make this commitment.*

To help me resolve this dilemma, I decided to make a mental list of pros and cons for adopting Mrs. Gonzales's baby.

Pro:

I waited and waited for just one pro to come to me, but I drew a blank. Perhaps it would be wise to start with the cons and wend my way back to the pros.

Con: I am alone. A child needs two parents.

Con: I have a job. I couldn't give a child the attention it needed.

Con: I don't know the legal ramifications of adopting a child whose family is being deported.

Con: Mrs. Gonzales could change her mind and return to claim her baby. Could I survive losing another child?

Con: I don't know anything about the child's culture. A child needs to know its heritage.

My con list was getting quite long, so I decided to give it a rest and get back to the pros. Yet when I tried to come up with valid reasons for being the mother to someone else's child, I still faltered.

Pro:

Pro:

Pro:

The only thing that came to me was, pro: she needs me.

But could I fulfill that need? Yes, I was certain I could be her mother because, as Joy said, I was already a mother. It seemed, though, that was all I had to offer. But was that enough? How about my being alone? I had said that being alone was a con, but many parents raise children alone. And as for my having a job, I had known many working mothers who managed just fine. Granted, there would be challenges, but even stay-at-home moms have challenges.

Then there were the legal issues? Could I manage the legalities of adoption, especially the adoption of a child whose family was being deported? Well, my dad was an attorney, had been for many years. He wasn't an immigration or adoption attorney, but surely he would know whom to contact to help us with those issues.

What if Mrs. Gonzales came back to reclaim her child? Well, nothing is certain. I could not allow an uncertainty to be a barrier to adopting a child.

And as for the baby's heritage, I could learn. I lived in a community of Latino residents. Surely they'd all help me teach my baby about her legacy, her traditions, her customs.

My baby. I'd said *my baby*. And instead of calling the baby *it*, I had said *her* for the first time. Eloisa. A little girl. A little baby girl who needed a mother, a mother to love her and care for her. A mother who would not be deported. I wanted to help Martina's family, but, more that that, I wanted to be the mother I already was. I wanted Eloisa to be my child.

My child.

But before I jumped in with my heart, I needed to reason clearly with my head. And even though I knew that this decision would ultimately be mine, I felt the need for my parents' support. This was a major, life-altering decision; I so needed their experience, maturity, and love—especially their love.

Twenty-three

By the time I returned to my warm, cozy cottage, it was well past midnight. Life-changing decisions take a long time to resolve, but I had only approached a resolution.

I dialed Christopher's number, since he'd asked me to call, had said he needed to hear from me. He answered on the first ring.

"No, I haven't made a decision," I told him. "There's a whole lot to be considered."

"You're right, Allison."

"I'm going to Raleigh in the morning. I need to talk to my mom and dad. They'll help me. They're so level-headed. I really need them now."

"Of course you do. Good idea. Want me to go with you?"

"Thanks for the offer, but this is something I need to do alone."

"Sure," Christopher said, trying but failing to hide his disappointment.

"I promise I'll call tomorrow night, though."

"Good. I'd like that.

"And one more thing, Allison—now, because of HIPPA laws, I am not allowed to share any of Mrs. Gonzales's medical information with you, but—and you can't breathe a word of this—she came in for her check-up yesterday, probably right before she came to see you. Her baby will be here soon. Real soon. I don't want to rush your decision, but I thought you should know."

"Thanks, Christopher. I'll keep that in mind. But, for now, I need to get a little sleep before I set out for Raleigh."

I had a fitful night but had managed to doze a bit. But when I was certain that I was awake for good, I rolled over and glanced at the clock. I figured Mom and Dad would be up and sitting at the Formica table, drinking coffee and reading the News & Observer. Now would be a good time to call them and let them know that I'd be coming home to see them. I didn't want to alarm them with my sudden decision to visit. I wouldn't say that I had something I needed to tell them and have them worry for hours. I'd just say that I missed them and wanted to see them. I reached for the phone and dialed their number.

Mom squealed when she heard I was coming and said, "Why, I'm just gonna go bake you a lemon meringue pie."

I knew she would say that. She is so predictable—about most things.

"Mind if I spend the night?"

"Oh, Ally, Daddy and I wouldn't have it any other way. Now, you come right on, and we'll be waiting for you."

"Thanks, Mom. See you soon."

Dad was watching from the front window when I pulled into the drive. He met me at the front door and took me in his arms.

"So good to see you, Honey. Missed you."

Then Mom was coming down the hall, wiping her hands on her apron, smiling broadly.

"Hey, Darlin'. Come on in. Your pie is cooling."

The house smelled so good, like my childhood—all tart and lemony and homey. Mom had already prepared lunch, and the Formica table was laid. So as soon as I dropped my bag, the three of us sat down to eat.

We made mindless chatter as I pushed my lunch around my plate and pretended to eat while trying to figure out how to break the news to my folks. I had practiced all the way from Pelican Isle, which was a breeze when I was alone. But now that I was face-to-face with my parents, it wasn't quite so easy.

Between lunch and pie I said, "Mom, can we wait a bit on dessert. I have something I need to tell you and Dad."

They instantly looked frightened, concerned, befuddled, all the postures they'd assumed to deal with their once-fragile, wounded daughter. They believed that I had recovered, that I had moved on, but my saying that I had something that I had to tell them had snapped them both to attention and turned them a ghastly white.

"What is it, Darlin'?" Mom asked.

"Do y'all remember my telling you about my student Martina?"

"Sure, the little girl who reads so well," my dad said.

"That's the one," I said, taking a deep breath. "Well, her family is being deported."

"Oh, Ally," my mother said, her hand flying to her mouth in horror.

"Ally," my father said, "my practice isn't equipped to handle deportation cases, but perhaps I can find someone to help."

"Thanks, Dad, but Martina's mom said they have exhausted all avenues, that the decision is final. They have to leave."

Crossing his arms over his chest in resignation, he said, "I'm so sorry, Ally. I know how fond you are of that little girl."

"Yes sir, I am. But there's more."

"What is it, Honey," my mom said, her brow knitted in preparation for more sad news.

"Well, Martina's mother is expecting a child. She is due any day now."

I waited for them to say something, but they just stared at me curiously.

Clutching my hands in my lap, I told them, "She has asked me to adopt her baby."

Mom reached for Dad's hand and emitted a frightened little squeak. One minute I was counting the flowers on my bedroom wall; the next I was telling them that a mother whose family was being deported wanted me to adopt her child.

They both stared at me, stunned silent. Finally my father said, "Ally, are you really considering adopting this baby?"

"I don't know, Dad. I'm just so confused. That's why I came to see you and Mom. I need some help sorting this out."

Both my parents relaxed, smiled, and reached across the table to me.

"Well, we're glad you shared this with us, Honey," Mom said. "The three of us can figure this out. We always manage to, don't we?"

"We sure do," I said, so relieved and smiling for the first time.

So we ate pie and talked. And talked. And talked.

Dad got out a legal pad and pencil, just as any good lawyer would do. He took notes as he and Mom asked all the pertinent questions and I answered as best I could. Of course, they asked all the questions I'd asked myself. They were concerned about my being alone and teaching all day; yet they both agreed that they'd known single, working mothers who had managed a family just fine.

When Dad had filled two legal pages with notes, Mom said, "But, Ally, what if the mother changes her mind?"

The question was inevitable. I'd asked it myself. I honestly didn't know if I could survive another loss, but I said, "Mom, Dad, this little girl needs me. Her family is being deported. Her mother feels she deserves to stay in this country since she will be a United States citizen. She trusts that I will take good care of her child, and I believe I can. And I can't let the chance that Mrs. Gonzales may change her mind sway my decision. I won't let uncertainty scare me away. All of life is uncertain."

They looked at each other and smiled, and then my father said, "Ally, your mother and I have no doubt you'd be a wonderful mother for this little girl. We never questioned that. We just don't want you to suffer any more hurt, but we also know that we can't protect you from pain. Now, if this is something you feel is right for you, we will support your decision. And regardless of what happens, we will be there for you."

"I knew you'd say that, but I just needed to hear it. I couldn't do this, or anything, for that matter, without both of you."

Then scanning his notes, my father said, "Okay, then, I think I have all the information I need. If you ladies will excuse me, I'm going to go make some calls. We'll have to iron out the legalities before we move forward."

I loved that my father was saying *we*. Hearing that made me hopeful that I could be a mother, that I could adopt Mrs. Gonzales's baby and teach her to read and to be a brave girl.

By bedtime I was exhausted from the emotion of the day before, the ride from Pelican Isle to Raleigh, and from trying to resolve the issue with the help of my parents.

"Mom, I think I'll take a shower and turn in. I'm tired."

"You do that, Darlin'. I'll be up a little later to tuck you in."

I was anticipating bringing a child into my life, but I would forever be Grace Macklemore's little girl. I would never be too old for her to tuck me in.

"Thanks, Mom, I'd like that."

Once I'd showered and called Christopher and Joy to tell them that my parents were rightly concerned but very supportive, I crawled under the covers and waited for my mom to come tuck me in. She sensed my waiting, as I knew she would.

"Hey, Sweetie, you settled?" she asked, peeking her head in the door.

"Yes, ma'am, all settled. It feels good to be back in my bed."

"And it's good to have you back in your bed," she said, smoothing and tucking and poking the sheets.

After she'd tucked and brushed my hair back and kissed me on the cheek, she climbed onto the bed beside me. I scooted over to make room for her.

Propping herself on one elbow, she stroked my hair with her free hand and said, "Oh, Ally, I've never been able to find the words to let you know how very much I love you, how proud I am of you. But once you have a daughter of your own, I'll no longer need to look for those words. You'll just know. You'll just know."

"I can't wait to find out how much you love me, Mom."

She just smiled and kissed me on my forehead.

"Mom, her name is Eloisa."

"Oh, Ally, what a lovely name."

"I would like to call her Eloisa Grace."

Her eyes misted and she tried to speak, her words caught in her throat. "I'd like that," was all she could manage. Then she smiled sweetly, cleared her throat, and said, "Well, it's been a busy, busy day, and you need your rest. And so do I."

Slipping from the bed, she patted my covers smooth and turned to leave. When she reached the door, she stopped and smiled.

"What is it, Mom?"

"I'm really proud of you, Ally, more than you'll ever know."

"Thank you, Mom."

I was asleep before she cleared the door.

The following morning I awoke to the smell of coffee and my mother's homemade cinnamon rolls. I dragged myself out of bed and down the stairs, barefoot, hair uncombed, teeth unbrushed. I realized I'd always love being a child in my parents' home. I was betting that even Eloisa's arrival wouldn't change that.

I found both of them in the kitchen, Dad reading the paper, Mom icing the cinnamon rolls.

"Morning, Sunshine," my mom said, as I gave her a hug and slid into my chrome-and-vinyl chair at the kitchen table.

"Hi, Dad," I said, stretching and running my hands through my bed-scattered hair.

"Hey, Princess, want to share my paper?"

"No, thanks. I believe I just want coffee and one of Mom's cinnamon rolls."

"Sounds like a better idea," he said, folding his paper and dropping it on the floor beside his chair. "The news can wait."

Mom poured us each a cup of coffee and brought the pan of warm cinnamon rolls to the table. She doled them out onto bread plates and passed them around. She and Dad ate theirs with a fork, like civilized adults; I ate mine with my hands, as I always had, so that I could lick the warm icing from my fingers. Mom just smiled as I ran my tongue over my sugary lips and stuck my sticky thumb in my mouth. Then she put down her fork, dabbed her lips with her napkin, and reached for my non-sticky hand.

"Ally, your Dad and I were awake late into the night, talking about your decision."

"I'm sure you were. It's a lot to take in. I know you are both concerned."

"One thing we need to know, Ally."

"What's that, Mom?"

"Are you adopting Eloisa to replace Rory?"

Her question stung like a slap. I'd never considered Eloisa as a replacement baby, but I understood Mom's asking.

"Oh, no," I promised. "I'll never be able to replace Rory. I will love her and will be her mother always. But this little girl needs me, and I need her too—but not as a replacement."

"Okay, we just had to make sure. So now that that's settled, what do you think of Tita and Tito?"

"Huh?"

"I went online last night after you were in bed to see what Latino children call their grandparents. Grandmother and grandfather in Spanish are *abuela* and *abuelo*. Did you know that?"

"No, ma'am, I didn't."

"Well, it's time you learned. You have a class full of Latino students, and you're about to become the mother of a Latina child."

"Yes, ma'am, I agree."

"And Latino children sometimes call their grandparents Tita and Tito. Do you think Eloisa would like to call us Tita and Tito?"

"But, Mom, you've always wanted to be called Gram and Grampy."

"I know, but don't you think it's important for Eloisa to hold on to her heritage, to know its traditions? I think it would be a good thing for her to call us Tita and Tito. Don't you think that would be a good idea?"

I had been so concerned about teaching Eloisa her heritage, her customs, her traditions. Looked like I was going to get lots of help.

"What do you think, Dad?"

"I like it. I believe your mother is right, Ally. I think it's going to be very important for us to teach Eloisa about her roots, about her parents."

"Tita and Tito," I said, listening to how it sounded when I said it. "Yeah, I like that."

"Your dad and I are very excited, Ally, but, of course, we're concerned."

"I know, Mom. I'm concerned too. It's a big step. But it's a step I want to take, a step I really need to take."

"You know we'll do anything we can to help, don't you?" Dad said, repeating what he had promised the night before. "I made a half dozen calls last night and left detailed messages. I expect to hear from some experts very soon. We'll get all the legalities worked out. You just concentrate on that little girl."

"Thanks, Dad. I knew I could count on both of you."

Licking the last of the sweet icing from my lips and fingers, I said, "Well, I'd better go gather my things and get on back home. We have lots to do to get ready for your granddaughter."

"*Nuestra nieta.*"

"Huh?"

"Our granddaughter. That's how you say our granddaughter in

Spanish," Mom said with a smug, know-it-all grin.

Twenty-four

Joy was at my door before I could drop my bag.

"Tell me everything," she said, taking my hand and guiding me to the sofa.

I told her, "Mom and Dad were wonderful. I knew they would be supportive, but they were more understanding than I ever dreamed."

"Oh, Ally, I prayed it would all work out for you," Joy said. "But of course they are very concerned. What parents wouldn't be?"

Just then the door opened and Christopher stuck his head in.

"Hope you don't mind my coming over unannounced. I saw you when you passed by my house, so I followed you home. I just had to hear about your trip."

Reaching out my hand, I said, "I'm so glad you came. I was just telling Joy about my folks' reaction to the news."

"Please start over. I want to hear everything," he said.

"Sure," I said, so happy that he was interested and wanted to be a part of my decision. "They were concerned, of course, but they are going to support me, regardless of my decision."

"And have you arrived at a decision?" Christopher asked.

"Yes, I have," I said. And looking from one to the other, I told them, "I have decided that I want to adopt Eloisa. I want to be her mother."

Joy and Christopher could not hide their glee. Joy cried out and clapped her hands excitedly, while Christopher jumped from the sofa and pumped his fist in the air, crying, "Yes!"

We all laughed aloud from sheer exuberance, excitement, happiness, and release.

"We didn't want to pressure you, Ally," Joy said, "but we were so hoping that would be your choice."

"I'm so glad you approve, but there is so much we need to do, not the least of which are the legal issues surrounding an adoption, especially the adoption of the child whose family is being deported."

"Gosh, you're right, Ally," Joy said. "I was so excited about the baby, that I'd hardly thought about that."

"But, as y'all know, my dad is an attorney. He's been in practice for so long that he has many colleagues in all areas of the law. He's already made calls to adoption and immigration attorneys. He says he'll iron out all the legalities and leave us to take care of Eloisa."

"That sounds good," Joy said. "Where do we start?"

"Well, before I go any further, I need to talk with Carter. He has entrusted me with his first graders. I want him to know that adopting a child won't change my commitment to my students."

"Good idea," said Christopher. "He really cares for you, Ally. He'll appreciate your confiding in him."

"I also want to talk with Dr. Brown, let her know that I'm getting a roommate to share her house."

"Well, knowing Betsy," said Joy, "I'm certain she'll be delighted to have a little girl living in her home."

It sounded so odd hearing Joy call Dr. Brown by her first name, Betsy. No matter how familiar I became with my former professor, she would forever be Dr. Elizabeth Brown to me.

"Hello?"

"Dr. Brown?"

"Speaking."

"Oh, Dr. Brown, I'm so glad I caught you in your office. This is Ally Albright."

"Well, hello, Ally. I was just thinking about you. I got a call yesterday from a principal in Charlotte. He's short a first-grade teacher and wondered if I had a recommendation. Ally, we need several dozen of you. You'd be perfect for the job."

I felt myself blushed. Would I ever be comfortable with her praise or feel that I deserved it?

"That's kind of you, Dr. Brown, but I think that Pelican Isle is stuck with me. I've renewed my contract."

"Oh, Ally, how wonderful. I know that Carter is delighted."

"No more delighted than I am, Dr. Brown. Pelican Isle feels like home. I love the residents, but, mostly, I love my students. They are all wonderful children. I am so blessed."

"That's good to hear, Ally."

"Dr. Brown, I can't thank you enough for sending me here. I know I balked at first, but I am so glad you didn't give up on me."

"I'm like a dog with a bone, Ally. When I want something, I won't give up till I get it."

"I'm thankful, too, that you allowed me to stay in your home. Now, that didn't take much convincing. I will never be able to repay you for sharing your wonderful cottage with me."

"My pleasure. I'm glad to have someone I trust looking out for it. I so hope you're finding it comfortable."

"Oh, I am. It's the most magical place I've ever seen. I couldn't have dreamed a more perfect home."

"That's great, Ally."

Clearing my throat, I said, "Dr. Brown, the reason I'm calling concerns your house."

"Oh?"

"What would you say to my getting a roommate?"

I held my breath, thinking, *Oh, please say 'yes,' oh, please say 'yes.'*

"A roommate? Why, I'd have no problem at all if you feel you can fit another body into those cramped quarters."

"Well, it'll be a tiny roommate," I said.

"Tiny?"

"Yes, Dr. Brown, a tiny baby. I'm going to adopt a baby, a little girl. She wouldn't take up much space."

"Oh, Ally," she practically yelped, "what exciting news! When?"

"Well, she's due any time now."

I tried to give Dr. Brown a synopsis of the adoption without unloading all the details on her. I just wanted to make sure she was fine with my bringing Eloisa into her home, but I also wanted to share my good news with her. Dr. Brown had been a part of many of the major decisions of my life; it just seemed right for her to know about my little girl.

"Ally, you must keep me posted. I'm dying to know details. Now, take lots and lots of pictures, and email them to me. I'll share them with all your professors. Oh, this is just so exciting. I can't wait to tell everybody."

I assured her that I would email regularly with pictures and updates and that my new roommate would help me take care of her home.

As soon as I said *good-bye* to Dr. Brown, I dialed Carter's office. It was Saturday, but I was certain I'd find him at work. His job was his life. He was dedicated to the children of Pelican Isle.

"Hey, Carter."

"Ally, what's up?"

"I need to talk with you. Are you going to be in your office for a while?"

"I can be here for as long as you need me. Hope nothing is wrong," he said, concern in his voice.

"Oh, no, nothing's wrong. Just have some news I want to share with you, and I'd rather do it in person."

"I'll be waiting right here for you," he said and hung up the phone.

I could imagine him straightening his desk and making sure there were cold Cokes in the fridge.

The day was sunny but brisk, so I rode with the curtains rolled down around my golf cart. I found myself smiling as I cruised north on the island, the island that I now called Home. Such a short time ago I had been so frightened by Mrs. Gonzales's request that I adopt her child, yet I had already embraced the notion and looked forward to being Eloisa's mother. I was convinced that, with the support of my mom and dad, Christopher and Joy, Dr. Brown, and surely Carter, I could be a loving, capable mother, even though I would be a single mom with a full-time job.

I passed Ricky Hernandez on his way to his job at the fish market, and he threw up his hand in greeting. Ricky had been so welcoming when I'd first gone to the market to buy shrimp. He picked out the biggest and freshest for me, saying, "Only the best for Miss Ally." I was so touched by this warmth, but I soon learned that everyone on Pelican Isle was as warm and welcoming as Ricky. I was confident that Ricky and all the residents of Pelican Isle would support me and do all they could to help me raise Eloisa.

When I pulled into the lot in front of Carter's office, he stepped out onto the porch and called, "Come on in here where it's warm."

I slid out of the cart and headed for Carter. His arms were open for a hug before I reached him.

"Want a Co-Cola?" he asked as he followed me into his office.

"Sure, I'd love one," I told him.

He approached the yellow Norge refrigerator which had developed a clank and a wheeze since I'd last seen it. He gave it a swift kick to calm it down and reached inside for two bottles of Coke. He popped the lids with the opener that was still hanging from the counter by a frayed length of twine and handed me one.

"Carter, that refrigerator sounds like it's on its last leg."

"Nah," he said, patting its side, "this old girl has a few more good years in her. At least she'd better. There's just no room in the budget for a replacement."

I took a swig from my Coke and sat in the same chair I'd occupied when I'd first come to Pelican Isle for my job interview.

Carter sat opposite me, across his desk, and said, "Okay, what's up?"

"Carter," I said, "I know you're aware that Martina Gonzales's family is being deported."

Pursing his lips, he said, "Yeah, I know. I'm devastated, but there's just nothing that can be done about it. As I told you when you came to the island, this is one of the perils of living here. You're privy to all the

168

heartache. I'm just so sorry that it's happening to one of your students."

"My favorite student," I said, the emotion cracking in my voice.

"Yes, Martina, so special," he said, sounding as sad as I.

"Well, you also know that Mrs. Gonzales is expecting a baby," I said.

"Yes, I understand they will be leaving just as soon as she delivers."

"That's right. That's where I come in," I said, leaving Carter looking quizzically at me.

"Huh?"

"Mrs. Gonzales wants me to adopt her baby."

"She what?" he nearly screamed and bounced in his chair.

"You heard me, she wants me to adopt her baby because she knows I can't be deported. Isn't that the saddest criteria for motherhood?"

"Oh, my, that is just so, so sad."

"But," I said, "I've given this a lot of thought, and I have so much support from my parents and Christopher and Joy. I'm confident I can be this baby's mother. I really want to be her mother."

Carter took a deep breath and placed his Coke on the desk. Making a steeple with his fingers and placing them to his pursed lips, he averted my gaze and knitted his brow.

I flushed and my heart raced, wondering what he was thinking and fearing his response.

Finally he looked me in the eye and spoke: "Ally, as your principal I feel I would not be doing my job if I didn't consider all the ramifications of your adopting a child whose family is being deported."

"I understand, Carter," I said, shaking and clenching my hands in my lap. Surely my boss couldn't prevent me from adopting Eloisa. And would he even try?

"Consider the precedent you are setting. What if all the teachers felt it their obligation or right to adopt a Latino child?"

I thought of the other three teachers at Pelican Isle Elementary. Mrs. Edna Thurmond was a seventy-year old widow who had purchased a two-bedroom bungalow on the island. She had come out of retirement and begun teaching again in order to afford her small home at the coast. She loved her kindergarteners—and they her—but I doubted she'd want to take any of them home with her.

The second and third grades were taught by never-married fiftyish sisters who lived together in New Oak and drove over the bridge every morning in their twenty-year-old rust-colored Chevrolet. They, too, were great teachers and loved their students; but at day's end they fled the island, never to interact with the residents of Pelican Isle after school hours. I doubted, as well, they'd feel obligated to adopt a child.

"Ally, I know what you're thinking—that none of the other teachers would want to take someone else's children into their homes. I'm sure that's the case. But future teachers may feel differently. I have to consider that."

"I understand, Carter," I said, somewhere between fear and sadness.

After an uncomfortable silence, Carter said, "Ally, I just may be looking for problems where there are none."

I just shook my head in agreement.

"But you do understand that it is a possibility, and I feel I wouldn't be doing my job if I didn't at least consider it.

"Yes, you're right. I just hadn't thought of that."

Carter picked up his Coke and held it with both hands.

"But that doesn't change my mind," I said, somewhat defiantly.

"I'm sure it doesn't, but it had to be said. And if, at some time, the issue arises, we'll just address it. Right?"

"Right," I said, breathing deeply and managing a wan smile.

"That having been said, I want you to know, Ally, that I'll do anything I can to help you. I know that you are sincere, and you deserve the support of your friends. Now, I pray I haven't thrown a damper on your wonderful news because I truly want to know all of the details," he said, finally smiling sincerely and putting me at ease.

So as we drank our Cokes, I told Carter every detail, feeling he needed to know everything about the family of one of his students. And about his first-grade teacher. Despite his trepidation, he appeared understanding and pledged his complete support. He offered me all the time off from school I needed to get Eloisa settled—insisting that he could find someone to cover for me. I knew that he'd be that someone, but I did not want to impose on him to that extent. His job was demanding enough without his having to teach a class of first graders.

"Thanks, Carter," I said when I'd drained my Coke and put the empty bottle in the yellow, wooden crate beside the yellow fridge. "Guess I'd better be getting on home. I have lots of planning to do. Thanks so much for listening. And thanks for your support." And wrapping my arms around him, I said, "Please know that I understand the position I've put you in. I hope it doesn't cause you problems."

Hugging me back and ignoring the potential for complications, he said, "Glad you extended that contract. Don't think any of us could manage without you."

I left Carter's office confident that I had the support of everyone who mattered to me. Adopting a child and being a single mother was not going to be easy, but with the help of my parents and my Pelican Isle Family, we could raise a little girl who would love to read, would know the importance of an education, and would learn how to be brave. She would know the sacrifice her parents had made for her, her heritage, and her customs. And she would be proud to be a United States citizen.

Twenty-five

Martina was reading to the class. Still downcast and reserved, she was apparently aware and saddened over her family's leaving Pelican Isle. But the students and I had coaxed her to read, and she ultimately gave in. She was at her happiest when she was reading, and her cares seemed to take a back seat when she was at the helm of our reading circle. Since she had joined my class, she was reading on a fifth-grade level, an extraordinary feat for a six-year old. Her fellow students loved to hear her read and were mesmerized, and perhaps a bit envious, by a child their age who was able to read so well.

That morning she had chosen FORTUNATELY, THE MILK, a silly story about a father's misadventures during a trip to the corner store to get his children some milk. So funny was the tale, that it was sending the class, including the teacher, into fits of giggles. Even Martina, despite her circumstances, laughed along with us. When the giggling subsided and Martina was able to resume her reading, my cell phone rang. I noticed the call was from Joy. I motioned for Martina to continue while I stepped into the hall to take the call.

"I'm on my way," Joy said. "Chris just called. The baby is coming, and you need to get on over to the clinic. I'll be there in about ten minutes to watch the kids."

In addition to everything else she did, Joy served as a substitute teacher at Pelican Isle Elementary. She knew every student by name, as well as their siblings and parents, and all the children were comfortable in her care. So I felt at ease leaving my sixteen in her charge.

When I stepped back into the classroom, Martina stopped reading, and all the children looked toward me questioningly.

"Guess who's coming to see you?" I said.

"Who?" they all screamed, wide-eyed.

"Miss Joy. And I bet she'll bring crafts."

"Yay!" they all cheered.

Their enthusiasm hurt my feelings a little. But I understood. Miss Joy made me scream, "Yay," too.

I returned my phone to my pocket and told Martina to continue reading. She picked up right where she'd left off, reading flawlessly, showing the pictures to her classmates as she finished each page. My heart broke. She had no idea why I had to be away from class. She did not know that her mother was in the clinic giving birth to her baby sister. She did not know that I would be leaving to claim that little girl as my own and take her home with me. She only knew that she was doing the thing she loved most in the world: she was reading. I prayed she would always have books, would always have someone who would encourage her to read.

I slipped to the break room to gather my purse and jacket as Martina continued to read and her classmates continued to giggle. By the time I returned to the classroom, Joy was bustling through the door, lugging her shopping bags brimming with crafts.

"Well, look who's here. It's Santa Joy," I said

The children all crowed and clapped and ran to greet her.

"Now, Miss Joy is going to stay with you while I'm out."

"Where are you going, Miss Ally?"

"I just have some personal business to take care of, Cara," I said and gave her a wink. "Now please return to your seats and let Martina finish your story. And I'm sure, if you beg her real hard, she'll read you another."

Martina looked at me and smiled behind her sad eyes.

Joy dropped her load and walked me to the door.

"Don't worry about a thing here. Martina and I, and Cara, of course, have everything under control." Then sensing my fear, she clasped my hand and said, "It's going to be fine, Ally. Everything will work out just the way it's supposed to. Now, go. Chris and Eloisa are waiting for you."

When I got to the hospital, Carmen was manning the front desk. She met me, took my arm, and said, "Come on this way. Dr. Chris is expecting you."

As we reached the delivery wing, she handed me off to a nurse who had me scrubbed, gowned and masked, and in the delivery room within minutes. We had discussed my being present at Eloisa's birth, but I hadn't quite made up my mind. Guess the clinic staff had made it up for me.

There was a nurse holding Mrs. Gonzales's hand while another stood by Christopher, who was seated on a stool in birthing position. The nurse holding Mrs. Gonzales's hand smiled behind her mask, making her eyes crinkle, and motioned me forward. Christopher looked up and gave me a wink before he returned his full attention to Eloisa's delivery.

Mrs. Gonzales was bathed in perspiration, her blue-black hair clinging to her face. Her eyes were closed, and she was panting. When she heard me approach, she opened her eyes and tried to smile. Then she released the nurse's hand and reached for mine. I offered it, and she clutched it tight as a labor pain seized her and she emitted a guttural wail. The nurse handed me a cool, wet cloth, and I dabbed at Mrs. Gonzales's steaming face.

"Miss Ally, you came."

"Yes, Mrs. Gonzalez. I wanted to be here when Eloisa came into the world."

"Not Mrs. Gonzales. My name is Graciela."

"Graciela? What a beautiful name."

"Thank you, Miss Ally. It means grace."

I just smiled. Of course it does. Eloisa would be named after her selfless, loving mother.

"Graciela, my mother's name is Grace. I had planned to name our baby Eloisa Grace. Do you like that?"

I tear ran from her eye and she said, "Yes, I like that," as another pain seized her and caused her to cry out and crush my hand with a vice grip. The discomfort shot to my shoulder, but I felt it was small price to pay for my daughter.

"She's crowning," Christopher called out to us. "You're doing beautifully, Mrs. Gonzales. Now, give me just one more great big push."

Graciela turned beet red and let out a blood-curdling cry before I heard a soft, sweet mewl.

And there was my daughter, all six pounds, five ounces of rosy splendor, purring like a sweet kitten, sucking her thumb.

"Oh, she's beautiful," I cried.

I turned to get Graciela's reaction to the birth and found her facing the blank, green wall away from her child, the tears now flowing freely. I turned my attention from Eloisa, knowing that I would have a lifetime to take her in. For now Graciela needed me, so I held her hand tightly and stroked her damp hair away from her face. And I let her cry. Leaving the nurses to tend to Eloisa, I followed Graciela to recovery where I fed her ice chips and let her hold onto me until she drifted to sleep. Only then did I leave her side to see my daughter.

I headed for the nursery where I scrubbed again and slipped into a clean gown. There were four newborns lined up in their little clear plastic cribs. All dark haired, dark eyed and beautiful, I knew immediately which was Eloisa Grace. A mother just knows her own baby. The nurses had cleaned her, and her skin glowed pink. Her beautiful, black hair formed soft waves around her head, and her large, dark eyes, ringed with long, thick lashes wandered the room inquisitively. And still she sucked her thumb.

"Hi, Eloisa Grace," I whispered.

She stopped sucking and stared, transfixed. I reached for her tiny, free hand, and she wrapped it around my finger and held tight. I talked softly to her, and as I did, she cooed back at me, as if she were trying to tell me something. We were chatting and I was caressing her downy head when Christopher joined us.

"Have you ever seen a more beautiful little girl, Christopher?"

He put his arm around my shoulders and said, "I've delivered a lot of babies, but she is, without a doubt, the most beautiful."

I knew he was humoring me, but I didn't care. I was certain I was right. "Is she okay?"

"She's fine, a perfect little girl. *Your* perfect little girl."

Christopher lifted my little girl and placed her in my arms and said, "Why don't you and Eloisa go over to that rocker and get acquainted?"

I held her close to me and kissed her downy head as we made our way to the rocker. By now I had rocked my fair share of babies and loved the feel of all of them as they nestled in my arms. But holding my daughter felt like no other experience I'd ever had. I was accustomed to comforting babies until it was time for their mothers to claim them and take them away. But I prayed no one would ever take Eloisa Grace from my arms because she was my daughter. I was her mother, and I would always have arms to cuddle and comfort her. Eloisa was back to sucking her thumb, and as we rocked, she studied me hard with her beautiful, big black eyes.

Eloisa and I were still rocking when school ended and Joy saw my students onto the tram and came straight to the nursery. She pulled up a chair and began rocking in tandem with Eloisa and me. She beamed at Eloisa, stoked her dark, wavy hair, and agreed that she was, indeed, the most beautiful child ever. I believed she was telling me the truth, not just humoring me.

"Oh, Ally, she's an angel," she said and, stretching out her arms, added, "okay, it's my turn."

Once she was nestled in Joy's arms, Eloisa performed by showing her how she could coo and suck her thumb. Only a few hours old, and already she was so smart.

Handing her back to me, Joy said, "Here you go, Mom." Then she added, "I'm just so happy for you. You're going to be a great mother to this angel. And you, Eloisa, are one lucky little girl."

Then she stood, hugged me hard, and was on her way, saying, "Gotta get some rest. Tomorrow I'm going to need a lot of energy for those students of yours. Either they're getting rowdier or I'm getting older. Probably a little of each, don't you think?"

Once I was alone, the nurses let me feed Eloisa. She took to her bottle right away, but she clearly preferred her thumb, plugging it back in as soon as her bottle ran dry. After eating she burped on cue and fell asleep in my arms, thumb still in her mouth. And as she slept, I rocked her, kissed her tiny, dimpled hand, and promised her that I'd always be there for her.

I stayed through several more feedings and diaper changings and would never have left if the night nurse had not tapped me on the shoulder and said, "Miss Ally, it's three in the morning. You need to go home and get some sleep or you're not going to be fit to take care of this baby."

I left reluctantly, returning three times to kiss Eloisa on her sweet head. Finally dragging myself away, I dropped my scrub gown in the laundry hamper, slipped on my jacket, turned up the collar, and headed out into the brisk middle-of-the-night air. I ran for my golf cart, hopped in, and headed off down a dark, deserted Beach Road. It was so cold out that I could see my breath, even with the curtains rolled down around my golf cart. But I wasn't bothered by the chill as I sang some silly childhood song that I had dusted off and was practicing for Eloisa. I laughed out loud all the way home.

I was on such an emotional high that I felt sure I wouldn't be able to sleep, but I was out before my head hit the pillow. I awoke four hours later, rested, excited, and ready to return to my baby.

I started the coffee while I grabbed a quick shower and a change of jeans. Then I filled my thermal mug, wrapped a bagel in a napkin, and headed back to the clinic.

"You look awful happy this morning," Carmen said as I whizzed by her station.

"Oh, I am, Carmen," I called over my shoulder and waved. I could hear her laughing at my enthusiasm as I rounded the corner.

Instead of heading straight to the nursery to see Eloisa, I stopped by Graciela's room. She would be leaving the clinic before noon and would be leaving the country within the week.

"How are you feeling this morning, Graciela?" I asked, reaching for her hand.

"I'm okay," she said, none too convincingly.

"Have you seen Eloisa?"

"No."

"Would you like to see her, hold her. She's a beautiful little girl."

"No, I can't."

"Oh, Graciela," I said, squeezing her hand and struggling to hold back my tears, "please don't do something that you'll regret. I want to be Eloisa's mother, but I want what is best for her. And for you. If that means she leaves Pelican Isle, you must know that I'll understand."

Yes, I would understand, but it would break my heart—again. I had bonded with Eloisa overnight, and I already felt as if I were her mother. I didn't know if I could endure another broken heart, but I had to let Graciela know that I would understand should she choose to take her when she left the country.

Guess that's what being a mother means.

"This is for the best. I've made up my mind. Eloisa is an American citizen. She deserves to be in America."

"Graciela," I said, taking her in my arms and holding her to me, "I can't be you, but I promise that I will love your daughter with all my heart and be the best mother I can be."

She clung to me as I let her cry for an unfair situation that had no perfect solution.

Twenty-six

I decided that Eloisa should stay at the clinic until the Gonzaleses left Pelican Isle. During that time, Dad's colleagues would draw up the necessary legal documents to move forward with the adoption. I just wanted to make sure that everything was in order before I took Eloisa home with me. Christopher, Joy, and my parents agreed that I'd made a wise decision.

Since Graciela's release from the clinic, she and I had seen each other on several occasions. We'd met on neutral ground, at Peli Pier, in order to keep our connection as impersonal as possible. To do otherwise would have been emotionally draining.

We would sit in a booth, facing each other, only Graciela couldn't look at me. I would order ice tea for the two of us, yet she never touched hers. She would just stare into her lap, her face a rigid mask, all the while twisting her napkin into a tight, stiff string.

Over and over I'd say, "Graciela, you don't have to do this. Graciela, you can change your mind. Graciela, I'm sure there is some other way."

But each time I mentioned other options, she insisted that she was making the only decision possible, that it was the right thing to do for Eloisa. She was thinking only of her daughter, not herself, not her family. Her baby was an American citizen. Eloisa deserved to stay in America. That's all that mattered.

When I was absolutely certain she wasn't going to change her mind, I said, "Would you like to keep in touch with Eloisa? I'd be happy to send you pictures and progress reports."

"No," was all she would say, no matter how many times I offered.

When I knew she wouldn't budge, I said, "I promise you that Eloisa will know the sacrifices you have made for her. I'll never let her forget you. And

I'll tell her all about her big sister Martina. I'll teach her to read and help her get to college." Leaning forward and clutching her arm, I said, "And I promise that I'll make sure she realizes how fortunate she is to be an American citizen."

Still she wouldn't look at me, wouldn't respond. I was convinced her doing so would have broken her heart.

When she rose to leave Peli Pier for the last time, I reached to hug her. She stood hunched and limp, like a woman defeated, and sighed from the weight of her life. She didn't respond, in kind, but just let me hold her awkwardly, her arms dangling limply at her sides. When I released her from the discomfort, she turned without looking my way. I watched her bent back heave and shudder as she shuffled out the door, across the dusty parking lot, and down Beach Road.

"Are you okay, Miss Ally?"

"I'm fine, Enrico," I half-smiled and patted his arm, "only daydreaming."

"Just so you're okay."

"Thanks for asking. I'm really okay. Honest."

I tossed some bills on the table to cover the tea and a tip, half-smiled once more to the skeptical-looking waiter, and headed for the door. Crossing the parking lot, I scanned lonely, cartless Beach Road. I saw Graciela in miniature, trudging, trudging, her head down, her body appearing too heavy for her to bear. I could turn in her direction and offer her a ride home. I was certain, though, that she wanted nothing more from me, that seeing me would only keep the wound raw. So I slid into my cart, steered away from Graciela, and headed to the clinic to rock my baby.

As much as I wanted to spend every waking moment with Eloisa, I needed to be at school. Mostly, I needed to be with Martina. Although I had been able to distance myself from Graciela, I had a physical and emotional ache to spend with Martina what little time she and I had left.

The other children knew that the Gonzaleses were leaving because there's just no hiding deportation. Such news spread like a virus throughout Pelican Isle. Though the children were no longer shocked when it happened, they were still saddened when their friends had to leave them.

I knew it was okay to be sad, but it was not okay to let Martina's time with us go uncelebrated. So I chose to make her last week with us a very special time. Without dwelling on her leaving, we would cherish the time we had left with her and rejoice in what she meant to us.

One day I brought cupcakes, veggie chips, and juice boxes to school, and we had a just-because-we-want-to party. Another day Joy brought her craft bags. We pushed the desks back, spread quilts in the center of the room, and sat in a circle and made friendship bracelets. At the end of the day, the children—without prompting from Joy or me—chose to give their friend Martina all of their bracelets. She slipped each colorful, woven ring onto her wrists, including Miss Joy's and mine, and wore them for the remainder of her time with us.

Martina gave her red, blue, and yellow friendship bracelet to me. I slipped it onto my wrist. Though it has gotten quite frayed and faded and is little more than a string, I wear it to this day.

I asked each child to make up his or her own story about friendship and to tell it to the class. Their stories showed amazing insight for six year olds. Their humor made us all laugh. Their kindness brought me to tears.

Then one morning I surprised my students with piñatas, and we pounded them mercilessly and ate candy all day long.

And we read. We read lots and lots of books. And Martina did most of the reading. The children and I wanted Martina to leave us with her remarkable gift. That last week I watched Martina glow under the care of her classmates. She would be sad to go, of course, but she would leave us knowing that her friends on Pelican Isle loved and cherished her.

At the end of Martina's last day, as the children made their way out the door to the waiting tram, I called, "Cara, please tell Mr. Ruiz to hold the tram."

"Yes, ma'am," she yelled back to me as she clattered down the hall with the others.

"Martina, may I see you for a minute?"

She came to me, and I dropped to my knees in front of her. Eye-to-eye with my all-time favorite student, I took her hands in mine and said, "I will miss you so much. You will always be my favorite student."

Martina ducked her head and whispered, "Thank you."

Then I handed her a small, wrapped gift, a vintage book I'd found on eBay.

"Martina, this book will always remind me of you. It will always be my favorite book."

She opened it, and a smile spread across her beautiful face.

In her sweet, quiet voice she said, "My very own SURPRISE DOLL. Thank you, Miss Ally. It will always be my favorite book too." She opened the book to the doll named Theresa and said, "This is Martina." Then she turned to Mary and said, "This is Miss Ally. We'll always be together."

As I said, six-year olds can show amazing insight.

Before I could cry—again—I opened to the front of the book and showed her the inscription.

She read: "To Martina, my surprise doll. I love you. Miss Ally."

She put her arms around my neck and said, "I love you too, Miss Ally."

Then I handed her her e-tablet, the one with the reading app with stories about brave girls.

"Take this with you, Martina. Read all about the brave girls."

"Thank you, Miss Ally. I will."

Cara came thundering down the hallway and yelled at the door, "Mr. Ruiz says he can't wait any longer. Hurry up, Martina."

"Thanks, Cara. Tell him she's on her way," I called to her.

I stood and took Martina's hand and walked her to the door.

"Never stop reading, Martina."

"I won't, Miss Ally."

I was confident she wouldn't need anyone's prodding, but I so hoped she'd have someone to encourage her.

She turned, and I watched a very brave little girl walk slowly down the hall. When she reached the front door, she turned, lifted an arm full of friendship bracelets, and waved bye to me.

Before I could dissolve into a puddle of tears, I turned my focus from Martina and her family to my child. Eloisa was waiting for me at the clinic. She needed her mother to come to her, to take her home, to nurture her, to teach her to read, to teach her to be a brave girl.

I ran to the break room and grabbed my coat, scarf, and gloves. Bundling myself against the raw wind that was whipping off the ocean, I grabbed my purse and headed for the door.

As I locked my classroom and rushed down the hall to the parking lot, I whispered, "Hold on, Eloisa, Mommy's coming."

Each morning I'd go to the clinic early to hold my baby and promise her that I'd love her and care for her forever. Then when school let out in the afternoon, I'd, once again, return to her to repeat my promise and cuddle her until it was time for me to call it a night and head home for a little rest. I was just counting the moments until I could bundle her and take her home with me.

Finally that day arrived, and Eloisa and I were alone in the nursery, rocking in our favorite chair for the last time. As I cradled her in my arms, she sucked her thumb and made happy, squeaking noises at me, unaware that her world was about to change.

"Are you ready to go home, Little One?"

She sucked hard and furrowed her brow as I talked to her.

"Your grandparents will be here soon, and they are just going to eat you up."

She studied me carefully and sucked even harder.

Mom and Dad were so anxious to meet their granddaughter. I asked them, though, to wait until the morning she was to leave the clinic to arrive on Pelican Isle. My daughter and I had had enough excitement, chaos, and hovering people in our lives, and I wanted to be calmed and settled before they swooped in and assumed grandparenting duty. And I also needed to make sure I could bring Eloisa home with me before they met her. I didn't think they could bear losing another grandchild.

But it was official. Eloisa was truly my daughter. My father had come through with his promise to take care of the legalities, and he had found the best advice to insure that the adoption would progress smoothly. Assured that Eloisa would be his little *nieta*, he and Mom were on their way to greet her.

Between the fear of the major commitment I had made and my joy at being a mother, I said, "I promise I'll do my best. It may not be perfect, but I'll do all I can to be a good mother. You'll like me sometimes and you'll think I'm a jerk sometimes, but we'll get through it together. Just you and me, Kiddo."

And as we rocked, I held her close to me and kissed her precious head, covered with soft, black, wavy hair. I caressed her rosy cheek with my finger, and she smiled around her thumb and squeaked her approval.

"Oh, you like that, huh?" I said, as I continued to rub her little cheek so she'd smile and coo for me.

And as Eloisa and I were talking, I heard a commotion in the hallway. I knew that the excited grandparents had arrived. I looked up to find my mom and dad at the nursery window, hands over their mouths, tears standing in their eyes.

I waved to them and said to Eloisa, "Well, it's time to meet your grandparents and go home. You ready?"

Christopher strode into the nursery and said, "Looks like your ride is here and y'all are ready to go." And reaching to stroke Eloisa's head, he said, "This place just won't be the same without this sweet little girl." Gathering all the baby paraphernalia, he said, "Eloisa, it's time to go meet those excited grandparents."

When we got to the hall, I found my mom and dad giddy with excitement, both reaching for Eloisa, eager to touch her, to hold her, to kiss her.

"Hello, little *nieta*," my mother said, adding, "that means granddaughter in Spanish. Oh, my, she's more beautiful than I ever dreamed. Oh, Ally, oh, Ally," she said, her voice trailing off when she could no longer find words to express her emotions."

Dad reached for Eloisa's hand, and she latched tightly onto his finger.

"Hi, Little Girl," he smiled and whispered, "me and you gonna be good buddies. What do you think of that?"

Again Eloisa furrowed her brow and squeaked at him around her

181

thumb.

"That's right," he said, "you know what I'm saying, don't you?"

Already I could tell that Eloisa and her grandfather were, indeed, going to be good buddies, just as he and I had always been.

And as we made our way down the hall, my mother scurried along beside me, patting Eloisa all the way, while my dad followed close behind. When we arrived at my parents' car, I found that they had installed a top-of-the-line baby seat to take Eloisa home. They were also pulling a small U-Haul trailer full of baby necessities: crib, stroller, dressing table, boxes of disposable diapers, formula, a baby seat for my car, and several shopping bags overflowing with baby clothes that the new *abuela* just hadn't been able to resist.

"Nothing but the best for our granddaughter," Dad chuckled.

"Thank you, Dad," I said, sliding Eloisa into her seat and buckling her into safety.

Christopher shook my dad's hand and gave my mother a warm embrace.

"Thanks for all your help, Chris," she said and patted his cheek lovingly.

"My pleasure, Mrs. Macklemore. And welcome back to the island. So good to see you again."

"Please, Chris, it's Grace and Gray. Why, we're almost family, what with you delivering our granddaughter. Don't you think?"

"I sure do, Grace," Christopher said, giving her another hug and a pat on her back.

Then he took my hand and walked me to the other side of the car where he helped me in beside my daughter. My parents hopped into the front seat.

Christopher leaned in to kiss me on the cheek, and I said, "Are you going to be able to make it for supper?"

"Sure. Norm is covering for me, but I'll need to get back tonight to check on everybody."

"I understand. But we'll have you for a little while."

He smiled at my understanding and said, "Bye, now," closing the door and waving us toward home.

As we made our way down Beach Road, Mom said, "You know, Ally, when I'm away, I forget how lovely this place is. There's nothing more beautiful than that white, sandy beach with those glassy, blue waves crashing to shore. I can see why you wanted to make it your home."

"It is beautiful, Mom, but that's just a small part of why I wanted to make it home. The people are the best part of the island. They make it home."

"And now there's Eloisa."

"Yes, now there's Eloisa," I said, as I stroked my inquisitive little girl who was taking in her new world with her huge, black eyes.

As we pulled into the driveway, I noticed smoke curling from my chimney. Joy would be waiting for us, a fire crackling in the fireplace, lunch simmering on the stove. She had promised from the beginning that she would be there for me all the way. And she had been—tending my students in my absences, caring for Eloisa in the nursery while I taught, readying our home for Eloisa's homecoming. But her help would not end there; she had also volunteered to care for my baby while I taught. I told her that I could find a nanny, but she insisted she was the only nanny suitable for Eloisa.

When she saw us drive up, she stepped out onto the back porch and called, "Come in out of the cold." She wrapped her bulky sweater around herself, stepped from foot to foot, and waved us toward home.

Dad stepped from the car and waved, calling, "Hey, Joy, good seeing you again."

"You too, Gray." And to Mom she called, "Hey, Grace, welcome."

Dad ran around to the passenger side, opened my mother's door, and helped her out. Then he opened the rear door, and, with the flurry of an expert, disengaged Eloisa's carrier from its base. Then he headed up the stairs to where Joy waited, Mom skipping alongside, ready to dive into grandmother duty. They left me to carry the baby items the hospital had given us, along with a few bags of new baby clothes.

"Come in, come in," Joy crowed, as we reached the porch. "Here, let me help you with some of that stuff, Ally," she said, grabbing bags from my hands.

Joy's fire crackled in the fireplace, and my house was warm and cozy. I smelled clam chowder simmering on the stove and Joy's famous jalapeno cornbread baking in the oven.

"Thank you so much for everything, Joy," I said and wrapped my arms around her.

Hugging me back, she said, "Oh, Ally, nothing could please me more than presiding over Eloisa's homecoming party. So y'all get yourselves settled. I have to get back to my lunch." And she disappeared into the kitchen.

Mom already had Eloisa out of her carrier and was rocking her back and forth in her arms, singing some Spanish nursery rhyme she'd learned from YouTube.

"Come on, Honey," Dad said to me, "let's get the trailer unloaded so we can set up Eloisa's room."

So Dad and I left Eloisa to Mom's care and headed for the trailer to bring in the crib and dressing table and enough diapers to last us several months.

I had decided to turn the little office alcove off the living room into Eloisa's room, and we were able to wedge the crib against one wall and the dressing table under the only window. Once her furniture was in place, there was just enough room left for one person to diaper a baby and put her to bed. But that's really all the room my baby and I needed.

Mom handed Eloisa over to Dad while she went to the kitchen to prepare bottles of formula. I stood aside and took mental notes as I observed how the experts cared for an infant.

My dad gently cradled his granddaughter as if he were handling a delicate egg. And all the while he rocked her gently, smiled at her sweetly, and chatted quietly to her. He mesmerized her. She stared intently into his face, sucked her thumb furiously, and squeaked appropriately to everything he told her. Yes, I could tell they were going to be good buddies, the best of buddies.

"Okay, Tita's turn," Mom crowed, charging out of the kitchen, warmed bottle in hand. "Here, hold this for me, Tito, while I change our little *nieta's* diaper."

Dad took the bottle and handed over his buddy to Tita, who retreated to the dressing table in the alcove to change Eloisa's diaper with an expertise that astounded me. It was going to take a lot of practice to be able to master that. When she was clean and dry, Eloisa nestled into the crook of her grandmother's arm to take her bottle and drift off to sleep.

"She's going to be an easy baby, just like you were, Ally," Mom said, holding Eloisa closer and kissing her forehead. When she finished her bottle in her sleep, my mother easily transferred her to her shoulder and rubbed her back gently until she burped. Then Mom slipped her into her crib. Eloisa didn't stir, just sucked peacefully on her thumb as she napped.

"Good timing," Joy whispered when Mom turned from the crib. "Lunch is ready."

We adjourned to the kitchen where we found the table laid with steaming bowls of chowder, as well as Joy's tossed salad with oranges, avocado, and citrus dressing. The breadbasket overflowed with homemade cornbread. It was the perfect homecoming lunch on a chilly Pelican Isle day.

After lunch Joy insisted upon washing the dishes and tidying the kitchen while my parents and I rested. I felt I was taking advantage of her good nature, but she insisted as she shooed us from the kitchen.

"Y'all go relax. Don't worry about me. I'll get my turn with the princess very soon," Joy crooned in her wonderful buttery voice.

Twenty-seven

Just as Mom had predicted, Eloisa was an easy baby. As long as she had her thumb, she was happy. She would suck and hum and play with her toes for hours to entertain herself. She was charming and loving and never met a stranger.

And it appeared she didn't even know how to cry. If she did, she never felt the need. When her diaper was soiled, she'd wail, "Eeeeeee," as if it disgusted her as much as it disgusted me. As soon as I'd reach for a diaper, her "Eeeeeee" would turn to a contented "Oooooo." And if she were hungry, she'd merely grunt, "Uhm, uhm, uhm." When she'd hear me preparing her bottle, she'd smack her lips and pat her hands together. And nap and bedtime were cause for celebration, not tears. When I'd put her in her crib, she'd smile, stick her thumb in her mouth, and hum herself to sleep.

Despite my easy-going, happy child, being a single, working mother had its challenges; I had to learn quickly how to juggle. But what working mother doesn't? It just comes with the territory. But my precious, contented baby made the juggling worthwhile.

Eloisa would wake me early each morning with her good-natured chirping, and our day would gleefully begin with her taking her bottle and waiting patiently and happily while I readied myself for school. Then I'd dress her, and off we'd go next door to Joy's.

Just like everyone else, Eloisa was besotted with Joy. She squealed with delight, as if seeing her each morning were a huge surprise. Initially it hurt my feelings that Eloisa never cried for me when I left her and was just as happy in Joy's company as she was in mine. I soon got over that. What mother wouldn't be wallowing in gratitude for such a perfect set-up. I couldn't have had a more contented child, and I couldn't have found a better nanny. I was thrilled with both. Sure, I missed Eloisa during the day, but I was always glad to get to school and to my students. I was a mommy, but I was also a teacher. Always had been, always would be.

And then there were still the babies at the clinic. I had made a commitment to Joy and to Chris and to the babies themselves to rock them in the afternoons. I tried, oh, how I tried, but I found that I was spreading myself way too thin. I had so wanted to do it all, but there just wasn't enough of me to go around. By the time I left the clinic and picked up Eloisa from Joy's, I hardly had the strength to feed and bathe my child and put her to bed.

"Ally, darling," Joy said one afternoon when I felt—and I'm sure looked—frazzled and exhausted, "you just can't do everything. And no one expects you to do everything. Being a mother is a full-time job. Being a teacher is a full-time job. You will find a way to do both. But we will excuse you from baby rocking. Perhaps when summer comes, you can take some shifts. But for now you need to concentrate on your baby and your students."

I was so relieved to hear her say that, but still I felt guilty. A commitment is a commitment. But Joy and Christopher and Carter and my parents all assured me, so I kissed all my babies and rocked them once more before telling them good-bye. I knew that I would see them out and about on the island and that I'd probably have most of them in my class in six short years.

Even without rocking the babies, my days were stretched thin. It takes time and coordination to learn how to be a working mom. But, in addition to Joy's help, Christopher was there for Eloisa and me, as well. He turned over more and more duties to his staff so that he could spend time with us, often coming for supper and staying to play and help me change and bathe Eloisa and get her to bed. He was so tender and nurturing, as if he were born for the job.

Then once we had Eloisa down for the night, Christopher would stay to play with me. His visits became more and more frequent and got longer and longer.

He'd say, "I just want to stay to make sure she's fine. I think she may be coming down with a cold." And, "I don't like the looks of that diaper rash." Or, "She was pulling at her ear. She may be getting an earache. And, you know, Ally, she likes waking up and finding me here."

Then he finally admitted, "I miss her so much when I'm away."

So his visits progressed to late nights and then to early mornings. And I was glad he wanted to stay, no matter his excuse. I knew that although he missed her when he was away, it was more than Eloisa. I was confident he came for the two of us. Our flurry of texting at Christmas had blossomed into something so special, so tender, so comfortable.

"You don't have to shamelessly use my child as an excuse to crawl into my bed with me, you know," I said, grinning and playfully slapping him.

Grabbing me and pulling me to him, he wrapped his arms around me, threw one leg over me, and smothered me with kisses, panting, "My being here in bed with you has absolutely nothing to do with you. It's all about Eloisa. How dare you suggest otherwise."

Giddy with happiness, I melted into him.

But, still, we both had an ear trained toward Eloisa.

As winter turned to spring, even in my happiness and Eloisa's contentment, I began worrying about my child's and my living arrangement. Come summer I would have to find another home for us. The thought of leaving our magical cottage for the summer months made my heart hurt, but that was my agreement with Dr. Brown. And, of course, at the time I came to that agreement with Dr. Brown, I was planning to leave Pelican Isle—for good—at the end of the school year.

But that plan was no longer in play.

Finding a place to rent on the island was out of the question. Rental rates skyrocketed during peak summer season, and my teacher's salary would not allow for a rental budget that rose overnight from zero to astronomical.

I didn't share my concerns with Christopher and Joy, because I was certain they'd both say, "Oh, you and Eloisa are welcomed..."

I'm sure they'd have both kindly taken us into their homes for the summer, but they had already done more than their share for us. I wouldn't feel right crowding them with me, a baby, and all our belongings. Helping was one thing; housing was quite another.

Guess I could have found a small place in New Oak to tide us over, but I wasn't too familiar with the town, and I just wouldn't have felt comfortable making that temporary move.

There was only one acceptable option: Eloisa and I would return to Raleigh to spend the summer months with my parents. I knew, without asking, that they'd both be in a glee over the prospect of having Eloisa all to themselves for the entire summer. In fact, I was certain they'd already thought of it and were secretly hoping and making plans. I didn't relish the idea of being away from Christopher, but we'd just have to make plans to visit each other—often. It wasn't ideal, and certainly not my first choice, but it was the only practical solution I could envision.

But before I could call my parents to insinuate Eloisa and myself into their home for three months, something remarkable happened. But I had ceased being surprised by the remarkable. My life on Pelican Isle had become a series of remarkables.

Dr. Brown called.

"Ally, Betsy Brown here. How's motherhood treating you?"

"Oh, Dr. Brown, it is wonderful. Eloisa is wonderful. And she is helping me take such good care of your house."

"You just never know the joys that are in store for you when you let go and take a chance," she said. "And I've no doubt Eloisa is a marvelous house guest.

"Ally, I want to know all about your baby, and I have loved the pictures you've sent. She is darling. But there's something else I need to discuss with you. I have another favor to ask."

Oh, no, was she going to ask me to go to Iceland to fill in for a first-grade class of little Icelandics who just couldn't do without me? Surely not since she knew that I'd extended my Pelican Isle contract. But whatever the favor, I could hardly turn her down. She had already done so much for me, had helped change the course of my life—for the better. Much better. I knew I would say yes to whatever Dr. Brown wanted from me.

"What can I do, Dr. Brown?"

"Well, I've just been offered a summer sabbatical in Spain."

"Oh, my gosh. That's incredible. Congratulations."

"Yes, I'm very excited. I'll do a little writing and some teaching. And lots of sightseeing."

"That sounds wonderful. I'm so happy for you."

"Thank you. And, yes, it is wonderful, but it also means I won't be able to spend the summer at Pelican Isle. That part saddens me. I haven't missed a summer on the island since I bought the house twenty-three years ago."

Where was this going?

"Now, I'm not saying my cottage wouldn't be safe, but I just won't feel comfortable leaving it unoccupied with the huge influx of vacationers. Do you think I could convince you to stay on through the summer, just to keep an eye on the place for me?"

"You mean live here all summer?"

"If you will, Ally, I would appreciate it so much. And, of course, it's yours for the next school year, if you want to stay on."

Without a second's hesitation, I cried, "Oh, Dr. Brown, I'd love to stay on through the summer—and next school year too. I promise I'll take good care of it."

"I know you will, Ally. And, thanks, again."

As soon as Dr. Brown said, "Good-bye," I screamed, "Yeeeeeee!" grabbed Eloisa out of her playpen, and spun her up into the air.

She giggled around her thumb, as if she understood our good fortune.

As the school year came to a close, I felt a profound sadness leaving my students. They had all claimed a spot in my heart, but I was aware that in the fall they would move on to another teacher's class and into another teacher's heart. I knew from past experience that saying good-bye to students was inevitable, but I'd never had a class like my first at Pelican Isle. Each child was special in his or her own way, and I had grown to love each one. And I was confident that they all loved me, as well.

As they each hugged me on that last day of school and looked up at me with broad, snaggle-toothed smiles, I was filled with a joy I'd never known. I walked them to their waiting tram and waved them away, all of them calling, "Bye, Miss Ally, I love you, Miss Ally."

As much as I would miss them, I still felt blessed with good fortune. First of all, I would be able to stay for the summer in my magical home on Pelican Isle, thanks to the generosity of Dr. Brown. I also had the friendship and love of Joy and Christopher, both of whom I cherished; and my mom and dad would come on weekends to spoil their little *nieta*. Best of all, I had a beautiful little girl, and I would be spending the entire summer being her full-time mom.

By June my honey-colored Eloisa was three months old and chubby, with a cherub's face full of dimples. She grinned perpetually behind her permanently shriveled thumb and giggled and batted her thick lashes at anyone who dared look her way.

Each morning after breakfast we'd pack a snack—a bottle for Eloisa, trail mix and water for me—slather on sun screen, strap on our hats, and head for the beach. I'd plop her in her mommy front pack, and along the way we'd gather shells and sea glass in anticipation of our Christmas tree. Though she couldn't understand, I'd tell her about our wonderful Christmas traditions and how she would love decorating the tree with Christopher, Joy, and me. I told her that on her first trip to the tree lot, Mr. Robinson would give her a candy cane and that we'd eat a greasy supper at Wendy's before returning to Pelican Isle with our pitifully scrawny tree. She giggled and clapped her hands as if she couldn't wait until Christmas.

We'd stop and talk with vacationers along the sandy shore, making new friends each day. My precious baby was truly a people magnet, charming each and every stranger with her throaty giggle and huge black eyes. I'd jump her up and down in the lapping tide, causing her to pump her chubby legs and squeal with delight.

Eloisa would become delirious with excitement at spying a colony of sand crabs, those strange little translucent creatures that scurry frenetically and stare warily at beachgoers with black, beady eyes perched high on sticks. They looked like tiny Mars Rovers, with their many erector-set appendages that traverse, sideways, the craggy, mini sandhill-terrain of the coastal landscape. But with Eloisa's first shriek, the skittish crabs would burrow into their sand-hole homes of safety. When they'd disappear, Eloisa's chin would quiver in despair, and her huge, dark eyes would begin to puddle, as if she were being abandoned and her heart were breaking.

But I would point out a sandpiper, and my perpetually-happy, easily-distracted baby would forget about the sand crabs and be enthralled by those cunning little birds with the long, straw-like beaks and knees that bend backwards. Even I was mesmerized by little birds that could outrun encroaching tides with long, skinny legs that resembled pipe cleaners and knees that were installed backwards.

When Eloisa tired of crabs and sandpipers and vacationers who pinched her cheeks, I'd give her her bottle, watch her nod off, and then hold her to my chest as she dozed. Then I'd stroll back to our magical cottage, snacking on trail mix and loving life on Pelican Isle.

Back home I'd put Eloisa down in her crib for her afternoon nap. Joy would drop by and sit with her while I cruised to the clinic to rock a baby or two; then when I returned home, Joy would take a shift at the baby nursery. I'd shower, and then I'd bathe Eloisa in the kitchen sink before I plopped her in her baby swing in the corner of the kitchen. She'd rock back and forth, entertaining me with her gurgles, while I fixed a light supper, in hopes that Christopher could join us for a while. More often than not he would.

That first summer on Pelican Isle with my daughter was charmed.

But the three months sailed by, and soon I was looking at a bulletin board that needed to be decorated, desks that needed dusting, a snack cupboard that needed replenishing. And as much as I hated to say so long to Eloisa and our carefree days, I looked forward to a new crop of freshly-scrubbed, angel-faced first graders, a good many of whom were siblings of my former students.

I couldn't imagine my life getting any better.

Twenty-eight

About a month into the new year, I trudged up Joy's steps one Friday afternoon after school to collect my child. It had been a particularly trying week, the children, for some reason, rambunctious, fretful and argumentative. Full moon? Who knows, but their behavior had flat-out worn me out. So when I let myself into Joy's house and called for her, I was eager to gather Eloisa and take her home for a restful weekend.

Joy met me, shaking her head and crying, "It's all my fault. I should never have taken her to the mainland. We're so insulated here on the island. It was foolish of me to expose her. I'm just so sorry, Ally."

Immediately I knew the cause of Joy's distress. My child's nose was running to her chin, her eyes were red and watery, and she had a ragged, croupy cough. She'd been a little sniffly that morning when I'd dropped her at Joy's, but I'd brushed it off as no big deal. Everybody sniffles once in a while. But, apparently, sniffles can be a very big deal. Lesson learned, and I'll know to pay closer attention next time.

"For heaven's sake, Joy, it's not your fault. Babies get colds. She'll get over it. And we'll get through it. Now, you rest so you don't come down with something yourself," I said, cradling my snotty-nosed child with one arm and giving Joy a hug with the other. "Remember, I'm going to need your help again come Monday."

"I'll be here," she said, "if you'll still trust me with your baby."

I gave her a weak smile and one more reassuring hug and turned to leave. As I headed for home, I could hear Eloisa's chest rattling as she barked a wet, raspy cough.

That night Christopher brought over a humidifier which he set up beside the crib, but still my baby rattled and coughed and gasped to breathe. She tried to take her bottle, but her nose was so stopped up she couldn't nurse and breathe at the same time. She was hungry and so frustrated that she flew into an angry rage, a rarity for my near-perfect baby who seldom emitted more than a slight whimper, even at her worst. And in addition to her wailing cry, she would shake until she turned purple. She wasn't even able to suck her thumb, and that was more traumatic than her inability to take her bottle. I spent Friday night and all of Saturday trying to calm her, but she just became rigid in my arms and screamed even louder. By Saturday night her symptoms appeared worse.

I called Christopher in tears. I was worn out from my efforts to care for Eloisa; and my failed attempts rendered me, in my mind, an utter failure as a mother. What's more, I was terrified.

Carmen answered the phone at the front desk of the clinic and must have sensed my desperation. "Hang on, Miss Ally," she said, "I'll page him."

Christopher, too, must have picked up on the urgency of my call because he was on the line within moments.

"Should I bring her in?" I asked, not really sure I had the energy to get us dressed and to the clinic.

"No, I don't want her exposed to anything else, and we shouldn't expose our patients to her cold. Just hold on, and I'll be there as soon as I can."

I was relieved but, out of courtesy, said, "But can you leave your patients?"

"Sure, the nurses can take care of things until I get back."

He showed up soon with a nasal aspirator, a nifty little invention every mother should own, something I will have in my medicine cabinet until the end of time. He took Eloisa from my arms, still crying and shaking and bathed in perspiration, and quickly sucked out each nostril with the little rubber bulb. She emitted one loud shriek but calmed immediately and let out a sigh when she realized she could breathe again.

"Hand me her bottle," Christopher said and headed for the sofa with Eloisa in his arms.

Like the pro that he is, he cooed and patted her and held her close to his chest. Soon he had her calmed and nursing, her eyes drooping from fatigue. She finished her bottle in her sleep. Then he gently transferred her to his shoulder, rubbed her back, and burped her without waking her.

"Stay right there," he whispered. "I'll change her and put her down."

I didn't argue. I don't think I'd have had the energy to argue or change a diaper, so I sat motionless on the sofa. I hadn't slept since Thursday night, hadn't bathed, hadn't eaten, and hadn't sat without holding a screaming, thrashing baby. My joints ached, and my stomach was tied in knots. Even my eyes hurt: burning, throbbing, with lids that scratched like sandpaper as I blinked. So while I gladly let Christopher tend to Eloisa, I curled into a ball, my body buzzing and twitching. I smoothed my tangled hair from my face and hung onto a handful, as if it were a lifeline.

Once Christopher had Eloisa dry and resting peacefully, he returned to me and settled himself on the sofa, gathered me in his arms, and pulled me onto his lap.

"It's okay, Honey. She's going to be fine," he said, dislodging my hand from my hair-lifeline and kissing my palm tenderly. He lifted my chin and kissed my eyelids, my scratching, aching, worn-out eyelids; then he held me close and rocked me back and forth. If I'd had the energy, I'd have cried—from exhaustion, from the feeling of failure, from relief of being cared for by the gentlest, kindest man I'd ever known. But I didn't have the strength to weep, so I just let Christopher rock and comfort me.

"Thanks so much for coming. I don't believe we could have made it through another night alone," I garble-whispered into his chest.

"Of course, you could have," he said, kissing my dry, burning hand and placing it on his cool cheek. "But everybody needs a little help sometimes. Taking care of a baby is hard work, especially when the baby is sick and you're alone and have a full-time job."

"But I should know how to do whatever that was you did to calm her. I'm her mother. I'm supposed to know these things."

"Mothering is a learn-as-you-go sort of job. You're not supposed to be an expert right away. And, Allison, you're not expected to do everything by yourself. Spread the baby care around. Remember, Joy and I said from the start that we were all in this together."

I was too exhausted to agree or say thanks.

"So tired?" he asked into my disheveled hair.

"Um hmmm…"

"Would you like for me to help you shower?"

"That bad, huh?"

"No" he chuckled, "not bad at all. I just thought a warm shower would relax you."

I would have enjoyed soaking in a nice tub bath, but my stand-up shower in my tiny bathroom was the best my home had to offer. It'd have to do.

"Yeah, I think I'd like that."

So he lifted me from the sofa and said, "Here, hold on tight," as he draped my arms around his neck and I rested my head on his shoulder. He carried me to the small bathroom, where he turned on the shower and gently stood me on the bath mat, saying, "You okay?"

"Yeah, okay," I said, limp and barely able to focus my eyes.

"Here, hold onto my shoulder," he said as he stripped my clothes from me and tossed them into the hamper.

He tested the water before helping me into the stall.

"Here, hang onto that rod. I'll only be a minute."

Then he quickly shed his clothes and stepped into the shower with me. Holding me gently around my waist, he shampooed my hair and soaped my body all over. Even my skin ached. Then he removed the hand-held shower nozzle and sprayed the soap and shampoo from by body and down the drain. It felt so relaxing, I melted into his naked body as the spray washed away the stress and anxiety. When the water began to cool, he turned off the shower and helped me back onto the bath mat, where he grabbed a towel and patted us both dry. Carrying me to the bed, he pulled back the covers, laid me on my pillow, and pulled the blanket over me.

Sitting on the edge of the bed, he said, "Can I get you something to eat? You must be starving."

"No, thanks, I'm really not hungry."

"How about some warm milk to help you sleep."

"I don't think I'll need any help," I yawned.

"Some tea?"

"No, really, I don't want a thing. You've done enough. Thank you, thank you so much," I slurred and tried, unsuccessfully, to keep my eyes open.

So instead of fixing me tea, he sat naked on the edge of my bed, caressing my head, holding my hand, kissing my cheeks, my eyelids, my forehead. I felt myself drifting into sleep.

That's when he whispered, "Allison, I am so in love with you. Will you please marry me?"

Women dream of sexy, romantic marriage proposals on the beach, on a cruise, on a mountaintop, over a fancy dinner, accompanied by roses, diamonds, champagne. But what could be more romantic than a man caring for your sick child, then tenderly bathing you and tucking you into bed, after which he sits naked and vulnerable by your side, offering his heart and soul to you?

I tried to speak, but my tongue was swollen and uncooperative. So moved by his love but unable to muster the strength to embrace him, I merely managed the weakest of smiles.

He took me in his arms and kissed my eyes again and whispered, "You don't have to answer me now. I just needed to let you know how much I love you. I know we haven't been together very long, but, Allison, I've wanted to marry you since the day I first saw you. The dating has been just formality."

Willing my eyes to open and my tongue to cooperate, I whispered, "Yes, yes, I will. I love you too."

Smiling broadly and flashing his dimple, the last sexy, romantic gesture I needed before sleep, he said, "Scoot over, I'll stay with you until you doze off."

So I scooted, and as he crawled under the covers, I nestled into him and drifted away as he gently rubbed my back.

I awoke to the smell of coffee. I cracked one eye and found Christopher stretched out beside me, fully clothed in jeans and tee shirt, propped on his elbow, smiling at me.

"Hey, you," I said, my tongue cooperating a little better than it had the night before.

"Hey, you too."

"I thought you were going to stay just until I fell asleep."

"I changed my mind. I couldn't drag myself out of this bed. You just felt too good to leave."

I smiled up at him through slitted eyes.

"And I wanted to make sure that you and Eloisa were all right."

My eyes snapped wide, and I threw the covers back.

"Eloisa?"

"She's fine, Allison," he said, reaching for my arm and stroking it reassuringly. "Her fever broke in the night, and she doesn't have nearly as much congestion. I changed her and gave her her bottle, and she went right back to sleep. Poor little thing must have been worn out."

Since Friday afternoon my life had been a blur of stuffy noses, sponge baths, temper tantrums, fitful rests, fevers, and a very frightened new mother. Then Christopher had shown up to calm my baby and me. He had tended us through our crisis and...

"Christopher?"

"I Immmm?"

"Did I dream...?"

"Dream what?"

"Did you propose to me last night or did I dream that?"

"Not a dream. I did propose to you last night," he said, scooting closer and kissing me gently on my lips.

"Did I say *yes*?"

"Yes, you did. I hope your answer is still *yes* in the light of day."

Now wide awake, I said, "Christopher, did you propose to me because you thought I needed to be rescued?"

"Of course not. Why would you think that?"

"Well, you didn't ask me to marry you until I was knee-deep in sick child and crying out to you for help."

Taking me in his arms, he said, "Allison, I don't think you need rescuing. You're perfectly capable of taking care of yourself. Look how far you've come. But I do think you need to be loved."

As I opened my mouth to protest, he put his finger on my lips and said, "And so do I. And no one else can love me but you. And I want to be the only one to love you. And Eloisa too. You know that I love her so much, and I want the three of us to be a family."

Smiling and confident that Christopher didn't consider me a rescue, I said, "Then yes, yes, I want to marry you. I want to love you. And I want you to love Eloisa and me."

"I do, I do," he said and gathered me in his arms, sealing his proposal with a deep, tender kiss.

When he released me, I said, "I need some of that coffee."

"Then stay right there, and I'll go get you some."

"Thanks, I was hoping you'd say that."

So I ran my fingers through my bed head, plumped my pillows, pulled the covers back over me, and waited for Christopher to return.

"Here you go."

"Mmmm, just the way I like it, sweet and light. Thanks."

Once the coffee revived me, I said, "What time is it?"

"A little after seven."

"Don't you have rounds this morning?"

"Yeah, but my patients won't go anywhere. They know I'll show up soon. I just needed to make sure that my best girls were all right before I left." And, laying his coffee on the bedside table and cupping my cheeks in his warm hands, he said, "Allison, you and Eloisa are the most important things in the world to me, more important than the clinic."

That's when I knew, for sure, that Christopher truly loved me deeply and wanted Eloisa and me to be his family.

"Guess I need to make another trip to Raleigh," I told Christopher. "This isn't something I can tell my folks over the phone. First, a baby. Now, a marriage proposal. They are going to suffer shocking-news overload."

"Want me to come with you?"

"Yes, but I think this is another one of those things I have to do alone."

"Don't you think I need to ask Gray for your hand in marriage?"

"That would be nice, but I believe I need to ease them into the idea first. Then you can pay Daddy a visit."

"I guess you're right."

Eloisa had recovered from her cold and was cooing at me as if she had never screamed and thrown tantrums and caused me a moment's distress. She squealed with delight as I carried her to the car. I attempted to buckle her into her car seat as she grabbed for her belt in order to *help*. Her attempt to help at only six months old was a clear indication of things to come. She would show early signs of independence, and some of her first words would be *Do it self!* So I gave into her help, and eventually the two of us had her secured in her car seat. Then she giggled and waved her arms at me, so excited that she was going for a ride. Had she understood that we were on our way to see Tita and Tito, she'd have passed out from sheer delight.

Once my parents had gotten used to the idea of my adopting Eloisa, they'd thrown themselves into grandparenting with a vengeance. They took to calling themselves Tita and Tito to everyone, as if that had been their names since birth. Regardless of what they had accomplished in their lives, their new and sole identity was grandparent. My dad went into phased retirement, and my mother bought new luggage. Then they traded their SUV for a fuel-efficient hybrid, and most weekends they burned up the highway to Pelican Isle to visit their little *nieta*.

"We just don't want to miss a single milestone. Why, what if she sat up by herself or stood up and we weren't there to see it. We'd just never forgive ourselves."

As my parents made Pelican Isle their second home, we, somehow, out of sheer love, I'm sure, managed to make do with our cramped magical cottage. Joy and Christopher had both offered bedrooms, but Tita and Tito would have none of that. They wanted to be where the action was, with Eloisa. And Eloisa and I wanted them with us, as well.

Though refusing Joy and Christopher's hospitality, they did come to know them both very well and to love them as I did. They especially loved that Christopher had delivered Eloisa and that Joy was caring for her while I taught. Whenever Mom and Dad visited, we'd have family meals with my two Pelican Isle friends a part of the family.

They knew that Christopher and I were dating, but they knew that our dates consisted mostly of wiping runny noses and sneaking an occasional semi-romantic Peli Pier meal and a private evening at his house. They approved, but they especially approved of having a doctor nearby for their granddaughter's health and safety.

But how would they feel about Christopher's and my plan to marry so soon? As with my news about adopting Eloisa, I had practiced my speech all the way from Pelican Isle to Raleigh. And just as before, it was much easier practicing on myself than it was telling my parents.

"Mom, Dad, I have some news."

My parents got that ghostly stare, and they glanced at each other with a what-has-she-done-this-time look on their faces.

"It's good news."

"Yes?"

"You know Christopher?"

"Yes?"

"As you know, we've been dating."

"Yes?"

"Well, he's asked me to marry him."

Clutching her heart and crying out, Mom said, "Oh, Sweetie, you had us scared there for a minute."

"And you're okay with this? You know, we haven't been dating long."

"Ally," Dad said, "your mother and I knew the minute we saw you with that young man that there was more than friendship between you two."

And Mom added, "Why, yes, I told your father, 'You mark my words, Gray, those two are in love. I can see it in their eyes. It's only a matter of time before he pops the question.'"

"Can't get anything past you two," I said to them, shaking my head in relief.

"Oh, parents know these things," Mom said, patting my hand maternally and rolling her eyes at Dad conspiratorially.

"So you do approve?" I asked them once more.

"Darlin'," my mother said, "we think Chris is a fine man. If he loves you and Eloisa and you love him and he makes you happy, then, yes, we approve."

"Oh, thank you," I said, putting my arms around them and hugging them close. "I do love him. I really do. I didn't think I could love again after Cam, but I believe I can."

"Ally," my mother said, smoothing my hair from my face, the way she always did when she talked seriously to me, "you deserve to find love again. Cam loved you so much. He would never have wanted you to be alone. You do know that, don't you?"

"Yes, ma'am, I believe I do."

Then my dad said, "I've seen Chris with Eloisa, watched the way he cares for her. You can tell a good man by the way he treats his children."

"You should know, Daddy," I said and wrapped my arms around his neck once more and kissed his cheek.

Mom joined us in a group hug.

Eloisa had been resting quietly in her kiddie seat, pulling off her socks and examining her toes, but when she saw my parents and me embracing, she abandoned her toes, clapped her hands, and crowed with delight.

My mother lifted her from her seat, hugged her to her and said, "You are one lucky little girl. You have the best mommy ever, and soon you'll have a wonderful daddy. Isn't that terrific?"

Eloisa shrieked, threw up her hands, and blew raspberries at her Tita.

Twenty-nine

When I told Christopher that my mom and dad had given us their blessing, he let out his breath in a whoosh of relief.

"Well, then, now that that's settled," he said, "let's set a date. And I say the sooner the better. I don't want to wait any longer."

"Me either. I want to be with you, and I want you, Eloisa, and me to be a family."

"I've waited so long for you to say that, Allison," he said, reaching for my hand and kissing it.

"Don't mind me," Joy said. "I'll just sit right here and knit and mind my own business. Carry on. Plan your lives."

Christopher and I both laughed. We had just finished supper and were sitting on Joy's back porch, watching the sun go down. Joy knitted while Christopher bounced Eloisa on his knee.

"Thanks, but we are your business," I said, "and don't you forget it. If it hadn't been for you, we probably wouldn't even be planning a wedding."

"Y'all didn't need me. Love finds a way. All you two needed to do was follow the sparks," Joy said, her needles clicking away as she talked.

"What do you say we get married right out there on the beach?" I asked.

"I was hoping you'd say that," Christopher said. "I can't think of a better place. It's the perfect wedding chapel."

I grabbed my phone, tapped my calendar, and began scrolling.

"How does October twenty-fifth sound?"

"That's just three weeks away."

"So?"

Seeing that I was undaunted by a three-week deadline, he said, "Well, if you can be ready by then, I'm sure I can find someone to cover for me at the clinic."

"If I can be ready? All we'll have to do is walk across the dune, stand on the beach, and say *I do*. Right? The way I see it, the only thing missing is someone to marry us."

Without hesitation Christopher pointed to Joy.

"What?"

"Joy."

"What about Joy?"

"She can marry us."

"You can marry us?"

"Sure can," she said casually, her needles going click-click-click without pause.

"I knew you could do just about anything, but I didn't know you were a preacher. When were you ordained?"

"I'm not an ordained preacher."

"Then what are you? A judge? A ship's captain?"

Joy laughed and said, "Neither. I'm a magistrate."

"A magistrate? How did I not know this?"

"I guess the subject just never came up."

"Well, it's up now. So how did you become a magistrate?"

"A judge over at the county seat appointed me."

"But why? How?"

"Well, it seems Pelican Isle needed someone to handle minor skirmishes and perform weddings for people who wanted to get married on the beach but didn't have a preacher."

"Like us."

"Exactly."

"No offense, but what are your qualifications?"

"Oh, no offense taken. It's a reasonable question. Let's see, my qualifications...nobody else wanted to do it. So, voila! I was qualified."

"Simple as that, huh?"

"Simple as that."

"And how long have you been a magistrate?"

"How long, Chris?" Joy asked, looking up from her knitting and furrowing her brow.

"Hmmm, about twenty-five years?"

"Sounds about right," she said, her needles clicking once again.

"Well, I guess I can trust that you know what you're doing if you've been at it about twenty-five years. So, will you marry us?"

"Can't think of any marriage I'd rather officiate," she said, resting her knitting in her lap and smiling over at Christopher and me.

"How many marriages have you performed?"

"Oh, goodness, I've lost count."

"Well, then, how many skirmishes have you settled?"

"Three. Two involved golf carts, and the other had to do with the rightful ownership of a crab trap. Real high-profile, controversial cases. They were all over the national news. All parties involved ended up in federal prison."

I laughed and said, "Thank goodness I don't own a crab trap, and I'll make sure to behave myself in my golf cart."

"You do that, young lady. I'm a stern magistrate," she said, stabbing a knitting needle in my direction.

Having found a stern magistrate to marry us on the beach, Christopher and I began making a list of all the things we needed to do, because, as it turns out, getting married is really not as simple as walking across the sand dune and saying *I do.*

So on Monday afternoon, when the tram ferried all of my students out of sight, I carted up to the clinic where Chris was waiting.

He hopped into the passenger seat when I coasted to a stop, leaned over and kissed me, and, squeezing my hand, said, "You still sure?"

"Still sure, so sure," and kissing him back, I said, "I love you, you know."

And as Christopher settled back for the ride, I pulled out onto Beach Road and headed for the south end of the island and the ferry over to New Oak. When we passed Carter's office, we found him locking up for the day.

I tooted the toy horn that emitted a reedy beep-beep, and he turned and threw up his hand and yelled, "Good luck, you two."

He knew that we were on our way to get our marriage license. He was taking credit for our relationship since he had been the one to introduce us, right in the sandy parking lot in front of his office.

We passed only five or six carts and a couple of cars on our way to the south end of the island, which was standard for off-season on Pelican Isle. Once we arrived at the village, though, we found a flurry of activity at the dock, where the mainland restaurant kitchen managers bartered with fishermen for the freshest catch of the day, and seagulls squawked and shrieked overhead, begging for scraps. The harbor open-air market, where vendors sold everything from herbs and vegetables and fruit to hand-made jewelry to leather goods and clothing, was abuzz.

The ferry had just pulled into the dock, and weary workers carrying hard hats and lunch bags spilled from the gate and made their way on foot toward their homes or second jobs.

"Just in time," Christopher said, as we hopped out of the cart and he reached for my hand.

I loved holding hands with Christopher.

Cam didn't like hand holding, said it seemed childish, as if I were a little girl he was helping across the street. He preferred that I take the crook of his arm as we walked—like adults. Even though it reminded me of my grandparents, I didn't tell him that. I just took the crook of his arm. Like an adult.

But not Christopher. He loved holding hands, and I glowed each time he reached for mine. His touch was gentle, his hands so soft and nurturing. From time to time he'd give me a little I-love-you squeeze and lean in for a sweet kiss. Cam also didn't like public displays of affection; he said our love was personal, just for the two of us. But Christopher wanted the world to know that he loved me and that I loved him back.

So hand in hand we raced to catch the ferry that would soon be making the return trip to New Oak. We filed on with a few dozen late-season vacationers and day-trippers and made our way to the front of the vessel. I clutched the railing as the early fall breeze tossed my hair and rocked the ferry while Christopher stood behind me, wrapping one arm around me and holding on to the railing with the other. He nuzzled my neck and didn't care who watched.

Several pleasure boats zoomed by, creating a wake that sloshed against the ferry, causing it to bob to and fro. The boaters waved merrily as they passed, and we waved in return, acknowledging their joy.

Then an ear-splitting blast from the ferry's horn told us that we were about to set sail from Pelican Isle, headed for New Oak.

We shielded our eyes from the quickly setting sun as we watched pelicans and gulls soar overhead. As we churned our way from shore to shore, we bumped elbows with our fellow passengers and shuffled for sure footing while we rocked in the choppy waters. In just ten minutes Christopher and I reclaimed our land legs as we stepped from the ferry onto the dock at New Oak.

As much as I love Pelican Isle, I always enjoy visiting the quaint hamlet of New Oak. The downtown streets are laid with cobblestones dating back to the 1700's, and many of the brick, ivy-covered buildings that face the oak-lined avenues are the original structures. The historic, ornate courthouse, directly across the street from the ferry dock, houses the Clerk of Court's office where we would apply for our marriage license. Taking my hand and squeezing it excitedly, Christopher practically skipped across the cobblestones and raced me up the steep, age-worn steps.

"Let me guess," said the tiny, blue-haired woman behind the front counter. "You two want a marriage license," she said, smiling broadly, her chocolate brown eyes dancing behind ornate fashion glasses.

"How did you know?" we both asked.

"Oh, I've been in this business a long time. I can tell. You've got that happy, gettin'-married look in your eyes."

"Well, you're right," Christopher said, squeezing my hand and smiling at me.

Reaching her hand toward us, she said, "Name is Roberta. Been helping people get married for forty-eight years. And every one is just as fun as the first."

"Good to meet you, Roberta. I'm Christopher, and this is Allison," he said, reaching to shake her hand.

"Nice to meet you folks too."

And with the precision of a finely-tuned watch and someone who had done this many times before, Roberta flipped and sorted and shuffled the papers that would make our union official and legal..

"Good luck, you two. I have a really good feeling about y'all," Roberta said, after we'd signed on the dotted line and she'd packaged our documents and presented them to us.

"We do too," Christopher said.

"Thank you, Roberta," I said, and reached across the counter to hug her good-bye.

Out on the courthouse steps, Christopher looked at his watch and said, "Oh, shucks, the stores are closed. I was hoping we could pick out an engagement ring over at New Oak Jewelry. Guess we'll just have to come back Saturday."

"Sure, Saturday, that'd be fine," I said, even though an engagement ring didn't seem important to me. I didn't need a sparkly symbol to tell the world that Christopher and I were in love, that we were committing to spending the rest of our days together. But if he thought it was essential, I'd return with him to New Oak on Saturday and look at engagement rings. "Saturday it is."

"It's a date," Christopher said, slipping our license into his pocket.

"A date," I agreed.

Then Christopher said, "I worked up quite an appetite in there. You hungry too?"

"Yeah, I am. I didn't have lunch today. Kinda had a case of butterflies and couldn't eat," I said, smiling sheepishly.

"You too? Glad to hear I wasn't the only one," he said, laughing and grabbing me in a hug.

Looking up and down the street, we settled on the Pepto-Bismol-pink former Esso station that had been converted to a hamburger restaurant. Serving only hamburgers, any way you like them, and French fries, Jo and Bo's had been in business for twenty-five years and had been written up in Southern Living, Coastal Living, and Our State Magazine, the triumvirate of southern-cuisine praise, a true indication that a restaurant has arrived.

Grabbing my hand and tugging me down the courthouse stairs, Christopher said, "I haven't had a Jo and Bo's hamburger in ages. I need a fix."

He'd get no argument from me. Who was I to dispute Southern Living, Coastal Living, and Our State Magazine's assessment of the place.

Jo and Bo's was packed with diners, as it always is. But a long wait for a Jo and Bo's hamburger is well worth it. We joined the snaking line behind a behemoth of a man wearing tight jeans and an even tighter white tee shirt. He sported numerous colorful tattoos on his rippling arms, as well as a tattoo of barbed wire encircling his neck. He stood glaring at the Latina cashier behind the counter, his legs splayed wide, his arms crossed in defiance, his biceps bulging menacingly. When it came his turn to place his order, he strutted to the counter and spoke in a booming, twangy voice, enunciating each syllable clearly, so that all the customers could hear.

"Si' si', Senorita," he said, with a sick smirk on his face. "I want uno hamburger, all the way, except no tomatoes. Gimme a super-size fry and a giant Co-cola. Comprende?"

The cherubic-looking cashier with a blue-black ponytail to her waist and sparkly, jet-black eyes flushed with embarrassment and quickly looked down at her order screen. She repeated the rude customer's order in broken English: "Yes, sir, one hamburger, all the way. One super fry. One giant Coke. Will that be all, sir?"

"No, no, my senorita. I said no toe-may-toe. Nein, nyet, nada toe-may-toe. Now do you comprende?"

"Yes, sir, no tomato," she said, adding his special request to the order. "That will be nine dollars and eighty-seven cents."

Licking his beefy thumb and counting ten singles from a wad of bills, he dropped them on the counter rather than handing them to the cashier, saying, "That'll be thirteen cents change, Senorita, in case you can't count American money any better than you can speak American English."

I felt Christopher tighten beside me and take a sharp breath. I looked up to see him narrow his eyes and clench his jaw. But he didn't say a word, just looked straight ahead.

When the man's order arrived, he picked up his tray, turned to us, shook his head in apparent disgust and said, "Stupid spic. If they're gonna come to America and take our jobs, the least they can do is learn to speak our God-given English."

First of all, I didn't realize that God had given us English, and, secondly, the woman certainly hadn't taken my job and I doubted his, either. But I wasn't going to challenge this Neanderthal in any way. He was awfully intimidating. I just looked away, as if he weren't there. Christopher, on the other hand, wasn't as cowardly as I. A head shorter and half the girth of the guy, Christopher apparently had held his tongue as long as he could.

"How's your Spanish, Bud?" he said to the rude customer.

"I don't need to speak no Spanish, Bud. I ain't going to Mehico. She come to my country, the good old U S of A. She needs to speak English."

"Well, it sounds like she's trying real hard, don't you think? The least we can do is show her a little patience and understanding. Perhaps some encouragement would be kind and neighborly."

"Hey, what business is it of yours, Bud?" he sneered.

"It wasn't any business of mine at all, until you engaged me in conversation and called the woman who was helping you disrespectful names," Christopher replied.

As he remained cool and just stared up into the red face of the mountain of a man, the guy clenched his jaw and balled up his fist.

I prefer to distance myself from public scenes, but I had no desire at all to distance myself from Christopher. As frightened as I was, I had never been so proud to be seen with him. So I reached out and grasped his hand in solidarity.

The guy, thank goodness, relaxed his fist, because I'm guessing his mama had taught him you can be as rude and disrespectful as you please, but you must never take a swing at a lady. So instead of taking a swing at this lady, he just squinted his beady, close-set eyes and scowled at us, turned, and clomped away on huge, high-heeled cowboy boots. As he clattered away, I noticed that the toes of his boots were laughably long, narrow, and pointed. They curled up on the ends, giving his feet a comically elfin look. It kept him from appearing quite so menacing, and I had to stifle a giggle of relief.

Christopher turned to the embarrassed woman behind the counter, smiled at her, and placed our order in fluent Spanish. I have no idea what he said beyond hamburgers and French fries, but I'm sure he included a heart-felt apology and a sincere thank you. I could sense the tension release from the woman's body as she relaxed and smiled sweetly at Christopher. Then she read back his order in Spanish and tallied his bill for him.

Christopher pulled bills out of his wallet, placed them in her outstretched hand, looked her in the eye, and said, "Gracias."

As we waited for our order, I looked quizzically at Christopher and said, "You know, my ancestors came to North Carolina hundreds of years ago. I'm not sure what language the Native Americans living in North Carolina at that time were speaking, but I'm pretty sure it wasn't English. And I'm certain my ancestors didn't learn the native tongue. Had they, I probably wouldn't be speaking English."

Christopher put his arm around my shoulders and kissed me on my head. "You so get it, Miss Allison. I couldn't love you more than I do at this very moment."

When our order arrived, Christopher released me, grabbed our tray, and headed for the only available booth—directly across the aisle from Neanderthal man. As we sat and Christopher doled out our supper, he began chatting animatedly in Spanish. I didn't understand a word he was saying, but each time he paused, I'd glance across the aisle, throw my head back, and laugh hysterically. As Christopher chatted and I laughed, the guy ate faster and faster, cramming hamburger and fries into his mouth, slurping loudly through his giant straw. When he finished, he grabbed his tray, gave us one angry parting glance before clomping to the trash receptacle, dumped his trash in the container, stashed his tray, and headed for the door. Just as he reached for the handle, everyone in the restaurant began clapping. Without looking back, he headed for his beat-up red pick-up truck and swung himself high into the driver's seat. I'm certain he could see all of us laughing through the window as he tried and tried and tried to get his engine to turn over. Once he'd successfully revved the motor, he sped from the parking lot, spewing gravel angrily as he disappeared.

"Sorry that guy got to you," I said. "What a jerk."

"Oh, Ally, it's not just that guy. It's every sanctimonious bigot who accuses the residents of Pelican Isle of taking jobs from actual, entitled United States citizens. Their words, not mine. Allison, do you know of anyone who would want a job gutting fish or scrubbing strangers' toilets?" When I just scrunched up my mouth and shrugged my shoulders, he said, "Yeah, didn't think so. That stealing-jobs excuse is nonsense, just a flimsy argument to discredit hard-working people. They do jobs that no one else wants, and they do them with dignity and respect. They are the hardest working people I know—just like my mom and grandparents—and they take their jobs seriously and are very grateful to have those fish-gutting and toilet-scrubbing jobs."

His eyes flashed with passion as he clenched and unclenched his fists while he spoke.

"Allison, not one soul on Pelican Isle is on welfare or unemployment. They all pay their own way. If someone is down on his luck, neighbors, friends, and family help out till he can get back on his feet. And even though many could qualify for food stamps, no one accepts them. They did not come to this country for a handout or to take something they don't deserve or haven't earned. They came to work hard and give their families a safe, fighting chance, a chance they couldn't have in their own countries. I wish people could understand that."

"I do. I understand it, Christopher."

"Yeah, Miss Ally, I know you do. Otherwise, I couldn't love you so much," he said, finally smiling at me and softening me with his dimple. "Now, finish that hamburger so we can make it to the ferry before it floats off and leaves us."

When we made our way to the landing, we could see the ferry heading our way, about halfway across the sound. With a little time to kill, we bought a sack of breadcrumbs from a vendor to feed the screeching, grateful gulls while we waited for our ride.

As we tossed crumbs at the greedy birds, I asked, "What were you saying in Spanish while we were eating?"

He looked at me, flashed his dimple, and said, "I was telling you about the time a friend and I went to get the scrawniest Christmas tree in all the land. After we'd found our perfect tree, the lot proprietor gave my friend a candy cane. On our ride home she shared her candy cane with me, giving me the crooked part, the best part. I was pretty sure that I was already in love with my friend, but her giving me the crooked part of her candy cane sealed the deal, made me know for sure that she was the woman of my dreams."

I stood on tiptoe, put my arms around Christopher's neck, and gave him an I-love-you-too kiss. I didn't care who was watching.

When the ferry chugged to a halt and the gate dropped into place, only two couples, dressed in tuxes and cocktail dresses, exited and headed toward town, the women teetering on spiky heels over the cobblestones, the men holding them steady and upright.

"Mayor Berkley must be having one of his soirees tonight."

"Well, if it requires spiky heels and a cocktail dress," I said, "I hope I never get an invitation."

Handing our bag, still half full of bread crumbs, to a young boy and his sister, we climbed onto the ferry in our comfy jeans and tennis shoes. Once again, we made our way to the front, where Christopher opened his jacket and welcomed me in to ward off the early-evening chill that was coming from the choppy sound. On the return trip, he held me close, and our bodies swayed as one to the sensual rocking rhythm as we watched the sunset turn the blue sky to a swirl of pink and purple.

When we reached Pelican Isle, the village was still bustling. The island businesses didn't maintain New Oak merchant hours. They'd keep the fishing docks and vendor market open until the last shoppers spent their last dollars, tired, and headed for home.

Clutching my hand, Christopher said, "Want to look around?"

"Sure," I said and headed for the open-air market.

"Hi, Miss Ally, Dr. Chris, can I help you with something today? Our herbs are fresh. And our fruit is always the best on the island." Then laughing gustily and looking over his shoulder, he said behind his hand, "But don't tell Carlos I said so. I'm sure he'd swear that his is the best."

"Well, Mr. Ortiz," I said, "I have no use for herbs since I rarely cook, but I'd love some of those apples and maybe an avocado, the very best on the island."

"For you, the best of the best," he said, as he sorted through his stock and bagged four apples and an avocado.

"Thank you, Mr. Ortiz."

"How is my Jose' doing in school?"

"He's a wonderful boy. Smart too. He's a delight to have in class."

Mr. Ortiz beamed.

I love telling parents how great their kids are. It makes their day and always leaves them smiling and proud.

Next Christopher and I passed a tent where a vendor was selling hand-smocked dresses. I stepped in to browse and came upon a stunning pale-pink sundress with shells embroidered around the hem of the skirt. The handwork was so delicate and intricate, the fabric so soft to the touch. I held it up to me and knew immediately that it was meant to be mine.

"Oh, look, Christopher, isn't it lovely?" I said, swaying from side to side, the skirt swirling around my legs.

"You'd look beautiful in it, Allison."

"I think so too," I said, admiring myself in the tall, smoky mirror with black flecks that hung from a pole in the middle of the tent. "Christopher, I want to wear this when we get married. Don't you think it would be just perfect," I said, so hoping he'd agree.

"Yes, perfect." he said, and turned to the proprietor. "We'll take that pink dress, Mrs. Hernandez."

"And, look, there are baby dresses too," I cried, when I discovered the rack of tiny pink, blue, white, and yellow smocked dresses.

They were so delicate, each hand smocked and embroidered in detail with tiny rosettes or daisies, shells, bunnies, ducks. They were all so precious, I had a difficult time choosing just one for Eloisa. But with Christopher's help I decided on a white one, embroidered with pink bunnies. I was certain my beautiful honey-colored baby with black hair and black eyes would upstage the bride in her darling little dress.

After we'd paid Mrs. Hernandez, Christopher said, "Anything else?"

"I don't believe so. I'm a little tired. I think I'm ready to head for home."

Taking the fruit bag and dresses from me, Christopher reached for my hand as we headed toward the market exit on our way to our cart.

"Wait, look," I said, when we passed a vendor booth with a display of silver and turquoise jewelry. "Isn't this beautiful?"

"Sure is," he agreed and to the vendor said, "Hey, Mauricio, you've been working hard, man. You've got a lot of new stuff here. It's great," he said and picked up a bracelet and turned it over in his hand.

"Allison, this is Mauricio Cruz, my cousin. His father, Mauricio, Sr., was my mother's little brother. Mauricio, this is Allison Albright," my fiancée.

"Oh, I know all about Miss Ally. Nice to meet you, and congratulations, you two."

"Nice to meet you too, Mauricio," I said. "Your jewelry is exquisite."

And while Christopher and his cousin chatted, I admired Mauricio's inventory. There were wide, silver cuffs embellished with turquoise, drop silver-and-turquoise earrings, pins with large turquoise stones, turquoise necklaces. Each piece was intricately hand-made and one of a kind. All were exquisite. Then I saw it: a simple silver band with varying shades of rectangular turquoise stones encircling it. I picked it up and slipped it on my ring finger. It fit perfectly. I held it up to the light.

"Look at this, Christopher. Isn't it beautiful?"

"Yeah, all of Mauricio's stuff is great."

But this ring wasn't just great. It was special. It spoke to me. And looking at it on my finger, I knew that it was where it was meant to be. It was supposed to be mine.

"This is my wedding band."

Taking my hand and looking closely, Christopher said, "It really is beautiful, but don't you want a diamond engagement ring?"

"No, I don't. I want this silver and turquoise band. It's perfect. I love it. It's far more beautiful than any diamond ring."

Christopher smiled and said, "I agree. It is perfect."

And turning to his cousin, he said, "Mauricio, do you have a ring like this in my size?"

"Well, not exactly. You know all my pieces are one of a kind. But I can find you something similar," he said, as he sorted through more inventory behind the counter until he found a similar ring in Christopher's size.

When Christopher tried it on, we knew, we just knew. They were the ones.

"I'm so glad the jewelry store wasn't open," I said and threw my arms around Christopher's neck.

"So am I."

After we paid Mauricio for our wedding bands, Christopher slipped them into his pocket and patted it, saying, "I'll hang on to them for safekeeping."

"Good idea.

"Now I'm ready to go pick up Eloisa and head home to crash. How about you?"

"Me too," he agreed.

Christopher drove the return trip. We rode with his arm around me, my head resting on his shoulder. I was almost asleep when we pulled into my sandy drive.

As soon as we deposited our purchases at my home, Christopher said, "Let's go get Eloisa. I bet she'll be happy to see her mommy."

"Ooooooo," Eloisa squealed and clapped her hands when she saw

Christopher and me come through the door.

"Hey, Miss Big Stuff," Christopher said, as he grabbed her and twirled her over his head. She shrieked with delight.

"Did you have a productive trip to New Oak?" Joy asked as she gave me a hug.

"Wonderful trip," I said, smiling at Christopher. "Not only did we get our marriage license, we also got Eloisa's and my dresses for the wedding and our wedding bands. And some apples and an avocado."

"Well, I'm glad to hear you got the apples and the avocado. Can't get married without those."

"Thanks so much for keeping Eloisa late for us."

"We've had a fantastic day," Joy said. "In fact, we're not through playing yet."

"What do you mean?"

"Eloisa thinks, and I agree, that you two deserve a whole night to yourselves. So she has decided to spend the night with me. She's already had her supper and her bath, so we're just going to play a bit more and read until bedtime."

"Are you sure, Joy?"

"Absolutely."

"What do you think, Christopher?"

"I think Eloisa is a very astute young lady," Christopher said and flashed his dimple, sealing the deal for me.

Thirty

"Okay, kiddos, sit down and stop fidgeting. I have something to tell you."

With the wedding less than a week away, I felt that I needed to let my first graders know about it. I loved my new crop of students and knew, for certain, that they already loved me, but no more than they loved their Dr. Chris. I figured they'd approve of our marriage just as much as my parents did. And I was certain their feelings would be hurt if I didn't let them in on our plans.

They all jumped into their desks, folded their hands, and began swinging their legs back and forth in anticipation of my news. As they stared at me with precious, innocent faces, their smiles wide, their eyes dancing with excitement, I said, "Dr. Chris and I are getting married this Saturday."

Before I could finish, there were whoops of delight, and four of my little girls jumped from their seats and rushed me, wrapping their arms around my waist, hugging me tight. When the rest of the class saw the group hug, they too raced from their desks and joined us.

Twirling and jumping, they squealed, "A wedding, oh a wedding, can we come? Please, please, Miss Ally. Can we come to your wedding? We'll dress up in our best clothes, and we promise we'll be real polite."

Christopher and I had planned to marry quietly on the beach with just Eloisa, my mom and dad, and Joy sharing our day with us. Yet I had opened a can of worms, and I feared there would be no getting that lid back on. But why shouldn't they come to our wedding? One might say they were partially responsible for my getting married or, at least, one of the reasons I had met Christopher. What's more, we certainly wouldn't be pressed for space; we'd have the entire beach as our wedding chapel. And I'd love sharing my happy day with my darling kiddos.

So I said, "Of course, you're all invited. I wouldn't think of getting married without you."

They ramped up their squealing several decibels, and there was just no settling them down. As hard as I tried, I couldn't get another minute's work out of them for the rest of the day. The girls wanted to talk about princesses and fairy-tale weddings and beautiful gowns and tiaras, and the boys just used the girls' excitement as an excuse to act like rowdy boys. I finally threw my hands up in defeat and took them out to the beach and let them twirl and leap their energy away.

Word spread, and soon the second graders, who had been my students the year before, came to my classroom and begged, "Oh, please let us come to you wedding. Please, please."

Then the third graders and kindergarteners felt left out. So I went from classroom to classroom and said, "Dr. Chris and I would love for all of you to come to our wedding on Saturday. In fact, we'd be very sad if you didn't come."

Mom and Dad arrived Friday night, and the four of us squeezed ourselves into my tiny home, a home that seemed to be getting tinier as Eloisa grew and acquired more baby paraphernalia. Mom brought Eloisa an adorable white bonnet with a wide brim to wear with her white smocked dress. She said it was to keep the sun off her face, but I knew she's gotten it because she knew just how adorable Eloisa would look in it.

Though we were taking a huge chance planning an outdoor wedding in the heart of hurricane season, we awoke to a perfect day. The sun shone in a cloudless blue sky, and a soft, balmy breeze kept the temperatures hovering in the mid seventies. Even the ocean, usually roiling and choppy in early fall, was turquoise blue and placid as a lake. The ever-present gulls and pelicans circled overhead. Only a school of dolphins frolicking off shore could have made the day more picturesque.

Dad took over the care of Eloisa while Mom helped me get ready for my day. Though I was capable of taking care of my own hair, we both wanted her to fix it, as she had when I was a little girl, as she had for my marriage to Cam. Since I'd moved to humid, sunny Pelican Isle, my dark blonde hair had turned into a halo of curls shot through with golden sun streaks, so Mom smoothed it away from my face, a few small, curly wisps breaking free, and secured it with two fragrant gardenia blossoms from Joy's yard.

"Mmmm, don't these smell wonderful, Mom. They remind me of Gramma."

She smiled and agreed that they did smell like Gramma's yard, but I could tell by the look on her face that she wasn't thinking of gardenias or Gramma. She was thinking of that first time she helped me pin my hair back and held my gown as I stepped in.

"I'm really happy, Mom."

"I can tell you are, Ally, and I'm so happy for you," she said, caressing my check.

"I love Christopher, love him a whole lot."

"I know you do, and I know that he loves you so much. It's written all over his face each time he looks at you."

"I know, Mom."

Kissing my cheek, she said, "Now, what else can I do to help?"

Checking the clock and realizing we had just thirty minutes, I said, "Could you give Eloisa a quick sponge bath while I finish getting ready?"

"I can't think of anything I'd rather do," she said, and was off to find Tito and her *nieta*.

I put on a little make-up—blush, lipstick, mascara—something I rarely did since my arrival on Pelican Isle, and slipped on my simple pink sundress and stepped into my strappy white sandals. Then I stuck Christopher's silver and turquoise wedding band on my thumb.

I found my mother and Eloisa in my daughter's tiny alcove of a bedroom.

"I think I'm ready, Mom."

"I know you are, Darlin'. You look beautiful, just glowing."

"Thank you so much for everything."

"Ally, your dad and I couldn't be happier for you. We love Chris, and we know that he'll be good to you and Eloisa," my mother said, kissing my baby on her chubby cheek and making her scrunch up her shoulders and giggle.

"Well, then, I believe it's time to get a move on, don't you think?"

"Here, take Eloisa. I'll go slip into my dress and get your dad."

Alone with my baby, I bounced her on my hip, pulled her shriveled thumb from her mouth, and said, "Say Mama. Ma. Ma."

She grinned and wrinkled her nose at me and returned her thumb to where it felt most comfortable. I was so hoping she'd call me Mama on my wedding day. But no matter how hard I coaxed, she just grinned around her thumb, as if she were taunting me.

"How about Dada? Da Da. Da Da."

She'd giggled and patted her chubby hands together, teasing me. But still she refused to say Mama or Dada.

I was still coaxing when I heard, "You look so pretty, Ally."

I turned to see my dad, looking spiffy but casual, in white linen slacks and a light blue shirt. Mom was on his arm. She was lovely in a blue flowered silk dress with a full, flowing skirt.

"Thank you. And thank you for being here with me."

"There's no place we'd rather be," Dad said and smiled like the proud father that he was.

He and Mom took Eloisa and me in their arms one last time and held us tight before we headed out the door and down the boardwalk to the beach.

As we approached the end of the wooden walkway, Joy and Christopher came into view, standing side-by-side on the beach, their heads together, the two of them smiling and sharing their secrets, as usual. And as I crested the dunes, I saw our guests—well over a hundred of them—waiting for us to join them. It appeared that every student from Pelican Isle Elementary had come to our wedding, each accompanied by a parent or grandparent, an aunt or uncle, or an older sibling. And there in the middle of my precious students stood Carter, his arms spread wide, corralling as many of the children as he could fit into his hug. He was dressed in his fancy attire—long, khaki pants and a button-down shirt—and his hair was combed neatly and slicked to one side. Christopher and I were special to him. This day was important to him. That touched my heart.

And when the children saw me, they all flapped their hands and whisper-screamed, "There she is. It's Miss Ally! Hey, Miss Ally!"

Carter smiled broadly and waved.

I, too, smiled, my eyes filling with tears of joy, and waved back as Eloisa clapped her hands and gurgled.

That's when it happened: it had taken over a year, but all the pieces just clicked into place like tumblers in a lock. And I finally got it. At that moment I realized that I was not the knight in shining armor who had ridden into town on her white steed and, as a favor, had saved the school children of Pelican Isle Elementary. No, it was they who had saved me. They and their families had brought me back to life and had made me realize that I was a good teacher, that I *needed* to be their first grade teacher at Pelican Isle Elementary.

Joy, beautiful Joy, with her butter-soft voice, had shown me, with great patience and kindness, what it means to be a good neighbor, a dear friend, and a loving, selfless, caring human being.

Carter had taken a chance on a broken, wounded young woman merely on the recommendation of a mutual friend, and he had proven to be the caring, jolly friend Dr. Brown had promised he would be.

Graciela Gonzales had made the ultimate sacrifice for my precious Eloisa and had trusted me to care for her child because she deserved to stay in America.

Eloisa had come into my life to show me that, yes, I was a mother.

And Christopher Cruz had come to shake some sense into me. He had also come to show me that I could move past grief to love and be loved again.

As I grinned at Christopher, I climbed down off that white horse that my ego had been riding since the day I'd appeared on Pelican Isle, kicked off my sandals, and made my way across the sand to my Pelican Isle family.

When Eloisa and I reached Christopher, he took my hand and gave the two of us pre-wedding kisses. Then our excited little guests, dressed in their finest and as polite as they had promised they'd be, made a ring around us and stared up at us, all grins and shiny black eyes. Joy smiled at Christopher and me and reached out to take our hands.

Just as she began, "Dear friends, we have come in love and happiness today to join Allison and Christopher...," Eloisa took her thumb out of her mouth, stretched her arms toward Christopher, and said, "Da Da."

We had decided, or so I thought, to end our wedding with a quiet lunch at Peli Pier. Since it is the hub of Pelican Isle activity, it seemed like the appropriate place to celebrate. Christopher, Eloisa, and I would go in my golf cart while Mom, Dad, and Joy would follow in Joy's. After racing Eloisa into the house for a quick diaper change, we headed for our carts. But when we reached Beach Road, we found a parade of streamer-and-balloon-decorated golf carts stretched into the distance. Mr. Ruiz's school tram, overflowing with balloon-toting children, was at the head of the parade. As we pulled onto the road and turned in the direction of Peli Pier, the procession of cheering wedding guests followed us toward our destination.

"What's going on?" I asked Christopher.

Shrugging innocently, he said, "Heck if I know."

I didn't buy it for a minute. I knew he was behind this, whatever *this* was. But as we traveled Beach Road, our entourage laughing and cheering and tooting their horns behind us, Christopher was the picture of dumbfounded cluelessness.

We could hear the mariachi band two blocks away, and as we neared Peli Pier, I saw that the doors and windows were thrown open, the building festooned with balloons and strings of twinkling lights. Still Christopher looked as astounded as I.

We maneuvered our cart into the parking lot, and my parents and Joy pulled in beside us, followed by our island caravan, everyone chattering with delight as they leapt from their carts and headed toward the music. Christopher slid out of the driver's side of the cart and came around to help Eloisa and me from our seats. Then Mom and Dad and Joy were beside us, all of them grinning slyly. That's when I realized that I was the only one who wasn't in on the plan. Everyone, all the people who loved me, had arranged this party for me. After hugging my parents and Joy and thanking them for their caring, I took Christopher's hand and entered the teeming restaurant, an excited Eloisa squealing and wriggling in my arms.

Franco Sandoval, the owner of Peli Pier, met us at the door, his arms spread wide.

"Welcome, my friends. And congratulations. Come, party. Let's eat and dance till the food is gone and our feet give out."

He took our arms and led us to the dining room, where we found the mariachi band, buffet tables groaning under the weight of food, and a huge contingent of Pelican Isle residents. Someone, I'm guessing Enrico, had moved the dining tables from the center of the room to make way for the band and to create a dance floor. I found some of my little girls already stomping away to the music, testing the dance floor with their sassy moves.

Rosa Soto, the mother of my student Perla, embraced me and said, "Miss Janice said the dusting could wait. She said Miss Ally's wedding was much more important than a clean house. Oh, I'm so glad. I wouldn't miss this for anything."

"Thank you so much, Rosa. That means so much to me. I'm so glad you and Perla are here."

Dominic Gutierrez, the manager of Island Grocery, had taped a BE BACK LATER sign in his front window.

"I didn't know how long this party would last, so I didn't give a time. But nobody is going to need groceries because everybody will be right here," he said, laughing and flinging his arms wide.

Miguel and Ramona were with Dominic. They were still in uniform, jeans and blue Polos with Island Grocery embroidered on the shirt pockets, having just come from work. But they were dressed perfectly, as reception attire seemed to run the gamut from jeans to frilly dresses.

"You look so pretty, Miss Ally."

I turned to find Bianca with her beautiful children, Cara and Mateo.

"Oh, Bianca," I said, giving her a one-armed hug while Eloisa leaned forward and gave her a slobbery kiss on her cheek. "I'm so glad you came. You know, you were one of the first people I met when I arrived on Pelican Isle. You were so kind and welcoming. I'll never forget that."

"Yes, I remember the morning you came in for breakfast for the first time."

"And you gave me free corn sticks."

"That's right, Miss Ally. We were all just so happy that you'd come to Pelican Isle to teach our children."

"Come, eat while the food is hot," bellowed Franco, and the children lined up politely and quietly, as they always had for me.

The tables were filled with all of Peli Pier favorites: fried shrimp, the best fried chicken this side of my mom's kitchen, cole slaw, hush puppies, butter beans, pecan and lemon meringue pies. In addition, every guest had brought a favorite dish—everything from salads to desserts to scrumptious, spicy Mexican foods. It all looked delicious, but I was much too excited to eat. I preferred greeting our guests, hugging my students, catching up with islanders who had taken time from work to share Christopher's and my joy.

"Come dance with us, Miss Ally," my little girls squealed from the dance floor. They were so adorable they brought a lump to my throat and tears to my eyes. Oh, what I'd have missed had I told Dr. Brown that I would not be taking the teaching job on Pelican Isle. The thought hurt my heart.

The dance floor was aswirl with their rainbow-bright dresses, all embellished with lace and sequins, each standing out from starched crinolines. The dancers pranced around on strappy little silver or white sandals with diminutive high heels, their tiny toenails painted shell pink or blue or green just for the occasion. Their mothers or grandmothers or older sisters had washed and curled their dark, lush hair, and it hung in shiny ringlets down their backs and bounced and swayed as they strutted and clattered and twirled. I was so in love: in love with Christopher and Eloisa and Joy and my tiny, twirling students and my newfound friends. I was in love with Pelican Isle.

"Go to Da Da," I said to Eloisa, as I handed her off to Christopher.

Then I kicked off my sandals and joined my delightful children on the dance floor. They giggled and squealed, as little girls do when they get excited, all of them clambering to hold my hands, hold my skirt, hold onto my arms, to teach me to stomp and twirl and be the happiest and most carefree I had ever been in my life. The floor shook as we kept time to the music, the children keeping better time than I, and soon the room was just a wonderful, radiant blur of color. I laughed a laugh I thought I no longer knew, as we dancers joined hands and circled round and round till dizziness and giddiness and sheer euphoria took over.

After three dances I was glowing with perspiration and panting, while the little girls were still going strong. Spreading my arms, I crouched and gathered them to me and told them how very much I loved them all. They assured me that they loved me back, and I kissed each and every one of them before returning to Christopher, Eloisa, Joy, Carter, and my parents.

Once I'd caught my breath, I realized that I'd worked up an appetite. So I made my way in bare feet past the still-twirling dancers and still-blaring mariachi band to the buffet table, where I loaded a plate with enough food for a family of four. But I planned to eat every bite myself.

I returned to my family and friends where I ate and greeted well-wishers and laughed and thanked God for the gifts of Pelican Isle.

When I'd cleaned my plate and leaned back and sighed, Carter stood, reached out his hand, and said, "May I have a dance with the bride?"

"Not more of that, I hope," I said, pointing to my still-gyrating students.

"Oh, no, that's not my style," he said.

And pulling me to my bare feet and leading me to the dance floor, he encircled me in his arms and glided me effortlessly around and around.

"Carter, I had no idea you were such a wonderful dancer."

217

Winking at me, he said, "I'll bet there's lots about me you don't know."

"Where did you learn to dance so well."

"I was raised over in Greensboro. My father was a heart surgeon. I went to private schools and attended cotillions at the country club. Squired me quite a few young ladies to the Debutante Ball in Raleigh too. Being a good dancer just went with that territory."

"Well, you dance beautifully, Carter. I'm impressed. Do you get to dance often?"

"Why, as a matter of fact, I do," he said, looking right proud of himself. "I teach dance lessons over at the Arthur Murray studio in New Oak."

"Carter," I gasped, "I had no idea."

"Told you," he said, and twirled me round and round.

"Thank you, Carter. Thank you so much for *everything*, my friend."

He just smiled and continued to show off his smooth moves.

When our song ended, he guided me back to my family, gave me a hug, and said, "And thank you, Ally, for everything."

Thirty-one

"Christopher, we just can't. I can't."

"Sure we can, my love," he said, smoothing my hair away from my face and flashing his dimple.

"Stop that right now. Your dimple isn't going to work this time."

"Oh, of course it will. It always works," he said, grabbing me and nuzzling my neck.

"Listen, Christopher, we've been married only two months. Eloisa is still an infant. She's not even walking yet. What's more, she's not out of diapers. And what about my students? I can spread myself just so thin. My kids need me."

Chris grinned slyly and said, "Oh, really, Miss Ally? I thought you'd just signed on for one school year."

I slapped him good-naturedly on his arm and said, "Point taken. I'm hooked, and you know it. No deportation for Miss Ally. But I don't want to slight them, Christopher. They've come to depend on me."

"I know they have, Allison," he said, scooting closer to me on the swing and putting his arm around me. The night was chilly, so I snuggled into his side and stuffed my hands into the pockets of my down-filled jacket. Then he told me, "I'd never ask you to take anything away from them. But I'm not expecting you to do this alone. You have me, you know. And there's always Joy."

"Always Joy. Don't you think that at some point Joy is going to cry uncle?"

"Never. Joy is with us for the long haul. She loves us and will always be up for another challenge. And then there's Tita and Tito," Christopher added to shore up his argument. "Why, they're practically Pelican Islanders."

"But another baby? Where would we put another child? We're cramped as it is, and I know very well that you'd never consider moving to a larger house."

After Christopher and I married, Eloisa and I moved from our tiny, magical home to Christopher's house, toward the north end of the island. It had three bedrooms, but it wasn't a great deal larger than Dr. Brown's home. But Christopher loved the place, and I knew that we'd be there, overlooking beautiful Parmeter Sound, until the end of time.

"That's right. I really don't want to move, but we can make this work. I know we can. I've already thought this through, at least the sleeping-arrangements part. The new baby can bunk with Eloisa for now so your parents can have the third bedroom. We'll revisit the situation when the children get older. So, you see, for now, problem solved."

The sleeping-arrangements part just might work. But that wasn't all that was involved in planning for a new baby.

"I just don't know," I whined when I'd run out of arguments, arguments that had gotten me nowhere.

"But, Honey, the mother isn't going to keep the baby. She's only fourteen. And the adoption agency thinks we'd be perfect."

"Christopher, just because we've adopted one child doesn't mean we'd be perfect to adopt them all."

"Not all, Allison. Just one more."

"Just one more is a lot to ask, Christopher."

"But just think how much joy Eloisa has brought into our lives."

Of course Christopher was right, but just how much joy could one mother handle?

Then he turned to me, took my face in his hands, and said, "It's a boy, Allison. He'll be our son."

I reached up and curled my fingers around his hands and squeezed as I watched his eyes fill with tears. I knew he was thinking about the young mother who could have easily chosen to give him up for adoption. Instead, she had given her life for him and had surrounded him with people who loved him and wanted a special life for him. But this little boy's mother was just a child herself. She didn't have the strength and courage of the young mother who had raised Christopher. So she was choosing to give up her son. Christopher wanted the special life his mother had given him for this little boy who could be his son. Our son.

And with the tears spilling over and dripping from his chin, Christopher said, "And, Allison, he needs a dad. Every little boy needs a dad. Please, please, I want to be his dad."

Since Christopher had legally adopted Eloisa, he had said on numerous occasions, "I want to be a good dad to her. Children need a father. I love being Eloisa's father."

He took his job as father very seriously, and he talked regularly of the importance of fathers in their children's lives.

Once I'd said, "Christopher, are you sorry you didn't look for your father?"

Biting his lip and thinking about it for a moment, he replied, "You know, when my mom offered to help me find him, I decided that I didn't want to. I felt looking for an absentee parent would have been disloyal to my mother, the one who had done all the heavy lifting, the one who raised me all by herself."

"I understand that."

"But it was my mother's decision to do all the heavy lifting. She didn't even give my father a chance. Who knows, maybe he'd have wanted to help. Maybe he'd have wanted to know me, wanted me to be his son. You see, I've never looked at it that way. Until now. Until I found out what it feels like to be a dad.

"Maybe I've missed a lot by not knowing my dad. Maybe my dad has missed a lot by not knowing me."

His admission made me so sad for him, so I said, "Christopher, it's never too late. I'll help you look, if you'd like."

"No, I think the time to look has passed. I'm a middle-aged man. Who wants to be a dad to a middle-aged man?" he asked, showing a grief in his beautiful green eyes that I'd never seen before.

I'd brought up the subject on several occasions, but each time Christopher just became more despondent and no closer to knowing his dad. I hated his sadness over never having had a father, but I didn't want to pressure him and cause him more pain. Also, it was a decision Christopher had to make for himself.

There was going to be a little boy who needed a father. Christopher didn't want him to grow up looking for a dad who wasn't there. I understood that, but, as I'd said, we couldn't adopt every child whose mother felt she couldn't keep it. Weren't there other parents willing to take this little boy?

I needed some time alone to think, just as I'd taken time alone to think about adopting Eloisa.

"Stay here and listen in on Eloisa," I said. "I need to go for a walk."

Smiling, Christopher kissed me on my cheek and said, "I understand. This is a lot to ask."

"Yeah, it is," I said, kissing him back.

I pulled the hood up on my jacket, shoved my hands deep into my pockets, and headed for the beach. Just as it was on the night I took a walk to think about Eloisa, the surf was roiling and rumbling, the waves huge as they crashed to shore. The stars overhead shone brightly in the absence of lights from the houses hibernating for the winter.

I walked and walked and thought about the little boy whose mother wouldn't keep him, a little boy who needed a dad and a mom. As I walked, I thought of my own parents who had always been there for me. I never doubted that they would be, so I took their parenting for granted. Christopher, on the other hand, had grown up never knowing his father. He had a very loving mother, as well as grandparents and other family members who cared for him. And he had Dr. C and Joy. But he did not have a father, a dad. And that was very important to him. He didn't want to run the risk that this little boy would be fatherless.

Christopher had loved me back to life and had supported my decision to adopt a little girl whose family was being deported. He not only agreed with the adoption, he helped me raise Eloisa, even before he was her father. Christopher deserved to be the father of this little boy. This little boy deserved and would be lucky to have Christopher as his dad.

It wouldn't be easy. Life never is. But Christopher wanted this little boy to be our child, and I so wanted more children with Christopher. I just hadn't expected to be a parent again so soon. I trudged toward home, knowing that adopting another child when Eloisa was still a baby would be a challenge. But I believed that Christopher and I were up to the task.

When I walked up onto our front porch, I found Christopher still sitting on the swing, Eloisa's baby monitor at his side. I sat down next to him, put my arms around him, and he rested his head on my shoulder. "You're right, Christopher," I said, "every little boy needs a dad. And a mom. It won't be easy, but I believe we should adopt this little boy.

"When is our baby due?" I asked him.

"What would y'all think about our moving to Pelican Isle—permanently?"

My folks were with us for a visit. We had just finished eating supper and washing the dishes and were relaxing on our back porch, overlooking the sound. Eloisa's eyes drooped as Dad rocked her and hummed to her. Joy and I had enlisted Mom to knit hats for the clinic babies, so she and I had pulled out the knitting bag and were working on tiny caps. Christopher was helping us, attempting to untangle a ball of yarn that had, somehow, managed to tie itself into a zillion knots.

He looked up from his untangling, smiled, and said, "I think that's great, Gray."

But before my father and husband, who had become BFFs, could seal the deal, I said, "But, Dad, you have a job. How can you just pick up and move to Pelican Isle?"

"Well, you know I'm practically retired, just going into the office a few days a week. I think it's time I go from practically to absolutely and make it official."

"Are you sure that's what you want, Dad?"

"Honey, I've always loved the law, but I find I love my granddaughter far more than I ever loved my job."

"And, Ally," Mom added, "with a new baby on the way, we think you might just need a little help. And then there's Joy. Surely, she'll need a hand caring for two babies. Don't you think?"

"Well, sure, Mom, but I don't want you to change your lives to accommodate my family and me."

"We don't consider it an accommodation, Darlin'. Your dad and I have talked it over. It's what we want to do—if it won't be an imposition."

"An imposition? You kidding?" Christopher cried. "There's nothing we'd love more."

"Well, then," my dad shrugged and said, "now that that's settled, I guess we need to be looking for a Pelican Isle home. Know anybody who wants to sell a house?"

"Hmmm, I just might," Christopher said, pointing to the house next door. "What do y'all think of that place?"

Dad stopped rocking, causing Eloisa to stir. He squinted his eyes and said, "Well, the yard looks mighty overgrown and the place seems as though it could use some work, but I believe it just might be doable. Is it for sale?"

"I think it could be. Herb Hammond owns it. Lives over at New Oak. He and his wife, Tillie, used to spend summers over there. Tillie died three years ago, and Herb hasn't been back to stay since then. Says it's just too painful. He hasn't mentioned selling it, but I just might be able to persuade him."

"And I'd love it," my Mom said, "being next door to y'all."

"Well, then, I'll go talk with Herb."

Christopher Cruz is a very persuasive man. Mr. Hammond was a little reluctant at first, but when Christopher told him about our growing family and my parents' desire to be near us, he knew we would love and care for his and Miss Tillie's cottage. Mom and Dad assured Herb that he would be welcomed at his beach home whenever he wanted, and within a month they closed on the fully-furnished house next door.

So my parents returned from Pelican Isle to Raleigh, where Dad made his retirement official, collected his gold watch, and backed a U-Haul trailer up to the garage door. Then he and my mother proceeded to fill the U-Haul with all their treasures and memories: silver and crystal, the artificial Christmas tree and the red and silver ornaments, Dad's record collection, their antique furniture.

When they couldn't wedge another item into the trailer, they toted the treasures of their lifetime together over to Goodwill and said, "Suppose y'all know some folks who'd like to make some special memories with this stuff?"

Then they filled their car with summer shorts and winter sweats and put the only furniture Mom couldn't part with, her mid-century modern Formica dinette set, into the now-empty U-Haul.

Then they gave the house key to their long-time friend and realtor, Peggy, and said, "Just call us when we need to sign on the dotted line."

Then they gleefully set off to begin their new life in their drafty, age-worn, shabby-chic cottage with mismatched furniture and an overgrown yard on Parmeter Sound at Pelican Isle.

It was an unseasonably warm winter day, and Dad was out digging in the yard. While Eloisa napped, Mom and I had rearranged the furniture the way she liked it and, against my protests, installed the pictures of me from birth to college on their paint-challenged walls. We had just taken an ice tea break when Christopher called.

"It's time. He's on the way."

"Be there as soon as I can. Love you, Christopher."

"Love you, Allison."

"Mom, the baby is on the way."

Taking the tea from my hand, she shuttled me toward the door, saying, "Go, run, Darlin'. We have everything under control here. Eloisa will be just fine with Tito and me."

"Thanks, Mom," I said, stopping just long enough to embrace her. "Again, I couldn't do it without you."

"Again, we wouldn't want you to do it without us," she said, smiling tenderly and patting me on the cheek.

And running out the door, I called over my shoulder, "Will you call Joy?"

I made it to the clinic in twelve minutes and was out of the cart before it came to a complete stop. When I reached the front desk, Carmen said, "Better run. The baby's coming now."

So I rushed to the birthing center just in time to slip into a gown and cap and scrub my hands. I was getting to be an old pro at this.

Christopher was seated on a stool, telling the young woman on the delivery table, "Push, Benita, push."

Benita just bellowed but didn't push.

"Just one more big push. That's about all it'll take."

"I can't, Dr. Chris," she cried, her dark hair sticking in ringlets to her wet, red face.

She looked like a child, a scared child. And she was all alone. Where was her family? Her parents? They probably couldn't get off from work to accompany their fourteen-year-old child to the clinic to give birth—more evidence that life could be so difficult for the residents of Pelican Isle. I took her hand and brushed her hair from her face.

"You're doing great, Benita. I know it hurts, but it's almost over," I said to her.

"Miss Ally," was all she said before she clamped down on my hand with the force of steel, arched her back, turned bright red, and, with a blood-curdling scream, gave birth to our son.

He was perfect, just as Eloisa had been. Nine pounds, eight ounces with a head full of black hair, he had lungs to match his size. He screamed lustily and shook his balled fists in the air.

"That's my boy," Christopher murmured and winked at me.

One of the nurses cleaned him up, weighed him, and swaddled him in a sweet blue blanket.

She approached Benita and said, "Would you like to hold him?"

Benita turned to the wall and said, "No, I want to go home."

"Are you okay, Benita?" I asked, still clutching her hand.

"I just want to go home," was all she'd say.

"Can I do anything for you?"

"No. I said I just want to go home," she said, raising her voice and gritting her teeth.

So I left her to the nurses' care while I followed my baby to the newborn nursery.

I found him quieted, his round little head covered in a blue-and-white striped Joy cap, wisps of curly, black hair peeking out from the edges.

"Oh, yes, I want to hold him," I said, when the nurse motioned to me.

He was so big, over three pounds heavier than Eloisa had been at birth, but he was beautiful, with large black eyes and fat, rosy cheeks. I settled in a rocker and held him close to me.

"Would you like to go home with me?" I cooed to him, as he tried to focus his eyes on my face and furrowed his brow curiously.

"Beautiful, isn't he?"

Lost in cuddling my little boy, I hadn't heard Christopher come in. He drew a chair near, sat, and began stroking our baby's cheek.

"Thank you so much, Allison," he said, leaning forward and kissing me.

"My pleasure, Dr. Chris. He's perfect, isn't he?

"Yes, in every way."

"Want to hold him?"

"Of course I do."

I passed our son to Christopher, and our baby was soon asleep in his father's arms.

I heard the door to the nursery open and turned to see Joy rush into the room, fully gowned and capped, grinning broadly.

"Okay, my turn," she whispered and reached for our baby. Christopher handed him over, and we watched Joy settle into her rocker.

"Oh, my goodness, he's beautiful. Have you decided on a name?"

"Finally," I said, smiling Christopher's way.

"Christopher Macklemore Cruz," Christopher said proudly. "We thought Gray and Grace would like that."

"Oh, I'm sure they will," Joy said.

"We're going to call him Mac." Christopher said. "Mac Cruz. Sounds like a cool dude, don't you think?"

"Yeah, a real cool dude," Joy laughed.

"Well, I'm going to head on home and leave the cool dude to you guys," I whispered. "And I'm sure Mom and Dad are anxious to get a look at their grandson."

"*Nieto.*"

"What?"

"*Nieto.* Grandson. Really, Allison," Christopher laughed, "you need to be boning up on your Spanish."

Kissing him on the lips, I said, "Sorry, Christopher, I don't have time to learn Spanish. I'm too busy taking care of children. Lots of children."

ALLISON

AND

CHRISTOPHER

AND

ALL THE REST

Thirty-two

"Well, dear hearts, I'd best mosey on home," Joy said, as she gave us all a hug and a peck on the cheek, hopped into her cart, and cruised toward her cottage.

"Yeah, I'd better head on out too," Carter said, inching toward his cart, reluctant to leave our group he'd come to call family.

Joy and Carter had joined Christopher, the kids, and me, as well as Tita and Tito, for hamburgers on the grill. We'd gathered around the picnic table in our back yard overlooking Parmeter Sound and, after eating, had watched our babies toddle in the grass and wave at the vacationers taking early evening cruises in their pleasure boats. Then Joy had stayed to help Mom and me bathe Eloisa and Mac and wrestle them into their pajamas, while the men washed the dishes.

Mom said, "I guess Tito and I had best get on home too. I noticed your dad nodding off after that second piece of Joy's pecan pie."

So after kissing Christopher and the babies once more and rubbing my growing belly lovingly, Mom kissed me on the cheek and said as she always did when she parted, "Love you, Darlin'."

Then she took Dad's arm and strolled through the bougainvillea hedge to their home next door.

My pregnancy had come as a surprise to me and a delight to Christopher. We'd been careful, or so we thought, but careful isn't always one hundred percent. Eloisa was just a year and a half, while Mac was only nine months old. But we had taken the news in stride and had embraced the notion of another little one to love. I knew Christopher was hoping for another boy, but he beamed with glee when he first glimpsed the ultrasound of Elena Joy.

When reality set in, I cried, "Where in the world are we going to put her?"

I swept my arms across our already-cramped, toy-strewn space, showing Christopher that we'd used up every square inch that we owned.

"No problem." Christopher said. "We'll just build a second floor, or Eloisa and Elena can bunk together, and Mac can have the third bedroom all to himself."

"Bedrooms are just the tip of the iceberg. Look at this place. We're wall-to-wall baby stuff."

My mother said, "We'll be glad to take the overflow, won't we, Tito?"

Dad had happily agreed.

But I knew the children would not overflow into the house next door and that we'd, somehow, make it work. We always did.

We stood for a long while after Tita and Tito disappeared into their house and let Eloisa tumble around on the lawn while Mac crawled after her.

Smiling and watching our little black-haired, honey-colored babies play, Christopher wrapped his arms around me and nuzzled my neck, saying, "I am the luckiest man on earth. I have the most beautiful children God ever created," and, caressing my tummy, he said, "and another perfect angel on the way. And I love you, Allison, so much."

"I know, and I love you, Christopher," I said, wrapping my arms around his waist and holding him tight.

As the sun began to sink into the sound, turning the sky bright purple, Christopher said, "Okay, time's up. We need to get these yay-hoos settled down for the evening."

So we corralled our giggling babies and headed indoors where we took our seats on the living room sofa for a bedtime story. Mac, straddling my round belly, leaned into me, his thumb in his mouth, his eyes getting droopy.

Eloisa crouched before the bookcase on her sturdy little legs and began searching through her books with her chubby, dimpled hands. When she'd found the one she wanted for story time, she trotted to the sofa and, with her Dad's help, climbed up between us saying, "Dolls, dolls."

She had chosen THE SURPRISE DOLL, her favorite book, the one she chose four out of five nights. She was too young to know about her sister, Martina, and her love for THE SURPRISE DOLL, but Eloisa's love of the book came as no surprise to me. Already she looked so like her big sister. Why wouldn't she share her interests?

Opening to the first page, Eloisa handed it to Christopher and said, "Daddy read."

"Okay, Sweetie, I'll do the reading tonight," he said, smiling and gathering her under his arm.

We were only a few pages in when there came a knock at the door.

Christopher stood and handed Eloisa the open book, saying, "Save my place for me, Kiddo," and went to greet our visitor.

"Dr. Cruz, I hope I haven't come at a bad time," said a tall, handsome man with salt and pepper hair and wire-rimmed glasses. He wore a turquoise Polo shirt, khaki Bermudas, and deck shoes that set off a deep, rich golfer's tan.

"Why, no, not at all. What can I do for you?"

"Well, I'm an old friend of your mother. I'm visiting here on the island and have just learned of her passing. I was so sorry to hear, and I just wanted to pay my respects."

"Thank you. That's so kind of you. Won't you come in?"

"Oh, no, I shouldn't. I don't want to intrude," he said, peering into the living room where the children and I were perched on the sofa.

"No intrusion at all. We were just reading our bedtime story. We'd love to have you join us." Christopher said, opening the door wider and showing the gentleman into our home.

"Well, thank you. I'd like that," he said, entering and sidestepping the minefield of toys.

"I'm sorry, I don't believe I caught your name," Christopher said, extending his hand.

"Oh, excuse me, I'm Thomas Thornton," our visitor said, accepting Christopher's handshake.

Christopher showed him into the living room and, offering him a seat, said, "Thomas, this is my family—my wife, Allison, and our daughter, Eloisa. The droopy guy there is Mac."

"So pleased to meet you all."

"Nice of you to visit, Thomas. Would you like some ice tea?" I asked.

"Oh, no thanks. I won't stay long. Don't want to keep you…"

When our guest's voice trailed, leaving us in awkward silence, Christopher asked, "You say you knew my mother?"

Smiling wistfully, he said, "Yes, yes I did."

"How did you know Mom?"

"Well, when I was just a boy, my parents and I used to spend our summers here on Pelican Isle. I met Elena the summer I graduated from high school. She was working in that restaurant just down Beach Road a bit, Peli Pier. I was smitten from the moment I saw her." Then chuckling to himself, he added, "Fact is, every boy of a certain age was smitten with your mother."

"Is that so?" Christopher asked. "Never heard that."

"Well, it's true. I was one of the lucky ones, though. She agreed to go out with me, if you call walking on the beach, listening to the waves crash, and sitting among the dunes looking at the moon going out."

Christopher laughed and said, "That's about all there is to do around here. I recall many beach-strolling dates."

"She was amazing, your mom. So smart. So funny. And such a lady. Why, she wouldn't even give me a kiss till our fifth date," Thomas said, blushing at the admission and smiling at the memory of their first kiss.

I was wondering if Christopher's mom had ever told him about the geeky little boy who held her hand and tried to kiss her. It was such a sweet story, the chaste kind of story parents like sharing with their kids.

"I really loved her, as much as a teenage boy can love a teenage girl."

"Loved her?"

"Yeah, at the end of the summer, I told her that I wanted to stay on the island and marry her."

"Marry her?" Christopher laughed, then realized that Thomas wasn't laughing. Or joking.

"Sounds silly now, seeing as how we were both just kids, but I was serious back then. She said, 'But what would you do to support us?' I told her I'd get a job waiting tables. She got kinda huffy and said, 'I'm not interested in someone with no more ambition than that. You don't think I'm going to be waiting tables forever, do you? I'm going to go to medical school. I'm going to be a doctor.' She was a sassy one, your mom. Determined too," he said, smiling wistfully and shaking his head at the memory.

"That sounds like my mother," Christopher said, sadly, knowing he, not Thomas, was the reason she had not realized her dreams.

"I told her I'd come back after we'd both finished school. And I promised that I'd have ambition, for what I didn't know. But she said no, that we were from different worlds and it just wouldn't work. About broke my heart. But what could I do?" he said, shrugging his shoulders dejectedly.

Then furrowing his brow and tapping his finger to his lip, he added, "I've been right successful. I think I'd have made your mother proud—with my ambition, that is. Fact is, about all I've done is work. Never had time for marriage, a family," he said, looking forlornly at the children. "I never had much interest in marriage. I think your mom spoiled me for other girls," he said, shrugging his shoulders. "All those others just didn't hold a candle." Then sputtering, he said, "I, I'm sorry, I don't know why I'm telling you all of this. I guess being here on Pelican Isle after such a long time has made me nostalgic. I have a lot of happy memories of this place."

Looking confused, Christopher said, "Thomas, was it my mom who brought you back to Pelican Isle?"

"Yes, yes, as a matter of fact, it was. I sold my business about a year ago, and I've had a lot of time on my hands. Time to think. And I've been thinking a lot about Elena. I figured she'd moved on with her life, and I can see that she did," Thomas said, motioning to Christopher. "But, mind you, I didn't want to intrude. I just wanted to see how she was doing, see if, by chance, she remembered me at all. Then I found out…"

Christopher and I exchanged uncomfortable glances. Thomas's story was a sad one, but I was beginning to question my husband's decision to invite him into our home, regardless of our open-door policy here on the island.

Then Thomas breathed deeply, composed himself, and said, "But, sadly, I waited too long. So please accept my condolences. I am so very sad for your family. And for me."

Christopher cleared his throat and said uneasily, "Well, Thomas, you were kind to come by."

Thomas began to stand but settled back down and, looking hopefully at Christopher, said, "I was sort of hoping she'd mentioned me."

Christopher smiled uncomfortably and said, "I'm so sorry. She didn't tell me about meeting you. In fact, she didn't mention many people from her childhood. Guess she was just too busy taking care of me to think about her past."

"I see, I see." Then rubbing his temple, he said, "Well, did she maybe mention meeting somebody named Chip?"

I heard Christopher gasp and turned to see the blood drain from his face, but Thomas was too deep in his thoughts of Elena to notice.

"You said Chip?" Christopher croaked.

"Yeah, that's what she called me. Chip. She said I was preppy with my Polo shirts and monogrammed shorts and that Thomas just wasn't a preppy name. Said Chip was more like a boy in Polos and monograms."

As Thomas recalled the girl he loved giving him a special nickname, he sniffed back his emotion, and I felt my husband begin to tremble. I slid closer and rested my hand on Christopher's back as Thomas reached into his back pocket and pulled out a monogrammed linen handkerchief. He removed his glasses and wiped his face. After taking a deep breath, he sighed and looked up at us with startling green eyes. Then he smiled faintly for the first time, and I watched the slightest sign of a dimple take shape in his right cheek.

Knowing the men needed to talk privately, I said, "Come on, Kiddos, time to hit the sack."

I took Eloisa's hand and hoisted Mac onto my hip as I said, "Thank you for coming by, Thomas. You're welcome in our home any time."

As I left Christopher and his father to get acquainted, I was reminded, once again, why I'd come to Pelican Isle—not to save anyone or anything but to be saved by the island's many gifts.

Then I added one more special gift to my very long list.

End Notes

[1]Williams, Maurice and the Zodiacs. "Stay." Herald Records, 1960, p.43
[2]Gipson, Morrell. The Surprise Doll, Wonder Books, 1949, p.134.

About the Author

Padgett Gerler was born on the coast of South Carolina but grew up in the Shenandoah Valley of Virginia. In the 1980's she relocated to Raleigh, North Carolina to attend North Carolina State University. Upon graduating with a BA in accounting, she passed the CPA exam and began her career as a certified public accountant, first in public accounting and then as a CFO in corporate accounting. In 2010 she left accounting to pursue a career in writing. Prior to THE GIFTS OF PELICAN ISLE, Padgett published her novels, GETTING THE IMPORTANT THINGS RIGHT and LESSONS I LEARNED FROM NICK NACK. LESSONS I LEARNED FROM NICK NACK was awarded the indieBRAG Medallion, as well as honorable mention in the 2014 Writer's Digest Self-Published Book Awards competition. She also authored the short story "I know This Happened 'Cause Somebody Seen It," which was published in the anthology SELF-RISING FLOWERS. She is the first-place recipient of the Southwest Manuscripters Short Story Award for her short story "The Art of Dying." Padgett and her husband, Ed, reside on pastoral and inspirational Winchester Lake in Raleigh, North Carolina.

Made in the USA
Charleston, SC
28 June 2016